ROBIN McKINLEY

The Outlaws of Sherwood

GREENWILLOW BOOKS, NEW YORK

Library of Congress Cataloging-in-Publication Data
McKinley, Robin.
The outlaws of Sherwood.
Summary: The author retells the adventures of
Robin Hood and his band of outlaws who live in
Sherwood Forest in twelfth-century England.
1. Robin Hood (Legendary character)
[1. Robin Hood (Legendary character)
2. Folklore—England   I. Title.
PZ8.1.M198ou   1988
398.2'1'0942   88-45227
ISBN 0-688-07178-3

TO MERRILEE,

WHO SAVED IT;

AND TO R.W.,

WHO SAVED ME

CHAPTER ONE

A small vagrant breeze came from nowhere and barely flicked the feather tips as the arrow sped on its way. It shivered in its flight, and fell, a little off course—just enough that the arrow missed the slender tree it was aimed at, and struck tiredly and low into the bole of another tree, twenty paces beyond the mark.

Robin sighed and dropped his bow. There were some people, he thought, who not only could shoot accurately—if the breeze hadn't disturbed it, that last arrow would have flown true—but seemed to know when and where to expect small vagrant breezes, and to allow for them. He was not a bad archer, but his father had been a splendid one, and he was his father's only child.

His father had taught him to shoot; he had also taught him to make and fletch his own arrows. Robin stopped to pull the treacherous arrow out of the ash it had chosen to fly at, and ran his fingers gently over the shaft. It was undamaged, he was relieved to see; he had a living to earn, and little time to spend making his own arrows. Mostly he sold the ones he found time to make; he had some slight local fame as a fletcher. He would rather have had any local fame, however slight, as an archer. But the money was useful; as one of the youngest sub-apprentice foresters in the King's Forest of Nottingham, he barely earned coin enough to feed himself—in fact he didn't earn even that, and he was struggling as well to keep title to his father's small holding. Every quarter saw him in rising panic as the time for the rents grew near.

Fortunately for his peace of mind, Robin was usually too busy, and too short on sleep and food, to have time and energy for thinking. And he was young and strong and still hopeful; this Chief Forester, who sent him on all the most disagreeable tasks, was old, and might be expected to die or at least to retire some day soon. With some luck the new Chief Forester, although inevitably another sheriff's man, might not hate young Robin for the sake of his mother, who had had the excellent sense to marry another man.

Today Robin had the great fortune to be free to go to the Nottingham Fair, and perhaps his holiday meant his luck was looking up at last. It was old Nobble, who had worked with his father as a friend, who had had the duty to decide which of the younger men might have the day to go to the fair. He had had the wisdom not to choose Robin first, for Bill Sharp, who was the Chief Forester's spy among the young men, was watching eagerly; but Robin knew as soon as Nobble's eye fell on him that he was to be permitted to go. He had to stop the smile that wanted to spread across his face from appearing till his name was called—a cautious third. Bill Sharp's name was not called at all, and that made Robin's happiness even greater.

Robin was to meet Marian and Much at the fair, and they would see the sights together: the jugglers and the players, the wrestlers and the knife-throwers. There would be no knights' contests. The best knights did not care to display themselves at so mercantile an event as the Nottingham Fair, much to the sheriff's chagrin, for the sheriff was vain of his town and his place in it. But his love of gold invariably won over even his love of pomp and ceremony; and while the sheriff said aloud that he was not willing to lay on a tourney that the best would not attend—for petty, illogical reasons that Nottingham need not concern itself with—the truth of it was that he was not willing to lay on a tourney that would end up costing him a great deal of money. He did consider, twice a year, as fair time approached, the noble—possibly even royal—favour he might curry by a fine tournament. But—as he told himself—royal favour was a notoriously chancy (and expensive) thing and at best a long-term one; and the sheriff of Nottingham had a short-term mind.

But the three friends did not care for such things, although Marian often heard gossip about them, and had many times made Much and Robin laugh till their sides hurt with her deadly imitations of the sheriff and his society. Once Robin said to her, "But your stories are second- and third-hand. How do you *know*?"

"I don't," said Marian cheerfully. "But I'm a good guesser—and a good actor, am I not?"

Robin said teasingly, "I will tell you what you already know only if you promise that you will not run off with a band of wandering play-ers."

"I will not have to," replied Marian, "so long as evading my father's questions when I wish to spend a day with you continues to exercise my talents so usefully. Come; Much will think we have fallen in a hole," and she ran off ahead of him before he could speak again.

There had been little enough time for the three of them to be together in the last months; but the fair was going to make up for all that. They would look in the stalls and admire the trinkets for sale, the bright cloth, the raw wool and flax, the charms and toys, the spices and wines; and everything would please them.

Robin had contrived to finish off another couple dozen arrows since Nobble had called out his name a fortnight ago, working late into the evenings at great expense of sleep and strength—and of eyesight, crouched over one flickering candle till his head ached so badly that he saw twenty fingers and forty arrows. But he knew he would be able to sell them to Sir Richard of the Lea, his best customer—and the kindest, though Robin tried not to think about that too much in the fear that he might realise he should not accept the kindness. Sir Richard was unusual in that he permitted himself, a knight, to be interested in this commoner's sport. He had first bought arrows from Robin's father, and had not only organised his own levies to practise with their bows, but he even learnt to shoot himself, and had caused something of a ripple in local aristocratic society by claiming that he quite enjoyed it. But, he said, it was only sense to wish to send archers to the Lionheart in Palestine since the news of the Saracens' at-the-gallop harassment of properly armed knights had come home to England.

It was a great pity, as everyone said, that such a good man (and forward-looking, said those who approved of his archery; if misguided, said those who did not) should have such a worthless son. There was a good deal of local consternation, among both the high and low, at the prospect of the son's eventual inheritance of the father's estates. The sanguine held that, barring an unlucky pox or dropsy, the son would kill himself at one of his headlong games before such a fate came to be. And there was no point in speculating—which everyone then immedi-ately did—whom the king might in such a case assign the estates to.

Robin himself was keeping an eye out for the son as he walked toward Mapperley Castle; he bore a small but slow to fade scar on the back of his neck where young Richard had laid his hunting-whip when Robin had not gotten out of what Richard perceived as his way quickly enough to suit. The son might have had more trouble if his father were less loved; as it was, yeoman farmers got both their flocks and their daughters under cover when young Richard was heard of, and elegant dinner parties in several counties were enlivened by tales of his exploits.

Sir Richard, who had not ordered any new arrows, still let his man show Robin at once into the room where he sat. He said, with the smallest trace of amusement in his gentle voice, "Have you an especial need for ready money, perhaps? Have you permission to go to the fair?"

Robin acknowledged, somewhat guiltily, that this was true. But Sir Richard willingly examined the arrows, as carefully as if he had long awaited them. "You have more than earned your fee with these," he said. "They are very fine." A blessing on that wandering goose, Robin thought, whose feathers he had ransacked before returning it, only a little the worse for wear, to its coop. Sir Richard stood up from behind his great desk and fumbled for his purse; and he pressed coins into Robin's hand and curled the young man's fingers around them as he turned him toward the door to the long hall that led down stairs and at last to the kitchens.

The smell of cooking made Robin's head swim. He knew he was accepting charity, but he was also relentlessly hungry and almost never ate meat; and Sir Richard had enough money to support not only his lands but his wastrel son. The odd extra meal for a craftsman worth his salt (Robin told himself) was no ignominy, on either side. It was not until his mouth was already full of beef and gravy and bread that he thought to look at the coins Sir Richard had given him; and found that he had been paid half again his usual price.

So Robin had enough money in his pouch to throw to a juggler who might particularly take his fancy (although he should be saving it for next quarter day); and enough to buy the hot fried bread there would be at the goodwives' booths for Marian and Much as well as for himself. He wondered for a moment, as he settled his bow and quiver over his shoulders, if perhaps he should throw the coin he would need to enter the fair's archery contest to that hypothetical juggler, and leave his arrows at home. He hesitated, looking at the tree his last arrow had missed.

He did not hate the fact that he was a second-rate archer; and Much and Marian knew him and were his friends. But there would be friends of the Chief Forester shooting too, and nothing would please them more than to taunt him when he stood up—and to take the story home of how young Robin had missed the mark with his very first arrow. Robin had learnt that it did no good to answer the taunting, and so he could hold his tongue; but he had yet to learn to ignore it, and as the anger—compounded of his helplessness and inability simply not to listen—beat inside him, it would throw his shooting out. The Chief Forester himself might be there to laugh his great, rolling, harsh laugh, though usually at such events he disappeared into the tent set out for the refreshment of the sheriff and his men, and was little seen.

Robin knew that any story of his own indifferent marksmanship would lose nothing in the telling. Bill Sharp would be telling it far and wide at least by the next day—and Robin thought it likely that he would have gone whining to the Chief Forester to be given permission to go to the fair after all, despite Nobble's decision, and would therefore be able to see for himself. There were those who said that Bill Sharp's real father was the Chief Forester, and not the farmer who had bred him up—and sent him off to be an apprentice forester at the earliest possible opportunity. Robin could readily believe it; it seemed to him that Bill was the Chief Forester all over again in small, for Bill was a skinny, weedy boy, and the Chief Forester was fat from many years of living off other people's labour, and eating at the sheriff's table. Robin particularly did not want to miss his first mark, with Bill Sharp watching.

But Much and Marian would be bringing their bows and would think it odd if he did not, for they were all to enter the contest. Privately Robin felt that Marian had a good chance of winning; she was one of those who always allowed for the breeze that would kick up from nowhere after the arrow had left the string. They might not like it when she proved to be a girl, but no one would notice in the crowd when the three of them signed up together, for she would be wearing boy's clothes, with her hair up under a hat; and after she won, Robin didn't think they'd deny her the prize. If he didn't enter, Marian and Much might decide they wouldn't either—he could hear Marian saying, "Oh, Robin, don't be tiresome. It doesn't matter. What is the prize—a lamb? *I* don't particularly want a lamb. Do you? I only came so we could spend the day together."

Robin had not told her or Much what his life had been like since his father died; and this was only too easy a decision to keep, as he had so little time to meet with them. They knew that his father had been a forester, and a man much admired and respected by the folk who lived roundabout. Too much respected, in the eyes of the sheriff, for there were those who felt that Robert Longbow should have had the Chief Forester's post; but he had been a quiet man who never took advantage of his popularity against the sheriff. And so the sheriff and his choice of Chief Forester had let him alone—in case his popularity might prove inconvenient if anything untoward happened to him. It had been their great good luck that he had died so suddenly of the winter catarrh; but he had driven himself very hard since his wife died, and was not so strong as he had been. No one thought anything of Robert Longbow's death but sorrow to see a good man gone; and Robin had known better than to mention the unnecessary call that came one stormy midnight after his father was already sickening. When Robert came back late the next morning, he was wet through, and he took to his bed, and did not leave it again alive.

His friends knew that the Chief Forester was hardly Robin's favourite person, but they knew little more than that. Let them think the unpleasantness was minor, left over from the old romantic story of how his father and the Chief Forester had courted the same woman, and his father had won her, despite the Chief Forester's better standing—and private income. He'd bring his bow to the fair, and enter the archery contest, and try not to miss at least his first shot. Even if Bill Sharp was not there, he was always at his worst with a lot of people watching him. But he really wanted to see Marian win.

He resettled his bow on his shoulder and gave another shake to his quiver, that it would hang straight, and not tease the back of his neck; he spent far too much of his daily life walking to be comfortable with an arrow-sack looped around his belt and banging against one leg in the common manner. That done, he set off solemnly through the trees— trying to feel that his decision was not only final but a good one, and that he was pleased with it besides. It was a long way to the town of Nottingham; it was probably foolish of him to have taken the time for target practice, particularly when practice wasn't going to tell him anything he didn't already know. He tried to whistle, but gave it up as a bad job.

He knew no other life than forestry, and if he left Nottingham he would have no choice but to give up his father's holding. His father's pride in England had extended to include his pride in tenant ownership of a cottage and small bit of land—land for a garden, and the cottage large enough to have separate rooms for eating and sleeping. There was even a separate coop for his wife's chickens, built against one outside wall of the cottage, where the birds were not only out from underfoot in the house, with their dirt and their feathers, but safe from foxes and other marauders as well. It was not only Robin's mother's family who was conscious that she'd married beneath her.

There was another reason Robin would not leave Nottingham, nor voluntarily give up his loosening hold on his father's land: Marian. And he could not help it that he often recalled that his gentry-bred mother had chosen to marry a mere forester with no prospects. But while the present Chief Forester remained, there was no chance of marriage for Robin, neither to a member of the gentry nor to the humblest village girl, who would never contemplate sleeping apart from her chickens were she so fortunate as to own any.

Robin knew the Nottingham woods hereabouts so well he did not need to think about where he was going, and his feet carried him responsibly forward while his mind was elsewhere. But he was not in the mood for any meeting with his fellows, and he was snapped out of his reverie by the sound of voices: one of them Tom Moody's, the Chief Forester's great friend and crony, and another Bill Sharp's.

Robin stopped, but it was too late, for they had seen him. There were half a dozen of them together, and they sat and watched him so expectantly that he wondered if they had been waiting for him, and what they intended to do.

Bill stood up to his full if insignificant height, and leaned casually against a tree by the narrow, tree-crowded path. Robin, if he continued, would have to pass so near him their sleeves might brush; and there was no graceful nor inconspicuous way to leave the path altogether. The others sat where they were; Tom had a very large grin on his face. There was what appeared to be the remains of a meal spread out around them; one or two were still chewing, and Robin could smell the sharp tang of the ale in the small open cask that lounged on the greensward among them.

"A very good day to you, Master Robin," said Bill, his arms folded across his negligible chest, the sole of one foot cocked nonchalantly against his tree. "I'm afraid I can't suggest that you join our feed—I fear there is little left but crumbs."

Tom stood up, and Robin recalled that Tom was the only forester his father, who could see goodness in almost anybody, had called bad. Tom was still grinning; there were small strings of meat caught between his teeth. He shot the king's deer for his own belly whenever he chose, and the Chief Forester looked the other way—so long as he got a haunch of it. "Perhaps young Robin would like the crumbs—he's a little too thin, don't you think, lads?" He reached out as Robin stood hesitating a few paces from where Bill leaned against his tree, and seized his arm.

Robin could not stop the spasm of disgust that crossed his face as the man's fingers touched him, and he jerked himself free with an unnecessary violence—a violence that he knew at once had cost him any chance he might have had in escaping this meeting without some kind of skirmish.

Tom laughed, for he knew it too, and it was what he wanted; and he was pleased that his prey had proved so easy to bait. He pawed at Robin again, circling the young man's upper arm with his thick fingers. "Too thin, eh, lads? Too thin to do a *man's* work as a forester?"

Robin flushed but stood stiffly and said nothing, hoping against his better judgement that Tom might yet let him pass.

But Tom only stretched out his other hand, and pulled one of Robin's arrows half out of the quiver—by the feathers, Robin knew, and he gritted his teeth, for he could not afford damage to even one of his arrows—and then let it drop again, and Robin heard the protest of the other stiff pinions as the dropped shaft forced its way downward. "And certainly too thin and weak to draw a man's bow like a man."

He laughed again, and the hot foul wash of his ale-smelling breath over Robin's face brought all the young man's frustrations to a boil. Tom knew as well as he himself did that he could not easily draw his father's bow, which was a hand's-length longer and better than a stone heavier to pull than the plainer, lighter bow he carried. He kept his father's bow in what had been his father's room, carefully wrapped and stored against damp and rodent teeth; and occasionally he took it out and practised with it, when no one was near. But he could not bear it that this man should gibe at him so, now, and just before anger stopped thought altogether he said to himself: They are here to trap me—well, let them do their worst. And then the anger overcame him, and he snarled at his tormentor: "I can draw a bow as well as you, or any other fat forester who can barely sight down his arrow for fear of stinging his paunch with the released string."

Now Tom let go of Robin and his own face began to flush up with anger, and Bill dropped his crossed arms and stood warily, and the other four men stopped chewing and got to their feet. What they thought of doing or might have done Robin did not know; but anger still darkened his mind and while it did he felt no fear. "If you choose to doubt me, then I will happily meet you at the Nottingham Fair later today, for I go now to that place that I may see how I fare at the archery contest. And I will say that I will shoot far more handsomely than you, whose greasy hands will let his bow slip, and mayhap his arrow shall pierce the sheriff's hat where he sits watching the performance, and then you shall win a prize specially for you, and yet like not what you might have chosen."

The seven men stood for a moment like a tableau in a Christmas pageant; and then Tom said thickly, "We shall not wait for the fair; we shall have our shooting match here. And by my faith, if you do not shoot as you choose to boast you can, be sure that I shall take great pleasure in basting your ribs till your sides are as red as any flayed deer's.

"Come," said he, turning on his heel. "What shall we use as mark?" He spoke, not to Robin, but to his friends; yet even they quailed before the fierceness of his gaze. Bill backed cautiously away from him, as if Tom might order him strung up kicking for a more challenging target. "There," he said, and Robin's heart sank in him as Tom pointed. "See the gnarled oak tree, two score rods distant, I judge, or thereabouts? And see the crotch halfway up that tree, and the small black burl beneath the crotch? At that we shall aim." He strode over to where his bow and quiver lay, next to the small open cask on the ground, and he snatched them up, tumbling the quiver through the loop on his belt, his knuckles white where they held the bow.

"As the challenged, I go first," he said; but Robin was too sick to protest that it was not this test he had offered as challenge; nor, he knew, would a protest have done him any good. At such a range he would be lucky if his arrows did not bounce—if they struck the correct tree at all. The anger that had borne him up drained away as suddenly as it had risen, and he was cold and weary, and knew he had been a fool. He wondered if Tom meant to kill him after. There was no doubt that Tom was the better archer, any more than it was uncommon knowledge that Robin was not the archer his father had been; Bill had made his ears burn often enough on this subject—for all that Bill himself could barely hit the broad side of a barn at six paces. Robin thought sadly that he had not known the old wound could still hurt so sorely.

Robin turned heavy eyes to Tom as the bigger man took his stance and pulled his arrow powerfully back—but he noticed that the man's hands were not quite steady. With anger? Robin thought. Or with ale? Either way he will take joy in beating me senseless.

"Three arrows each we may try," Tom said between his teeth, and let go his first shaft. It flew straight, but a little awry, for it buried itself at the left edge of the burl, and not the center. The second struck so near to the first that their feathers vibrated together; and this second one was nearer the burl's center. But the third, which should have struck nearest of all, went wild, and sank in the trunk a finger's-breadth from the burl. Tom threw his bow down savagely and turned to Robin. "Let us see you shoot yet half so well," he said threateningly.

Robin slowly moved forward to take his place, slowly unslung his bow, bent it to slip the string into its notch, and pulled an arrow from his quiver. But his hands were steady as he drew the bowstring back and sighted down the arrow.

His first arrow struck the far right side of the treetrunk, a good hand's-breadth from the burl. There was a snicker behind him. It might be Bill; he doubted it was Tom. And yet his arrow was, for him and indeed for most archers, good shooting. It was not for his archery that Robin's father had called Tom Moody bad. He notched and drew his second arrow, and it flew beautifully, to strike at the veriest right-hand edge of the burl; and yet it was nearer the mark than only one of Tom's, and Robin had already shot two.

He fitted his last arrow to the string, staring at his hands, which went fairly about their familiar work without acknowledging the trouble that they and the rest of Robin were in. The arrow was his best; from the same fine-grained bit of pine he had made a half-dozen arrows Sir Richard had paid handsomely for, so handsomely that Robin had let himself keep the last, the odd seventh, in the wistful hope that so excellent an arrow might have an effect on his marksmanship. When he raised the bow, for a moment his eyes clouded over, and he could not see the tree he was aiming for; and he wondered, as his arrow quivered against the string, if he would ever shoot another after Tom and his lads got through with him.

He murmured a few words under his breath—a prayer, perhaps, or a farewell to Marian; or an apology to his father—and loosed his last arrow.

Another vagrant breeze arose from nowhere, and kissed his arrow in its flight; Robin felt it brush his cheek as well. And the arrow, perhaps, wavered.

And struck true, dead center, in the burl.

A barely audible gasp rose behind him: a hissing of breath through shut teeth. Robin stared at his arrow, its shaft still vibrating, and for a second time his vision briefly clouded. He blinked, and heard footsteps behind him, and stiffened to prevent himself from cringing away from what he felt sure would be a heavy hand on his shoulder, preliminary to the beating he would still receive, from many heavy hands, despite his lucky shooting.

But Tom strode straight by him, toward the tree, and after a moment Robin followed him without looking around.

There was no doubt that Robin's arrow was beautifully centered, and that neither of Tom's better shots came near it. Tom growled something, jerked the perfect arrow out of the tree, and trod on it. Robin heard the shaft break, but said nothing, thinking of his ribs, and of the sound of approaching soft footsteps behind him. But Tom still made no move toward him. He pulled his own arrows out of the tree and then stepped aside, glaring; and Robin, in a daze, stepped forward, retrieved his two remaining arrows, and restored them carefully to his quiver. He would

11

check them later. After a moment he also stooped and hastily picked up the splintered halves of the broken arrow; and these he thrust under his belt.

Still no one said anything, and he moved cautiously away, toward the path, toward his day at Nottingham Fair, his day with Marian. He had to turn his back on Tom to do this, and he walked jerkily, as a man passes a growling mastiff which he knows would be happy to tear his arm off if he makes a false move; and he had regained the path and turned down it, carefully not looking back, when there was a strangled shout behind him.

"And do you think then, that you shall go unhindered to Nottingham Fair, and boast to your friends in the dirt that you did best Tom Moody at archery?"

Robin, too conscious of what was happening off to one side, was not conscious enough of what lay under his feet on this rough woods path; and he stumbled, ever so slightly, and his head nodded forward to save his balance. And an arrow whistled past his ear.

It whistled so nearly that it creased the nape of his neck, gently, and the narrow place where it rubbed was red and painful for many days. Fear jumped back into Robin's throat and stopped his breathing, and his bowels turned to water: He means to *kill* me, he thought, and he turned like a creature at bay, crouching against the possibility of a further shaft from his enemy, groping over his shoulder for his bow, which he had providentially not unstrung. He notched an arrow and let fly back at the little group around the gnarled oak tree.

He aimed for Tom Moody's right leg. He had aimed neither well nor carefully, and he took no thought for the consequences, should he succeed at so tricky a shot—or should he fail. But he was nonetheless appalled as he saw the feathered shaft appear as if by magic in Tom's broad chest, as he heard the man's hoarse cry of pain and terror. Tom looked down a moment, and clutched at the great spreading red stain around the thing that grew now so abruptly from his breast; and then his knees buckled, and he fell forward on his face and lay still. The snap of the shaft as Tom's weight crushed it was very loud in the stillness; and then, like a long echo of that sharp, final sound, a squirrel appeared on a branch of the oak tree, and shrilly protested the invasion of his peace.

CHAPTER TWO

Robin had no memory later of taking to his heels. He ran, his traitorous bow still clenched in one hand, till he could run no more; and then he walked till he caught his breath, and ran on. Once or twice he fell. He did not know where he went or where he was going; as he lay on the ground the second time, the wind knocked out of him, the ragged ends of the broken arrow in his belt digging into his flesh, his foot aching from the root that had tripped him, he thought, I will run till it kills me, for I have killed a man, and my death is demanded by the king's law. And he got up, limping a little, and ran on. He ran till he was blind with running, till he thought he had lived his entire life running, one foot pounding down in front of the other endlessly, till his bones were on fire with it, and every time either foot struck the ground his whole body cried out against the jolt. He set his teeth and ran on.

But his body betrayed him at the last, and the next time he fell he could not get up but lay, face down, in the leaf-mould, stirring only faintly, like a baby first learning to crawl. And then even that movement ceased, and he turned his cheek to the earth and gave up; and after a little while an uneasy sleep took him. He drifted in and out of sleep, vaguely conscious that the sound of water was very near and that he was more and more thirsty; and he noticed also that the light was growing dim, and at first he thought that in truth he had run himself blind. But he realised that it was only twilight, as happens every evening, whatever the events of the day past have been. And he sighed, and turned his other cheek to the earth, and shut his eyes.

But then he came wide awake, more alert than he had been since Tom Moody first stepped up beside him that day and seized his arm. For he heard, faintly, careful footsteps coming through the trees—coming toward the place where he lay. He rolled over—and his cold exhausted muscles groaned with the effort, and he gasped, and moved more slowly. With numb swollen fingers he snatched up his bow, and scuttled, stumbling, to stoop painfully behind the boulder to his one side. Behind him, now, as he waited to see what was before him, was the stream; and the sound of the water made his mouth suddenly ache, and he turned away from what he expected was his last doom to scoop up the cold water in the hand that did not hold the bow.

The taste of it on his tongue shocked him to full consciousness, and he realised what his actions meant: that he wanted to live. Even with Tom Moody's blood on his head, and the king's men looking for him as a murderer—he wanted to keep his life.

He was too tired to run any more; either luck was with him and the footsteps would go away, or he would try to give himself up with dignity. He had several good arrows left; but even if he had the strength to draw his bow—and he was not at all sure he did—he would not seek to take any more life. Even his own.

The mercurial luck that had played with him all this day seemed to turn its face from him now, for the footsteps came ever closer. It sounded like two people—only two; and he thought wistfully of his several good arrows, but he did not move to ready one. The footsteps were approaching with rather too much haste at the expense of care; while they belonged obviously to woodsmen and not common soldiers, he could follow their progress without difficulty. And they seemed to be coming directly and deliberately toward his place of concealment.

He closed his eyes briefly, for his head swam with weariness and an urgent will to live; and when he opened them he thought he dreamed, for he did not see two grim king's foresters reaching out to drag him to gaol and the hangman's noose, but—Much and Marian, their faces pale and taut with worry.

He stood up, not knowing what he could say, and staggered around one end of his boulder. His head felt light, and Marian's face was surrounded by tiny bright twinkling stars. She ran forward, heedlessly dropping her bow on the ground, and threw her arms around him, pressing her cheek to his; her hair tickled his nose. Much, with a sigh, laid his bow carefully against the boulder that had hidden Robin. Another squirrel chattered somewhere close by, and the stream made small *gloop*ing noises as it ran, as fish broke the surface to swallow water bugs and bits of leaves.

14

Marian said, "I was so afraid we wouldn't find you—that you'd go straight away, take ship for the Holy Land—be sold as a slave to the Saracens—that we'd—that I'd never see you again."

Much said, "We heard they had some trouble planned for you today —but we only heard this morning. 'Twas a friend of my father's told him. If there had been time we would have tried to stop you coming; but it was too late."

Marian, unmoving, said to Robin's shoulder, "I was worried today, at the fair, long before there was any reason to worry—before you were even late."

"And then you were late," said Much.

"And then you were later, and then we started looking," Marian said, and turned her face at last; there were tear marks on it, and Robin felt a pricking behind his own eyes, that Marian should cry over him. "This place was my best hope—and my last—that you might think to come here and look for us."

Robin looked around, puzzled, and then recognised what he had not thought to look for. This was the little river where Much's father's mill lay, below them where they now stood by over a mile. But here, with its splendid boulders for playing King of the Mountain, and a pool just upstream for pirates and leaf-sailing races, was where Much and Marian and he had spent happy hours as young children. He murmured, half to himself, "I've been running—as I thought, away, or somewhere—all day. Since morning. And this is where I end: barely a league from—from where . . ."

Marian stepped back, but only to put her hands on Robin's shoulders, as if she feared that if she did not hold on to him he might still go to the Saracens. "Robin—has it been so bad, since your father died?"

Robin almost smiled. "Not so bad as right at present."

But Marian would not be distracted. "Why did you never tell us? I —I thought you grieved for your father, and did not wish to press you as you seemed not to want to speak. But—someone could have done something—my father—or you need not have been a forester."

Robin shook his head. "Your father—or anyone else—could have done nothing, had I been willing to ask. Hush," he said, as Marian opened her mouth. "It doesn't matter. Forestry, and the making of arrows, is all I know; and you know what Will Fletcher in Nottingham

---

15

is like—he would have stood no competition, and I could bear him less as a master even than the Chief Forester."

"It is not Will who would have brooked no rivals," said Much, "but the sheriff, who might have found you a little less willing to pay his tax."

Robin shrugged. "It matters not. What is done is—done." And then the sight of Tom Moody clutching at the feathered shaft rising from his red-stained tunic was before him, and the shrug turned to a shudder and he closed his eyes.

Marian's hands shifted and tightened on his shoulders, and she said softly, "What happened, then? We know you met with trouble, dark trouble, but we do not know its name."

Robin looked at her in surprise. "You don't know? You—" But he could not get the words out.

Much said, "My father's friend thought they might accuse you of killing the king's deer; someone was bragging that he had stolen one of the arrows you've made from Sir Richard's son, who was too drunk to notice."

Marian whispered, "That's a hanging offense—if they could do it."

"They could do it," Much said briefly, and a little silence fell.

Robin could hear his friends trying not to make the silence too hectic with expectation. He shook himself free of Marian's hands and took two steps back, carefully not looking at his friends' faces. "I—I killed Tom Moody. I killed him." Then he turned and knelt stiffly by the stream, and bent over for another drink; not because he was thirsty, but because it gave him something to do. He had said aloud the awful thing that he had done, and the saying, in some way, made it irrevocable, as it had as yet not been. Or, no, he thought, dipping his hand into the freezing water again. It is not that I have doubted the thing I did; it is that I have acknowledged the burden of it now, by telling my friends of it.

Marian sat down beside him, heavily, as if the spring had gone out of her muscles; as if she, too, had run for hours. Much said, over their heads, "How did it happen?"

Robin told them, haltingly, but he told them, and he tried to tell everything, leaving nothing out but that this was only the latest, last, and worst of his trials under the Chief Forester who had hated his father. Last. His heart even tried to lift a little at that thought: whatever came next, he would never have to take orders from the Chief Forester again. "It is, at best, a very stupid thing I did."

"It is stupid only because you lived and he did not," Marian burst out. "He meant to kill you—he would have killed you if you had not stumbled."

Robin rubbed the back of his neck thoughtfully. The arrow-crease burned with the salt of his sweat. Marian began plucking up the small weeds and grasses that grew on the bank of the stream, and casting them angrily into the water.

Much said, "My father came out of the mill and called me just before I was to set off; there had been several folk there who had just left. He said, 'You are meeting your friend young Robin at the fair today, are you not?' and I said I was. 'Tell him then to have a care; for I have heard that the friends of the Chief Forester have a mind to remove him from their master's sight, and beyond any man's care.' "

"I wonder he did not kill you outright, at the very beginning," Marian said, tearing a particularly long weed into bits before she flung it into the water.

Another faint smile crossed Robin's face. "That would not have been nearly so enjoyable," he said.

Marian's fingers paused. "What should we do now?"

Robin gingerly stretched one arm and then the other; they felt like blocks of wood, and creaked like badly hinged blocks of wood, although wood, presumably, did not ache like this. He thought that perhaps he felt as he would if Tom had held to the original plan of merely beating him—but from Much's words, that had never been the plan. He wondered if there was some comfort in this, but he was too tired to consider it. "*We* should not do anything; though I am very glad to have seen you one last time. I would not have dared to come looking for you. You should go home, and forget you ever saw me this day, and—"

"And you will go sell yourself to the Saracens," Marian put in. "Well, you won't. We came to help you, and help you we will."

"And you can't stop us," said Much, with almost a grin. "It is hard for you, Robin, but you know, this could almost be a good thing in the long run—"

"A *good* thing?" exploded Robin. "A man is dead, and—"

"And his death is going to give the Norman dogs an excuse they'll love, to bite down on us Saxons; yes, I know. But there's another side of it. Everyone hereabouts knows who your father was. It would be an easy thing to put it about that the trouble you're in comes of being your father's son; that the lying Normans can't bear an honest Saxon around them long—and it's the truth, too. So, if word goes round that Robin, son of Robert Longbow, is—is living free—well, I think a few hardy like-minded folk might wish to join him. The Nottingham woods are huge; quite a few of us could lose ourselves in them beyond ken of any sheriff's or king's men forever. I think a few hardy like-minded folk might be pleased."

"Pleased? Pleased to do what?" Robin said, throwing a few weeds of his own into the brook, despite the ominous creaking through his back and shoulders. "Pleased to skulk around in the shadows, pleased never to have a roof or a home, or anything over their heads but a price to see them dragged before the sheriff? This kind of talk was amusing when we were children and didn't know any better, Much. You always told the best stories—I envied you the way you told them, the way you believed them. But that's long ago—more than just years. It's nonsense. You must know it's nonsense."

"It's not nonsense," Much said patiently. "You've been too preoccupied with staying out of the Chief Forester's way for too long to listen to us. Henry had stopped caring about anything but quarrelling with his sons by the end; Richard stayed in England barely long enough to be crowned, and then it was off to the Holy Land—"

"Henry gave us the law," argued Robin, "and Richard is an honest man."

"Richard is an honest man in Palestine," said Much, "and what we have is a Regent who is not. Do you suppose one of Henry's handsome travelling justices is going to listen to a lot of ragtag Saxons against the word of a Norman sheriff who is a personal friend of the Regent? Think, Robin. You could be our rallying point."

Robin shook his head. "It sounds fine," he said. "I'm sure you are often in demand as a fireside speaker. But it won't work."

"And if we are going to put it to the test," Much continued without heeding, "this is the season. It's spring; we have summer and autumn ahead, when staying alive will be easy, and we have time to make mistakes before winter begins, and we'll have to be serious."

"Be serious! It is you who are not being serious," said Robin. "Have you given any practical thought to your shining notions of Saxon revolt against Norman tyranny? It is too late for me, so I do not matter. But do you have any idea what using me as a so-called rallying point would mean for those who rallied? Do you understand how absolute the no going back would be? I can't believe that you do, or you would not suggest it. What kind of a man do you suppose me to be, that I could permit these 'hardy like-minded folk' to come to me, knowing that by so coming they could be hung for my offense if they were caught? Hardiness alone grants you no woodscraft, and woodscraft— do you understand what the isolation of living in Sherwood would mean? It would be a short life, for one thing: we would only be able to kill the king's deer to feed ourselves for as long as our arrows held out, for we would not be able to buy steel and twine to make more. Even if we knocked a travelling fletcher on the head for his supplies, where could we leave the wood we need for shafts to season, when we had not even a place to sleep dry? We could not build anything, for large as Sherwood is, I can tell you that the foresters might find their way to any part of it by lucky or unlucky chance; it is what we are for. Is what *they* are for. And they will hear the same rumours that your like-minded folk will, and they will be looking. The occasional rogue in Sherwood is a common thing and no one cares overmuch so long as he kills no one important; but an entire band of them, waving a banner saying 'Down with the Normans' virtually in the sheriff's teeth? Be sensible, man."

"This is why we need you," said Much comfortably. "You're a pessimist and a good planner."

"I have not *begun* to plan and be pessimistic," said Robin angrily. "You are simply not listening; you wish to ignore me—beyond my symbolic status, of course, which you find valuable—because the price on my head, you think, is oppressing my spirits—as it damn well is, I agree, and as it should. Stop telling yourself beautiful stories, Much. How many examples do I have to give you before you will listen? Perhaps after we run out of arrows we can learn—before we starve—to make snares out of gut, to catch our food. Perhaps. But are we to raise our own sheep for wool to make our clothing? Do any of your like-minded folk know how to card and spin? A meadow, deep in the heart of Sherwood, full of sheep that don't seem to belong to anybody might cause a little curiosity too. And where did the sheep come from? Do we steal lambs from the farmers who are already being taxed past bearing by the sheriff who wants my head? In that case we might as well go on stealing lambs —and calves and chickens—and eat them too. I'm sure snares would be a nuisance. Of course then we wouldn't make so grand a rallying point for our fellow Saxons. We would look, from the farmers' perspective, quite a lot like Normans."

Much and Marian exchanged glances. "We will not be entirely cut off from the outside world," said Marian carefully.

"You cannot be a part of this madness, Marian," said Robin sharply; "you always had less patience with Much's will-o'-the-wisps than I did."

"Nor am I an overtaxed farmer or an outlaw in hiding?" said Marian. "It is possible that it is exactly that that leaves my head clear now to judge what you cannot judge—"

"Judgement!" said Robin. "Neither of you is judging anything. Neither of you wishes to look past a friend in trouble, and I honour you for it, but there is no future in it—I must make you see that there is no future in it."

Much said, "You are right that not everyone who believes in us will have both the strength and the desire to live as an outlaw—I do know what you're trying to say. But we will not be completely isolated. We will be able to get arrowheads and wool and other things through our friends."

"Bought with leaves and twigs?" inquired Robin.

"Our skills will still be saleable; it is the marketing that must be done by others," said Much.

"There is, of course, a great deal of call for bagging flour and meal in the king's forest," said Robin.

"You can still make arrows," said Much. "One of my friends, Harald, is a leather-worker, caught in a position something like yours might have been under Will Fletcher. There are other examples. And I—oh,

I can experiment with snares. And someone will have to dig privy vaults. You see? I do have some notion of what I'm proposing.

"But I'm not going to argue with you tonight. You're tired; you couldn't be anything else. You can sleep in the old barn at the mill tonight, and tomorrow night as well. Just promise us—for this evening —that you won't try to sacrifice yourself to your stubborn idea of justice to a Norman king. No sacrifices till you've had at least one good night's sleep, and something to eat."

"And have let you talk at me some more," said Robin.

"That's right," said Much.

There was a long pause. Robin looked at his two friends, seated now on either side of him, and it occurred to him that they were going to take him into custody as inexorably as any king's foresters might: their faces told him that. "Oh, to the devil with you, and your troop of merry bandits with you," he said. "I promise."

CHAPTER THREE

Robin woke up with an intolerable headache and a sense of impending doom that it took him a few moments to define. When he had remembered the events of the day before, fear tried to shoot him bolt upright—and his abused body, which had turned to stone overnight, jerked an inch or two in its bed of straw and refused to move further. The jerk, however, woke up a great many more, not only physical, protests, that cast the headache into comparative shadow. Robin lay still, staring at the roof, and his thoughts were bleak.

He rolled over—cautiously—at last, and found lying beside him not only a loaf of bread and a bottle of water, but his father's bow, still in the wrappings he was used to keep it in.

He ate the bread, drank the water, and contemplated the bow. He was still too tired to think sensibly—he felt as if the night before had been more a period of unconsciousness than of sleep—and his bruised emotions could not decide if they were chiefly of gratitude for the mysterious rescue of the one possession that meant more to him than any other, or fear of finding out how, exactly, it had been restored to him.

He muffled a sneeze. He was stowed away in the smallest, highest loft in Much's father's old barn; in Much's grandfather's day they had kept a few beasts, but the mill's custom had increased to the point that the animals were more trouble than they were worth when the miller could trade for anything he might need. "If there had been six of me instead of only me and a few sisters," Much had said once, "that barn might still be used; but there isn't, and there's more than work enough for my father and me at the mill." Robin thought of that now: and Much was suggesting that he turn his back on his father, to run wild in Sherwood. He had tried to balk the night before, when Much brought him home; Much was known as a friend of his, the sheriff's men would come to the mill to ask—possibly to search. "Oh, they'll come and they'll ask," said Much, "but they won't search. You don't know my father when he plays stupid. He'll be beautifully offended when they ask if his only son might be harbouring any known criminals, and he'll be even more offended when they suggest, none too gently, as gentleness is not part of their training, that they might just have a look in the old barn. He's still the miller hereabouts; they'll leave him alone for now—and now is all we need."

The straw in the loft was older than he was; it was hard to tell if his tongue would have tasted mouldy this morning anyway, or if the unsubtle flavour was a result of breathing ancient strawy dust all night. He muffled another sneeze, and crawled to the edge of the loft to look down. A shadow darkened the narrow doorway, and he flattened himself immediately; but it was only Much.

"You're awake, then," his friend said softly. "I was beginning to think that what we do with you next was irrelevant because you were going to sleep for the rest of your life. Are you feeling any better?"

"No," said Robin.

"Oh. Well, it's a bright clear day out, my father dispatched the sheriff's men without half trying—a timorous lot to be sure, to be set hunting a desperate man—and some of my friends are coming round tonight to talk to you." Much had climbed the first rank of wall beams as he spoke—the ladder that would bring him the rest of the way to Robin's loft was in the loft with Robin—and his head was now only a little below his friend's as Robin hung over the edge.

"How did my father's bow get here?"

"I brought it up when I brought you breakfast," said Much.

"You know what I mean."

Much would not meet his eyes. "You'll have to ask Marian. She'll be here tonight."

"She'll—what? She's *not* to get mixed up in this."

Much's face was invisible as his fingers groped along the edge of the loft for the legs of the ladder. "I seem to have pushed it a little too far back," his voice said. "If you could—"

"Did you tell Marian she could come?"

Much's face re-emerged, looking cross. "You don't exactly tell Marian she may or may not do things."

Robin had noticed at their parting by the stream the night before that she seemed preoccupied; but there was an abundance of material to be preoccupied with. Much was leading him off to his refuge, Marian said only, "Good night," as she left them, and Robin, too tired to do anything at all—including follow Much—assumed that she was going home, and was relieved that she had gone so quietly. He had been afraid she would insist on coming with them, and every minute she was in his company was another minute's terrible danger for her. If he had been more alert, he might have noticed a gleam in her eyes.

"She is not to get mixed up in this," he repeated.

"You get to tell her that," said Much. "Never mind the ladder; you're not fit for conversation if you're going to brood, and there's work waiting at the mill." He stared, exasperated, at his friend's inward-looking face for a moment. "Robin, I do know enough *not* to know what you're going through just now." Robin's gaze flicked back to him. "But —don't take it out on Marian?"

Robin said nothing. Much shook his head, and started to climb down. "When you need to go out—the back of the barn's sheltered from any peering eyes; there's a broken board you can squeeze past." He reached the floor. "Try not to drop the ladder; we might hear it at the mill, and mice and bats don't drop ladders. I'll be back to bring you indoors after dark."

Much's two sisters still at home were bundled off to stay with friends, and his father, who knew about the temporary occupant of the old barn, tactfully (and strategically) left the house to his son and what friends might appear. Did anything go wrong with the evening's affairs, he would have been seen by at least a dozen of his own acquaintances, safely and innocently drinking ale and discussing crops at the Singing Lark on the road to Nottingham.

Marian was the first to arrive, and this did not help Robin's mood. He had meant to be calm and well-reasoned, although he was already angry that she should so casually (he thought) continue to put herself in danger by associating with him, and while he began by asking only how his father's bow had come to him, his own voice sounded curt in his ears.

She did not react to his tone, although she looked at him sidelong. She had simply stolen Robert Longbow's bow out from under the sheriff's guards' noses, for what had till yesterday been Robin's little holding had been under close watch by yester eve. She had done it at black midnight, after Robin and Much were both asleep. The very manner of her telling infuriated him, for she spoke flatly, and made no acknowledgement of her foolhardiness. It infuriated him further when it occurred to him that even had he noticed a suspicious gleam in her eyes the night before, there would have been nothing he could have done about it. When he began to remonstrate with her, she cut him off impatiently.

"I could not let your father's bow into their hands if I could help it," she said. She tried to smile at him, but the grimness of his expression made it hard for her. "I could not. Robin—you haven't listened to what Much wants to tell you; you are too anxious to make us believe we aren't listening to *you*. He—we—need you, and we need the—the heart of you. I thought perhaps the heart of you is that bow; or at least it was all I could save." She looked at him measuringly, trying to gauge how black was his mood. "The cottage would have been a little difficult to carry away secretly."

His temper flared then, and hers flared right back, and Much told them, half in alarm and half in amusement, to keep their voices down.

"And do you think you may tell me what I will and will not do, for our friendship's sake—or for aught else, perhaps?" said Marian. "Do you think that you have either the right or the wisdom to preach so to me?"

"Had I wisdom I would have eluded Tom Moody yesterday, and we would not be speaking so now. But, yes, I tell you you put yourself at risk needlessly—"

"Needlessly? And how do you mean 'needlessly'? Have you further decided the future of the Saxon race on our green island that it does not include the small measures that each of us Saxons may take? Even to the needless risk of helping a friend?"

"It is not seemly—"

Much said hastily, "I don't think you want to talk about seemly, Robin, unless you really want to be thrown head-first into the fire. But—"

"A *bow*!" cried Robin in frustration. "A few feet of ash-wood bent and bound in such a way as a Welshman once showed my father would hurl an arrow farther than his old bow ever could. For this—"

"We haven't got an army to throw the Normans out of England," Marian put in, her cheeks flaming from Robin's last remark. "The only thing we have to fight with is symbols. You are become a symbol, or you will—"

"*If* you will," murmured Much.

"And, I thought, a symbolic prop might be of help to you," said Marian, and the anger seemed to drain out of her. "Besides putting you in a better humour. I was wrong."

"Did you know what she was about last night?" said Robin.

"No," said Much. "But I wouldn't have told you even if I had, you know."

Robin looked from one to the other. "You have discussed this revolutionary force between you before."

"Yes," agreed Much, "but only because you refused to join in the discussions. We have not kept you out."

"And I have developed some taste for theory—and will-o'-the-wisps," said Marian.

"If you mean to reproach me," said Much, "I don't blame you. But—"

"But there is Norman blood in my veins, and your friends are not sure of me," said Marian. "I have never gone cold or hungry, that is true. But you do not know, because I have not told you, what it is like to have a half-Norman father who despises all things Saxon, including his wife, who I believe died of it; including his own tainted blood and his daughter's. He believes that he would have done much greater things in his life had he had the good fortune to marry a Norman woman; unfortunately no Norman woman with the dowry his estates needed would have him. I have quite a romantic view of the Saxons, you know," she said with a bitter smile; "I blame all my faults on my Norman blood, and my virtues on my Saxon. I like Much and his notions."

Robin said, trying to sound patient, "But you have just admitted to a ridiculously romantic idea of the Saxons; we will not prove any better than the Normans at close inspection."

"I disagree with you there," said Much.

"I did not say ridiculous," said Marian. "I said romantic. I will settle for the truth; and I find myself quite anxious to seek it."

"You're both hopeless," said Robin, hopelessly. "The king will catch us if the sheriff should fail to; and then the Saxon race can be symbolically and romantically hung by the neck till dead."

"If you want to talk romance," said Much, "do you really think the Lionheart is going to win Palestine? But it's a glorious idea, and he's the only Norman I've ever thought of liking. If he came home and tried ruling, I might pay attention." There was a rather implausible owl-hoot from outside, and Much's head snapped around. "If he can't get it better than that, he might just as well shout," he said, and got to his feet to let the next member of the Saxon revolution indoors. "You know, Robin, you can ask Marian to promise not to do it again; after all, your father had but the one bow."

Robin made an inarticulate sound and stood up; Much threw up his hands in mock terror and said, "See here, you aren't going to start on *me*. Besides, you'll make a bad impression on my friends," and opened the door.

Robin was embarrassed to discover that by the end of that first evening he was involuntarily feeling a reluctant hope for Much's plan of a few stalwart outlaws harassing the Nottingham sheriff and his fellows from a base hidden in Sherwood Forest. It was perhaps as well that he decided to think positively, if for no other reason than that his was one voice against several, all of them good talkers. Much himself was better than good; he was inspired. "Do remember that we are starting small," said Robin, amused, at one point, when Much was outlining a grand idea for releasing all the prisoners in the sheriff's gaols. "You will soon have us believing we can walk on air and pick locks with our fingers."

Much had been right that his friends would be glad to meet Robin; and they seemed to accept Marian as well—perhaps because she proved as fanatical as they were, he thought. But he found also that he was a little ashamed of himself for pouring water on the fire of their enthusiasm, when the bottom of that enthusiasm was that they were keeping him alive—they who could earn a welcome purse of coin instead by turning him over to the sheriff's men.

That first even there were seven of them: Robin himself, and Much and Marian; the leather-worker, Harald; Jocelin, a carpenter; and Simon and Gilbert, both yeomen under the same Norman lord. The hours passed swiftly, and Robin's head swam with talk and smoke—which refused to rise and go through the hole in the roof as it should, but preferred to snake around nose-level through the room—and exhaustion. He was still tired from the day before; and his nerves were pulled their tightest besides at the knowledge that for all the days that remained to him the threat of that purse of coin would follow him. He also had small patience with theory, however finely and logically it went together; and half to keep himself awake and half in pursuit of some small shadowy thoughts of his own, he began to draw bow-shaped marks on Much's hearth with a piece of charcoal. "You get to clean that off again," said Much, when he noticed; "my father is a tidy man and my sisters are worse."

"Um," said Robin.

It was probably nothing but a way of distracting his mind; but then his mind was pitiably grateful for anything by way of distraction. The next day, hidden again in his loft, he strung his father's bow for the first time in months and tried to pull it. Various things pinged and popped across his chest, down his shoulders and back; he pulled it, slowly, as if to control the flight of the arrow he did not notch: once; twice; thrice. He could not pull it a fourth time. His wrists shook with the strain; he looked at them dourly.

He did not have a great deal of time for such exercise after that. At his own insistence he left Much's barn the third day; the sheriff's men had not been back, as Much pointed out, but they would be back, as Robin pointed out. He carried with him a parcel of food and two blankets, both bows, what arrows he had left, a small axe, and a small shovel. "I feel like a pedlar," he said to Much, as his friend tried to help distribute the load. "I shall probably make as much noise as one, too— crash, crash, bong, clang, clang—oh, stop it. You're just making my shirt ruck up underneath with your tugging."

"If you were a donkey you'd bray," said Much cheerfully. "You're welcome; I'm glad to have been of assistance to you."

Robin grinned, but the grin fell away. "Come to think of it, I'm glad to have something *not* to thank you for." They stood looking at one

28

another for a moment. "Thank you," said Robin. "Thank you for my life."

"Pfft," said Much. "You know me, I just like to tell stories. How could I resist getting close enough to this one to tell about it later? I'll see you in a day or so." And he turned and went back downhill, toward the mill.

Robin went the other way; up into the undergrowth behind the barn which soon enough became Sherwood Forest, for Whitestone Mill lay with the forest at its back, where the stream that turned its wheel first emerged from the great trees. He was going to a place he knew, a place he thought was as safe as any might be for such as he, a place he had discovered once while chasing a (legitimately) wounded deer. He'd noticed it then for no particular reason—he thought—as somewhere that might be rendered both relatively comfortable and relatively defendable; and dismissed the notion at once for fear of what thinking about it might lead to. It had permitted itself to be dismissed, but it had never quite gone away completely, and he'd visited the little glen once since then—only once, because it was far off the usual way of the king's foresters in Sherwood. There was no need to visit it, awkward as it was to get at, through a jungle of hundreds' years' growth, undisturbed by humankind; and yet at the heart of the jungle was a bare space, sheltered on one side by a tumble of boulders extended by a tangle of two fallen oaks and the vines that laced them round; and, most wonderful, with a stream running at one edge of it, and a quiet pool at one end.

On the second evening round Much's fire he had suggested the place, hesitantly, knowing that his words would be the doom of the seven who listened to him—a man named Humphrey and a man named Rafe had joined them this night, and Marian was not there—and all had at once agreed to it. He did not like it that they deferred to him so easily. The most comforting explanation for it was that he was the only forester among them, and might be expected to know Sherwood best; and he would have liked to leave his musings there. But whether he wished to acknowledge it or not, the price on his head gave him an aura; however accidentally he had gained it, and however greatly he wished he could be rid of it, in their eyes because of it he was the real thing, and thus they would follow his lead.

Three days after he left Much's barn he crept back to it, to leave a pre-arranged mark for Much to see there; and retreated to wait at that place they had played in as children, where Much and Marian had found him, less a day still than a sennight since. "I was beginning to think you were simply going to disappear," was Much's greeting.

"I thought of it," said Robin.

"'Tis a good thing you did not think of it long, for we'd have ferreted you out, did we need to hire king's men to do it."

"That's rather what I thought," said Robin. "So here I am."

The first trouble was that it was soon obvious Much would not be able to find his way again to Robin's new—hiding place. Robin could not call it home, not yet; he carefully thought only one hour, or at most one night, ahead. Much was a competent woodsman as folk go who do not earn their living by it; but he did not have the points of the compass in his bones as a man must when he cannot see the sky. "I'll lead you here and back for now," said Robin. "At this rate, whether we have arrows or not we will not have time to shoot them; everyone will be fully occupied by getting lost."

"I can learn a track," said Much with dignity.

"But we can't afford to have a track," said Robin. "The existence of a track suggests that it leads somewhere. You—all of you—will have to learn *where it is,* and work obliquely. More obliquely than a forester. Never mind. Here we are."

Much ducked under the last concealing branch, and found himself at the cave mouth. "You have been busy," he said admiringly.

On the first day Robin had discovered that the boulders leaned into a bit of a hill, hidden by trees, and that there was a bit of a cave in the bit of hill, which he thought might later be enlarged. He began to build out a half-roof, half-screen from the cave opening, weaving green branches till his hands were raw and sticky with sap. He also found a spot, not too near, not too far, to dig the first privy.

He also strung his father's bow again, and drew it, gritting his teeth against the instant pain in his shoulders, which were already weary from digging. He tried to recall what his father had told him about the making of it, about the man who had given it to him; but all he could clearly remember was the obvious thing: that a bigger bow threw an arrow farther. He knew from his father's example that there need be no loss of accuracy. He worked his shoulders back and forth a minute till the rubbery feeling faded a little, and pulled the bow again. What remained to be seen was whether mere dumb desperation could accomplish anything.

He led Much most of the way back to the mill again, trying not to let it dismay him how long a lead Much needed before he began to recognise where he was clearly enough to make his own way. He promised to meet Much again in another two days.

Much was not alone the next time; Rafe and Harald were with him —and Marian. "I wished to come before," she said, "but Beatrix has been sick, and the world centers on Beatrix when she is sick. It would have been conspicuous had I left her." She grimaced. "Much as I would have been grateful to. But see here: I have brought you something useful, and not in the least symbolic." She undid the pack on her back and revealed the first fold of a long length of heavy green wool. "Is it not splendid? It is just the thing for outlaws who must sleep in the rain, and who will be tearing themselves on twigs and thorns. It is very stout stuff," she went on, pulling it between her hands to show the closeness of the weave, and not looking at Robin. "Here are needles and thread too—although I suppose I will have to show you how to use them."

A little silence fell, as Robin looked at Marian, Marian looked at her pack, Much looked at both of them, and Rafe and Harald looked puzzled. "What do you say, Robin?" said Much, with the air of a man who needs to bridle a horse whose ears are flat back and whose eye is rolling.

Robin swallowed. "I say—I must say—thank you. You are right that you will have to show me—us. I can sew up the holes that thorns have made, but I do not know how to cut and shape."

"I can do most of the cutting for you," she said, lifting her eyes at last to his, "and leave the seams for you, if you promise to have a care to sew them straight."

And it was Marian who said, when they had come again to Robin's camp, and Robin was trying to find out how much more of the way Much might have learned this time, "I can take us all back, Robin; you can stay here and start on some seams while daylight lasts."

The four men blinked at her. It had not occurred to Robin to question Rafe or Harald, for a horse-coper and a leather-worker were not expected to have much woodscraft. But it had not occurred to him or to

31

Much to look to Marian either. "You can come with us a little way if you like, and be certain I am not bragging," said Marian. "But I know where we are and where we came from."

"And furthermore she will do it obliquely," said Much. "How *do* you do it obliquely?"

Marian stared at him. "What are you talking about? It is only that I have long preferred the company of trees. My father's house, with Aethelreda there, runs very well without me; I spend more of my time at Blackhill than at the city house, and there is only so much embroidery I can do without going mad. I taught myself years ago, when I was still young enough to be thrashed for coming in late for dinner, not to get lost, for fear of being forbidden to go among my friends again. I cannot stop Beatrix from quarrelling with everyone, but I can get our party back to Whitestone Mill."

"Oh," said Robin.

"Now," said Marian hastily, "is there anything you need at once that I might get for you more easily than some other? Leather, perhaps. It is your craft, is it not?"

"Yes, lady, it is," said Harald slowly. He and Rafe were trying not to be dismayed that the lady with Norman blood in her was the only one besides Robin himself who could go freely through Sherwood. But the blankness of Robin's and Much's expressions was comforting, for there was no fear in it for the lady's loyalty. And it was true enough that Robin's folk would have need of friends, and a lady would be useful. "It—it would be a great boon to me to have leather in my hands again."

"Not to mention letting you off much of the digging and the stone-piling and the getting slapped in the face by the sharp edges of things like leaves that aren't supposed to have sharp edges," said Much. "It's that for you, Rafe, you know; there are no horses to trot out in Sherwood."

"Where did the wool come from?" said Robin.

"It was a bad dye lot," said Marian. "You will see. They were glad to have it go away at almost any price; but the cloth is good, and leaves and trees are rather streaky too, aren't they? You'll blend in the better for the streaks. Let me measure you across the shoulders, and I will cut out the first shirt."

CHAPTER FOUR

Spring passed swiftly as Robin and his small band began to make, or tried to make, or blundered toward making the ways and means that would enable them to live in Sherwood; if not beyond the reach of, then relatively safe from discovery by, any of the sheriff's men or the king's foresters. There was a little coming and going as prospective outlaws made their final break with their previous lives—and Robin began to mutter under his breath about using the thread Marian had brought for tying to the wrists of would-be outlaws who could not go six steps from the home camp without getting lost. Marian was still his only other truly reliable guide, although Much went wrong seldom, and Rafe through sheer tenacity was learning. "An eye is an eye, isn't it?" he said. "And I've a good eye for a horse. Wish trees had four legs." Harald made a pair of shoes for Gilbert, who had none, and even spring in Sherwood is hard on bare feet.

As folk arrived after leaving their old homes for the last time, they brought bits of their lives with them; but few had more than bits to bring. Humphrey brought three good bows and the seasoned wood for four more; and the gear to make several dozen arrows. "Call it a dowry," said Humphrey with a grin half-sheepish and half-proud. "Old Alcock's been drunk for years," he said; "he'll never notice they're gone. And if my lord does, it'll be too late to guess the truth and Alcock will have to think up a good tale quick to save his own skin—which if you want to ask me he should have lost long ago."

Now, how many among us can shoot what they aim at? thought Robin. About as many as can be sure of the north side of a tree. "Very well done," he said aloud; "and the sooner you get those arrows fletched, the better. You couldn't have chosen anything we needed more."

But the first night that he was not alone in the little half-hut, half-cave he could not sleep, listening to the breathing of the other human beings who now shared his outcast condition. He still could not quite believe that anyone would willingly throw over a living, however meager, to live as an outlaw. "Ah, but Robin, that's just it: we *are* choosing," said Much, when Robin admitted a little of this to him. He looked at his friend a time, finding, Robin suspected, new circles under the eyes and lines in the forehead. "None of us wakes in the night speaking the name of the man he killed by accident," he added.

Everyone was too tired come nightfall for many second thoughts. With the basic requirements of survival to attend to, which were daily urgent enough, Robin compelled—or was compelled to compel—practice sessions in woodscraft and archery. "If we had a smith among us, perhaps it would have been swords, but it is just as well it is not, because I know nothing of swords except that you should hold on by the end that isn't sharp. And we cannot afford to let anyone live among us who cannot sometimes bring home meat to feed us." Humphrey was a decent archer, about even with Robin himself; and Rafe, again, learned quickly. These two and Much he took aside and had practise further, with his father's longbow. "You must be mad," said Much, when he drew it the first time; "Good God," said Humphrey when he did. Rafe lost hold of the string altogether and put his wounded fingers in his mouth without saying anything.

"It is not possible to be accurate with anything so big and stiff," said Much.

"It is," said Robin; "my father did it. We have need of some edge over those who would pursue us. I have it in my mind that the longbow shall be that edge; it is little enough. I know something of bow-making; you and I, Humphrey, must see what we can do."

Humphrey looked thoughtful. "I might make another visit to Alcock's armoury after all. There are untrimmed lengths that might answer, or discarded ones that no one has looked at closely."

"Let us wait on that till we hear if there is any gossip about the six strong men who bound the heroic Alcock hand and foot and stole his twenty best bows from under his helpless eyes," said Robin. "There are other armouries and other bow-makers."

"To what purpose?" said Much. "Your father was an extraordinary man; we're all superlatively ordinary. Even if we could learn to draw such a thing as this longbow of yours, we are supposed to be woodsmen, are we not? We'll be whacking the ends of our bows off at every tree."

"The bow will be the size of the man," said Robin, "no more."

Much sighed. "Then I am the wrong one to complain, I guess, as mine will be the shortest in the company."

Marian, when she heard, liked the idea. "I have heard that the Welsh have been using longer bows than ours for some time; and they are not a tall people. May I try?" Robin handed her the longbow; she pulled it, but her eyes widened. "Ouch," she said. "I will have to begin carrying a wolfhound under each arm at home to develop my strength."

Exhaustion at day's end did provide a thankfully dreamless sleep for most of the little band. Robin, who dreamed more than the others, had something else to be grateful for: a marked lack of philosophy. Robin was much better at choosing hidden spots for secret meetings than he was at getting through the meetings themselves; no longer at the miller's clean hearth, he drew plans for huts and trenches in the dirt with a stick while the conversation went on without him. He did not wish to be either a king or a king-maker, and did not see that kings or philosophies kept the rain out. He said this latter so often that Much threatened to carve it in wood and hang it around his neck on a thong. Much missed the tale- and future-glory-spinning by an evening fireside; since he had left the mill for Sherwood, he spent his days doing the work of two or three people and therefore was one of the first to fall asleep at night. But Robin was happiest building huts and digging trenches, and it was hut-building and trench-digging that were important now.

The passing months were hard ones and grew no more easy; for as the green young outlaws grew a little older in skill and experience, the tale of their existence gained momentum. The tale had been launched by the sheriff's reward for the taking of Tom Moody's murderer, and it had lost nothing in the telling as the first weeks passed and the murderer was not taken. If Robin had not gathered a band of outlaws around him, the tale-tellers would have had to invent one for him. But the band did exist, and none of its members was taken either—the tale-tellers did not have to know how close one or two of Robin's dumber and more eager folk occasionally came—and this, too, improved in the retelling. There had been outlaws around Nottingham and in Sherwood before, but this sounded like something new—outlaws who believed in king and country, and good English law; who merely rebelled against the heavy hand of tyranny. The outer reaches of Sherwood became positively thick with people who, for practical or impractical reasons, wished to find these honourable outlaws; and some of them, too many from Robin's perspective, penetrated deep into the forest whose vastness was to be his and his people's security. The foresters and sheriff's men were avoided. If they were a dangerous problem, at least they were a straightforward one.

But other men came too, and a few grim and weary women, to seek just that haven that the tale-tellers had made of Sherwood and of Robin. And they were a much more complicated problem. The first few self-chosen outlaws were all Much's friends; their loyalty to Much's cause was not questioned, only their adaptability to the hard facts of their new life. The folk who came searching for Robin now were unknown. But their usual method of search was merely to plunge as far into Sherwood as they could get and then, completely lost, to wait hopefully to be rescued by the intrepid new scourge of Norman corruption. Robin could not ignore them, for it was on his head as certainly as the sheriff's reward that they were there at all. And so they were rescued and brought, if not to the home camp, at least somewhere that they might meet a slightly-built, ordinary-looking young man who spoke to them courteously. They tended to be surprised when Robin introduced himself. Some realised, or were persuaded to realise, that life as an outlaw was not the answer to their troubles. Some stayed.

The ones who did not stay were led back to one of the public ways through Sherwood, and given enough food to see them to the nearest town—and sometimes a coin, even if only a farthing. Much observed the first act of alms-giving with an ironical eye; he himself had brought the outlaws' first earnings back to Sherwood from the sale of some arrows Robin had made from the materials Humphrey had brought. The money was to have gone to buy more materials for more of those desperately-needed arrows to keep the outlaws fed. "I saw the extra loaf of bread in that parcel, too," said Much. "Fortunately my snares are working nicely, and I also brought flour."

Robin hunched up his shoulders and scowled. "The man had been wandering for days; you could see his ribs through his shirt. What would you have me do?"

"What you did," said Much. "Didn't I just say that my snares work nicely?"

Robin's band had settled, more comfortably than might have been expected, into the little hillside glen with the stream and pool nearby. The hut-cave had been enlarged enough by the first half-dozen of them that it was possible to creep out in the middle of the night without necessarily treading on any of one's fellows. The position of the boulder-fall had made it possible to build a semi-permanent hearth for a fire, which was protected from the worst weather, and which could be prevented, mostly, from smoking in too tell-tale a fashion; and which enabled them to eat cooked food. No one remembered when the camp began to be called Greentree. One day it was merely a patched-together and unreliable temporary shelter for folk who had no better; and the next day it had a name, and had become home.

Many of the king's deer that Robin had once earned his bread to preserve went to feed the pinched bellies of his outlaws; and as anyone's marksmanship improved, he began to learn to set his arrows where the beast was least likely to fall and break the shaft, that the arrow might be salvaged and used again. It occurred to Robin that it might be possible to grow tired of venison; but there were rabbits as well, and squirrels and pigeons, and several of the folk that now sheltered with him proved handy with roots and herbs, and the stews then produced became savoury as well as nourishing. Much brought flour from Whitestone as his father could spare it, so that they might also have bread and dumplings. The miller was well off as Saxon yeomen went, and could spare it, and so Robin tried not to think of the debt, only too likely to prove unpayable, that his company was running up to the miller's generosity. It was a little easier not to think about when he looked around him at the wan discouraged faces filling out, and the wary glint of hope seen in more and more eyes.

"Any man may be called merely *Robin*," grumbled Much one day; "we need a better name for you."

"Normanslayer?" Robin suggested ironically. "Deerthief? Sheriff's-bane?—would that I were."

Much shook his head. "My second sister's husband's name is Robin, and a duller stick of a man you could not hope not to speak to."

"Speaking well or ill does not keep the rain out," said Robin automatically. "If he—"

"No," said Much. "We all know by now about your single-minded lust for the practical. But word's gone out, you know, just as we told you it would. Anyone we'd want who got you confused with my sister's husband wouldn't come, for fear of being bored to death. You need another name. Or we need something to call you." Much brooded. "I rather like Sheriff's-bane."

"I do not," said Robin. It was a grey and louring sort of day, and a damp, sticky drizzle fell or crept through the trees. Summer had arrived, and the woods were thick with the smell of it, and the rain was warm and felt almost like sap—no less unpleasant running down the back of the neck. Robin pulled his cloak up around his head. "Robin of the Hood," he suggested. "It rains enough here, God knows."

"It'll do," said Much. "I know you too well to expect better."

Marian came to the camp at least once a sennight. She was, if anything, even more tired than Robin himself, although he never asked her if her dreams woke her in the small hours. Nor did they ever discuss her coming to live in Sherwood as Much had done, who still went outside, when it suited him, as the miller's son. But then his father was sympathetic to his son's cause, and Marian's, had he known of it, would not be. Marian continued to live at her father's house, and she learnt what people said of the sheriff, and of the small band of unusual outlaws lately gathered in Sherwood; and she brought the tales with her as she brought leather and twine and salt and pots for cooking. It was a dangerous task she had set herself, and a dangerous journey, both for herself and for Robin and his people. The strain—beginning with the fact that Marian did not permit discussion of what it was she was doing —told on both her and Robin, and they quarrelled almost as often as they met.

It had been ten days since last she had been to Greentree, and not only had the company cautiously accepted two new members, but there were two families sitting in a subdued and worn little huddle near the fire. The small available space of the glen was bursting at the edges, and

Robin was twitchier even than usual. There were too many people to keep utterly quiet, and he wanted any forester so implausibly scrupulous in pursuit of his occupation (or the price on Robin's head) as to come anywhere near the camp to hear nothing more for his trouble than the sounds all trees make alone in a wilderness. "I did not think there would be so many," said Marian wonderingly.

"Neither did I," said Robin grimly. He had not had the heart to send the families immediately on their way, as he usually did with the clearly unsuitable. They had been wandering too long and were too weary; each had children who were wearier yet. They would be sent on—soon; but not till they were fed and rested, and meanwhile they had, somehow, to be taken care of till they had regained their strength.

Robin, looking at the faces around the fire, and then back at Marian's, thought there was not much difference between them. Love and fear turned in his heart, and he could not have said which was stronger; but the two of them together produced a spark like anger. "You cannot keep on like this," he said. "It is too hard for you. It is too hard for me, watching you."

Marian sighed; she and Robin hadn't had their quarrel yet this visit. She pulled herself to her feet. "I will go on like this because I am the best spy you have. I cannot trust the Norman gentry any less than you yourselves do," and Robin saw the shadow of her father on her. "You need not fear that I will be followed; the sheriff's men wonder, to be sure, and they watch me when they have a few minutes to spare; but they will not believe anything too mutinous of a mere daughter while the father still pays his taxes and salutes the sheriff in the streets of Nottingham. And I have taken care to be seen drooping and ashamed as persons of better judgement tell me what I might have expected of such a scurrilous friend as the son of old Robert Longbow. Robert was not a bad man, you know, but his son . . ." She looked at Robin and half-smiled. "I will try to bring more cloth the next time I come; you are still sadly ragged."

"Robin keeps insisting on clothing the ones who need it worst first," said Much. "I've told him that that colour really doesn't suit him, but he won't listen."

Robin stood up beside Marian. "Truly you must not risk yourself this way. I know I say this to you every time, but I cannot help it. If anything should happen to you—"

She laid a hand gently on his lips. "Nothing will happen to me, barring an inconvenient tree limb falling on my head, or that Beatrix contrives to fall ill again. You have other, better things to concern yourself with."

Robin smiled beneath her fingers, and took her hand in his own and kissed it. "No," he said.

She held his hand a moment longer when he would have released hers. "Thank you," she said, and then she turned and was silently gone. A baby cried, and Robin returned to his present responsibilities with a shudder. "A crying child's voice will carry half across England. Is there still no news?"

Much shrugged. "I'm sure Jocelin is running his feet sore even now, but it's only been three days, and it's not so many towns that will take families who have so obviously run away from their last places—particularly farm families without town skills. It will take time."

"Time which we will not have," said Robin. "We must split the camp. If they are caught here, not only are our heads forfeit, but likely their own as well, for being found with us."

Much nodded. "That's true. There's shelter at Growling Falls, and it's an easy way from here, and we could still feed them and keep an eye on them."

"There will be shelter, you mean," said Robin. "We'll start on the roof tomorrow." The child wailed again, and Robin grimaced.

"Or perhaps tonight," suggested Much. "There's a good moon for it."

It would be at least another day and more likely two before, in conscience, the families could be shifted to Growling Falls. In conscience? thought Robin. How does my conscience feel about *not* moving them? There was no news from Jocelin; the only news was of the sheriff's braggadocio, and how he would have Robin Hood's head on a pike before the season was passed. Robin had spoken to the baby's mother, but colic was colic; and even once they were resettled at Growling Falls they would eat as much as they did at Greentree, and how much they ate was—as people who have not had enough to eat for months will eat.

Not for the first time, it occurred to him that Much could run their company, particularly now that it was more or less going, now that there were at least three or four of them who could be trusted not to get lost, now that there were folk to hunt and dig and cook as well as plan. If he gave himself up into the hands of the sheriff's men, much of the enthusiasm for tracking the others down would evaporate, and they might not be in much danger. He knew however that he was not capable of giving himself up in cold blood; and his thoughts went round in a circle not so dissimilar to the one he had been caught in on the day he was to meet Much and Marian at the Nottingham Fair. He recognised the similarity, and decided that he was not in a very good mood.

The path took a sharp bend and dived over the stream Robin could hear through the trees. There was no proper bridge, but only a great log, wedged on either end where it lay on the land by stout pegs hammered into the earth and braced with stones. Beneath ran the stream, deep enough here to be treacherous, deep enough to give a man a thorough wetting if he tried to wade across it. The log bridge had been set there by the king's foresters years ago, but it was the only dry way to get across the stream for some distance in either direction. Robin should have had all his wits about him for so public a crossing, but he did not. He stepped up on the great treetrunk, still preoccupied; steadied himself momentarily; and began to walk across.

He didn't go very far. There was a man—a very large dark-bearded man—standing in the middle of the narrow way, leaning on a long blackthorn staff. Robin, suddenly aware of the unmoving shadow that stood in his way, paused and looked up, thinking: how stupid can a man with a price on his head be? I never noticed the fellow; and he is a bit large for overlooking.

"I'm a stranger here, to be sure," said the shadow, "but it seems to me that you show scant courtesy; for I was already a quarter way across this slender bridge when you jumped on the far side and strode toward me."

Robin didn't like the man's tone, and he was a shaggy and draggled-looking figure besides; arrogance did not sit well on him, or so he told himself, to drown out the lecture his better judgement wished to give him on caution. What if the man had been a forester? The man was not a forester, that's all; and Robin now wanted to get past him and forget the whole incident as quickly as he might. He looked up into the man's eyes—and quite a way he had to look up to do it—and his voice was not friendly as he said, "Very well, I was in a hurry and was not paying attention, and I did not see you. As you apparently stopped to watch me, for you are still only a quarter of the way over and I am more than half, I suggest that you go back and let me by, and then you may cross at whatever leisurely pace seems best to you. You may even sit bestraddle and dangle a hook for fish if you will, so long as you have an eye out for other travellers who may, like me, wish to proceed at a normal pace."

"No," said the stranger. "I like not your plan, and I seem to have forgot my fishbait. You shall give way before me and prove that the folk here are not the knaves they seem to be."

Robin's nerves were still jumping from the quick, awful wash of fear when he had first seen the stranger and had not known if he faced a doom brought on by his own carelessness; and his temper, never slow to follow up an opportunity, would not now allow him go the long way back to the far shore and let this unpleasant giant past. "I shall not. I say that the folk of your county must have thrown you out for your manners, and you come here to plague us."

Something flared in the man's eyes at these words, and he uttered a sharp bark of laughter that had no humour in it. He said, "Then I shall have to make my own way—as I have often done in this life." And, as if he thought of using it to clear his present path, he took a fresh grip on his staff.

"A brute and a bully you are," said Robin angrily, his temper gone for good, and, instinctively, one hand strayed toward the quiver on his back.

"And a coward I call you," said the stranger, his brow lowering in a terrible frown; "for you would shoot me with your arrows when I have naught but a staff to defend myself with."

Robin's common sense tried to make him say something conciliatory; what came out was a snarl: "A coward I will not be called!"—and he ran freely back to the far side of the stream, but with his hands shaking with rage. He cut himself a sturdy oak staff that might hold against seasoned blackthorn, and trimmed it, taking a few deep breaths to steady himself. The stranger had not moved from his place a quarter way across the log bridge.

Robin left his bow and arrows hung on a tree limb, and went to meet his challenger. He was, or had been, good with a staff, for he was quick and light on his feet, and vagrant breezes had less effect on staves than on arrows. But he had not practised with a staff in many long months, and his footwork would avail him little whilst he stood on the narrow curved back of a log bridge; and he knew besides that he would be no match in physical strength to the giant before him.

But he stepped up on the log nonetheless, and held his staff warily, and advanced against his enemy; and his enemy straightened up and moved forward to meet him.

Robin feinted and, as the stranger lowered his staff to parry, raised his own in a lightning stroke to smash the stranger across the brow; only the quickest shift on the stranger's part saved him from a blow that would certainly have landed him in the stream. "You strike well," he said, surprised; and, surprising Robin, his voice sounded almost pleasant. He began an attack of his own, but deft and wise though he was, Robin parried ably, and threw the blows back upon him.

They stood so for many long hard minutes, neither moving but for the rare half-stagger as his opponent drove past his guard and rapped him with his staff; for they were better matched than they appeared. Robin was the smaller by a good deal, and, as he soon knew, the less practised, but he was strong and wiry—and stubborn; and he had the knack of the thing besides. The stranger was just the littlest bit slow, and never quite managed to deliver a blow that had his full strength behind it.

Their breath came in great gasps, and a red haze was in their eyes. Sweat ran down Robin's face and sides, and his ribs burned from the stranger's bludgeoning. And this for who gets to cross first, he thought in disgust, for his bruises were cooling his temper. Perhaps it was that ill-timed thought, or the sweat running into his eyes, that put him out, for of a sudden a blow he did not see knocked his staff aside and caught him fairly between the last rib and the hip, and swept him into the stream.

"*Ugh,*" grunted Robin, floundering to the surface, and spitting water.

43

The stream was *cold,* and his body seemed to contract inside its skin with the shock of it after the heat of the contest; his bones ached with the chill. He stood up awkwardly; the strength of the current pulled him off balance, and his backbone felt as if it had been split in half by the stranger's final blow. He glared up at the man still standing on the bridge. The stranger was looking down at him with a curious expression on his face. "Well, you have won," Robin said ungraciously. "I would count it a favour if the victor would now proceed on his way and leave me in solitude."

"You fought well," said the stranger, as if he would make peace.

Easy for him to say, thought Robin, who only grunted again in reply, and pushed his dripping hair away from his face; it clung to his neck like weeds. The cold made his teeth chatter, and he could feel the blood blackening the skin at all the places the stranger's staff had struck him, as if the water were a charm to bring up bruises. He found himself ungenerously hoping that a few of his own blows were making the stranger's sides throb as well. He set out for the nearer shore—and to his annoyance found the stranger came to meet him, and held out a huge hand to pull Robin through the mud and water-weeds of the slower-moving water near the bank.

"My thanks, sirrah," Robin said grimly. "Why do you not go? I have acknowledged that you have won the right to cross the bridge first; or you have acknowledged it for me by removing me from your path. Yet you are still on the side of the stream where you began."

"And you, on the contrary, are where you wished to be," said the stranger with something like humour.

Robin had taken off his boots and was peeling out of his tunic, and he looked at the stranger with dislike, but something in the man's face brought a weak flicker of humour to his own. Now that the stranger was not standing like a small mountain in the middle of the bridge, nor scowling like a medium-sized thunderstorm, Robin found himself thinking that he looked like someone whose company Robin might have enjoyed in other circumstances.

"Just where I wanted to be indeed," said Robin, and began discouragedly to wring out his tunic.

"I will offer you an apology, if I may," the stranger said after a

---

44

moment. "My temper is not so good as it might be, and I—well, it is of no matter."

"My temper is nothing to boast of either," said Robin ruefully, now squeezing the water from his shirt, and shivering in the light breeze. "Perhaps times are hard with you; and such weighs on a man's mind."

The stranger went suddenly still, and Robin looked over at him—at first curiously, and then with some alarm. What if this man had been sent by the sheriff after all—? Robin's hands paused, and for a moment the only sounds were the voice of the water and the rustling of leaves, and, audible perhaps only to himself, the sodden slow drip of water striking the moss around his feet.

"Times, in truth, are hard, " said the stranger slowly, "and I have come a long way in a short time, and am not—at ease in the new country where I find myself."

Not a spy, thought Robin; or I doubt the sheriff could hire any spy so good at his craft as to put on such a look of weariness. He squeezed again, and a heavy splatter of water sank into the wet moss. Although the sheriff is holding little back of late.

"May I set you on your way, then, if you are unfamiliar here?" he said aloud, trying to sound disinterestedly courteous. He picked up one soggy boot and looked at it with gloom.

The stranger heaved a great sigh, and spoke as if he made a hard decision. "I seek the man they call Robin Hood."

Robin dropped his boot, more in surprise than apprehension. "What for?" he said aloud.

The man sat down, which made him look, as he drew his knees up to clasp his hands around them, rather like a short thick mountain than a taller thinner one. "I come from the far side of Nottingham," he said; "but we know your sheriff there, too. My lord needed no help to raise the rents on the yeomen who worked his land; but the sheriff and his taxes gave it him anyway, and generously. They have been this three years at driving me off my farm, and they have done it at last. I could not meet the rents when my lord raised them once more. . . . I had lately heard of a man named Robin Hood; I little knew whether to think him real or a tale to torment such as I. But I have nothing left to risk, and so I thought to look for him. . . ." He paused, and swallowed. "Forgive

---

45

me, but I have had little to eat this past sennight, and our battle, which I brought on myself—I have ever had a hasty temper; my lord would not else have taken notice of me among his other Saxon slaves—seems to have taken my strength.

"It was seeing you, well-clothed and fed, and hurrying to your business with such firm purpose that you did not see me, that brought a sudden blackness to my mind, and I challenged you."

Hurrying to my business with such firm idiocy, thought Robin; I suppose such preoccupation does make me look honest, for only an honest man could afford it. He undid his damp leather wallet from his damp leather belt, and opened it. "It is your own fault that it is wet," he said to the man on the ground, "but the bread's made of the miller's coarsest meal, and should have held up to its soaking pretty well." He held it out to the stranger, noticing for the first time how hollow the man's eyes were beneath the weariness, and how his ragged clothing hung over a frame too thin for its great bones.

The man looked at the wallet and then at Robin, but he made no move to touch the food. "I thank you, but I do not ask for charity," he said, with a slight return to his old threatening manner. "I would ask, if you will or can give it, a direction to this outlaw, Robin Hood—or perhaps the information that you are a sheriff's man, and will clap me in irons."

Robin grinned. "I would like to see me try it. It's not charity—may I say that the temper you wanted to apologise for is showing again, even if you have not the strength to back it just now? Take the food, or I'll stamp it into the mud." He found himself growing embarrassed. "You see—*I* am Robin Hood. It's your first wages, if you like, although we cannot pay wages, and we have yet no spoils to divide, as successful outlaws are expected to do. But if you think I look well-clothed and well-fed, you will be better off with us than without us."

But the man only went on staring. Robin took a step closer. "Take it," he said, "or I'll drip on you."

The man reached up and took the wallet, but then he bowed his head, and still he did not touch the food. "I do most humbly beg your pardon," he said to the ground.

Robin, putting on his boots and grimacing at the clammy feel of them, said, "Yes, as well you may, but don't go on about it, if you please. I think we might as well go back to Greentree, where we—live. I can bring you in and get dry too."

The man broke the bread in half, and offered half back to Robin, who, after looking at the set of the stranger's mouth, accepted it. The man thoughtfully ate his half, looking at the stream. "Would you wish me, for my first command, to fall off the bridge into the water?"

"It's an idea," said Robin. "But while I am considering it, you could tell me your name."

The man climbed slowly to his feet again, and Robin wondered how he could not have noticed before how very thin he was, and how worn his clothing. "For the size of our holding, my father was called Little; and so I became John Little after him, or *Johnlittle,* as it amused those who looked up a certain distance to see my face to call me." He paused; his beard made it hard to read his expression. "But that was when I had a home and a holding, and friends to call me by name."

"We shall baptise you again as you enter your new life," said Robin, tipping his own head back to look up the certain distance. "I call you Little John, and so you shall be known from this day forward."

"So then I shall," said he, and, ignoring the bridge, waded into the stream, and crossed so to the other side. He was wet to the neck when he came up on the opposite shore.

CHAPTER FIVE

obin lost count of how many bowls of stew Little John ate that evening; it might have been six or seven. That was besides the half a pie and the ends of two almost-stale loaves (nothing edible in Greentree lasted long enough to get really stale) he'd eaten when they first arrived.

When the two of them squelched back to camp, they headed at once for the fire. All the children were lingering significantly in its neighbourhood, where the big pot that was one of the Sherwood band's dearest possessions sat on its short iron legs and steamed; its aroma said, vegetable soup, heavy on the turnips and too few marrow bones. The old woman who was tending the fire looked at Robin and then at his companion; and her face went abruptly blank, and her cheeks hollow, as if she were sucking in at the corners of her mouth. She turned and busied herself at the woodpile, and threw several good chunks on the fire, that it would blaze up better, to cook the soup faster or to cause wet clothes to steam dry more quickly.

One of the children went up to Robin and grabbed a corner of his shirt. She squeezed it disbelievingly, and looked up into his face with an expression of deep disapproval. This was a child who had been thrashed by her mother the day before for playing in the pond, and getting her only whole suit of clothes wet.

"*You'll* get no soup," she said with profound certainty. Someone behind them chuckled, and there was a rustle, and utter silence fell.

Robin said mildly, "There was a little trouble about a bridge that was too narrow. But all has ended well, and I wish to introduce you to our latest member: I give you John Little, henceforth to be known as Little John."

Much appeared from wherever he had been and said, "A *little* trouble, say you?" He lifted one of the staff-flayed strips of Robin's tunic. "And with, we understand, a little man." He gazed up at the newcomer loom-

ing over Robin's shoulder. "Be it so; I would not cross your judgement."
He dropped his eyes to Little John's staff—Robin had lost his green oak
to the stream—and said, "I am sure you will be a very useful man to
have around. With your little staff. I welcome you."

Little John's mouth stretched and curled as if he were not accustomed
to smiling; and he said, "I shall try to be useful. And your name, my
new friend?"

"Much," said Much. "Much of Whitestone Mill, as I was; although
the person of that name seems to be gaining some notoriety of late, and
I believe I shall start leaving him at home in Sherwood."

The outlaws were lucky in their first winter. Snow fell rarely, and
only a little of it sifted through the many branches and stubborn brown
oak leaves of Sherwood to cover the ground. The center of Greentree's
glen gleamed white in the sunlight occasionally; but what snow there
was melted quickly. Thanks to Harald, by the time there was ice underfoot everyone had shoes stout enough to walk without fear of frostbite,
and a leather tunic to cut the winter wind. As the season stayed mild,
the animals the outlaws depended on for food and clothing were in good
condition, and most of them continued to stray through the forest as
they did during the rest of the year, and did not take hibernation too
seriously.

The winter chill and the shortness of daylight did, however, cut down
on the number of folk who left what homes they had to seek Robin
Hood, for which favour Robin felt that a little snow and a permanently
cold nose was worth it. Even the sheriff and the king's foresters seemed
willing to live and let live for a time, and take things, even outlaws, a
little more leisurely, be grateful for the boon of a gentle winter, and wait
for spring.

By midwinter Robin could hardly remember a time when Little John
was not at his elbow, patient and hard-working, ready to carry out
orders, and to suggest improvements on those orders before he followed
them. As his frame filled out to its proper proportions, he suited his
nickname even more illustriously than he had when Robin met him on
the log bridge; and yet for all his size he moved quietly through the
laboriously preserved tangle around Greentree. He also never got lost.

And he unexpectedly knew practical things about the design and

49

shoring-up of earthworks. "From farming a landscape that doesn't want to be farmed," he said. And from being the largest man in several villages and automatically expected to do more than an equal share of the heavy work. "I learnt to have an eye for hills and ditches in self-defence," he said.

"Self-defence," said Much. "Ah. A man the height of a Midsummer bonfire would find himself preoccupied with self-defence."

"Even as horses are plagued by horse-flies," said Little John. "I learnt wrestling when I was a boy, when I got tired of being knocked down by boys half my size and twice my age."

Nonetheless no one was sorry when the little green knots of young leaves began to appear on the tips of twigs, even though the stream at the edge of Greentree's meadow promptly overflowed and the hut-cave where they mostly slept was flooded, and almost everyone caught cold. No one became dangerously ill, only a trifle snarly.

"Have you noticed that Robin hasn't complained about the stink of the arrow-glue and Harald's stretched hides for over a week?" said Much. "Because he can't smell 'em. Maybe the foresters all have head-colds too and won't wonder why someone has set up a tannery in the middle of Sherwood."

Perhaps it was the end of his head-cold, or the relative peace of the winter just passed, which made Robin sharp when Much brought a stranger to Greentree one day in early April. The man was the first stranger Robin had seen—or rather, been seen by—in several months.

In any company that did not include Little John this man would have been large; and he towered over Much. But where Little John had come to them dressed as a man dresses who has had an empty purse and no home for some time, this man dressed as a prince might, in smooth red-dyed leather unmarked by age and little by use. There was even a touch of lace at his wrists and throat, which caught Robin's attention more than the size of the bow over the man's shoulder, which under other circumstances could have pleased him.

Robin said harshly, "Why came you to Sherwood? This is no place for the likes of you." To Much he said, "And why did you bring him here? It would have been better to have led him to Growling Falls—where it matters less who finds us."

Much said, "I led him nowhere. He arrived."

Robin, appalled, was silent. When he looked back to the stranger, the man smiled, a surprisingly sweet and wistful smile. But his first words were badly chosen: "I come willing to pay for my pleasure," he said.

Robin's brows snapped together, and a few of those standing near moved to leave a little space around their leader and the yellow-haired stranger. But Much held up a fat and jingly purse; perhaps he shook it a little too forcefully to be in keeping with his casual expression; and he was careful that Robin's eyes should be upon him when he raised his shoulders and eyebrows as if to say he did not understand it either but was willing to give the benefit of the doubt.

"I heard," the stranger said, "of a band of folk deep in Sherwood, who, having become outlaws because they were not permitted to earn an honest living, have been sending those poorer than themselves along their ways with coin in their pockets. And—" the stranger looked bashful but optimistic—"and I thought that this was an outlawry I would wish to ally myself with. And I thought I might begin by replacing a little of the coin spent in so honourable an undertaking."

The guilelessness of the stranger's confidence was not lost on Robin; the worst of having been brought up in easy comfort was the notions it gave you about the fairness of life and the supremacy of virtue. It had crossed his mind once or twice, listening to Much in full cry, that too much high-mindedness could tantalize some careless scion of a great family into thinking outlawry romantic; but Much had no more use for the aristocracy than Robin did himself. Much's mother had been a lady's maid before she married the miller, and the tales she had told of the life of the gentry were similar to the ones that Robin's mother had told—and that Marian could tell but rarely did because she did not like being reminded of them. Robin had hoped that they would be safe from scions in Sherwood because the more whimsical of Much's philosophical raptures would fail to reach so high for lack of a messenger.

"You are but playing with words," said Robin. "Speak plainly."

The stranger let his breath out with a grunt, and his voice was no longer light and charming. "Speak plainly, say you. I am the younger son of a father who has chosen to accept any ignominy the Normans wish to inflict on our family—and my older brother takes after him in all ways. We have lost much of our own substance in currying favour; let a Norman admire a thing and my father will press it upon him as a gift. So it has happened that a Norman lord has admired my sister. He is nearing fifty, and my sister is seventeen; he has buried two wives already, but he is soon to have a third." The man stopped speaking and stared at the ground, and Robin felt his first belief in him, for his expression was now one he recognised; made up of anger and desperation, Robin had seen it on the face of everyone in Greentree. The man looked up and said, sternly, as if he would command belief, "I am a Saxon, sir."

"How did you find us?" Robin asked, more gently; but still first in his mind was the safety of his people. Second he thought that this man was too confident to make a good outlaw; and third he permitted himself some sympathy for a young man who had found his easy life less easy than he wished. And fourth he wondered if the young man's sister was anything like Marian.

"You are . . ." said the stranger, and hesitated. Robin was pleased at the hesitation, of the awareness that he was among strangers. "It is not a simple thing to hide so many as you are, even in a forest the size of Sherwood," he said at last.

"You tell me nothing I do not already know," said Robin with a little impatience.

"By the sheriff's long nose," burst out Much. "Is that all you can say? Robin, we can use this man—two-thirds of our company still can't be trusted out of sight of the camp to not get lost. And he may have found us easily tracked, but has anyone else showed up on our door-step like this?"

"Thank you, Much," said Robin calmly, "for telling this unknown gentleman truths I would rather we had kept to ourselves. Besides, not more than half of us get lost that easily any more. We could use you," he went on, turning back to the yellow-haired man. "What I need to decide is whether we should. And I would have a clearer answer from you as to how you found us. The suit you wear is not commonly seen on those who possess such woodcraft as you claim."

"Meaning—?" the stranger said in dismay. "Meaning that I was brought here like a lamb on a string and left bleating outside your lair

while the hunters wait in ambush?" He looked down at himself. "I—
I did not think of that. I thought I was being practical. Leather is tough
and long-wearing. I like red. I—er—the colour is not practical, is it?"

"Not very," said Robin dryly. "One could run a pole across your
shoulders and stake you out at any corner of a tourney ground with the
other banners. But I acknowledge that a spy probably would choose
better than to wear a signal-flag on his back when he went among
rogues. You were about to tell us how it is you make so light of finding
your way through a league of bramble-bushes as trackless as we can
keep them."

The young man stood silent a moment, recalling his wits. "I—I have
friends, who have heard things, and I have eyes." He paused, and Robin
made a sharp gesture with his hand as preface to a sharp word, but the
young man threw up his own hand. "No, wait. I'm not—trying to play
with you. I've always been able to find my way. It was a joke when I
was younger, that I could find lost arrows. Our old huntsman hated me
because the first time my father brought me out, I found the deer we'd
wounded after the huntsman had missed the way. I'm at home among
the trees." The smile, tentative now, reappeared. "Even if I don't dress
like it.

"I cannot tell you my friends' names," he added slowly, "if that is
your next question; the reasons you yourselves would honour, did you
know them."

"Had you considered that you might be seeking merely another gang
of cutthroats, who honoured no laws whatsoever?" Robin put in, all the
more quickly for the ringing of Much's words in his ears. They *could* use
this young man who could find lost arrows. But many men had Normans thrust into their families against their will; and running off to
Sherwood was of no particular service to his sister. This young man
would wake up, a week hence, missing his feather-bed, and he would
be gone—and the number and the plan of Greentree with him.

"Yes, of course I have thought; I have thought long, for my sister was
betrothed at Christmas." He looked around at them, and something
glittered in his eyes. "I do not wish to boast, but I am stubborn, and
skilled in ways of use to you. It did not need your companion's impetuous words to tell me that. I would not have come had I not something

to offer besides the contents of a purse. If you have doubts of me, take me out and let me show you I can do what I say I can. If you still have doubts . . ." He paused, a little at a loss. "Well, chain me to a tree at night and post guard."

"Post guard," said Robin thoughtfully. "We might have enough people to begin to do so." The yellow-haired man's shoulders slumped. "No —I did not mean on you, although I will accept your offer of a demonstration.

"I know of no other haven as satisfactory as this to set camp," he continued; "I would rather we not try to shift, if I can shut my conscience—or my fears—up enough to hear myself think. I, too, am stubborn. But I wish I were sure this was a feature entirely missing from the sheriff's men and their fellows the king's foresters."

"They will not find you here for some time at least. Those who are not stupid and might tell them where to look mostly do not love the sheriff," said the yellow-haired man.

"But it is not something we can count on, as you betray by the words *at least* and *mostly*," replied Robin.

"'Tis true enough that the sheriff's men do not come so deep in this forest they claim to rule—and so do not know the knolls and clearings that might harbour a camp such as ours," said Much, subdued but hopeful.

"And the foresters dislike tearing their fine tunics on the brambles we have hereabouts," said Robin. "So I think we will compromise. It has long been in my mind that we should set regular guard—at some little distance from the camp, that those who guard might have time and opportunity both to warn and to mislead."

"I—" said the stranger and paused. Robin wondered how much consideration he had given, in the months since his sister's betrothal, to the possibility of a lack of warmth in his reception when he found his band of honourable outlaws and suggested he throw in his lot with them. "I might be able to lessen the risk in another fashion. I have some knowledge of the—construction of fortresses—"

"Book-learning," said Little John, in the tone of voice of a short-tempered man blocked from crossing a narrow bridge by the discourtesy of a fellow traveller. "Your father bought you a dusty old man to tell you how the Greeks did it, didn't he?"

The stranger looked thoughtfully at the one man present even taller than he was. "It began with my tutor, yes; I can tell you how the Macedonians did it and the Romans did it, as you say, as well. But—"

"There's no harm in book-learning," Much interrupted, having recovered his spirits, and addressing Little John's belt-buckle, "if you know what to do with it."

"Throw it out," said the stranger pleasantly, and he smiled again, as if he had found his footing after being too hard-pressed for his skill. He turned his smile full on Little John, and Robin thought, perhaps he has learnt to use his charm so forcefully because his life has not been so easy as I would make it.

There was a little stir at the edge of the circle of folk watching the scene; and Robin saw the top of a head he recognised as Marian, who stepped around Much, who made way for her—and then stopped in her tracks. "*Will?* Will of Norwell? What are *you* doing here?" But the tone of her voice was trusting, and no more than surprised, and Robin saw that everyone at once relaxed.

"Of Norwell no more," said Will.

Several things flashed over Marian's face, and at last she said, "Will Scarlet, then, for your old nickname has always suited you best since you discovered dyed cloth." And she walked forward and held out her hands, and Will Scarlet grasped them. Robin felt a twinge of jealousy, not that Marian should have so handsome a friend whom she was glad to meet, but at the gracefulness of their hands clasping. Greentree, relentlessly tidy as its leader required it to be kept, and he himself, Robin Hood, were infinitely the more shabby for one brief touch of hands.

"My father is an old friend of Will's father," Marian said, turning back to Robin. "I have known Will almost as long as I have known you." The explanation made Robin's heart beat the more hollowly, for Will, who was so old a friend, was someone he had never met before, though he had heard the name, now that she had named him: no stranger to her, but a part of her proper life. She had leaves in her hair from her passage through the forest, and a brown streak, where she had rubbed against rotten bark, down one sleeve; the sleeve had a darn in it. He thought, as he always did, she should not be here.

Will said, "You see, perhaps, sir, why I would not speak to you of my friends. When Marian stopped talking of you I could not, in courtesy, pry at her—or your—secrets. I heard that the sheriff sought you, and I heard why; but Marian was not unhappy about you, even as she turned away any attempt to question her about you. By that I felt I knew what I needed to know about your—band of cutthroats. Then it was only the finding."

Marian said, "I heard some—little discussion as I approached. If my word will help, I give it for Will of Norwell's good character, Will Scarlet as I have known him."

"Welcome, then," said Robin, and Will said, "I thank you." The little crowd about them began to disperse; to Rafe, Much, Little John, Will, and Marian, who lingered, he said, "Now we can begin to plot how best to set our new system of guards. We shall have a network over the length and breadth of England, at this rate, between what we have begun to do about finding new places for the displaced—and keeping them and ourselves safe in the meantimes."

"It is an army we become," said Rafe with satisfaction.

"Good for us," said Much.

"Maybe," said Robin. "Of a sort."

The sentry system took a little while to design and set in motion; and a few people fell asleep, and out of their trees, in the process. Col sprained a wrist this way. "Your punishment shall be merely that I do not let you off your present schedule," said Robin. "Fear of spraining your other wrist should keep you awake."

"Do we have to be *in* the trees?" said Much. "Wouldn't *behind* one do?"

"In is better," said Robin. "You're out of more of harm's ways when you're up a tree. A cross-tempered stag can't mistake you for another stag trying to steal his does; and foresters look down and behind things, rarely up. You'll get used to it."

"Like I'll get used to your abominable longbow, I suppose," said Much; but he took his sentry duty obediently up a tree.

Will also had an idea for a simple rope-trap for an unwary sheriff's man, to guard some way that outlaws could not have two eyes on, and Much looked at him admiringly: "What a poacher you would have made. I must have you look at our rabbit snares."

"Let you stay with snaring rabbits," said Robin. "A man-trap may cause more trouble than it's worth; if we fail to catch one of our own —or some innocent—then we will merely cause undue interest in the trap's whereabouts. Even to foresters' minds will occur the slow thought that a trap is a signal that something important may be close at hand, and worth looking for."

CHAPTER SIX

Will became almost an ordinary member of the band as his aristocrat's hands grew callused and his carefully trimmed hair grew shaggy. He no longer tied it back with a red ribbon, but with a leather thong; and he laid aside his lace-edged shirt for the rough cloth shirts the rest of Robin's folk wore. Neither he nor Little John would ever be lost in a crowd, for they stood head and shoulders above most men; but there continued to be just the faintest air about Will, however dark and worn his clothing.

"Vanity," said Marian with a chuckle. "He used to tell us that clothes are a serious business," she said privately to Robin. "The rest of us would be climbing trees and so on, and he always took his tunic and shirt off first—later, of course, he did it to impress us girls with his chest muscles, which are impressive, you know. But if you want to know the real, awful truth about Will, he used to wash his own shirts because the laundresses never got them white enough to suit him. He said that laundresses didn't care about clothes; they were just paid for a job."

Her smile faded. "I've found out little enough about what goes forward at Norwell, though. There's some mystery there, and I haven't been able to ferret it out; and I must be careful about asking too many questions." She frowned, and Robin saw the cloud in her face that gathered there whenever she thought of her own father's household.

But then as the pale spring greens darkened into summer, till even the shadows of Sherwood were as green as leaves, Robin Hood's aristocratic outlaw fell into a desolate mood. Robin's first thought was that Will was reverting to type after all; despite Marian's faith in him, he had begun to miss his soft bed and a plenty—and variety—of food on his table, as well as the table itself and a hall to put it in. Robin was cross for permitting himself to expect otherwise; and crosser still for feeling so disappointed. He put off speaking to Will for a day, a sennight, wondering if he should offer to let him go and get it over with, or whether he should force Will to come to him.

But it was nothing to do with Greentree that had changed Will's mood.

Marian had discovered that Will's sister had not married her Norman betrothed after all; on her wedding day her maids found her door locked from the inside, and she refused to open it. She had been stormed at and threatened—through the door—but there was no graceful way to come at her, as her room was at the top of a bay, and her windows overlooked the old trench from the manor house's days as a fortress.

"And, in the last bitter end of things," said Marian, "she cannot be forced by physical means to say vows she will not say. She'd only moved to this new chamber the beginning of this year, and Will has realised that she must have planned rebellion from the first. I don't know what all he's thinking, but I can guess that he has thought of it that she did not come to him for help. . . . She said at the time to the family that she wanted to be a little apart from the household she was soon to leave, to consider her new life before she entered it. She put this over with a great show of maidenly modesty," Marian said, with a grin of appreciation, despite the precariousness of her friend's situation. "Her father bought it, and he's an old so-and-so, but he was stupid with delight at catching a Norman. And Will, who should have had better sense, only saw this as the proof that Sess's spirit had been broken by the prospect of marrying one of the enemy." She paused. "I thought it was a little strange at the time myself, but I don't see Sess as often as I was used, in our early tree-climbing days—she's several years younger than Will and me—because her father has kept her mewed up increasingly as she was increasingly inclined to kick against his rule. It was at least possible that he had broken her at last. I thought he must have done, when I heard of the Norman suitor. Sess always had a great deal of character, but quite the wrong kind."

"And Will feels now he's failed her by running out," said Robin. "Maybe he wants to run back."

"I permit that remark only because you are responsible for all your people," she replied. "Will would never break a promise; nor would he want to break his promise to you. You have no complaints of him besides a little current sullenness, do you? He's a member of your band till you throw him out, and the more fool you if you want to."

Robin sighed. "On the contrary, I want to be convinced that I don't have to. I don't in the least want to lose him, and have been putting off trying to find out what his doleful looks are about, for fear of what I would hear. But what comes now to the sister?"

Marian frowned. "I don't know, but I will try to find out, for Sess's sake as well as Will's—and the curiosity of a certain outlaw leader. Now that the story has got out a bit, I can ask leading questions; better yet, I can set Beatrix to asking them. Her long nose has been twitching with eagerness since Hawise came back with the first bit of the tale some days ago. It is the favourite topic as we sort colours for our latest epic tapestry.

"Sess must have the loyalty of one of her maids, to bring her food and water, but they'll find out who it is, and then I feel almost as sorry for the girl as I do for Sess. This can't last long, one way or another. I suppose Sess is hoping the embarrassment she's causing her Norman's dignity will bring him to break off the engagement by the time they dig her out of her earth; but I have not heard that he has done so thus far." She chewed her lower lip. "What I have heard of Sir Aubrey is not comforting. She is lucky—if you want to call it luck—that it was marriage he offered her." She stopped abruptly, and when she spoke again her voice was light and careless. "Her betrothed is a lout, her father is a boor; and now her brother is trailing around looking like a thunderstorm about to burst. Men are not sensible creatures."

"Thank you," said Robin.

"But I would be looking like a thunderstorm myself if it were my sister," she said, "so I except poor Will after all."

"What about me?" said Robin. "Am I to be excepted from the ban?"

She looked at him, smiling, but the smile changed in some way he could not follow, and he both badly wanted to know what she was thinking and badly wanted not to know. "I except you only so long as you do not try to make it impossible for me to go on visiting you here," she said.

"Your ban is ill-defined, then," said Robin, "for you would now tell me to let my heart have all its own way over my good sense—what there is of it."

"Is that what it is that I want?" said Marian. "Then, yes, I would."

There was another ill bit of news that spring. Edward returned from a visit to Nottingham town one day while everyone was still sneezing and the high road was no road at all but a badly rutted mud slide, and said that there were queries out about a man wanted by the sheriff; and that the description was of a very large man with dark hair and beard, who might be known as John Little. The queries were rather urgent; more urgent than the disappearance of a failed farmer late last autumn would warrant.

"I cracked the skull of one of the soldiers who came to put me in debtors' gaol," said Little John quietly. "Perhaps the man died."

His guess proved true, and then Little John also fell into a bleak mood. Robin sent him off on a new errand every time he returned to Greentree, that he might have little time to brood. There was never time for idleness, but even so, Little John recognised what Robin was doing very soon, which Robin privately thought was a good sign. When Little John said rebelliously, "I am no babe, that needs to be nursed, as you would nurse me through the blame and responsibility of my own deeds," Robin smiled.

"I would trust no babe to bring me news of the Chief Forester; a babe would get lost in the forest, or mistake the Chief Forester for a fat, stupid old man."

"I can promise not to lose myself in Sherwood; but for the other, it may be a hard task."

"I have great faith in you," said Robin.

The Chief Forester and the sheriff of Nottingham had shaken themselves out of their winter sleep and begun to readdress the tiresome question of the new band of outlaws infesting Sherwood. This band had, unfortunately, survived the winter; the weather had taken care of certain similar questions in years past. But the Chief Forester was, from the outlaws' point of view, the lesser evil, for the king's foresters were largely taken up with their legitimate business. It was the sheriff of Nottingham who had more leisure, money, and a wider scope to expend on whim and personal vengeance. This had initially been to their advantage, for while the sheriff could be relied on to bestir himself against any probable threat to his own comfort, and local outlaws of all styles and political persuasions must be numbered on such a list, Robin Hood's company had not, at first, directly troubled him. (Indeed, he had grown a little tired of the Chief Forester's fixation on the subject. The Chief Forester, thought the sheriff, suffered a slight excess of self-importance.)

So while the sheriff had not been idle in pursuit of these outlaws, his harassment was irregular, as if he was not entirely convinced that he needed to care that they existed; or as if he was still hoping, if he tried very hard to forget about them, that his forgetfulness would have the salutary effect of making them forget to believe in themselves, whereupon they would burn away like fog in sunlight, and stop troubling him. "He believes his own lies," said Much; "chief among them that he is the law, and not merely the bully with the biggest stick, in Nottingham."

But Robin's folk had grown harder to ignore. They grew less and less inclined to remain quietly in the heart of Sherwood, nursing their subversive notions—and eating the king's deer. They had begun preying upon the high roads. There was even talk of some kind of spy network among them and other subversives in other parts of England, where local malcontents might go and begin new lives, and cheat their rightful Norman overlords of rents and taxes.

By the time of the spring fair in Nottingham there was a lively new topic of gossip among the small farmers and merchants who set up booths. Robin Hood had already become quite a favourite among them; more and more of them had friends or relatives who had been assisted, or thought they had been assisted, by some member of the Sherwood outlaws (Robin would have been astonished at the amount of philanthropy he was responsible for at several retellings' remove.) The conversations went: So, had everyone heard of this Robin Hood and his band of folk in Sherwood Forest? Yes, yes, of course everyone had heard. Well, the latest was that they were not merely offering a helping hand to those cheated by greedy Normans—they were now *robbing* the greedy Normans directly. Pause for appreciative laughter and the rubbing together of hands. Was this not the classic end of thieves? Was this not how the Normans *must* be treated? Did it not seem as if this Robin Hood was—well—some instrument of fate?

The preying upon the high roads had begun as the longbow practice abruptly became rather successful. After lengthy moaning and groaning and the rubbing of pulled muscles, accompanied by lingering reproachful looks at their leader, suddenly there were half a dozen outlaws capable of hitting what they aimed at—capable of knocking a deer down from four hundred yards' distance; capable of putting an arrow through a forester's hat from the same distance (although the fellow who did this was nearly drawn and quartered by Robin, when he heard of it). Then there were eight of them who began to carry longbows; then fourteen.

Robin said nothing to his once-reluctant pupils beyond generous praise, but he knew that what had done the job at last had as much to do with pride as with practice. Little John and, later, Will had joined the longbow sessions after the general tenor of aggrieved complaint was well established. Much was among the loudest, and certainly the most articulate, of the complainers, although Robin had noticed when he had begun to hit more targets than he missed, and that there was a look of sneaking pleasure on his face when he saw how deeply the arrow from the bigger bow had bitten into the target. But it was when Little John had hurled several arrows better than a hand's-breadth into the gnarled, thick-skinned old oaks of Sherwood with no more remark than a look of faint surprise, that Much shut up and concentrated on shooting. Little John did not pick up a bow by choice; his staff was readier to his hand. But when he held a longbow, specially made to fit his long length—"To think I almost cut that one down not a sennight since as impossible," said Humphrey—the arrows went where he sent them.

Will had been shooting from a conspicuously oversized bow for some years. "Since I found out I could," he said cheerfully; "I like to show off." He had brought his own bow with him, and demonstrated his prowess by breaking off the tail-feathers of his first arrow with the point of his second, so close did they strike. "Wasteful," he said afterward, looking at the damage; "it will have to be retied now." He looked at Robin. "You are not saying that showing off can be like that."

"I am not saying it," agreed Robin.

But there was a second material matter in the acquiring of the outlaws' close attention to mastering the longbow. Marian had taken practice with the rest, when she was present; and could be seen practising on her own when she had been very many days away from camp and had missed her turns; nor did she ever complain, though she sometimes grew a little white around the mouth after she had pulled the string a few times.

And there was now another woman in the camp, a widow named Sibyl, who had lost her farm after she lost her husband, and arrived in Sherwood soon after Will. "I knew it was hopeless alone, but . . . I did not think, till I heard of Robin Hood, that I had anything left to do but wait to die; it would not take long, and I would be with my husband again." Her look of grief faded and was replaced by one of faint bewilderment. "I did not at first see that Robin Hood was aught to do with me; but I knew that, were Walter alive, and we lost the farm, he would have come to Sherwood; and so I came."

Robin had first thought to send her along to the next place that their spy system heard of that she might fill; but by the time there was such a place, Sibyl was taking her regular turn at standing guard, and had learnt, more easily than most, not to get lost. There was, besides, someone else by then who worse needed that place in the world outside Sherwood. And so she stayed. When another suitable place was heard of, there was again someone else, someone who could not learn not to get lost, and who was oppressed by the heavy encircling green of Sherwood besides; and so Sibyl stayed. By the third time there was no longer any notion of asking her to leave; she did not wish to, and she—and Marian—were among that first half-dozen who could reliably draw a longbow.

The presence of women as a spur to the men among Robin's outlaws did not trouble the sheriff; its results did. Bolder now, longbows in hand, they prowled the common ways through Sherwood, woodscrafty enough to remain invisible, pleased with the success of their experiment thus far; pleased still to be alive and untaken. But their relocation activities cost money; and their various saleable skills could earn only so much when the craftsmen in question had often to stop their hands' work to chop firewood or stand guard. They peered through leaves at the gaudily dressed Normans making their unknowing ways here and there; and they plotted.

Much returned to camp one day with the news that the canon of Turham was travelling to Nottingham to deliver up the latest taxes due the sheriff. The canon's rents upon his Saxon farmers were known to be harsh; to this canon the sheriff had often looked, and for each look, it seemed, the rents rose again.

It was, as Much said, and as even Robin was compelled to acknowledge, ridiculously easy. A dozen outlaws burst from behind the trees and surrounded the canon's company; the two guards among them were so surprised, they were taken before they had a chance to grab for their weapons. The outlaws relieved the canon's palfrey of the weight of its saddlebags, and led him and his companions, blindfolded but otherwise unharmed, to a place near the main route to Nottingham. When Rafe slapped the palfrey's flank to make it trot forward, it kicked him.

"A steed to suit such a master," said Much cheerfully, as Rafe sat panting in the leaf-mould, rubbing his thigh and grimacing. The canon's farmers later discovered mysterious small clinking bundles hung on their cows' horns or in their mangers, or slid under thresholds, or dropped in cradles. The price of fair rent the outlaws kept, and two or three of the oldest and youngest of them, the ones best able to look innocent or ordinary, were dispatched to various markets to buy what the band most needed.

"It won't stay this easy for long," said Robin.

"You are the worst killjoy honest rogues have ever been forced to bear," said Much.

Jocelin, squinting over needle and thread in the flickering light of the fire, was heard to say something wistful about roofing timbers. Jocelin had been a carpenter.

"Think again," said Rafe. "Are you going to peel them up and tuck them under your arm whenever we must go out to play follow-the-leader with a few foresters? Let's not make it any easier than we have to for them or the sheriff's men to guess what they're looking at."

"You've turned as gloomy as Robin since the canon's horse kicked you," said Much; "it must have rattled your heart loose. I'm tired myself of my face hitting my blanket with a splash instead of a thump every night. We'll have moss growing on us soon."

"Nobody is making you sleep under the leaks," said Rafe, "nor stopping you from plugging 'em. I've a bit of canvas you could have, if you asked."

"A real roof—" began Much.

"But if I hear any more about it," added Rafe, "you will eat that canvas, instead of sleeping under it. We're becoming very grand for homeless outlaws, aren't we? Roofs, my faith. Next you'll be wanting tailors."

"Maybe we should stop a thatcher on the road," said Jocelin.

The sheriff tried sending a group of hired soldiers led by several of his own men into Sherwood soon after the canon had had his baggage lightened; but Sherwood is a vast forest, and the sheriff's men were not nearly such good trackers as Will Scarlet. Robin and his folk crept after the noisy group—"Do you suppose the sheriff's bright mercenaries have never seen a tree before?" whispered Will, as one of them reeled back from a slap in the face dealt by a branch released by the man he had followed too closely. In the course of his reel he cracked himself against another tree and fell to his knees. It was not difficult leading them astray.

It was not difficult, but they were a long day at it; and there were a few grim looks from those with the most bruises and least sleep when Robin said, "Now we must do it a second time. After the fox has hunted the mother who flutters her broken wing at him and then flies away, he may return to the place he first saw her, and look again."

So the next day they did it again. One of the sheriff's men was caught in a trench Little John had dug—one of his first efforts and not, he protested, one of his better ones—and one soldier was caught by the leg and dangled far above the heads of his fellows by one of Will's snares. There were several of Robin's folk at hand when this happened, who turned purple with repressed laughter at his yelling. "He screeched like a babe too hardly woken," said Much that evening. "If his friends hadn't been so busy looking for ways to cut him down without breaking his crown when he fell, they might have noticed some leaves trembling without a breeze nearby, where we were biting the bark to stop ourselves laughing aloud."

The sheriff's men found nothing and went home, two with scrapes and sprains, and all with anger and wounded pride. But the sheriff did nothing more for the moment, and when the canon of Turham tried to extract a second rent, there was such an outcry that the sheriff told him to desist. The sheriff again decided—or decided to decide—that Robin's folk were merely the latest pack of the usual riffraff, perhaps a little cleverer than most, but nothing more. He could lose occasional rents; and it was the risk taken when a civilized Norman tries to administer the barbarous Saxons. The failure of his first skirmish was disheartening but not serious. He did, however, raise the price on Robin's head.

"We do not want the sheriff to come to believe that all mischief in all of Nottinghamshire is of our doing," Robin said severely to his people, who showed some tendency to be flattered by their new reputation. One or two of the men who had girlfriends in town shifted uncomfortably; they had told their Sues and Nancys nothing—or nothing they remembered; and they guiltily remembered one or two more glasses of ale than were perhaps wise—but they had been glad to listen to the tales the women told, and to bring them back to Sherwood. And it was possible they had retold them with a little too much enthusiasm.

"In the first place it is not true," Robin went on; "and in the second we do not need the sheriff declaring a private feud on us. Let us attempt to look like the common sort of outlaw, that the sheriff may be permitted to believe us so."

And accordingly the next wealthy travellers waylaid in Sherwood were some London friends of the sheriff's, nothing to do with local rents and Saxon farmers; and these lords and ladies from the distant city were simply relieved of their jewels and money. When they complained of this outrage to the sheriff, he was so pleased by the ordinariness of the robbery that his reaction was almost perfunctory, and his friends were offended. When they returned to London they took a very long way around to avoid all forests—no mean feat in the heart of England.

CHAPTER SEVEN

The little band of outlaws had stabilized by late spring—by the time of the Nottingham Fair, and the end of Robin's first year as a man with a price on his head. The folk that remained at last remained by choice—a combination of theirs and Robin's. And if those that wished to remain (as Robin thought sometimes, particularly late on a sleepless night) too often had more of Much's view of their life and prospects than his, he supposed it couldn't be helped.

Greentree itself was often nearly empty; there were too many watches to be stood now. There were look-outs at several, varying locations on the main roads through or near Sherwood, waiting for well-dressed travellers who peered so nervously into the shadows as to suggest they would be worth stopping; and other green-clad folk lay hidden in (occasionally, when they thought they could get away with it, behind) trees, to see who walked the more private ways that the outlaws walked. There were the two smaller outlying camps to be attended to, Growling Falls and Millward; and there were several tiny go-to-ground havens for the hard-pressed. And, most dangerous and exhausting, there was the running of the system of secret messages and messengers that provided for the folk who did not stay in Sherwood.

As the season progressed, Will's and Little John's moods lightened somewhat; Will no longer sought solitary errands, that his oppression of spirit might not oppress his friends. In this the real difference between the two men was apparent, for Little John had always preferred duties he could perform alone. And while everyone was sympathetic to Will's trouble (even those who thought privately that he was a little odd to be so distracted by the fate of a mere sister), only Robin guessed what the one other member of his band with a price on his head might be thinking. The other outlaws were a little in awe of Little John.

Marian had brought no more word of Sess's fate; but Robin still watched Will with an edge more of anxiety than he did Little John. Robin, in his dislike of philosophy, had a blind spot about some of his volunteers' reasons for volunteering; he knew only that the blind spot existed. Will had given up, or lost, more than anyone else in his company. And since some of Robin's blind spot was a guilty conscience about Marian, and as Marian and Will were friends, the conscience, or at least the uneasiness, tended to bleed over to stain Will too. It was all the worse that Will was a good friend to Robin; like Little John, Will Scarlet was one of the few of Greentree's members he could talk to without feeling as if CHIEF was branded on his forehead and his every word must matter.

And Marian gave him something further to worry about. "I fear that Will may take it into his head to attempt his sister's rescue; he has friends among us, you know, and could perhaps do it even if you did not like it," she said. "There are those who would like the romance of it well."

Robin had been thinking about the pleasant weight of her head upon his breast, and his arm around her shoulders. They were half-lying between two great roots of an enormous oak tree, and the earth was warm with the approach of summer despite the evening chill in the air. Overhead he could see a few stars through the scalloped leaves. It was not often that they slipped away from the cares of his people to be alone together, and Robin thought that this was just as well, since when he was alone with her his brain seemed to cloud over and . . . He shook himself gently, and sighed, and sat up, pulling his tunic down where it had rucked up during his quarrel with a few twigs and pebbles digging into his backbone.

Marian sat up as he did, but leaned against him, and turned her face to his, slid her fingers along his jaw, and kissed him. His brain clouded over in a rush, like a thunderhead obscuring the sun. Then he took his arms from around her, where he discovered they had put themselves, apparently of their own volition, and stood up.

There was a little silence, and Robin said, in a voice that did not sound like his own, "I am sorry for Will's trouble, but you are right that I would not like it if we tried to rescue her. I do not like it that any woman should be married against her will, but I think we would overreach and risk what little gain we have made—did we decide to concern ourselves about such as she, who has at least a roof over her head, and food to eat."

Marian was silent so long that Robin stooped down beside her again. "Mari, I—"

She stopped his mouth with her fingers, as she did so often when the tone of his voice warned her what he would say. "Don't say it. I don't want to hear it again."

He took her hand in both his, and so they sat for some little time. With his hands locked together he could not give in to the desire to stroke her hair, and her face was turned away from him. "I think I will go . . . home now," she said, and her voice was thick with misery.

"Your father—"

"Robin, I am a woman grown. I need not stay with my father forever. And—"

But she said no more, and he dared not prompt her, and the silence stretched out between them till it was as impenetrable as the shadows around them. "I will try to talk sense to Will," she said at last, with a little of her usual brisk manner. "For you. But if I were Will's sister, I would want to be rescued." And she was gone into the forest.

A few days after Marian's warning, Robin was sitting on the ground near the camp at Growling Falls, making holes in the dirt with a stick, puzzling out plans for a new hiding-place with Little John. There were still great stretches of Sherwood where there was nowhere for Robin's folk to disappear when danger approached them too nearly. Now that they were putting themselves at greater risk by robbing the high road, such alternatives to disaster were terribly necessary; there had been a near miss for Harald and Gilbert just a week before. Little John had suggested that they begin to go underground. "Is not privy duty enough digging for you?" said Much. "But no, I daresay not, for your grandfather was a badger."

Robin looked up, frowning, when two sets of feet presented themselves at his elbow. Humphrey was not afraid of his leader's frowns, but the strange young man with him blanched. Robin stood up, as did Little John; and Robin said, "Forgive my lack of attention. Who is it you bring here, Humphrey?"

The stranger dragged his eyes away from Little John, whom he appeared to recognise as something out of a childhood nightmare, and looked at Robin. "My name is Alan-a-dale," he said; his voice was a light tenor, but there was a curious, creamy undertone to it. He could make folk do what he wanted them to with that voice, Robin thought, but looking into the young man's eyes he saw that the boy did not know this. At least not yet. Alan bowed, and Robin registered that the bundle on his back was of a specific shape, and the specific shape was that of a lute; the long stem of it was visible over his shoulder when he straightened. "I have recently heard tales of a band of folk who live in the deeps of Sherwood and prey upon the wealthy Normans who have gained their wealth through injustice to the good Saxon folk." He paused, but Robin had only half-listened to the familiar compliment, and waited to hear the purpose behind it.

"Indeed, perhaps I have heard of this band for enough of time that I have written a ballad or two about them; a ballad or two received well enough at market day among the yeoman farmers and goodwives, but not so well among those who live in great castles and feel the need to have an eye to their own wealth." He paused again, but this time as if his thoughts had overtaken him, and as if those thoughts were burdensome.

He plays the part very well, thought Robin. Little John, who had moved a little to one side, as if to loom better with a magnificently branching yew tree at his back, caught Robin's eye; the same thought was reflected in his own. The young stranger cast his own look toward Little John, spoiling his characterization; then he pulled himself together again. "I have remembered the tales of this band of folk," Alan-a-dale went on slowly, "in the back of my mind, perhaps, but still there, and as more than a tale to turn to song. I have thought of this company as a court I might apply to for justice in extremity—an extremity I feared I might find myself yet come to."

"Which we guess has fallen upon you as fated and foreshadowed," said Little John, who had little patience for poetry.

"You speak truly," said the young man, with a glance at Little John that was, to Robin's amusement, humble, and with no awareness of irony. "I love a lady," Alan-a-dale said, and his voice lifted and fell so that he almost sang it. "I love a lady . . . fair and pure as dawn, as the first bud of a rose-tree in spring. . . ." Little John made a strangled noise, and Alan quailed and broke off, looking surprised and hurt.

"This lady has fallen to some ill fate?" suggested Robin, making a mental note to have a little chat with Humphrey about his eliminatory methods of dealing with strangers who wished to present cases of trial and trouble to the noble outlaws of Sherwood. Humphrey was perhaps better off making arrows.

Alan's face darkened, and his long-fingered musician's hands clenched into fists. "The blackest of fates! She is to marry a Norman she loathes, because her father is greedy of the favour the alliance would bring him; and—my lady loves *me,* and would have me, but I am but the younger son of a small Saxon lord, and I have no Norman favours to offer."

Robin offered a small prayer to fate that Will Scarlet would not walk up just now. "And what would you have us do?" Robin said, wondering whether the comparatively simple—as he thought—economic basis for his company's defiance of Norman rule was soon to be set permanently awry by the demands of star-crossed ladies. Meanwhile he added Humphrey's name to the list of folk he thought would go with Will to the succouring of his sister. "Why came you to us?"

"They are to be married a fortnight hence," Alan-a-dale said eagerly, "in a small chapel held by the Norman brigand who would steal my lady as he stole the lands he holds. It is a chapel in a corner of Sherwood far from Nottingham, and far enough from known haunts of Robin Hood that this Norman hound feels safe in bragging that he fears no outlaw."

"What might the Norman hound's name be?" inquired Little John in a tone of voice that made Robin look at him sharply. Alan answered, "The Baron Roger of St Clair."

Robin said, "Has this name some meaning for you?"

"Indeed it has," Little John answered. "I had not thought to steal the bride of the man who drove me off my farm, but that trick would do as well as another."

"Then you will do it?" Alan said, with hope so bright in his eyes that Robin wished that the yew tree might fall on his friend. "We cannot decide at once, nor so easily," said Robin. At least the boy had enough sense to look merely disgracefully hopeful, rather than certain. "If revenge were to become our sole motive, the great vengeance of the Saxon against the Norman, we would have no time for sleep, and the trees of Sherwood could not shelter the vast numbers of us. Not to mention trying to keep all those people fed." He looked again at Little John, who appeared unmoved, and then at Alan-a-dale, who stood looking at the ground like a scolded child. To the top of his head Robin said reluctantly, "I do not say we will not do it."

"Will not do what?" Marian asked. Will Scarlet stood behind her. *Blast,* thought Robin. They both carried strung bows, and Marian had a brace of rabbits over one shoulder.

"Roger of St Clair has taken it into his head to marry this man's sweetheart," Little John said. "He would have us take her away from him before he succeeds."

"I sympathize with love's loss," Marian said lightly. "I will not say against the plan."

"Nor I," said Will.

Little John snorted.

"I know you have little use for love and love's dolours," said Will; "surely you do not speak in favour?"

Little John replied, "I speak not in favour of the relief of love's trouble, but in favour of doing Roger of St Clair some hard mischief, for it was he who drove me off my farm."

"Then we are in agreement," Marian said, "and we have not yet quarrelled. Unless you wish to quarrel, my Robin."

Robin looked at her where she stood, lithe and slender, wearing one of the dark-green woolen tunics that nearly all his forest folk now wore; probably one originally cut for him, for they were nearly of a size. Her hair was tied back, and her boots and breeches tied too as the outlaws did; she might have been a young man. "I never wish to quarrel, Mari," he said. "But I do wish to tell of this at least to Much before I agree."

"Much will not support you," said Marian gaily; "he will like the flavour of this adventure very well, for he is the worst romantic of us all."

"Allow me to direct your eyes away from the romance of love and outlawry," said Robin patiently, "and to direct them toward the cold heart of the matter at hand. I do not wish to risk our folk at such an undertaking without some gain, for I have more in common with Little John than with Much. The gain I have in mind is of the sort that weighs in the hand; we have had an expensive fortnight—our fortnights seem to be growing steadily more expensive—and our coffers, if I may call them so, are low. Again. Little John, do you know of aught lying easy for robbery in St Clair's holding?"

"The chapel will be full of valuable things for the wedding," Alan said, but Robin shook his head.

"We will not steal from that final judge of our lives and hearts that some call God," he said. "The Norman church is full of the corruption of man, but the idea of God is not yet corrupt, and I will not poison our small efforts by showing any lack of respect to—"

"—even to take back what a Norman hound has wrongly seized?" interrupted Alan.

"Aye, even to that extent," said Robin.

"This could mean trouble, did it get out," murmured Little John. "The sheriff would carry his treasure-house merely to within the nearest church doors, and sit back at his ease."

"Let us not gallop to meet future difficulties," said Robin. "A walking pace is enough."

Little John said thoughtfully, "The other side of this is that on the day of the lord's wedding, everyone on the lord's estate may be expected to be thinking chiefly of the lord's wedding. I know the grounds and ways of the estate well, from days before St Clair came to it. Perhaps I still have a friend or two at the great house itself—if they have not been turned off for knowing me, or their own worth. I could find this out if you wish it, Robin, and gladly would I lead a few of our company to the great house while you spent your attention on the chapel. Though I would be sorry to miss facing St Clair on my own legs."

"Do you find out what you may," said Robin. "We have only a fortnight's time—if we do it," he added, with an eye to Alan, who was obviously struggling to remain silent; his fingers twisted themselves together, untwisted, and clutched each other again. "*If* we do it, we should have been planning long since."

Marian said, "There is one more question."

Robin murmured, "Would you spoil your position for so little a thing as practicality?"

"I assume that you would wish to marry your lady in place of the doggish Roger?" she said to the boy, ignoring Robin.

Alan's eyes flashed, as if his honour had been impugned. "Of course."

"The priest will be St Clair's own," Marian said, "and he will not marry to your orders."

Alan said angrily, "He will do what he is told to do with a dagger at his throat!"

"Not necessarily," said Marian. "He will know that killing a churchman is counted as a peril to your soul, even deeper than the black sin of murdering an ordinary mortal; and he may know that Robin Hood's band is known not only for their outlawry but for the curious ways they seem to pursue it: and, pertinent to this case, they have spilt very little blood. Third and most important, if your Roger of St Clair is the kind of master I guess he is, your priest may feel his life is not worth saving, if he goes against his master's orders."

Little John said, puzzled, "What need you with a clergyman at all? Alan and his lady need only make their vows to each other, and if this goes as it looks to be going, there will be folk in plenty for witness if they wish it. The Church cannot yet force us to marry to its rules, any more than the Normans have found a way to force us to theirs; although it is a near thing sometimes. It is the Normans, now, who have our church by the throat; and if it were my wedding, I would want none of their words read out over me."

There was a little silence, and Marian said, "I was in truth guessing. And I am guessing that your lady would wish the clerical forms?"

Alan said, "Indeed," rather hotly. "She is *very* gently bred."

"I see," said Little John, dryly. "We speak of gentlefolk and ladies, whose tendernesses I do not understand. Where, then, are we to find a tame clergyman to quiet our lady's nerves?"

"I like *not*—" began Alan.

"I recommend you learn to like it," put in Will, "for yon small John is necessary for this adventure. Forget you not that we have not yet won our leader's vote for this thing, and Little John's support for your cause is to be nursed by whatever means come to your hands. At present the means are to permit his quaint sense of humour its rein. So: we must provide our own clergyman. And I have just the man."

"You do?" said Alan, enmity forgotten immediately.

Will looked at him a little whimsically. "I do. He is a priest and a friar who has forsaken his order for the deep woods and solitude; but he is a priest still, and I think he would listen kindly to our story."

"Story?" said Much, returning from patrol. "What story? Here, Robin, that old despot Stephen of Dunbury is riding for Sherwood, and the weight of his panniers will founder his poor horse if we don't relieve it. What story?"

"When did you hear of Stephen?" said Robin.

"Just now; I came to report. Sibyl brought the word. Stephen should be where we want him tomorrow afternoon. What story?" His eye fell at last on Alan. "And who might you be?"

"The story," said Robin, "incarnate. Alan of the Dale is the story's name, and he has a lady love he wishes us to steal from under the nose of the Norman lord who means to have her himself. What say you to this?"

"I greet you, Alan-a-dale," said Much; "I am Much of Whitestone Mill that was; plain Much now, I guess. And I say this story pleases me well." Marian laughed and turned it into a cough. Much went on, "Pulling the nose of a Norman always puts a sparkle in my eye and a lightness in my step. Any excuse is sufficient. When do we do this thing? Have we time for Stephen?"

"Yes, we have time for Stephen," said Robin, a trifle crossly. "And the morning after Stephen we will go to seek Will Scarlet's friar."

CHAPTER EIGHT

It was Robin and Will and Much and Marian who went to find the friar Will had spoken of, and whose name was Friar Tuck.

It was a small and secluded place where the friar lived, and it was near noon, though they had set early upon their way, when they came to it. Will had been casting dubious looks into the surrounding greenery for some little time, when he thought his companions did not see him; and Robin had bitten his tongue at least twice against asking if the man with the gift for finding things did, perhaps, find himself lost. But then Will's face cleared, and he strode toward an opening in the trees. It was a curious opening, made of the arched and entwined branches of two tall oaks, which stood as if planted to be door-jambs. "There!" said Will, and Marian let her breath out with a long sigh. Robin grinned at her.

Will was first between the guardian trees, and as he stepped into a little patch of sunlight beyond there was a great baying and barking, and three enormous dogs appeared as if from nowhere. His friends' bows were unslung quicker than thought, but quicker still Will's voice rang out: "Now, there, Beauty, my pet, and young Sweetheart, and bright-eyed Brown-eyes. Would you eat an old friend?" The dogs stopped, confused, but the bows behind Will's back stayed stretched. "I have the right-hand one in my eye," murmured Marian; "and I the left," replied Robin. "I am content with the center," said Much.

"Did you hear that, Beauty?" said Will, without turning. "Your lives are forfeit, should you forget yourself so far as to mistake me for dinner. You are a great ugly beast, Beauty," he continued; "perhaps I should forgive you that you do not recognise me at once, for I had forgotten how charmingly your lips curl when you snarl"; but Robin thought the tension of his back said something his words did not. The dogs were huge; Will had rather to raise his hand to pat the nearest on the head, than to stoop for it. "There, Beauty," he said. "You and I were always the best friends." The dog's long tail slowly lowered and after a moment wagged musingly back and forth, once or twice, as the ears gradually flattened and the lips dropped down over the dismaying teeth. The other two then came forward to sniff at Will's flanks, and he called each by name, and was suffered to pull their ears gently, and the brutes' great ruffs at last lay down flat against their necks.

Robin lowered his bow cautiously, though he kept his hand on the string. "That's all very well for him, but what about us?" There was a soft grunt from Marian, and her hand, too, stayed on her bowstring; Much, for once, had nothing to say. The dogs had not yet looked into the shadows behind Will, and the slight breeze was blowing toward the three friends, away from the dogs.

"Well, Beauty, Brown-eyes, Sweetheart, what have you caught here?" came a new voice. "A great hulking tatterdemalion like this and you have not treed him? I'm ashamed of you. You shall have pease porridge for supper, so you shall." The new voice was a merry bass, not quite so deep as Little John's, but with more velvet, for John's had ever a bitter edge. "So, my tatterdemalion, what do you do here, scaring my dogs?—for how else but by terror could you have kept them from chasing you up a tree? Don't you know I chose this place for my den specially for those two fine oaks you stand so carelessly before, to give unexpected visitors an easy leg up when they meet my welcoming party, my butler and my footmen? Hey, Sweetheart, why do you not bare your teeth, and only look at me in that puzzled fashion? It is not I who should command your attention."

The dogs went prancing back to the small round figure Robin could now see through the trees, approaching Will from the opposite end of the small meadow. "Perhaps your dogs have a taste for pease porridge," said Will, "but I always believed you chose this dell for the fact that it was the only unoccupied chapel you could find that was small enough that you need spend little of your time sweeping the floor. I had not realised the oak trees entered into your calculations."

"They did not," said the round man peaceably, "any more than the dogs did, when I first left my order. But while I found I did not overly mind being robbed, here in the wilderness, as I had little to steal but my thoughts, which I have ever safely preserved, I discovered an uncharitable aversion to being beaten and kicked. I prayed to be delivered of this sin of overminding the discomfort of the flesh; and the answer to my prayers came in the shape of a pedlar, whose bitch had recently whelped. The puppies, at four weeks of age, had feet the size almost of mine, and the pedlar told me much of the usefulness of dogs to a lone man. . . . But who are you, who knows so much about me? I am ashamed that I cannot decide if I know your face or not. I seem to recognise it, and then recognition flees as soon as I think to put a name to it."

"I have perhaps changed since last we spoke, and in more ways than in the manner of my apparel; but you may remember my face better if you recall it rising above a linen collar, and a red leather jerkin."

"Will?" said the round man wonderingly. "Will, it is you, then? But you are scarlet no more—Will Brown would I call you, Will Green—"

"Will Tatterdemalion," he supplied with a grin. "And I have some green and brown friends with me, who, I guess, remain shrinking in the shadows while they contemplate the size of your butler's teeth. May I call them out?"

"They are welcome," said the round man, and Robin took a deep breath and walked forward to stand beside Will, Marian and Much a few steps behind. The dogs' heads snapped around, and one stood up from where she had sprawled at her master's feet, her hair bristling up at once in a ridge down her vast back. "There, Beauty," said the round man, "you need not tree this one, for he has been vouched for." Beauty sat slowly down again, but her ears stayed up, and she did not sprawl.

Robin thought the look in the round man's eyes was not so dissimilar to that of his dogs'. "I am called Robin—Hood," he began. "And I—"

"Robin Hood!" exclaimed the round man. "I do not know if I am pleased to meet you or not, for I do not approve of outlawry, and I have the scars that persuaded me. You keep strange company, Will Green."

"We have never spilt the blood of an honest or an unarmed man," said Marian hotly, and the round man laughed.

"A lady outlaw," he said. "The tales I have heard did not encompass so much. Well, my daughter, I might query how you choose to define honest, and if the decision were not sometimes hard to make quickly beneath the glint of steel; but Will and I are old friends, and I would choose to have some faith that he exchanged his lace collars for good reason."

"I do not recall that you had very many kind things to say about the fopperies of wealth when still I wore those collars," said Will.

"I do not condemn the change; I merely wonder a little; and I have ever had an over-ready tongue. My brotherhood was perhaps not entirely sorry to see me leave, for all my virtues. But I understand, perhaps, about taking sharp swerves off the path laid out before us."

Will said grimly, "The fopperies of wealth meant too much to my father, and my sister at last was to marry Aubrey of Dent, that he might not lose them. Then I decided that to be Will of Norwell, son of John, was no longer what I wished to remember, or be recognised as."

The round man folded his hands over his belly, and looked at the ground. "I am sorry for your news," he said after a short silence. "I remember your sister when she was a baby, when I saw more of the world than I do now. I will lay my suspicions aside, and you will tell me why came you here, and perhaps your companions will forgive my hastiness and tell me of themselves, and I will listen and not talk so much. For I have been often wrong, and whilst the training of the Church has taught me to admit it, somehow I have never learnt not to be wrong in the first place.

"Perhaps you would eat with me as we talk?" he went on. "There is food waiting not far from here, and there is always more than I need, for I am very fond of food, and am therefore careful that it be so." He patted his belly. "Robin Hood, I now know. Me you may call Friar Tuck; and you, daughter?"

"I am Marian," Marian said, a little sharply, biting it off as if she would rather remain anonymous. Both Will and the friar eyed her, a little surprised, for her accents betrayed her, and a lady had more of a name than one received at the baptismal font. The friar stared for several moments as if he would draw more out of her with his gaze; but Marian said nothing further, and he turned, disappointed, to the last of the companions.

"I am Much," said he, "and my father is the miller at Whitestone."

"Ah!" said the friar. "I knew your father. A good man, as many say —not all, for if all called him good it would not be the truth. And so his son chooses—mm—this honest outlawry? I confess myself interested." He led the way, and the dogs followed closely, as did Will; the others followed at what distance seemed suitable in consideration of the four-legged members of the group. Robin came last, a little forlornly.

They came to a low, wide wooden door, which the friar threw open. Nestled into the side of a knoll it was, and hung over with vines, and looked like no home of man; but inside it was a snug haven, and Robin found himself making mental notes of the method wherein the forepart, which was made of wood, was fitted up against the shallow cave that lay behind. There were even two small windows, which let in a little light in the wake of the breeze that slightly parted the curling leaves. There was a faint, not unpleasant smell construed of green things and damp earth and cooking—and dog; for the dogs had crowded in with them and immediately flopped down with happy sighs, rendering the small amount of floor space impassable, giving over their role as guardians once they had all crossed the threshold together.

The friar stepped delicately over the recumbent Brown-eyes, lifting his long skirts up as he did so, and displaying a dilapidated pair of old boots, one of them held together with knotted string. He opened a cabinet that hung from a beam thrust into an earthen wall, and from it took down a loaf and a half of bread and something Robin guessed was cheese in some rather unwholesome-looking wrappings, and a covered bowl; these he set on the wooden slab of table next to the cabinet. He prodded a half-visible dog, whose hindquarters emerged from the shadows under the table, with his foot. "You may not lie there, Sweetheart," he said. The dog scrambled out, looking reproachfully at his master, and stood. He did not look as if he planned to stand for long.

The friar dragged a bench out from under the table. "I suggest you sit hastily, before he lies down again," he said. "The one of you left over can come with me; there is a pot to be carried, and two stools."

Robin was the one most reluctant still to accept the friar's hospitality, and so proved the one left standing. Something must have shown on his face, for the friar looked amused. "It is only a short errand I take you on, good Robin, away from the protection of your friends. I cease building a fire in my dwelling here as soon as spring warmth permits, for I am clever at neither thatch nor hearth, and my roof is a source of greater anxiety each year. My bed is thrust under the farthest corner of my little cave not for the sake of my visitors' legs, for I have very few visitors, but because the cave roof is the only portion that does not leak."

"And the occasional small confused insect crawling across your face and searching for its burrow is a small price to pay," said Will.

"I perceive some experience in sleeping under the earth in your words," said the friar. "Yes; I find it a vastly smaller price than the drenching a good rain brings. And beetles, I find, are mostly benign creatures; unlike, say, men." He opened the door again. "We will shortly return."

Even a few minutes in the dark little room made Robin blink in the sunlight. The friar led the way down a short path to a small, rather tumbledown stone chapel; smoke was drifting gently out of one glass-less window. "There is only one window left with glass," said Friar Tuck; "and it is cracked; but somehow the taxes levied against the farmers, which seem quite enough for many panes of real glass, are never enough; and yet it is a curious thing that the priest of this district has not only a fur cloak, but rings on his fingers, and many windows of glass in his house."

"Very curious," agreed Robin. "Perhaps you should bring the condi-tion of your chapel—and your thatch—more closely to his attention."

"As you would do?" said the friar, although his voice had no malice in it. "I have thought of it. But at present I find that if I build a fire just under the second window of the south-east side of my poor neglected chapel, the smoke goes nicely out the window that isn't there, and blackens the ceiling very little—or little more than the candles did, when more people came here." He heaved open the door of the chapel, which was no longer properly on its hinges, and they went in. It was cool inside, but it was not a pleasant coolness, and the air felt old, in spite of the fire. There was a faint smell of hot iron, but none of cooking. The stone walls were as thick as the length of Robin's arm, and the stonecutters' marks on them were worn with age.

Friar Tuck went to the fire, which was tidily built in a small half-ring of stones against the wall under the small, deep window. "If I could trouble you to carry two stools," he said, "I am better equipped to carry the pot." He picked up a corner of his skirts, wrapped it around his hand, and lifted the covered pot off its stone hearth. Above the boots, Robin observed, were ragged trousers which were short enough to expose hairy shins. Robin picked up two stools from a little row of them by the door, and they made their way back to the house-cave, where the quality of the silence that greeted them suggested that they had been the subject of a discussion abruptly ended.

The covered bowl proved to contain pickles so powerful that the reek of vinegar when the friar removed the lid made Much's eyes water, who sat nearest. The pot contained a vegetable stew of uncertain origin; and the dubious wrappings did contain cheese, of a potency, in its way, to rival the pickles. But these motley items made up an excellent meal (although, Robin thought, the friar's bread was made of a flour much inferior to that which Whitestone provided), and the meat-pies that his little troupe had brought for their noon meal lay almost untouched in the center of the table, where Will and Much had virtuously laid them.

They went outside again afterward and drank what the friar said was the end of last year's cider, and lay in the sunlight—Will and the friar each had dog ribs for a pillow, while the others had to make do with their crossed arms. Robin thought about drinking the end of last year's cider, which meant that this year's pressing would come, and after cider-pressing did winter follow; and the summer sunlight lay on him less warmly than on his fellows.

He sat up and stretched, and Much passed him the cider jug, which he dangled between his bent knees, listening to the cheerful giggle of the cider within. "We came to beg a favour of you, Friar Tuck," he said.

"I did not suppose that Will came again to find me for friendship's sake only," replied the friar. "Churchman that I am, I have a bleak vision of human nature."

"And so you bury your sorrows in food and drink," said Will comfortably, his eyes closed, his face half-obscured in Brown-eyes' ruff.

"Flesh is weak," agreed the friar. "But within my limitations, I try to be a good friar. How may I serve you?"

Robin found that Alan's story sounded pretty silly without Alan's young enthusiasm to give it colour; but Alan had been left, not without violent protest, at Greentree, for Will and Robin had both felt that the friar should be spared the boy's single-mindedness. "I think *we* might be spared his single-mindedness," said Will, aside, to Robin. "Melodrama makes admirable ballads, and I have sung a few myself, but it's a little wearying in a companion."

"A young man has come to us," Robin said, more tentatively than he wished, "with a tale of his Saxon sweetheart's fate to be married to a Norman lord she fears and despises. He wishes us to steal her back for him; and if we do so, we need a cleric to marry them."

"A curiously romantic undertaking," said the friar mildly, "for an outlaw band pragmatically dedicated—as I understand—to a more judicious distribution of wealth than the Normans find necessary toward a conquered race. Or perhaps this is a particular Norman lord?"

"Roger of St Clair," said Will.

"I see," said the friar, and fell silent. "Very well," he said at last. "I know tales of Roger of St Clair that, if only half of them are half true, prove that he is no fit husband for a lady, Saxon or Norman. And if half the tales of Robin Hood are half true, it is perhaps not a bad thing that I thus align myself with you. But I would ask—"

"We will bring the pair to you here," Will interrupted. "You need not fear showing your face to the heavy-browed Roger."

"It is not the weight of his brows I wish to avoid confronting," replied the friar. "But I was going to ask that you not tell me what else may be happening while Roger's attention is caught by the thieving of his bride."

Will laughed, but the others were silent, and there was a scowl on Much's face.

"I would also ask," said Friar Tuck, "since you remind me, that you endeavour not to be followed when you bring me the happy couple."

"I would not be here to ask favours of you, Friar Tuck, were we not able to avoid being followed," said Robin sharply; but the friar merely smiled.

"You comfort me," he said.

"Then we will be on our way," said Robin, and jumped up, suddenly angry that he had enjoyed the friar's food, and had lain on the greensward drinking the friar's cider. He set the near-empty jug down with a thump.

The friar and the others rose more slowly, though Much's face was still unfriendly, and Marian looked sardonic. "As you have a long walk —I guess—before you, I will not press you to stay," said the friar, "though there is little cider left to tempt you besides. But go not away in anger, Robin Hood; I am perhaps more of a coward than your other folk; and if this is true, then you should be glad to elude the crisis that could force me to take permanent refuge with you. And for the rest, if you have no doubts about what you do, then you are less of a man than I think you."

"Cleverly phrased," said Robin.

The friar looked at him. "Perhaps you should come again, when you are at leisure, and we will discuss it further."

"So long as I am not followed."

"My visitors, when there are any, are a contradictory assemblage; I draw the line only at a guest leading a bloody-visaged Norman to my very door-step. But yes, I should say you should come to me unpursued by those who seek the price on your head, because I am an old man and lazy as well as a coward, and I will not see the trap till it springs shut around you. And it would curtail our conversation as well." He paused. "Truce?"

"Truce," answered Robin. "It is perhaps chancy for my immortal soul to be in conflict with a churchman."

The friar laughed. "It is. Believe it."

"We believe it that thus you have lived to such an age and girth," said Will; and so they parted on good terms. As they passed through the oaken gateway, Robin paused and looked back. The friar was looking after them; one dog had its head raised and was looking too, but the others lay flat and motionless, like mossy brown stones cast surprisingly far from the stream that ran at the foot of the knoll. "I will send you a man named Jocelin," called Robin. "He was once a carpenter, and he frets, sometimes, at living in trees. He will weep for joy over your cottage."

CHAPTER NINE

heretofore the Sherwood outlaws' battles had been small skirmishes, and fought mostly from the rear—and, as Marian had said, with surprisingly little bloodshed. Over the recent weeks they had developed rather a flair for detaining the heavy purses of certain people unwary enough to wander little-guarded near the forest of Sherwood. "Once I thought it was a crime that news travelled so badly through England," said Much; "now I bless the Norman carelessness that cannot be bothered to warn its own folk. I will grow to love the race after all."

But the assault on the Baron St Clair was a different thing. Never before had Robin's folk gone out seeking trouble on the trouble's own home ground; nor on such a scale. One of the reasons they had been able thus far to perform their purse-cutting so neatly was that they were careful to take on only the smaller, softer, and more foolish varieties of wealth. Roger of St Clair was none of these reassuring things.

"The decision's been made," said Much.

"I am well aware of that," said Robin. He added broodingly: "I could almost wish that Little John's scouting had been less successful. I still do not understand why a man like St Clair is not hiring a cathedral, and filling it with a hundred guests; it feels almost too good to be true that he prefers to skulk off to a small chapel in our forest, where we can so readily get at him."

"You do not know him," said Little John. "For this suits him exactly, to own the chapel as he owns his estate—as he thinks he is about to own his wife. In a cathedral there might be one or two folk looking at the cathedral instead of at the gripping fist of St Clair."

"I believe you," said Robin; "it merely seems to me odd. But we have too many uses for the money this adventure should bring us to ignore the opportunity."

"You mean that the adventure *will* bring us," said Will Scarlet.

"Money!" cried Much. "What about reuniting the young lovers?"

"Young lovers be hanged—as we hope not to be," replied Robin. "We shall at least find out if our hiding-places are as good as they must be; a test of fire. After that day's work there will be Normans after us thick as witch-hunters after a poor old woman with a cast in one eye."

"I like not your picture of our doughtiness," said Will. "I can see out both my eyes."

"Should we succeed," said Much, "we'll have coin enough to bring twice as many as we are through the hardest winter England has ever seen."

"Your grasp of the economics of weather is sadly feeble," said Marian. "If it is that hard a winter, you will spend it in the cellars of Blackhill, and a tight fit it will be."

Much grinned at her. "Ah, but the wine we could afford to drink while we waited for spring!"

There was a faint *twang* from where Alan had been playing his lute for a group of folk at a little distance. Alan-a-dale was still shy of the court, as he thought of them from his days of playing for lords: Robin and Much and Marian, Little John and Will Scarlet; but neither could he stay away from them far or long as the day he dreaded and prayed for came ever nearer. The result was that the "court" knew his music very well without having quite paid attention to it or having had it performed specially for them. His shyness was not soothed, either, by Robin's general noise-ban; any occasion when his muse was particularly present, his muse being a creature who loved volume, was sure to result in a curt order from his new leader to be quiet. It was also not lost upon him that Little John was no music-lover and grew frozen-faced in his vicinity.

But the relationship between Little John and Alan-a-dale was dubious at best. Little John had, finally, after low-spoken protest and some mulishness, agreed to arrange for a message to be delivered to the lady Marjorie.

"She must know to keep her courage up!" cried Alan, looking like a rabbit shouting at a lion. "You would not be so cruel as to deny her some token!"

"Wouldn't I?" said Little John. "I wonder about this fair maid of yours, who has so little courage as to bend to others' bidding so quickly, even to marrying a man she loathes."

"You do not know her!" Alan cried, cheeks crimson with fury. "She is all gentleness, all sweetness, all softness!"

"I know the type," murmured Marian, sotto voce, to Will. "She is going to find hauling her own water and mending her own stockings a fate past comprehension. And when her stockings wear out, and she has to wear coarse wool next to her skin, she will have blisters, and then she will weep."

"She will have been weeping right along," said Will, "from her first glimpse of Greentree."

"—and she believes her first loyalty is to her father, which is just as it should be, not to—to—me, who only loves her," finished Alan, and his beautiful voice broke on a sob. Little John, sitting on the lopped-off trunk of an old tree, was still only half a hand's-width shorter than the standing Alan. He looked up under his dark straight brows at the pale boy trembling in his passion, and said nothing, but the set of his shoulders suggested that he was restraining himself. Alan put a long elegant hand over his face a moment, gave one last shudder, and took his hand down again; his eyes were suspiciously bright. "You *will* take a token to my lady," he said fiercely.

Robin, Marian, Much, and Will watched with great interest as Little John won the struggle with himself not to stand up and loom over Alan, who did not take being loomed over well. He bent down, instead, picked up a branch at his feet the width of an ordinary man's forearm, perhaps the size of one of his wrists, and broke it in half. He looked musingly at the ragged edges of the wood rings thus revealed, as if he would tell Alan and his lady's fortune there. At last he said: "Very well, I will take your token." He threw half the broken branch into the fire, where it crackled with sap; Alan half-turned and startled away, as if the fire were an enemy approaching him from behind. Little John added: "I will even try to deliver it."

Alan whirled back to Little John again, and opened his mouth twice or thrice, but nothing came out. At last he seized his lute round from its strap across his back, and clutched it to his breast as if it were the token he wished given to his lady; or as if it were the lady herself and, having her, he need not bear Little John any longer. His breast heaving and his knuckles white against the frets of his instrument, he stalked off; they could hear him crashing through the undergrowth for several minutes. Robin sighed.

"He is making no more noise than a wounded boar," said Marian. "Don't distress yourself."

"I hope he takes care of that lute," said Will. "It's a fine one, and 'twould be a waste to use it for kindling."

"You push him hard," said Robin to Little John.

"Would you risk this adventure—and our lives—on a silly boy's love-struck whim?" said Little John. "The girl will live with the waiting. If she's anything like her lover, she dreams of him every night and, dreaming, every night he rescues her. Upon waking she is sure that it is true."

"What a lot you know about the dreams of romance," said Will.

Little John gave him an inscrutable look and went on: "She does not need the doubtful proof of any token. But I will try, and she will get it if I can make it so. But I cannot say I like it."

On the evening air came the muffled whine and *ting* of long running chords played with ill-suppressed fury.

"If he were to stay with us, he would have to learn to be pressed hard," said Robin; "I do not understand why he thinks he would prefer such a life. I hope we may find some more suitable place for the two of them—soon, before, as you say, Marian, his lady wears too many holes in her stockings. I must acknowledge that the boy does his work and does not complain; and I have not spared his musician's hands."

"It has happened that a lady could surprise you," said Marian to the fire.

Robin smiled faintly. "Try to deliver the token as you can, my friend, but take no more risk than you wish or deem wise."

"That I can promise," said Little John.

"And meanwhile, he must stop that appalling noise," said Robin, and got to his feet.

For a token, Alan-a-dale produced a bit of ribbon which, he said, the lady had once given him, and it broke his heart to give it up. ("Good," said Little John. "Let us forget the whole matter.") The token was handed over to a man, who gave it to a maid, who, heart fluttering in excitement, gave it to the lady; and then the sending was reversed, and a little silk purse was given to the maid to give to the man, who gave it to Little John, who tucked it away with a snort. But when the purse was laid in the surprised hand of Alan-a-dale, a smile so sunny and brilliant broke out on his face that those who had grown used to him in the last ten days looked at him in amazement and did not recognise him.

So the plan was laid, and the players appointed, each to a part; and Alan grew frantic—and absent-minded—with hope and fear. On the day before Roger of St Clair's wedding day, Alan contrived to free a rabbit from one of Much's snares instead of killing it, and the usually good-natured Much lost his temper. Food was always the first thing on all the outlaws' minds, and an extra rabbit in the stew would have been welcome the night before so hazardous an enterprise. But nothing could discomfit Alan now; he looked hazily at Much, pulled the little silken purse from a pocket (near his heart), kissed it, and walked away smiling.

"I shall set him digging a privy vault ditch long enough for all of Nottingham town," said Much. "He can dig till he has no skin left on his hands, and cannot play his wretched lute."

"Tie him up and leave him in a cave, more like," said Will. "A pity it is we need him for the day."

"Brides have been married by proxy ere this," said Much. "And brainless boys too."

Robin laughed. "Now that he would not forgive us—and I think I cannot blame him for that. We will carry him tomorrow fettered and gagged, if it seems necessary."

"And I shall jerk the rope," said Much.

Little John and his companions left before dawn, to lie in wait near the manor house till the bride party would leave; and to those left behind, the air became frangible with tension, and struck at the eyes and in the breast like splinters of glass. There were several hours to wait till it was their turn to make their way to the chapel in the forest. Even the sound of beeswax smoothed on a bowstring was troubling; and when the string slipped away from its handler and snapped against the bow, everyone jumped.

"This won't do," said Robin. "We shall set out at once."

"We might go the long way round," suggested Will, "and wear the fidgets out, as with a fractious horse."

Robin shook his head. "We shall have need of all our edge to face down our Normans; for I think St Clair will not yield quietly."

"Quietly?" said Will, who had jumped the farthest when the string cracked. "I should hope not."

The ones that were to go picked up their bows and staves and knives, and settled their boots and belts and tunics, and then all melted discreetly into the undergrowth. There were very few left behind; most of them were already departed on other errands, watch-standing and message-bearing. Greentree became merely a quiet glen deep in Sherwood, and birds sang undisturbed in the branches at its edge, and the sunlight fell in a small bright patch in its center.

Those that followed Robin stepped, as always, on rock and moss and leaves, that would not take a footprint, and avoided soft low ground. Robin automatically looked for water to cross; his folk's boots were stiff with wax and grease as a result of this habit of their leader, and there was little grumbling, if one or two sighs, as they waded upstream through one of the many rivulets that wandered all ways through Sherwood, as proof of insufficiently treated toes or ankles became apparent.

They had a longish wait when they arrived at the chapel, but it was easier, lying on cool earth or outstretched on huge branches behind screens of oak leaves, and watching for what they knew would come, than waiting purposelessly in camp had been. No one fell asleep and only a few noses itched. Robin observed at his leisure that the baron's chapel was smaller than Friar Tuck's, but in better repair; there was not merely glass, but coloured glass with leading in all its windows, and the stone walls were shiny with fresh scrubbing.

There was a brief distraction in the form of Friar Tuck's arrival; it had been decided that the quicker the rearranged bridals took place, the better. "Not that I have any great doubt that if St Clair wishes to find out who performed the service he will be able to, whether or not he sees me. But I like the thought of doing it with dispatch, however disrespectful this may seem," was Tuck's reaction to the proposal.

"But can the fat friar walk so far?" said Will.

"Hmph," said Tuck. "Just tell me when it is—I already know where —and attend to your own part of the business."

Alan-a-dale was put in the charge of Much, with a severe warning to behave himself. Fortunately he seemed tractable enough now that the day was finally here; his face was pale and he looked everywhere around him very anxiously, his eyes opened so wide that the rest of his features seemed pinched. "I hope she will have the strength," he murmured at intervals, whether or not there was anyone to hear—or to pay heed. Robin's and Will's eyes met sardonically once after this comment, each wondering if some of the young lover's apprehension might be for himself.

Will heard the approach first, but as he turned his head to attract Robin's attention, Robin's own head turned and his eye brightened: there was the faint but unmistakable sound of a party of horsemen who did not care for the noise they made, or to what distance it might be audible. Thus it was still some little time before any of Robin's party could see anything. Soon it was apparent that the approaching parade was a celebratory one; someone was singing a merry song, and the horses' harness jingled with the sort of trappings left off more sober processions.

Even to eyes peering through leaves the bride was readily detectable among the other riders. She sat upon a white horse with flowers in its mane and tail, and she wore a long bright gown suitable for a noble- woman on her wedding day. She did not truly ride, for her horse was led, its bridle in the hand of a man in the dark plain garb of St Clair's men at arms. But she did not have the demeanor of a prisoner so much as of one so frail as to need protection from most of life, even the direction of one's own horse. (Robin thought of Marian, and wondered where she was. Curled up in a window embrasure somewhere in Black- hill, perhaps, staring out over Sherwood, and thinking of the adventure she was not a part of. There had never been any question of her accom- panying them—to Robin's profound relief. She knew as well as anyone that she could not risk the ill chance of St Clair's recognising her. But, perversely, Robin missed her presence at his side; he would have liked to hear her breathe through her nose when the bride came into sight.) The bride's hands were delicately crossed before her on the pommel,

92

and she swayed lightly, like a flower, to the horse's slow pace. Her head was a little tipped down, and her shoulders a little bowed: not as one in fear or sorrow, but as one content to wait on events.

They rode to the door of the chapel, and the priest was helped down from his pony and went bustling into the small building, with two clerkly figures carrying bundles hurrying after him. There was a general hubbub of dismounting, and then the guardsmen sorted themselves out into a double row, as if their only purpose were to honour their master's wealth and pride by their numbers; and they stood on either side of the chapel door as the lady's horse was led up. There was a pause; it seemed to be expected that the baron would wish himself to help his bride dismount; that on his arm only she should depend this day. But a little gesture of his gloved and ringed hand changed this; and two guardsmen sprang forward, one to hold the lady's stirrup, and the other to offer her his hand.

She seemed to drift down from the saddle, as if she weighed no more than the flower she seemed; as if she hid a flexible stem beneath her long skirts instead of ordinary human legs with particular joints capable only of particular movements. She barely touched the outstretched hand, and her stirrup never trembled. The man who had held her horse led it away; as it flicked its tail, one of the braided flowers detached itself and fell to the ground. The lady stooped—a pause; this gesture had not been a part of the day's pattern—and picked it up; and then stood, idly turning it in her fingers, as if surprised it was only a flower.

The guardsmen stood back to their places, and the bride's waiting-women came forward, and flung a scarf over the bride's head and shoulders. She looked up, momentarily, into the trees, as if she was looking for the succour she hoped for; but Much, who lay close enough to see (Alan was stowed several trees back, for safety), thought she looked dazed, and her eyes glanced where they would, without her thought to direct them.

The baron turned, still without touching his bride, and strode into the chapel; a faint twinkle, as of lit candles, gleamed at the leaf-shadowed windows. The flower-lady followed, her waiting-women close behind, as if they anticipated propping her up when she drooped; and several of the guardsmen followed. The others remained in their ranks on either side of the chapel door; a little way off, the horses stood and stamped. There were three other Norman-looking men who might have been friends or debt-bearers of St Clair who also entered the chapel, though with no great enthusiasm in their step; and these were followed by a little nervous man the watchers guessed was the bride's father.

"It will perhaps be not so uneven a match," said Robin in Will's ear; "they are not conspicuously armed, for all that there are unpleasantly many of them."

All in range were looking to Robin now, and he nodded. Those who saw him turned and nodded to others watching them, and the signal so went round the circle of outlaws.

Who dropped out of their trees, and sprang up from their underbrush, and fell—almost silently—upon the guardsmen. Rafe and Jocelin so neatly seized the man holding the horses that the horses were not disturbed, and only one or two even put their ears forward in curiosity.

All did not go quite so smoothly at the chapel door. One of the guardsmen managed half a shout before he was felled by a stave-end briskly applied to the back of his head; and there was some unavoidable stir caused by the violent collision of struggling human bodies. Even so, by the time those in the chapel had realised that something was amiss, Robin's folk were the victors; and Much and Will were occupied in tying the hands of the two baron's men still conscious—who were gargling angrily through the cloth gags that had been shoved none too gently halfway down their throats. More desultorily Gilbert and Simon and Sibyl were knotting together the wrists and ankles of the unconscious men, in a long untidy row. The guardsmen inside with the baron burst out the door, to be adroitly tripped up by some casually but firmly held staves just above the level of the threshold. The first went down like a poleaxed ox, and the others were too hard on his heels to do otherwise. As they yelled and thrashed at each other, the outlaws jumped on them.

St Clair himself came last, and he had taken the time to draw his sword; and he stood in the doorway with the women behind him, and none could, for the moment, get at him. The outlaws dragged the bound guards out of the way; and the tip of the baron's sword waved gently back and forth, in rhythm with his seeking gaze; nor did either tremble.

The sword was a dress-sword, such as a man might wear to his wedding; but it was good steel for all that, and the wrist that held it was brawny.

Robin stepped forward to face the baron, planted his staff on the ground and leaned upon it, as if it were no more than a walking stick. St Clair could not come at him without having been felled several times by Robin's folk on the way; there were several staves eagerly raised just for that purpose. But the baron did not acknowledge the opponents ranged against him; only his arm moved, till the glittering tip of the sword paused, drawn to Robin as to a lodestone. The gesture was smooth, graceful, and easy; as if the two of them were about to square off alone in a friendly match long anticipated. But St Clair's eyes were not friendly.

"There is some purpose behind this outrage?" said Roger of St Clair, and his voice was as steady as his eye and hand.

Robin thought of Little John, and wondered if the baron might himself be thinking of what could be going forward at his home, while he was so delayed.

"There is," said Robin; and then there was a rustle behind him, and St Clair's eyes flicked away, over Robin's shoulder; and first they widened, and then they narrowed, and St Clair's face turned a shade redder, and Robin's folk gripped their staves more fiercely.

"Can you not guess what our purpose might be on your wedding day, Norman pig?" said a young voice, so thick with hatred that its natural beauty disappeared under the burden of it. "Can you not guess that the good Saxon earth might rise up under your pig's feet and throw you down rather than let you marry an innocent Saxon maiden?"

Robin, from the corner of his eye, saw the spasm cross Much's face, and the jerk of his staff as if he felt Alan's neck beneath it. On threat of being left behind in a sack hung from a tree, the boy had promised, upon the spotless virtue of his lady fair (his choice of oath), to stay well back while the outlaws dealt with the baron's men. "Your hands know the shape of a lute, but not of a bow or staff so well; and on a matter so close to his heart any man might slip," Robin had said, with a patience growing rapidly threadbare.

Alan began to speak of honour, and—

"Stop your noise," said Little John; "cowardice is not spoken of. Do you want to risk—possibly the white neck of your lady—on your own fumbling? For I doubt not that you would fumble."

Alan, who would have died before he admitted that he was still afraid of Little John, was persuaded to agree to terms; but Robin, not for the first time, found himself wishing Alan-a-dale had found some other band of outlaws to ask for help.

Robin had hoped to take all the Normans, neatly, at once, though he had guessed that St Clair's was a cold mind, not easily clouded by anger or crisis; and Alan had stayed out of the fighting, sticking to the letter of his promise if no more. From where Robin stood he could just see the flower-lady, glowing faintly in the darkness of the chapel, behind the baron's raised arm; he was sure Alan could see her too. It was hard to blame the boy too much; but it was equally hard not to.

"Fine friends for a young worm," said St Clair. "And you, the leader, I guess, of these other worms, why do you waste time with such a worm's tale as that of my late bard? I thought he sang too little sweetly for listening long when his throat lay under my roof-tree." The tone of St Clair's voice was a more effective goad than a slap with the flat of his sword might have been; and now Alan's was not the only flushed face among those that faced the Normans. "I had heard of the new bandits within Sherwood, but I did not think they would crawl so far."

Much started forward, and the baron turned to him in a flash; but Robin cried, *"Much!"* and he paused, wavering, and St Clair laughed: a laugh that a killing offense by itself. "But I would rather begin, as I doubt not the beginning was, with the bard-worm's tale. Shall I call my bride out-of-doors that she may see your blood flow?" The baron's sword-tip moved from its aim at Robin's vitals to a point a little to Robin's left; and Alan, with a strangled noise, leaped forward.

But Robin caught him as he went by, and was swung round violently with the wild running weight of him. "You fool," he said to the panting boy. "Do you think to come at him with your bare hands? He would spit you on the point of his sword like the pig you call him—and you would deserve it for your foolishness."

"Harken the shepherd, little lamb," drawled St Clair, but he had been paying too great attention to the scene before him, and now a wiry noose was dropped round his neck and twisted tight by the strong hands of Will Scarlet. The baron made one wild backward lash with his sword, but Will yanked him round by the neck as he dodged the stroke.

"Do not kill him," said Robin, as the baron's knees buckled. "Why not?" cried Alan, and wrenched himself from Robin's grasp and ran to his fallen enemy, and snatched up St Clair's sword. "He deserves to die."

"He may," said Robin, "but his death is not your responsibility." The boy stood staring down at the baron's face, and Robin did not like his expression. "Drop it, *now*," said Robin harshly. Alan looked up, and met Robin's gaze, and blinked; his shoulders relaxed, and he let the sword fall.

And the flower-lady slipped past Will, as he bent over the baron, and fled to her lover; and he put his arms around her, and she put her head on his shoulder and wept; but what they murmured then to each other the outlaws were careful not to hear.

The men who had followed Will through the narrow side door—carelessly left unbolted—of the chapel ushered more folk outside. The waiting-women clung to each other and looked around with frightened eyes; the sight of Alan and their lady seemed to give them no comfort. The last guardsmen were dragged out by the heels, and roped to the ones already lying outside: "As daisy-chains go, I have seen more attractive specimens," said Much. The other Norman gentry looked as though it was all in a day's outing to be threatened by ruffians, and seemed only politely interested in their situation, and far less worried about the unconscious baron than the women were for their lady. The little nervous man looked as if he had been sentenced for execution upon the morrow, and kept up a listless, nerve-wracking keening till Will, saying, "Oh, shut *up,* man," clouted him over the ear, and he crumpled and lay on the ground like a bit of dropped laundry.

"Have you forgotten the function of a gag?" said Robin crossly. "He was hardly threatening your life."

"Only my temper," said Will.

"Then your temper is far too fragile," said Robin.

The flower-lady seemed not to notice her father's fate, if indeed the little man was her father, and now turned a radiant if tear-stained face to the other women and declared that they saw before them her own true love who she had known would rescue her from the shame of her Norman wedding.

"Faith is a wonderful thing," murmured Much, giving a last self-satisfied yank on the prisoners' bonds.

"It is indeed," said Friar Tuck, who had emerged from his hiding-place when the baron had been felled. "But I believe we might now, perhaps hastily—" He made little herding gestures at Alan and the lady. "And, young Alan," he added, "if it is any comfort to you against the knowledge that your enemy still breathes, I should have refused to marry a man who killed another while he lay unconscious at his feet, however richly that man might deserve such a fate."

Alan-a-dale at these words wrenched his eyes away from the flower-lady's face long enough to focus on the friar. He half-smiled, with an odd, old look, and said: "Just now, Friar Tuck, I have no enemies."

He turned back to the lady and took a deep breath. "Are you *certain*?"

"A fine time to be asking that," said Much, rather louder than necessary, and Will bit his lip to keep from laughing. But neither Alan nor the lady showed any consciousness of anyone but each other.

"I am certain," said the lady, in a thin, clear voice. "Certain am I that you are my own dear love." He clasped her reaching hands to his breast and knelt before her; and several of the waiting-women, who seemed to have believed their lady's declaration, sighed themselves, and clasped their own hands at their own breasts.

And then the priest and his attendants were led out of the chapel, the priest squeaking about the outrage, his eyes as large as an owl's, his hands fluttering like atrophied wings. There was a ripple of laughter around the ring of outlaws, in relief that the scene Alan and his lady were presenting to their unwilling audience was interrupted. "Come," said Robin, firmly, and seized Alan by the shoulder. The boy unfolded himself to his feet reluctantly; and Robin and the friar, with the two lovers, went into the chapel.

CHAPTER TEN

ittle John and his folk were already at Greentree by the time that Robin and his company, including the newlyweds, returned at dusk; the former were looking very pleased with themselves. The latter looked mostly tired. Robin felt bone-weary in a way that he rarely did; and yet the day had gone, over all, smoothly. But he found himself often and uneasily looking over his shoulder at Alan-a-dale, leading his lady, back again upon her white horse.

Marian was at Greentree too, and she came to Robin and touched his cheek, and smiled into his eyes, which unreasonably made his anxiety over the unlikely burden his outlaws had taken on by listening to Alan's story more sensible than the taking on itself was. Even Much's sense of romance had little to do with young lovers too innocent to come in out of the rain; and Alan's megrims had grated on Much as severely as on anyone.

"I will leave Little John to tell you what a fine haul he has made," said Marian; "I see that you too have been successful."

The flower-lady was flowing off her horse into her husband's arms. "I guess we must claim success," said Robin. "Those two are wed, and none of us is the worse for it except a few bruises."

Marian said gently, "The horses can be made useful. Except the white palfrey; she is much too conspicuous."

"And the baron's stallion," said Robin. "We couldn't travel far enough to make the risk worth selling him, for all the price he would bring."

"Sell him?" said Little John. "I know a few farmers who would give us a winter's food for the covering of their mares."

"And what of the farmer whose ill luck led one of St Clair's men past his field on the day St Clair's stallion was settling his mares? No. We'll take the stallion and the palfrey near the baron's lands and release them.

We can take the others to the horse fair in Nottingham. Rafe, I don't want you seen abroad again so soon; that was a near thing for you less than a month ago. Have we any other horse-coper?"

There was a silence, and Edward said, "I know one end of a horse from another—pretty much."

Marian laughed. "Sell them to me. I will make a very handsome story to my father's friends of the young man who pretty much knew one end of a horse from another who sold them to me. Our man at Blackhill can sell them again. Our steward can use the money; there's a certain out-building that needs repair. The rumour is that outlaws have been using it, if you can believe it. And our steward is fond of me, and will make no inconvenient protests."

"*I* will make the inconvenient protests," said Robin. Marian had her mouth open to reply before he went any further, and there was the beginning of a general furtive movement from those of the outlaws nearest at hand to become less so. It was common knowledge among them that the Blackhill steward knew perfectly well who Marian's friends were, and he and the woman who looked after the house agreed placidly when Marian's father or other folk commented on the amount of time she spent at the country house. But it was a sore point with Robin, and any reference to Blackhill was likely to start a row. But there was a timely interruption.

"What say you, that you would release my Lily?" said the clear, carrying voice of Alan's new bride. She stepped into the circle of fire-light, and very lovely she looked, her bright skirts shades of gold in the glinting light, and her pale hair tawny. The upward-flung shadows made her eyes huge and dark, and her cheekbones showed as clean and pure as the edge of a chalice. "Why must I lose my Lily? She is my only friend here, but my dear husband, for I come with no other, nor my portion either."

There was a dismayed silence. "We cannot have the keeping of beasts, as we live," said Robin; "and I fear you must resign yourself to the way we live—for now, till we can make other arrangements for you and Alan, away from Sherwood."

The small chin came up. "I resign myself to nothing but what my husband tells me. Lily will be no trouble; I will comb her myself."

"Combing is the least of it," said Robin. "We have neither fodder nor stabling for her. We live as you see us—we barely have shelter for ourselves. When it rains, we usually get wet."

Involuntarily she glanced at the sky, in which stars were beginning to appear, and then looked down again at Robin, who had not moved from his seat on a convenient log-end. She was frowning, and it occurred to him, tiredly, that she was accustomed to men standing when they addressed her, and calling her "my lady."

"As I see you?" she said, haltingly, and Robin felt a faint stab of remorse that he had misinterpreted her frown. "But this is—but a camp. A temporary thing. Alan said that Sherwood was now our home. You must have a—a house?" She drew her skirts closer around her; already the hems were draggled and dirty. Her eyes grew even larger as she looked at Robin. "You do not—live—here?"

Robin stood up. His right hamstring was extremely sore where one of the guards had kicked him. "My lady—we are outlaws. If we had a house we would not long survive, for we would be soon taken from it. This camp is a temporary thing because we live temporary lives."

"Alan said—" she whispered. And silence fell. No one moved. Then she turned abruptly and went off into the shadows, toward the tiny turf hut that the outlaws (on Marian's suggestion) had hastily cleared out, that Alan and his bride might have it this first night.

The hut usually held what goods and tools as the outlaws possessed that were not in such constant use as to render a place to store them unnecessary. Everyone was zealously wishing for the weather to remain fair overnight, that the heap of miscellaneous objects now reposing at the edge of the glen would not demand to be suddenly transferred into the hut-cave some time during the small hours—which would then oblige half the company to sleep in the rain instead. Everyone else might sleep through the sound of rain beginning to fall, but Robin would not, so there was no hope there.

"I don't think she'll appreciate the flowers you hung over the door," said Much to Marian.

"Poor little girl," said Marian.

"Or the luxury of privacy," said Little John.

"Luxury?" said Much. "On your wedding night, maybe. But I

101

wouldn't want to make a habit of it. Too many draughts. Temporary living has a lot of cracks in it."

"Bartlemey and Rafe can take the stallion and the—and Lily to where they may be released. Tomorrow," said Robin. "Who knows? Perhaps his stallion's recapture will make the baron somewhat less thirsty for our blood."

"You're dreaming," said Little John. "He was, as I understand it, rude enough when you parted him from his bride; he did not yet know that he was parted from much of his substance as well. That glad surprise awaits him yet, unless Will does not know how to tie knots."

"Or unless you do not," retorted Will. "I guess you overlooked a kitchen maid who ran round with a paring knife as soon as she saw the back of you, and there has been a rescue at the chapel this very eve."

"The maidservants were all in fits," Little John acknowledged. "They were the hardest to tie up, 'tis true, for they feared the wrong things; I shut two or three in wardrobes and threw the keys in the pond. But I think Alan's lady has given us a good portion, if you reckon what we brought away with us."

"I doubt she'll look at it that way," said Marian.

"She will if Alan tells her to," said Robin.

By the time a week had passed, the tale of Roger of St Clair's humiliation had spread far and wide, and the outlaws had brought a good bit of it back to tell at Robin's fireside.

"I hear we're all seven feet tall," said Much, "instead of only the one of us. And as this was told by one of the guards at the chapel, I find myself wondering what he might have made of Little John."

"I hear Little John threw wardrobes full of maidservants into the lake—alone, and with his bare hands, you understand—and miraculously none was drowned," said Marian. "It is fortunate that I am so well disciplined to keep my face ladylike, that is to say, blank, for such a terrible story should, of course, make a lady blanch. John, however—our steward at Blackhill—laughed when he heard, and said he could use that man on our holding, did he want to cease to be an outlaw."

"Have you maids that want a wetting?" said Much.

"I do not think that was what our steward had in his mind, but as you ask, I can think of—"

"Robin," said Bartlemey, who materialized out of the leaves and branches just beyond the fire-niche. "There's a young lad making his way here. . . ." He ended as if he didn't mean to end, but could not decide how to go on.

"And?" said Robin.

"Well—he looks angry and exhausted, and I think his clothes were good once, but they don't fit him very well and I do not think they belonged to him when he put them on. And he plunges through the forest like a blind thing and yet he looks like he will come on here; our usual ruses he ignores as if he did not notice. We could spring a snare on him, of course. And yet—I do not think we need fear him, but I have no cause to say so, except his face bears the anger of hard usage and not of arrogance."

"Um," said Robin. "Then I shall go ask him what he wants, if you will show me the way."

"I would come too," said Little John. "He might want knocking in a stream to cool his anger."

"I will come too," said Much, "to fish him out again, and to reassure him that not all of us have this queer craving for hurling folk in water."

Bartlemey guided them swiftly back the way he had come; and then Col dropped down beside them from one of their watching trees. "He is stopped, a little way from here, near Rosebrook," he said. Much chuckled. "He looks done in," added Col.

"Then we will offer him food as well as conversation," said Robin.

"Polite conversation," said Much.

The stranger was on his feet and looking in their direction much sooner—thought Robin—than he should be. This boy might be a dangerous enemy; but then perhaps he would be a good friend.

"Good morrow," said Robin, trying not to eye the boy's white knuckles clenched around his bow. The boy was slight and the bow was not; even among Robin's folk, who, along with being seven feet tall, all drew bows made of hundred-year-old oak trees torn up by the roots, this bow was a massive thing, little smaller than Will's or Little John's. Robin wondered if he had come by the bow the same way he had come by his clothing, which, as Bartlemey had said, had clearly been made for a larger man. But the tendons that stood out on the backs of his hands looked strong, and the hands did not look like a young boy's hands, despite the slenderness of the wrists.

"Are ye Saxon or Norman?" said the boy fiercely, and half raised his bow; his other hand made a convulsive little gesture toward the quiver on his back, though he must have known that Robin and the two men with him could have disarmed him before he pulled an arrow free. Perhaps this occurred to him too, for he took a step backward and paused on the verge of the stream, looking rather like a cornered deer as he threw up his chin and eyed them sidelong. And yet, thought Robin, he had already decided not to nock an arrow before he saw us, for he had time then. Do we look so dangerous? Aye, I guess we do. As dangerous as he looks desperate.

The boy's baggy hat, which fit no better than the rest of his clothing, fell over one eyebrow, and the boy shoved it up; whereupon one of the bunched-up sleeves unrolled, and the hand disappeared to its finger-ends.

"We must be Saxon," said Much cheerfully; "Saxons have not cloth to spare for clothing that hangs too large upon us."

"I am no Norman," said the boy, and the free hand made another cut-off jerk toward his quiver. "And were you any good Saxon, you would make no such jest."

"Then I am not a good Saxon, but a bad one," said Much, not in the least put out.

"Enough, Much," said Robin; and the boy's eyes flickered to Robin's face at the sound of the name.

"Much is perhaps a name I seek," he said.

"I do not recall wishing to be sought by any starveling boys in stolen Norman clothes," said Much, and Little John spoke for the first time:

"I begin to think it is you, Much, who needs hurling into the water for cooling off. I thought we were to make polite conversation?"

The boy's face had reddened, and he shouted: "It is no thievery to take from the Normans!" But he heard Little John's last words and paused, looking puzzled.

"That was the plan," said Much, "ere I—"

"One more word and we shall not merely throw you in, but hold you under," said Robin; but he noticed that the boy's knuckles were not so white, and his other hand hung quietly at his side. He looked at each of the three of them in turn, and something almost like a smile touched the corners of his mouth. "I would offer my help, good sirs, to hold that one under," he said. "I think he talks too much."

"I yield!" said Much, and threw up his hands. "Besides, I am hungry. If I take back my rude words about your choice of costume, will you eat with us?" He leaned his unstrung bow against a tree, and unslung his satchel. Robin saw that as the boy's hands relaxed, they trembled a little. "I have nothing to offer in exchange," he said gruffly.

"But I am in your debt for not throwing me into that water, which is too cold for bathing even this time of year," said Much. "The others are in your debt for your offer of assistance, because I can tell you I would not go quietly, and I am stubborn for my size." As he spoke he was laying out bread and dried venison. Little John dropped down on his knees beside him and produced a large stoppered bottle.

The boy looked cautiously at Robin, who leaned his own bow beside Little John's cudgel, and sat down at his elbow. "You could tell us your name," suggested Robin.

The boy looked ill at ease all over again, and took a fresh grip on his bow, and scowled. "And if I do not?" The recalcitrant sleeve unrolled again, and the boy looked down at it sadly.

"If you do not, I suppose we must loan you a knife to cut your sleeves to size," said Robin. "It might put you in a better humour—or dispose you to like us."

"Sit down," said Much. "I cannot talk comfortably with you looming over me."

"Don't tempt him," said Little John.

"Little John, you do not understand the art of conversation," said Much.

"I understand the art of silence," said Little John.

Robin saw the boy's eyes flicker again, at Little John's name. He pulled the dagger from his boot-top and tossed it, hilt-first, toward the boy's feet. The boy stooped to pick it up, paused, and sat down the rest of the way, a little distance from the other three. He picked at a seam

105

with the knife-point and with a small grimace grabbed the edge as soon as it was free, and yanked. It ripped out with a gratifying noise.

"Some housewife sewed a very careless seam there," said Much, and the boy gave him so evil a look that Robin was surprised. He took a corner of the cloth in his teeth, and tore it across; and in a moment one bony white forearm had reappeared. He turned his attention to the other sleeve, eagerly, as if his hunger were suddenly of little importance; and yet Little John had recognised the grey circles under the boy's eyes as Robin had noticed the tremor in his hands. He laid the second bit of rag beside the first with a happy sigh, and held his wrists out admiringly.

"No things of beauty, your arms, boy," said Much, "though they would look a bit better with a little flesh on them. Eat something before we finish it by accident."

Unfortunately the boy noticed the quizzical look Much was careless enough to let slide directly from the boy's thin arms to the huge bow he had let lie on the ground near him. "I *can* pull it," he said. "I will draw against any man here." He shot to his feet, staggered, recovered himself, and stood glaring. "If you are Much, and you are Little John, then perhaps *you*," and he flung the word as if he were a knight tossing a gauntlet at a rival, "perhaps you are he they name Robin Hood, king of Sherwood. I would draw bow against you and stop your rudeness."

Robin winced at the "king." "Blast your wandering eye, Much," he said. "Permit me to point out, youngling, that I have not offered any rudeness."

"Do you now mock me?" said the boy. "Are you not Robin Hood, who introduced the longbow to Sherwood, that all the Normans now go in fear of his reach?"

"I am he they call Robin Hood," replied Robin. "I am also calmly eating venison and would recommend you do likewise."

"I have come this far to seek Robin Hood, and to demonstrate my skill with my bow that he might accept me a member of his band," said the boy; and he raised one arm and wiped his forehead on his newly shortened sleeve.

Robin stopped chewing. "I was afraid you were about to say that." He looked up thoughtfully, for the boy was still standing while the three of them were still sitting. He wondered if the boy suspected the presence of Bartlemey and Col hidden behind leaves above them at no great distance. "How old are you?"

The boy stooped to pick up his bow. "If you will let me show you my skill, you will see my age is of small moment."

"Twelve," suggested Robin.

The boy's jaw dropped open and his eyes shone briefly in disbelief, and then pure hatred. "I am eighteen," he said; it was almost a howl. He marched to where Robin's bow stood, and half-threw it at its master.

"Now that, lad, is an insult, if you are in truth eighteen and like to be a man," said Little John. The boy looked at him, wavering, for a moment, and then put his chin up. "A mark! Choose a mark!" He whirled around as if a suitable mark might be creeping up on him unawares.

Robin stood up, but there were lines showing around his mouth, and his own temper was beginning to fray. If the boy is in fact any good with his stolen bow he will make me look silly, he thought; and I don't particularly like looking silly, with a short or a long bow. The lines around his mouth deepened. Blast the overweening dignity of the young. And that of the king of Sherwood too, I suppose.

"The mark is that ash with the little crook in it," said Robin. "There, across the stream." He bent his bow to slip the string into its groove, drew an arrow, fitted it, and let it go, almost before he finished speaking: partly because he was angry, and partly because if he was no great marksman still, he had shot too many arrows since he had become an outlaw not to do it smoothly. For now, whether or not his folk ate often depended on his speed. Marian almost never needed a second arrow to finish the kill; Robin could at least send the second into the creature's heart before it knew it was struck.

His arrow hit the ash, but rather more below the crook than he had meant. The boy was taking a few deep breaths—to steady his hands or his temper—and carefully drew and notched his arrow with all the formal grace of the castle yard. His arrow struck the ash tree at the exact center of the crook; and he drew another, concentrating, his feet planted perfectly, his back beautifully straight, and let it go; it struck a few fingers' breadth from the first. The third struck between the first two, and the boy then dropped his arms and his stance and turned a shining, hopeful face to Robin.

Robin's dislike faded as he looked into the boy's blue eyes, and a suspicion he had felt earlier stirred again, and then he suddenly and bewilderingly thought of Will Scarlet. Will had had the same glib balance of a man trained to shoot at straw bales, and yet he had become a highly valued member of the band in a very short time: as soon as he could remember to shoot first and check his posture second. . . . But if this boy was eighteen, Robin would eat all four arrows presently sticking in that ash.

"Now may we have our meal in peace?" he said, as gently as he could, and his dislike disappeared entirely and he began instead to like the boy as he saw him struggling not to let his face fall in disappointment.

"Shall I fetch the arrows?" he said, humbly.

"An excellent idea," said Robin, and watched as the boy waded uncomplainingly into the cold water.

"Did you plan this when you chose that mark?" inquired Much.

"No," said Little John, softly, also watching the boy.

"No," agreed Robin ruefully; "I was, as usual, not thinking much at all."

"At least you hit the tree," said Much encouragingly; the boy was out of earshot, and Robin laughed.

"Speak a little louder," he suggested.

The rest of the meal was passed in a silence that might almost have been companionable. Robin approved of the way the boy looked over his arrows before replacing them in his quiver; nor did he make any more protests about sharing their meat, and ate everything that was given him, ravenously, and did not notice that the other three chewed what they put in their mouths a very long time to give him the largest share.

At the end Little John put the stopper back in the empty bottle after he rinsed it in the stream; and they all rose. The boy was trying his best to look ordinary, familiar, unimportant, and unassuming, and Robin had finally to tap him on the shoulder because he could not catch his eye. The boy looked up, nervously.

"If you wish to come with us"—the boy caught his breath—"you must give us a name. *A* name," Robin repeated firmly.

Light dawned. The boy looked thoughtful, opened his mouth once or twice, and finally said, "Cecil." An evil little smile turned the corners of his mouth up. "Cecil is my name."

"Very well, Cecil. Try not to sound like a herd of crippled goats breaking down a fence, please? We attempt to move with discretion through the trees. The sheriff does like to send men after us now and again, you know."

The boy's face clouded, but it seemed to Robin that the possibility of being pursued had reminded him of his own problems, and that it was not fear—or the overweening dignity of the young—that troubled him. Let him not be some mad lord's only son, thought Robin, suddenly daunted. Some day we will accept someone into our company whom Sherwood cannot hold.

CHAPTER ELEVEN

lan's bride was receiving a cooking lesson. Her fine hair was roughly tied up, her eyes were red, and she was wearing a dress that did not fit her, but she was biting her lip in concentration, and Matilda, waving the ladle under her nose, did not look particularly cross, only earnest. Cecil looked at them and winced. "Are there—women—in your band?" he said.

"As you see," said Robin amiably, looking around; besides Matilda with her ladle and the lady Marjorie, Sibyl was unstringing her bow and frowning, and Eva was running her fingers along the curve of it and shaking her head. Neither Sibyl nor Eva, in leggings and tunic, was at first glance distinguishable from the men, and Cecil seemed rather caught by the scene over the cooking-fire. "Oh," he said. He finally turned his eyes in another direction, passing without break over Sibyl and Eva, to where Jocelin and Gilbert were deftly whacking up a gutted deer into joints. Cecil's pale face went paler, his eyes bulged, and he turned hastily away.

"Robin," said Harald. "A fat stag comes this way—" He paused, surprised, at a small, not quite suppressed moan from Cecil.

"This is Cecil," said Robin.

Cecil bobbed his head without taking his eyes from the rowan which so absorbed his attention. Harald looked at him in puzzlement and then turned back to Robin. "A stag of the two-legged variety, and so fat, I would say, as to have trouble walking, and so he goes in a litter hung with silk."

Robin whistled gently through his teeth. "A prize, I do think. Who have we here that might go and help hunt such a stag?"

The old lord in his silk-hung litter was not the least amused by the hiatus in his journey; he was not pleased to be divested of the gold chain around his neck or the rings off his fat fingers (Much had thoughtfully

---

110

brought a slip of their rough soap to grease the fat knuckles), or the heavy roll of coin poorly concealed among the cushions he rode upon. But he seemed more annoyed at the prospect of any loss of comfort than of the loss of his property's worth. His servants seemed at least as anxious about the temper of their master as about the tempers of their ambushers. "Not a merry meeting," said Robin, when their guests had been permitted to continue their journey.

"No," said Much, consideringly, "but not a wasted one either." The roll of coin had proved to be of silver and a few gold coins. It was laid out presently to wink in the firelight, as the outlaws who had shared the adventure took a little time before early bed or going on watch.

Cecil, who had spent the afternoon digging at the latest privy ditch, sat with them. Robin had noticed his hesitant arrival but had not commented; and Cecil seemed to have nothing to say for himself—perhaps from exhaustion. But when he reached to pick up a chunk of bread, Robin also noticed the hand twitch upon contact and the involuntary hiss of breath between the boy's teeth; Robin could guess at the blisters because he had been well-acquainted with shovel-handle blisters in his own first weeks in Sherwood. And Cecil still said nothing, though he frowned broodingly over the palm of his hand for a moment. When Much picked up one of the gold coins and held it for a moment over the flames till it gleamed like a tiny sun, Cecil looked at him thoughtfully, and then around, slowly, at his new mates; when he caught Robin watching him he dropped his eyes immediately. *I wonder whom he imagines in the old lord's place?* thought Robin. Even with a dark tunic like those worn by most of the outlaws belted over his ragged and outsize Norman-style clothes, he was visibly unassimilated; and he rested on his elbow as if he might leap twenty feet sideways at any moment.

Not a bad attitude for an outlaw, especially a new one, thought Robin, *but he's so—intense about it. He'll wear himself out. And we can use an uncomplaining digger.*

Cecil still wore the floppy cap they had first seen him in, which made him look more waifish than ever, like a kettle with a lid too big for it. *Fourteen,* thought Robin uncomfortably; but his eyes drifted down to rest on the boy's big capable hands dangling from their thin wrists, and he felt a little better. *Maybe sixteen. And he will learn. I think I will*

---

not be sorry that I let him join us. I will send him hunting with Little John, who will not laugh when he is sick, learning to gut a deer.

"I hear I missed sport," said a familiar voice, and Robin looked up; a very dirty and travel-worn Will Scarlet was unslinging his bow and an assortment of bundles and small furry corpses over a convenient branch. "Is there anything left a ravenous man might call supper?"

"An interesting question," said Much. "A ravenous man, I assume, will eat almost anything; but is he more inclined to call food one thing than another because of his hunger?"

"Because of your tongue it shall be fried and I will eat that," said Will, picking up half a broken loaf and spearing a piece of meat congealing in its pan over the low fire. There was a minor skirmish at the edge of the clearing; "Who was that?" said Will, chewing. "He was in a fever to be elsewhere."

"Your face, no doubt," murmured Much.

"No doubt," said Robin, looking at the suddenly vacated space by the fire. "You will have to meet our newest member later. His digestion, perhaps, is rebelling against our diet."

"Nothing wrong with our diet," said Much; "unless you're a Norman. Our guest this afternoon would have made a poor supper companion, I feel sure, and we were wise to detain him no longer than necessary."

"What is the new member's name?" asked Will. "And I was bolting at frequent intervals for the privy at least a fortnight after I got here, Much, my friend, and if you tell me I am a Norman, I will fry more of you than just your tongue."

"Cecil," said Robin. "And a very stripling."

"Cecil?" said Will in an odd voice. "Oh. There are surely a good number of Cecils in England; it stands to reason that one of them should make his way to Sherwood." He stood up, stuffing in a last mouthful, and shrugged back into his gear. "These will not keep the better for being warmed by the fireside. Much, would you like a tippet of the skins?" And he stumped off.

"Mmph," said Much. "He is as rude as a Norman."

"Little John," said Robin. "When Cecil re-emerges, tell him you are to take him hunting tomorrow. He can't dig for a day or two till his hands heal or they'll get infected—find him something to tear up for palm-guards while you're at it."

"The tender skin of the gentry born," said Much. "You and I wouldn't know."

"Bartlemey brought word that there is fresh spoor, down near Tuck's chapel, of a sizeable herd. Find out if he can shoot at a moving target."

Robin was contentedly trimming a new arrow when Marian returned to the camp the next morning. He watched her through his eyelashes as she crossed to him, his hands easy and knowledgeable along the clean narrow flank of the arrow as his heart beat faster. It was not . . . well, the alternative was that he might never have met her at all; and that did not bear thinking about.

"News," she said, dropping down beside him. She picked up a few of the feathers laid out on a ragged bit of leather at Robin's feet, and smoothed them with her fingers.

"You can make yourself useful, if you like," said Robin. "There's needle and thread in the pocket."

"That reminds me—I brought more thread," said Marian, pulling it out. "It was bargaining for the best of it that let me linger where I would hear the news." She chose her feathers and then looked at them uncertainly. "You know I never stitch them well enough for you," she said.

"Ah, but you stitch them well enough for almost anyone else, dear heart," said Robin, "and I am not the only fletcher in our company. I shall have the arrow you finish—and you shall have mine. Ben has several that need feathers."

"Ben?" said Marian. "My stitching is not that bad."

Robin grinned. "He has grown greatly in skill while he has been waiting for that leg to mend; I am a gruelling taskmaster, when I choose. And our company depends upon our arrows. Little John and Cecil went out with a few of his today."

"Cecil?" said Marian, threading the heavy needle. "A new man?"

"A new boy," amended Robin. "His bow is much too big for him, even by our standards; stolen, of course. He probably chose the largest he could find. I doubt he could pull it more than a half-dozen times before his shoulder came out of its socket; but he shot three arrows very sweetly with it yesterday."

"Three should be enough," said Marian.

"He plants his feet as if he would grow roots," said Robin.

"Little John will cure him of that," said Marian.

"That is what I hope," replied Robin. "And he can teach him staff-work as well, which will give him something new to think about. I cannot figure the boy out; he is obviously well-born, and yet he knows archery. A few do, of course, but this boy doesn't seem to know anything else—and fired up when I tried to ask him about it. He is over-ready to fire up; Little John is the teacher for him on all counts. But I hope his peevishness is not important. I do not like secrets; Greentree is crowded enough without them. What is your news?"

"Shall I tell you what you will least like to hear first?" said Marian. "For it concerns you."

"You have begun now," said Robin.

"The sheriff of Nottingham grows fierce over the depredations of the outlaw band in Sherwood; he declares that it is all the fault of their chief rogue, that Robin Hood, who is perhaps the devil himself, or at least devil-inspired, to incite men to such pillage. As God is his witness, he treats men fairly and taxes them only as befits a king's loyal man and is in all ways a good and honest master."

Robin snorted.

"It is astonishing, is it not, that the only truly wicked outlaws in the entire length and breadth of our green England should be here where they can plague that flower of justice and charity, the sheriff of Nottingham? Fate is a funny thing. I hear also, by the way, that some purse you took was to buy a young girl's father's permission that the girl should come to the sheriff's household. . . . So one girl in Nottingham has cause to love you, and the sheriff hates you with a particular ferocity just now, as I believe the girl is very lovely. She, meanwhile, has run away, or so her father says; I hear that he told her where to run and gave her what little money he had in coin."

"You know her?" said Robin.

"I supplied the coin," said Marian. "She'll be with the Sisters of Watersmeet by now, and when the sheriff guesses—if he does—it will be too late.

"But to finish my story: the sheriff, thus pricked, has decided he must have you, even at cost, even to the extremity of dipping into his own pockets—those pockets you have already stolen so much from—to bait the trap. The foresters, who love you as little as he does, perhaps because of the stripes laid across their backs by their chief on this account, cannot come at you. And so he has decided that he must lure you to come at them."

"You fascinate me," said Robin.

"So there is to be an archery contest in Nottingham, at the harvest fair; and the prize for the contest is to be a golden arrow."

Robin sighted along the shaft of his new arrow. "So?"

Marian smiled. "So the outlaws of Sherwood, renowned, as they are, for their archery, cannot possibly stay away from such a contest."

"Why not?" said Robin, genuinely surprised.

"Why, for the golden arrow," said Marian.

"Golden arrow? And what would we do with a golden arrow? Give it to Alan for a lute-string? I could hang it around my neck on a chain, perhaps, and let it stab me in the ribs when I tried to sit."

"And your honour as an outlaw?" Marian suggested.

Robin set down his arrow and laughed. "My honour as an outlaw concerns staying alive; and presenting my neck anywhere near the sheriff of Nottingham, who feels it wants lengthening, did he recognise it, runs directly counter to that honour. Besides, you know I can't shoot worth a pig's sneeze."

"The sheriff will be gravely disappointed," said Marian.

"That's the best news I've heard all week," said Robin cheerfully. "But you said you had two pieces of news?"

"I do not think this will make you laugh," said Marian, and paused. "You will remember Sir Richard of the Lea?"

"I remember him over every arrow I fletch," said Robin. "Your news will have to do with his son?"

"Yes," said Marian. "He has gone beyond what his father can protect him from at last; the wonder is only that it has taken so long. You may not know that Sir Richard began to mortgage his lands some time ago to buy young Richard out of earlier misdeeds. The mortgages are held by Blaise de Beautement—who, as you will know, is a friend to our friend the sheriff. It is thought that it is upon the instigation of our sheriff that Beautement is calling in his loan now, when Sir Richard has not a chance of saving himself. He long ago sold anything that might fetch ready money."

"Mortgaged?" said Robin. "I had not heard. I did not think he was so hard pressed."

"Young Richard killed a man," said Marian.

"A pity it is the man did not kill him," said Little John, looming over them a moment before he folded his long legs and sat down. "I had heard a rumour of this, but I did not know it would come true so quickly. Young Richard has killed men before."

"But never a Norman," said Marian.

"Beautement I do not know," said Little John.

"I know him," said Marian; "he is merely a creature of the sheriff's. Sir Richard was desperate indeed to turn to such a one, who he must know would wish to do him ill. The sheriff has made little pretence of liking a Saxon lord who too often is heard wondering when the king will return from the Holy Land to set his own country to rights."

"And now they will strip Sir Richard of his lands," said Robin. "Is the day set?"

"The meeting is a fortnight hence. Sir Richard is gone to the city to see what might be done; but he knows as we do that the answer is, nothing."

"It will please the sheriff's fancy to do this deed at Sir Richard's own home, I suppose?" said Robin.

"Of course. I'm sure the sheriff is greatly looking forward to that day."

Robin's eyes met Little John's. "Perhaps we may add something to his enjoyment," he said. "So, John, how does our new recruit?"

"He shoots stiffly, as you know," said Little John; "but with a bow that outmatched her as his outmatches him, even Marian might be provoked into shooting stiffly."

"Thank you," murmured Marian.

"I told him as much, and he wished to rant at me; but he did not refuse the smaller bow I offered—"

"Offered?" said Robin.

Little John smiled. "Firmly offered him, and we have gone some way this day in teaching him not to plant his feet as if they were the cornerstones of some great building."

"Do you like him?" said Robin.

Little John looked bemused. "I hardly know. It is an odd thing that you ask, for I've been asking myself, and it's not a question I care for; nor is he the first raw young man I have—um—"

"Intimidated into behaving himself," said Robin. "It is a thing I value you for. I am over-inclined to yell, and I cannot loom as you do."

"He is not the first raw young man you have given me for a first lesson," Little John said peaceably. "But he is—different. He is not without talent or brain—or wit," he added, a little ruefully. "But he has as many moods in an hour as I have in a year, though that may only be the strangeness of his new life. And he is mortally afraid of something; he is halfway up a tree while I'm still turning toward the sound of a broken twig."

"Poor boy," said Marian. She looked around. "Where is he?"

Little John shook his head. "Hiding in the shadows somewhere. I suggested to him that he make his report to Robin—I wanted to hear myself what he would say—and he could meet the lady Marian as well, but he gave me such a look as the creature in the snare when it sees the hunter's knife. It is the same look he casts over his shoulder as he climbs a tree to escape the breaking of a twig. He begged that I let him off, and so I did. For all his nerves, I have hopes of him when he has looked around him a little more."

"And when he has grown accustomed to sleeping on the ground," said Robin. "He probably hasn't had a good night's sleep since he left his home. He also has to learn to duck. I heard him walk into what passes for the lintel of our cave-door last night."

"His home?" said Marian. "Where is he from, then? Is there a reason he is afraid of meeting me?"

"He is well-born," said Robin, "but we know no more; he has not told us that much, but everything about him proclaims it. He fears, I guess, that he knew you in his former life."

"I see," said Marian, and her face cleared momentarily; but it clouded again. Robin looked at her inquiringly. "I am trying to recall what news I may have heard of recent runaways," she said; but if she remembered anything, she did not tell it.

Further details of Sir Richard's disgrace were soon brought back to camp. Rafe, who had a girlfriend who was a tavern-girl, returned from an evening in her company so preoccupied with the tale that Much teased him for being a poor lover: "She'll not tell you things if you forget her in the telling; and then you'll lose both her and her tales. She may be a comely wench enough, but *we* shall miss the tales."

Rafe said, very much on his dignity, "Lucy understands that I may occasionally think of things that concern her little; she likes me for it."

"No one, man or woman, ever liked such a preference," said Much, but Will broke in, grinning: "Not everyone, Much, demands such perfect attention to himself as you do. Why do you not have the fortitude to get yourself a town girlfriend who might tell tales that Rafe's Lucy knows not? Because you cannot spare your own attention long enough."

"I—" said Much, just as Will said, "Confess!" and Robin said across them both, "Is this an outlaw band or a nursery?"

Alan-a-dale, who lacked, perhaps, humour, nonetheless had an admirable sense of combustible situations from his years as a bard in Norman halls. He struck a gentle chord on his lute, and began to sing. He had dextrously learned to muffle each string as he played it, so that the aftertones died away almost immediately. He became so clever at this that his music had taken on a magical, ethereal quality, till it was easy to believe that his songs were from the faeries, who were standing just out of sight in the shadows. And, as Robin wryly said to Marian, as the faeries' music was said to choose its listeners, presumably no unfriendly ear heard it.

Marriage had been kind to Alan; his moodiness was all but gone, and he smiled more now, even if most of the outlaws' jokes puzzled him. Robin was still hoping to hear of some kindly Saxon baronial hall that wanted a bard, but it was not the sort of thing an outlaw spy-system was over-liable to be informed about—and, meanwhile, Alan seemed to think that he belonged where he was. He sat near the fire now, when he played; he had even learnt to ignore Little John.

What Marjorie thought, she never said—not even, Robin believed, to her husband. She was sitting next to him now; she lifted her head from his shoulder when his hand slipped up the fretwork to find its place. When he sang, she sang harmony in a weary little voice no louder than a sparrow's. The song Alan had chosen was a song of love, and it was hard to tell if it was a melancholy song or not. Robin thought, looking at the two singers, that Marjorie would have said that it was, and Alan would have said that it was not. The song ended, and Alan gave his young wife a kiss; she smiled, and put her head back on his shoulder, but she did not look away from the fire.

"I have it in my mind that we shall make a merry meeting of it for the sheriff and his friend Beautement, when they do come to rob Sir Richard of his home," said Robin. "Rafe, you have my leave to spend the next day or two in town; I will give you some small coin for supplies we must have, and you may spend your evenings making it up to Lucy so long as you spend your days gossipping in the market-place."

"I like such a task on both counts," said Rafe. " 'Tis lucky for me that Much has not a town girlfriend, for he could gossip the devil himself to a standstill, and I should spend every day in a tree, straining my eyes after foresters, and never see my Lucy at all."

"Hmph," said Much. "It is Will who owes me the apology."

"In a perfect world doubtless you would receive one," said Will cheerfully. "But you must make do with this world, in which you will not."

"Enough," said Robin. "Alan will wear himself out playing peace between you two."

Simon appeared at the edge of the firelight and touched Bartlemey on the shoulder, who sighed, stood up, and disappeared into the darkness. Several other such exchanges were taking place nearby. "There will be purses to empty before the week is out," said Simon; "Sir Miles has been heard saying loudly that the outlaws of Sherwood are a bad knight's excuse for carelessness, and he means to try us as we deserve. He should be here by sunset, the day after tomorrow."

"Good," said Robin. "I had feared that his friends would talk sense to him, and he would go the long way around; and we have need of every groat soon. Rafe, your most particular care is to find out what the sum of the mortgages comes to; gossip always exaggerates, so if we take twice over what you can tell us, we shall be safe."

"I shall cast my ear abroad also," said Marian.

"Be careful," said Robin sharply.

"Be careful, Rafe," said Marian.

CHAPTER TWELVE

Sir Miles did a great deal of bellowing when eight men in Lincoln green fell on him from the treetops, roped him neatly off his horse, caught that horse's bridle as it would have plunged away, knocked his men off their horses likewise, and began to delve into the saddlebags without further ado.

"If you do not be quiet," said Robin conversationally, as Sir Miles thrashed on the ground and roared that if there were a man among them he would challenge Sir Miles to single combat and that Sir Miles would then water the ground with his blood, "I shall gag you. I begin to think that I should enjoy gagging you."

"This is not honourable behaviour!" shouted Sir Miles.

Robin grinned. "I hope not. I am, after all, an outlaw and a rogue."

"I could slay you with one hand tied to my belt!" howled Sir Miles.

"Very likely. Which is why, you see, I took the precaution of tying both your hands to your belt, as well as your feet to each other, before venturing to discuss our business with you."

"Business!" shrieked Sir Miles. "I'll show you business! I challenge any man of you to single combat! I—"

"Yes, we've heard all that. You are not listening to us," said Robin. "If any of us wished to face you in single combat, I assure you he would have come forward by now. Cecil, gag this man for me."

"Gladly," said Cecil. Sir Miles bucked and gurgled and grew red, but the noise level dropped instantly, as Cecil finished his knots and stood up. He still wore his hat—Robin had observed that he slept in it—but he had tied it around his forehead with a bit of ragged twine, and with the camouflaging dirt smudged on his face and a grin wider than Robin's own, no one looking at him could have guessed that a fortnight before he had been—wherever he had been, sleeping in a real bed, wearing linen shirts, and firing at straw marks. "How do the saddlebags look, youngling?" said Robin.

"Good," said Cecil. "Heavy." There was an exceptionally frantic grunt from the now purple-faced man on the ground before them.

"Heavy with the right kind of contents, I trust," said Robin.

"You need have no fear of that," said Little John, nodding toward Sir Miles. "If he carried lead he would be calmer."

" 'Tis not lead," said Cecil. "Gold coin and a few gems." Robin opened his eyes and whistled. "And sausages, too. I find," Cecil added sheepishly, "that I miss sausages."

"There are worse vices," said Robin.

Little John moved dispassionately out of the way as Sir Miles rolled toward him. "It is well you gagged the fellow," he said. "His noise could have brought foresters fifty miles. They are not such bad woodsmen that I want to build a church tower and hang a bell in it to toll over our doings."

The other men were roped together and blindfolded, and made to walk with gentle, or mostly gentle, prods from staves to tell them which way to go. Sir Miles would not walk. When they hauled him to his feet, he attempted to kick the man who untied his ankles. Robin thrust his staff between his legs, and without his hands to save himself, he fell heavily. "That is a curious trick for an honourable man," said Robin, watching the knight roll back to the tree he had lain against and struggle that way again to his feet. He tried to kick Robin this time, and Robin did not try to be gentle when he bashed his staff between Sir Miles' ribs and pelvis. This time when he fell, he lay still for a few moments.

"Tie his legs again," said Robin, "and untie his mouth; but hold that bandage ready, for my ears are sensitive.

"We are taking you and your men to a place where we can pick you over at our leisure; but we have no wish to be kicked while we are about it. You will be blindfolded anyway, and more liable to kick an unoffending tree than any of us."

Sir Miles was a little curled up where he lay; he looked as if his side probably hurt him. "I will not co-operate with my captors," he said hoarsely, "who took me and my men all unfairly."

"You will do what it suits us you shall, and it suits us to prevent you from arriving in Nottingham yet. Your choice is merely of how uncomfortable you wish to make it for yourself."

"I will not co-operate," said Sir Miles, beginning to get his voice back. "And my family will not ransom me."

"He thinks we are Saracens," said Little John. "Trust a Norman not to know the difference between a Saxon and a Saracen." Cecil giggled.

"Your family will be put out by no such demands," said Robin. "We have no dungeons for the keeping of prisoners, even if we wanted the trouble of them."

"As a knight and a man, I will not co-operate with my captors!" bellowed Sir Miles, fully recovered, though he winced as he drew breath. "I challenge any—"

"Gag him," said Robin, and Cecil leaped to obey. Simon, who was in charge of the other captured men, looked inquiringly at Sir Miles and then at Robin. "Er—what *do* we do with him?"

"If he thinks it more manly to be thrown like a sack of meal over a horse's back and hauled, then we can oblige him, I guess," said Robin. "He had his choice. I will add, sir," he said to the man on the ground, "that we would have led you by smooth ways, and you would not have fallen, unless, of course, you were trying to kick the trees. Blindfold him, and bring his horse."

Sir Miles was not a happy sack of meal; he flailed so much that he made his high-bred war-charger uneasy ("Silly beast to be riding through Sherwood anyway," said Cecil. "Perhaps he was expecting a tournament," said Little John), and they had to shift him to a more tranquil mount. "We should tie his hands and feet to the stirrups," said Simon crossly, after they had made the transfer. "That would quiet him."

"No," said Robin. "If the horse fell or bolted I would not have even an enemy so vulnerable."

There required three men to hold him at last; one to lead the horse, one to hold him at the neck, and one at the ankles. It was not a pleasant journey. "Less comfortable for him than you," said Robin over the horse's back, as he took his turn at ankle-holding, to Simon, who had Sir Miles' collar. Sir Miles contrived to overbalance himself once, and only Robin's strong hold on his feet prevented him from falling over the other way to the ground. "If you do that again I shall let you fall," said Robin, "and break your neck, if fate wills. My patience wears thin."

"At last," murmured Simon.

Sir Miles was tamer after that, but from Robin's words or from exhaustion, only he himself could have said, and no one wished to try inquiring. The other men went submissively enough and, as Robin had promised, none fell, nor had trouble keeping his feet, for the outlaws gave warning when necessary to a blind man.

Sir Miles got no supper that night, for the three or four times his gag was briefly removed he immediately began shouting; and as Robin was as cautious about noise in the smaller camps at Growling Falls and Millward as he was at Greentree, Sir Miles was not given more than half a word's roar before he was shut up again. Perhaps from his example all his men were very well-mannered, and while they looked uneasily at the green-clad folk who faded in and out of the shadows, they were willing enough to eat the food given them.

Upon the next morning, rather lighter of the greater portion of their gear, they were taken to a different part of the forest than where they had been waylaid; and Sir Miles rode face down across the back of his charger this time, for that was the one horse too conspicuous for resale. But the sack of meal rode listlessly today, and seemed rather troubled by saddle-sores. The parting was simple. Little John loosened the bonds on one of Sir Miles' men, and left him to struggle free and help his fellows as the outlaws went silently away.

Rafe came back with one sum for Sir Richard's mortgages and Marian another, but they were not so far different, and Robin doubled the higher one. "Usury," said Little John. "The *lower* figure is usury."

Robin shrugged. "The taxes the Normans would hold us for are usury; I see little difference. And we shall be paying Norman usury with Norman gold."

"Got from Saxons," growled Little John.

"The system isn't perfect," said Robin with a grin; "keep your eye on the short term, my friend. If we look farther than tomorrow's stew or keeping Sir Richard's lands in the hands of the last local Saxon lord with power enough to be a nuisance to the Normans, we shall merely go mad."

"Which would be no fun at all," said Much; "and there has to be some fun in exchange for all the long boring hours lying on tree limbs never designed for the support of human flesh."

Nottingham was so loud with talk of Sir Richard that as the day of confrontation grew near, the outlaws of Sherwood felt they could almost hear the distant murmur of many voices from the isolation of Greentree. Even the foresters were more active, as if the sheriff's excitement at the prospect of a final stunning blow against that last strong Saxon lord in his jurisdiction was infectious.

Little John and Cecil had a brisk set-to with four men in an area of Sherwood Little John had chosen for its comparative safety from the depredations of sheriff's men and foresters. Cecil, as a new member of the band and one of the youngest, was obliged to spend much of his time washing dishes and hauling wood. The hero-worship he was developing toward Little John was magnified by the fact that it was a tremendous treat for him to escape the grisliest camp chores and go scouting—like a real outlaw, as he felt, although he was very careful that Robin should have no complaint of his dish-washing and wood-hauling. But Little John continued to deal with him as if with an infant Little John was merely too polite, or too obedient to Robin's orders, to leave behind; and Cecil resigned himself as best he could to his master's always selecting the least dangerous territory for guard duty when the infant was accompanying him.

But it was Cecil who gave the alarm: Cecil who, in Little John's words, was halfway up a tree while Little John was still turning to look. Cecil gave the low whistle Robin's folk all knew as warning, and as Little John wriggled an inch or two farther along his branch to bring Cecil's tree into view, he saw Cecil drop on the heads of the foresters. It was neatly done; the man Cecil landed on fell to the ground at once and lay stunned; and Cecil had felled a second with his staff before the other two knew he was there. Little John by this time was out of his own tree and halfway to the fray, cursing (silently) the impulsiveness of children; and as the two remaining men turned to make short work of the boy, who had used the only good staff-blow thus far in his repertoire and was now faintly nonplussed by its demonstrated effectiveness, Little John's readier staff caught one of the two under a shoulder-blade and spun him round, and cracked his head against a tree. The other one, gaping, made a fatal error in judgement and failed to decide which enemy to meet first, with the result that he was lifted off the ground and thrown to one side by the combined strength of Cecil's one good blow, reapplied with vigour, and another swift stroke from Little John.

"You damned young idiot!" Little John said. "What did you mean by that show?"

Cecil set his jaw. "I gave warning and attacked. We are near Greentree here; we are not merely to watch; we are *supposed* to attack. I did as I should."

"You did not wait to see if I would aid you!"

"Wait!" said Cecil, with scorn. "I knew when I whistled it would make them pause just a moment, and I wanted them to pause under my tree. And they did. I knew you would come."

They were patting down the unconscious men for anything worth stealing, or any broken bones; automatically they took the arrows from the quivers of the two men who carried them; Robin enjoyed shooting the king's deer with the king's foresters' arrows, despite their shorter length. "You did *not* know I would come," said Little John, pausing over one man's purse, which contained a few small coins. "You did not wait for the counter-sign."

"Pfft," said Cecil, flaring up. "What do you take me for? I told you why I could not wait; they would have moved on."

"I might have been asleep," Little John went on doggedly, returning the purse to its place untouched. He remembered Robin's tales of his days as a king's forester, and this man's face did not look as if it belonged to a bad man.

"Not you," said Cecil, as if it disgusted him to have to make any answer to such a suggestion. "If you had sent me out with—with Aymer, I would have waited for the counter-sign." Aymer's skill with longbow and quarterstaff had led Robin to make one of his few mistakes in accepting someone into his company; a mistake corrected barely a sennight before, when he was sent on to follow up news of work in a small Northumbria town. "Where his opinion of himself can get in someone else's way," said Robin. "Maybe the weather will dampen him a little," said Much.

Little John almost smiled. "Aymer. Mmph. You have learnt flattery somewhere. Promise me that you will wait for the counter-sign if you are sent out with anyone else. I ask you this, I, Little John, who never sleeps."

"Or Robin," said Cecil, ignoring the sarcasm.

"Or Robin, who, as leader, certainly never sleeps. Promise."

"Or—"

"Only Robin or me," said Little John firmly. "Promise."

"I promise," muttered Cecil. "I fear I have dislocated this man's shoulder."

Little John felt the arm delicately and agreed. "Leave it for now. We'll try to carry him a bit gently. We don't want to risk him coming to himself now by trying to snap it back; they'll all have headaches enough later without giving any a second knock." He stood up and gave the sharp burst of short whistles that Robin's other scouts in earshot—were there any—would know meant help was asked.

"You know," said Cecil demurely, still sitting on the ground, "you wish to punish me for doing exactly what you would have done in my place."

Little John looked down at his pupil. If Cecil had looked up he would have seen a real smile on his teacher's face. "Not with Aymer."

Cecil did look up then, but Little John had pulled his face into its usual long lines again behind the disguising beard. "Come," said Cecil. "Confess."

"I shall do nothing of the kind. That was a nice stroke you made, taking down the second man."

"Thank you," said Cecil. "I have an excellent teacher."

"A good thing too or he would never keep up with you," replied Little John in a tone of voice that would have terrified Cecil less than a fortnight earlier. "But it is time you learnt a few more basic strokes; if these fellows were anything but mutton-heads they would have blocked so plain a blow easily. And perhaps in the lessons your teacher may also knock a little sense in that hot head of yours."

"If I had waited for the counter-sign and they had moved on, I should have missed my leap, for I do not leap well either," said Cecil. "Do not think that I am not grateful that they are mutton-heads," he added, a little sadly.

Little John gave a snort that might have been a laugh, and then several of Robin's folk faded out of the trees around them, and the carrying of the victims to safer—that is, more confusing, or so the outlaws hoped, from a forester's point of view—territory began. "We heard the warning whistle, but we were at some little distance," said Bartlemey, who was the first to appear; "and I see you needed no help. You the glory and we the brute work," and he smiled at Cecil, because he remembered his first weeks as an outlaw, and had learnt a bruising lesson or two from Little John himself.

"Don't give him any encouragement," said Little John; "he should have waited. An outlaw interested in glory will have a short life."

Bartlemey winked at Cecil, who smiled sheepishly and looked side-long at Little John, who was bending over the man with the dislocated shoulder. "Take his feet," he said, addressing no one in particular, but it was Cecil who jumped forward. "If we are lucky, and these men run to type, they will not remember exactly where they were when the wrath of God fell upon them from above; but we had best tell Robin to set an extra watch this way for a little time to come."

It was hard to go quietly through trees anyway, and, Cecil thought, the sweat running in his eyes, impossible to go quietly while carrying half a man; but Little John made no protest about the noise they were making. He was intent on where they were going, and Cecil, trying not to stumble, was glad merely to hang on and follow. The other men seemed to recognise where they were when Little John stopped and they all lay their burdens down; only the man with the injured shoulder had the luxury of being carried by two pairs of arms. Cecil looked around, trying to behave as if he didn't feel entirely lost; Little John was frown-ing. "It is curious there are foresters this way at all, but perhaps the weight of the sheriff's frustration is making even the Chief Forester a little cleverer." He turned to Cecil. "Rip off a bit of this man's tunic and bind his eyes; if he wakes while I set his shoulder, we will get away before he figures out which hand can pull the bandage off for him. Now kneel on his chest and hold that other hand down—and watch that he doesn't kick."

There was a very unpleasant noise, the man cried out, thrashed briefly, and went limp again. "That will do," said Little John; and they headed back to camp.

*　　*　　*

Little John ended his description of the day's events by reporting that Cecil had addressed himself to the experience of his first face-off with the king's foresters "with what I am forced to call glee."

Cecil, who knew he was being reprimanded, flushed to the roots of his ugly hair. The hat had finally come off a few days after the episode with Sir Miles, and the ragged mop then revealed was striking in its awfulness even among the outlaws, who were not noted for personal or sartorial elegance. "He must have chewed it off," Much said to Robin.

"Yes," said Robin. "It's a pity one can't offer to—er—tidy it for him. But I was challenged by him before on less pretext, and am not anxious to repeat the performance—particularly after Little John has had a fortnight's training of him. He's also our most reliable dish-washer if not disturbed. The hair will grow out."

"He's an odd young one," said Much. "He seems to have hated growing up a young lord much worse than Will did."

Meanwhile Cecil had scraped what was left of his hair into a short tail that looked like a small thornbush at the nape of his neck, from which little scraggly wisps escaped and were relentlessly pulled behind his ears and, whenever he was near water, plastered in place. As he bowed his head under the weight of Little John's words, tufts of hair were sticking in all directions from his hairline.

Looking at the thornbush with some sympathy, Robin said, "He is obviously the most promising pupil you have had; I can't recall your ever maligning any of the others for gleefulness." Cecil looked up, blinking in surprise, and Robin smiled at him. "You don't know Little John as I do. The more somber he gets, the better pleased he is." A number of things passed very quickly across Cecil's face, and his eyes turned to Little John; but Little John, at his most inscrutable, was rubbing grease into a leaky boot.

"But I take the warning seriously about the extra watch," said Robin a little later. Cecil had gone off with a sigh in answer to a summons from Matilda; and Marian had just heard the tale of the day's doings—from Robin, because Little John had responded only in a grunt when applied to. "He's sulking because I've ruined his authority with Cecil," Robin said cheerfully. "The boy did very well today, but Little John thinks praise is bad for the young."

"As I recall," said Little John, "the reason you prefer me to do the schooling of him is that you felt I was most likely to keep him in line."

"I wouldn't want him to think that he was *not* supposed to knock foresters on the head when the opportunity presents itself," said Robin. "One does wish—cautiously, of course—to encourage certain attitudes. I didn't invite Cecil to join us for his services only as a dish-washer."

There was a glint of teeth in Little John's beard, but he did not reply.

"The forest is as busy as an ant-hill someone has just stepped on," said Marian. "I will be glad when the affair at hand is over—if for no other reason," she went on, as she saw Robin's mouth open, "than that I do not like to think of Sir Richard lying awake nights and knowing there is no hope for him."

Robin was not distracted. "Perhaps you should stay away for a time —at least till this business is over."

There was a little silence, and all the things that had lately grown harder and harder for them to say to each other hung in the air between them; Marian felt that she looked at him through a curtain. "I have heard," she said, her voice light and easy, as if nothing dismayed her and as if her heart did not hurt in her breast, "that young Richard has been packed off to the Lionheart's army; let them do with him what they can. But I hear too that the boy is shaken, at last, by the events he brought upon himself—and upon his father. The one virtue he does not lack is courage, so perhaps he may make a soldier."

She stood up, and looked down at Robin's dark head. He did not move. "Perhaps you are right. Perhaps I shall stay away from—from you—for a little time. Till this particular business is over." Robin's hands closed over the cup he was whittling from a knot of wood, and his knife stopped moving, but he did not look up.

"Good night, Robin Hood."

She was too far away to hear him when he finally said, "Good night, Lady Marian."

Cecil, standing in the shadows at a little distance from the circle of firelight, looked after Marian with an expression that would have made Much even more curious about his hatred toward his previous life; his hand touched his ragged hair, and then rubbed at his throat, as if he were having difficulty swallowing.

CHAPTER THIRTEEN

Marian was not seen in Sherwood for the next several days, but such an absence was not without precedent, and Robin chose not to think about it. She was being sensible, that was all, and staying out of the way till Sir Richard's fate had been decided. The working out of that fate which Robin and his folk had in mind kept them all busy enough: the best way to Sir Richard's castle had to be agreed upon and then spied out for traps, unexpected traps, and places where unexpected traps might be set between the present and the day to come. The recent forays of foresters and sheriff's men into parts of Sherwood usually left alone suggested that the sheriff had thought of the possibility of Robin Hood's scoundrels making trouble in defence of the last important Saxon lord in Nottinghamshire.

The outlaws' collected booty also needed its value guessed with enough certainty that they might not make fools of themselves when they threw the mortgage payment at Beautement's feet. "Or rather," said Robin, "our reckoning must be so unmistakably in excess of the amount owed that Beautement dare not protest."

"You'll have no trouble with Beautement himself," said Friar Tuck. "He's afraid of raindrops and falling leaves and clouds across the sun —and sees signs and omens in all of them. He has a taster at his elbow for every meal, I understand, although no one has as yet cared to make the attempt to poison so miserable a fellow."

"He sounds the sheriff's favourite kind of tool," said Robin; "the kind that has no mind of its own to distract it."

"Exactly," said the friar.

"You here?" said Will, coming upon them. "There must be fresh venison for dinner."

"Your respect for my grey hairs never fails to astonish me," said the friar. "It is no wonder I prefer the less taxing companionship of my dogs."

Much appeared at this moment, bearing a wooden plate, and Marjorie followed him, bearing another. "It was baking day," said Much, "and I felt that we should have the opportunity to try as much of what there is to try as we can—in honour of our guest, of course. Matilda has much respect for a man in orders—even if such respect is a little thin elsewhere in our company. You could put that down there," he said to Marjorie.

"I thought," she said shyly, glancing at Robin, "that you would tell me if these are—are acceptable." Between the two trays there were three loaves and a mound of rolls and buns enough for the Lionheart's army.

"I'm sure you have learnt to bake," said Robin mildly. "But you have not learnt to handle Much. The phrases that you need, my lady, are 'No'; 'No, you can't'; and 'No, get out of here before I throw something at you.' "

She put her shoulders back. "I am not 'my lady' here," she said. "I am an outlaw, and an outlaw's wife." The spirit went out of her again and she said, a little wistfully, "Alan doesn't care about food, you know; I think he would eat the leaves off trees if they would nourish him enough to go on writing songs. And Matilda is very kind, and no one else will—will tell me anything."

"Sit down and have a roll," said Much. "Have you tried eating one yourself?"

"No, I—" She sounded surprised. She glanced over her shoulder. "I should go back. Matilda will miss me."

"Not for a quarter hour. Take dinner with your leader, Robin Hood. Lady—that is—Marjorie, this is Robin; Robin, Marjorie. You met once under somewhat trying circumstances, I believe. This is a very good roll."

"Is it?" she said hopefully.

There was a small commotion, swiftly quelled, from the direction of the kitchen area, and Marjorie started. "I must go," she muttered, and fled.

Will caught Robin's look and said involuntarily, "Good God, man! That timid little thing is nothing like Marian!"

"True," said Much, with his mouth full. "Marian can't cook."

Whether or not Robin would have had anything to say to this was to remain unknown; there was a low, urgent whistle from just beyond Greentree's environs, and all heads snapped around as Eva burst into view. "Bartlemey's been hurt," she said, panting; "oh, friar, good fortune that you are here tonight."

"Is it bad, then?" said Robin, standing up and beckoning to a few of the faces turned toward them; Much and Will had already reached for their bows.

She shook her head. "I do not know for sure; I hope not. I fear . . . We were surprised by a group of foresters. Seven or eight of them, I believe, and we only three." She tried to smile. "Of course the losing party always sees two enemies for every one. But there were more of them than us. We knocked them down and got away; one of them has an arrow through his leg. But so does Bartlemey. Gilbert is with him; I came ahead for help."

Bartlemey was carried to Greentree white and sweating, but the friar pulled the shaft out easily and declared the wound shallow, "as such things go. You will come to no lasting harm, my friend, though you find it hard to believe now, if you follow my instructions." And he gave his orders for the making of a poultice.

It was deep night by this time, and the friar agreed to stay: "I am too tired to walk far, and I would like besides to see Bartlemey once more before I leave him to your doubtful mercies." Room was made for him, and a blanket found, not too threadbare nor too troubled by its life in a damp cave and its memories of the sheep who had originally worn it.

There should not have been foresters prowling—particularly in such numbers—through that bit of Sherwood where Eva and Gilbert and Bartlemey had been, any more than there should have been foresters where Cecil and Little John had met them only a few days before. Robin's outlaws were too many to remain invisible and too few to withstand a determined effort to get rid of them. Robin knew he would not be able to sleep soon that night. He returned to the fireside and poked a corner of the low-burning embers to make them catch again. He stood staring at the little tongue of flame, and then picked up the cup he had been whittling when Marian had last visited Greentree; he had not touched it since. There was not enough light to see accurately; but his fingers knew the shape of both cup and blade—and not all of the outlaws' drinking vessels sat straight anyway. At least he would not cut himself. Probably. He could not bear to sit doing nothing, and he

---

132

was too tired to stand an extra watch and let someone sleep who could. Everyone else had gone either to bed or back on guard; the camp was very quiet, except for an occasional pop from the fire and the scrape of knife against wood. So he heard the almost silent tread behind him; and then Will Scarlet dropped down beside him with a sigh.

"I've never known you unable to sleep," said Robin, after a minute.

Will smiled a little. "The good friar takes up the space of two men —and that's you and me, I guess. I'm grateful it won't rain tonight, for it's a tree for us." He paused. "Besides . . . I have wanted to say something to you."

Robin's knife seemed at a loss; it groped its way over the surface of the knot, but found no chip ready to be cut out.

"You might want to know," said Will. "Or you might throw me into the fire. But you might want to know—"

"Out with it, man," said Robin to his knife.

Will looked at his hands as if he wished for something to chop at also. "Marian has a suitor. She has had them since she was fourteen, I know —but the years draw by, and her father grows older, and . . . the months pass and nothing seems to change. Marian is from home a little more often is all, but not so much more often that a man who does not want to know cannot ignore it. And so his thoughts ease back into the well-worn way that is most comfortable to him."

A curl of shaving fell at Robin's feet. "Go on."

Will sighed again. "This suitor is a man named Nigel. His father was a Norman, but his mother was Saxon, and wife to his father. He levies the taxes that the sheriff requires, but he keeps his lands in good repair, and his people have a fair chance. None goes hungry. Marian's father would be pleased if she accepted him."

The cup was taking shape. "How do you know all this?"

"The whole camp knows of it," said Will, a trifle grimly. "I know a bit more, for Marian has long been my friend, and often I can read her face when she will not speak; and I am the only one of us who knew her father well. . . . I knew Nigel too, long ago, when we were all children."

"The whole camp knows, you say," said Robin. "I did not."

"Who would tell you?" said Will. "You of all of us are the most dependent on the tales others bring here. The fate of Marian's father's lands is not without interest in Nottingham, and so the fate of Marian herself as his only child is not without interest." He paused again. "I would have kept silence—Marian would not love me for telling you, did she know—but I think perhaps her father is pressing her. She was used to laugh about Nigel; but she has not laughed about him lately."

Robin was silent for so long that Will yawned involuntarily. "Time for you to go looking for that tree," said Robin. "I can recommend the ash over there," he said, pointing with his knife. "There is a hump of root on the south-western side that might almost have grown there to be a headrest."

"Oh," said Will, and yawned again. Robin's head had bowed again over the cup in his hands. "Um. Thank you." He stood up uncertainly, but Robin said nothing more.

Marian's other piece of news proved correct also: there was to be a grand fair in Nottingham, and an archery contest was to be a central attraction. There had often been archery contests at previous fairs, and they always drew a good crowd, both of archers and of onlookers; but the prize of the golden arrow made this contest unusual. It was not only that the prize was, to the sort of folk most likely to be shooting, of less interest than the usual one of a sheep or pig; it was that everyone knew that the sheriff was determined that this contest would trick the outlaws of Sherwood into exposing themselves.

"He wants a rumour put about that good shooting will win a pardon and—this is the best part—an honest job with the foresters, specially arranged by himself. But the right sort of folk don't talk to the sheriff's men, so that is precisely how the rumour goes: that he wants it put about. And then the man who tells you this grins, and you grin back, and you both know what the sheriff's pardon is worth, which is almost as much as a place with the king's foresters," said Rafe.

"There will be plenty who'll be glad to shoot for the other prizes, though," said Simon; "there's still a sheep and a cow and a horse. . . ." He sighed. Greentree had several times found itself sheltering sick or wounded or lost baby animals that Simon brought back with him. Robin had once found him hastily building a rabbit-hutch for the nest of baby rabbits he'd found a fortnight before the day he rescued a fox-cub. He'd scowled at his leader. "I'm not on duty!" he'd said. "I'm free the rest of today!"

"Did I say anything?" said Robin. "At least animals are quiet. I am, however, admiring your work. I will remember this talent of yours, you know."

The scowl lifted, and Simon rubbed his sweaty forehead. "Oh, well, Jocelin showed me what to do, first."

The fox-cub was no longer a cub, but it showed no inclination to leave an easy life of fireside supper-scraps. (The rabbits had been released when they reached adult size, to Much's disgust, who felt that the proper fate of all plump young rabbits was in stew.) It was sitting alertly behind Simon's ankles as he sighed, and he reached down to scratch it gently behind the ears. It was shy and wild with most of the others, but Simon it adored.

"That golden arrow is likely to make the best archers shoot a little awry," said Little John. "Who wouldn't prefer a sheep?"

"What I fail to understand is why he thinks an archery contest is going to lure *me* anywhere," said Robin. "It was common knowledge when I was a forester that I could hit the broad side of a barn only if it wasn't walking away too quickly."

"I don't think the good sheriff remembers you as that young forester," said Much thoughtfully. "You weren't a major public nuisance and private terror to him then; therefore you are somebody else."

Little John grunted. "By that reasoning, all any of us need do is trim our hair, wear some of the fancy clothes we take off their owners, call ourselves by other names, and walk gaily down the main street of Nottingham."

"It would be amusing, would it not?" said Robin.

"My favourite amusement takes the form of knocking fat Normans off their horses and stealing their purses," said Will. "I am sorry I missed Sir Miles."

"He was good sport," said Little John. "Watching Cecil's face as he gagged him was best of all. I had forgotten what it is like to have just knocked one's first Norman off his horse."

"Do you know I have still not met your young protégé?" said Will. "My curiosity grows sharp. Is it not strange that I have never seen him?"

Robin shrugged. "There are too many people in this camp," he said.

"There speaks the man who worries about keeping us all fed," said Little John.

"Especially you," said Much.

"You eat more than I do to keep that mouth of yours going," said Little John. "Cecil ducked meeting Marian too. Robin and I thought he knew her in his old life. Maybe he knew you too, Will."

Will frowned. "So? We are all outlaws together now. Why should we not meet?"

"You shall," said Robin. "Have patience with the boy."

"You only want someone to talk linen shirts and lace to since Alan and Marjorie are too high-minded to look back on what they lost," said Much. "I don't blame Cecil for avoiding you."

Robin sent everyone else into hiding before those who were to go to the meeting at Sir Richard's Mapperley set out. "There is nothing to tell me that we've been found or that we'll be successfully followed, but we are about to twist the sheriff's tail for him very hard, and he will try his best to turn and bite us for it. The energy of sheer rage can do remarkable things sometimes." And who should know better than I? he thought.

Everyone carried a longbow, and most carried a staff besides. The bow Will carried could put an arrow through an oak door, did he draw it strongly, as could Little John's, though the latter preferred to rely on his staff. "I am glad I am not a sheriff's man today," said Robin, looking them all over before they set out. Most of their tunics were patched; many had sewn leather pads over their shoulders where their quivers chafed, and there were dark shiny strips down their dark-green breasts where the straps hung. Their leggings were ragged and not all their boots had begun life paired; but their faces were eager and their eyes bright.

The last of the Greentree folk shouldered their small personal bundles and bulkier bits of common camp gear and disappeared into the trees. "What an unholy racket," said Robin, wincing.

"Harald knows better how to make boots than to walk in them," said Little John.

"Now that is Matilda," said Will, listening; "she has just been slapped in the face by a branch and she wants to chop the tree down."

It was a beautiful day; the birds sang behind the leaves, the bits of sky visible overhead were blue, and the little breeze was kindly. Robin and Little John carried the two heavy purses that were to buy Sir Richard's freedom; Robin felt that the Norman gold was balefully dragging at his belt and trying to bruise his hip with every step. It doesn't like being put to a good use, he thought, and smiled; and saw, out of the corner of his eye, Little John shifting the purse at his belt to hang more comfortably.

They came to the edge of Sherwood when the sun was high. They stood in the last row of trees, blinking out at the bright meadow that lay nearest them, below the farms around Sir Richard's moated stronghold. Robin looked around at his folk and said cheerfully, "Remember that we are an army of the faithful, come to rout the heathen enemy, and step out boldly." He was the first into the sunlight, Little John close at his side; the others shook their fears from them, and followed, trying not to huddle. Their lives had become too much like the king's deer they hunted, and sunlight and empty spaces were strange to them.

"The sun never shines like this on the Nottingham market," murmured Rafe with half a laugh to Simon, who, looking around wide-eyed himself, wryly agreed. Simon wished he were a fox himself, thought longingly of the cool familiar reaches of Sherwood, and sighed.

CHAPTER FOURTEEN

arian sat bent over her embroidery, that she need meet no one's eyes; and she kept her fingers moving, that no one watching her might guess she was troubled by anything but following the pattern of her stitchery. Her fingers knew as much as they needed to about pushing a needle through the heavy stuff that would hang on a wall some day; they did not need any further guidance from her brain. Tidily they followed as her eyes directed them, around the curve of the red deer's flank.

She had never quite decided if she approved of her skill with the needle or not; she knew she enjoyed designing clothing, and sketching tapestry scenes she would later fill in with coloured thread, but the rather idiotic patience it took to do the needle-work itself scared her a bit. Mostly she didn't think about it; what it had provided her with for many years was time and peace to follow her own thoughts undisturbed; what was frightening was how much time, especially over recent months, she needed for those private thoughts.

The other women chattered on; but Aethelreda, the only one of them who knew the story behind Marian's lengthening silences, deflected most of the attention from her cousin.

Robin and Little John and Will—would Will dare go?—went to Mapperley tomorrow—blithely, Marian thought. Without any fear that Sir Richard's real danger might be a trap for the man known so far and wide as Robin Hood had come to be; known as the man who daily made a fool of the sheriff of Nottingham for every day the sheriff failed to catch and hang him. The Baron of St Clair was quite specific on this point. Sir Richard was about to lose everything, and the source of this had naught to do with her Robin; but she thought that the noise made about Sir Richard's imminent downfall was a little too loud, even for a man of Sir Richard's rank, unless someone wished very badly that the news penetrate far and deep—even into the fastnesses of Sherwood where the sheriff's men did not go. The recent over-activity of the foresters was a blind to the purpose. . . .

No; she did Robin an injustice; he knew he put himself in danger. But the sheriff was growing shrewd; what direct threats and the dubious strength of his own men could not accomplish, perhaps tangential threats against someone who could not protect himself—and to whom Robin had reason to feel sympathetic—might accomplish instead. Would even the sheriff be quite so vindictive, without such added purpose, against Sir Richard in his troubles? He risked certain ill feeling among Sir Richard's powerful friends—Sir Richard was known to be on friendly acquaintance with the Lionheart himself—by stripping him. The sheriff was no fool. But his other goal had come to obsess him.

But what to do? Any mere emissary sent on Sir Richard's behalf would be suspect; and worse than suspect, once those purses were upended and some of their contents recognised—very likely by one or two of the sheriff's friends brought for the spectacle, the previous owners of this or that jewel. So vast a sum as Robin had had to put together left the outlaws little leeway to be careful with.

Beatrix appeared at the door of the chamber. "Marian, Nigel is come. Again," she added, with the smile Marian had intensely disliked for years. "He and your father"—again the smile—"specially request you join them."

Silence fell while Constance and Hawise and Euphemia exchanged glances. Marian composedly began to fold up her work; she had learnt composure since Beatrix came to live under her father's roof, Beatrix with her sharp eyes and sharper tongue. "Aethelreda, if you will accompany me?"

"Of course, my lady." Much of Marian's composure had come of watching Reda; she had not understood, when she was younger and gayer. Perhaps she should be grateful to Beatrix for forcing the lesson on her before Robin shot Tom Moody, and she found herself with a terrible secret to hide.

The two of them went down the cold stone stairs and into the great hall, where a fire always burned, the table where her father always sat drawn near. From the far side of the big room the fire was no warmer than the tapestry of a fire might be, and even in high summer the room was cool with a damp, insinuating coolness that was unpleasant:

unpleasantly cold right up until the rare moment in August that it became clammily too warm.

Her father sat in the same chair in the same place summer and winter; she preferred her smaller private rooms unless there was some occasion or company that needed entertaining in a way too grand or too proper than the women's rooms permitted.

Her father, she thought, had no cause for dreaming of being lord of a castle—a castle whose real Great Hall could contain their entire house. As he grew older he grew more timid, less able even to give the house servants the orders to lay a table or see to a neglected room—orders that had been his wife's, that should have been Marian's, that devolved more often on Aethelreda and Cerdic, their seneschal. But her father did not see to his estate either—such as it was—nor to its books; that, too, came to Marian, and to Reda and Cerdic. The master sat, day after day, by the fire in the hall of his cold stone house, and dreamed.

But he did not, thought his daughter bitterly, dream any longer of being lord of a castle, but, instead, of his daughter's being the lady of one, and of a greater fire in a greater hall that he would sit beside in his declining years, with no burden upon him even to pretend to see to anything. His son-in-law would take care of business, and his daughter would at last become the daughter she should be—bustling and house-bound, and probably fat, Marian thought, with children clinging to her skirts.

She looked at him now, and, hearing their footsteps, he looked up and their eyes briefly met; he did not often meet her eyes. The hope in his was as clear as that in a hound's who sees his master belting on his hunting gear.

Would it have been so bad to be plump and to have children and to gossip about small things while she counted linens? It was too late now; it was too late since her mother had married her father, over twenty years ago, her mother who was the closest friend of the young woman who chose to be cast off by her family rather than give up the man she loved, a young forester named Robert. Marian's mother had been her only loyal friend over the first hard years, and had brought her baby daughter to play with her friend's baby son. Because of his mother, the son had learnt to read, where the father could barely sign his name; because of her mother's friendship with the wife of a forester, Marian had begged and whined for a bow when Robin had been given his first bow. Robin had been very quick at his letters, quicker than Marian; but Marian had been quicker with her bow.

It was unfair to blame Nigel on her father. If it had not been Nigel, it would have been someone else, and it could have been someone worse. Except that someone worse would have been easier to turn away again, and again, as she turned Nigel away. He rose to greet her now with a cautious smile on his face; she thought his knees stayed slightly bent so that he could drop back in his chair at once and arrange his face as if he had not noticed her arrival, in case she proved to be in one of her "moods." A worse man would have let himself be turned away; a worse man or a better.

She was never sure if this bit of defensive behaviour on his part made her want to laugh, or run him through with the sheep-spit hanging from its hook by the fireplace. She paused a moment, halfway across the room, and surveyed him. Encouraged by this, his knees straightened the rest of the way, and his smile settled in upon his mouth. "Good morrow, sir," she said.

"Good morrow, my lady; Aethelreda." He was tall when he unbent to his full length; taller than Robin, if not so tall as Will or Little John. It was a joke, a bad joke, to think of any of the folk of Sherwood when she looked at Nigel; he was short-sighted from peering long hours at his accounts, and he went everywhere in a litter or carriage. He did not care for walking or for riding horseback; either was likely to stain his clothing with sweat, and he was fastidious about such things. His hands were flabby, though there was a callus on the second finger of his right hand, from the pressure of a pen.

Aethelreda murmured something polite, and turned to move a chair closer to the fire as Rawl, the master's elderly body servant, brought one for Marian. Marian quelled a shiver; it was colder here than in the heaviest downpour in Sherwood; some internal voice told her that this had something to do with the company. When her father's hall was full of people on the feast days it was warm enough—then the air turned steamy, and caught at her throat, and the hall seemed too small, and again she wished for Sherwood, and the dappled roof of leaves that never weighed upon her. She pulled her scarf closer around her and thought, I would rather live in a hut in the woods; a hut like the one of my first memories, with a clean-swept dirt floor, and a brown-eyed boy watching me from behind his mother's skirts as I watched him from behind mine. Overlapping that thought was another one: And how many times a day do I tell myself so?

I wonder if Robin would simply send me away—as he has sent other awkward or unsuitable folk away—if I declared that I was staying?

I wonder if he would like me to try?

And then, very quietly, the thought that stopped her from trying: I wonder if he loves me as I love him?

She found herself staring at Nigel, whose smile was beginning to falter. She sat down. "Fetch wine," said her father, and Rawl hobbled quickly off. He took his duties as first squire very seriously; he didn't let it bother him that there was no second squire, or that he had been first squire to a man who never left his fireside for thirty years and more.

Marian tightened her composure with her scarf and said, smiling, to Nigel: "Forgive me my absent-mindedness, sir. I am preoccupied with the troubles of a friend."

Nigel's face smoothed out. Now he was preparing to be sympathetic. Marian kept her smile in place by force of will. "A friend?" he said.

"Do you know Sir Richard of the Lea?"

The melancholy lines that appeared on Nigel's face at Sir Richard's name looked honest enough. "Indeed yes. A good and worthy man. It is a thousand sorrows that he should have been cursed with such a son."

Marian felt Aethelreda's quietness freeze into stone at her elbow, and she put a hand on her friend's arm, but casually, that the men might not think anything of the gesture. "A thousand thousand yet, when you think of one fewer noble holding falling from the good hands of the Saxons and into the clutching ones of the Normans."

"Now, Marian," said her father nervously; but the half-Norman Nigel only smiled again. Marian knew this time she definitely wanted to run him through with the sheep-spit. "It is my earnest belief," he said sonorously, "that Saxons and Normans will learn to live together in peace in this beautiful land. Perhaps even within our lifetime we shall see it." He looked at her through his eyelashes.

That, thought Marian, is what Reda calls his covetous look, and she's right. Her own eyes wandered to the fireplace, and Reda perhaps felt the hand on her arm close before Marian drew it away, for she turned to her lady and under pretext of arranging her scarf for her—which Marian kept fidgeting with—caught her eye and smiled her slow smile. The halo of her flaxen hair blocked the sheep-spit from Marian's gaze as she bent toward her. Marian sighed; Reda knew her very well.

"There are better-looking, better-dowered girls within a day's ride," Marian had said once, furiously, to Reda—Marian did not waste her composure when they were alone. "Why *me*?"

"Maybe he likes a challenge," Reda replied. "You *and* your father's estates."

Marian snorted with laughter—a muffled snort, that Beatrix might not hear from the next room and come to inquire the cause; Beatrix felt that laughter was most often the expression of some vice that needed to be put down or tied up or locked away. Reda rarely laughed; that time too she had only smiled her slow smile.

It was hard to tell about Reda sometimes; her composure went to the bone. She rarely spoke—and only to Marian—of her own youth, when she had watched her father die of a wasting disease in a year and a half, and her mother die of grief in six months; and a wastrel younger brother go through the family estate at such a pace as to have come to the end just as he fell off his horse and broke his neck. Reda had bought her composure dear; and she was less than three years older than Marian. She was pretty and, as Marian had cause to know, both practical and kind—and able to keep her peace. She might have married, had any man had the sense to see past her dowerlessness. None had, and Marian had convinced her father to send for her; she was but a second cousin once removed after all, and had no nearer family left her.

Rawl returned with wine and cups and then retired only far enough to hover at her father's elbow, almost quivering with eagerness to be sent on another errand. They were lucky to have Rawl and Cerdic and Aethelreda; very lucky.

"Rawl," she said, and his spaniel's eyes shifted at once to her face. She was not the master, but she would do; any errand was better than none. "Would you ask Cerdic to join us here?"

"I asked," she said, when Rawl had disappeared, "for any news of Sir Richard; Cerdic has cousins there."

Nigel's face had rearranged itself once again into its melancholy lines, but this insistence upon the topic of another man's ills (another unmarried man, Marian thought suddenly, with amusement; Sir Richard was a widower of long standing) obviously did not suit him. Perhaps any tale of a landed man's loss of land was upsetting to a land-proud account-clutching man like Nigel. She had a pang as she thought this, for would she not be devastated if her father lost his lands—and he could be foolish enough to do so without Cerdic's sharp-eyed loyalty —this home that she had grown up in, however much she had grown to dislike it of late? And, she thought, something that cuts even closer to the heart: would I like it if all Robin's conversation with me began tending to the sad plight of a good-looking widow. . . .

"If there were only something his friends and well-wishers could do," said Nigel.

"As you mention it," Marian said quickly, relieved that he should have fallen so neatly where she wished him to fall, and fearful that he might back out again if she let him go on talking, "I had thought of riding there tomorrow to offer him what comfort a friend might"— Nigel's eyes flickered—"and to tell him that if he is in need of bed and board for the immediate future we would be honoured to be of use to him."

"But, Marian," said her father. "You cannot go—alone—" His voice wavered, for as they both knew she went alone where she would, and he had long since learnt he could not stop her. But Nigel need not know these things, and it was fitting that a father should disapprove of so indelicate and unfeminine an errand. His eyes slid away from hers, as they usually did, but they both knew they were playing a father and daughter role for their guest—so why, thought Marian at him irritably, can you not keep your voice steady?

"I thought to ask you to accompany me," said Marian silkily. Her father's gaze jerked up at that, and they looked at each other with no great affection on either side. Then, as if unified by a single thought— which I guess we are, Marian said to herself: that of fear that Nigel won't play this game with us—they looked to their visitor. "Perhaps our guest would care to make another of this party?" Marian's father said feebly.

"I should be glad to offer my support," said Nigel, and now he cast his eyes down in no good humour. I think I can rely on your clinging to my shadow, thought Marian, and shedding the light of your dreadful respectability upon the proceedings. All the proceedings.

Cerdic entered then and Marian said, "What news of Sir Richard?" and everyone turned quickly, Reda perhaps quickest of all.

Cerdic shook his head. "Sir Richard has locked himself up, and will speak to no one; nor does he eat and, they think, sleep. He is returned from the city but a few days past, with nothing to tell, and the cloud upon him as dark as ever. His candle is seen shining from his high window at all hours of the night, and they see a shadow of a man pacing."

"His people—?" began Marian, not sure exactly how to phrase the question.

Cerdic, who knew of his mistress's absences if not of a certainty that the company she kept when she was from home might have a dangerous interest in his answer, said calmly, "Sir Richard did issue orders that no one shall attempt to bar the lawful execution of Blaise of Beautement's visit tomorrow."

Marian was wondering if she dared ask if they would obey, when her father, who was quick enough to notice anything that might rub his timidity too near, said nervously, "They will obey, will they not?"

"I am sure they will not disregard the last orders of so good a master," said Cerdic gravely, and a taut silence followed, broken just before it became panicky by Marian, suggesting that perhaps Nigel would gratify her by playing a game of chess.

"You will come tomorrow?" Marian said, pleadingly, to Reda. She had tucked her hand into her cousin's elbow that she might speak quietly enough that Beatrix, close behind them, might not hear. Beatrix had deplorably quick ears.

Nigel was staying overnight; he often did anyway, as it was a longish journey to his home for a man who had no taste for the usual forms of travel. But in this case he stayed because they would set out early on the morrow for Sir Richard's Mapperley; and as he obviously viewed this eventuality with less and less pleasure as the evening hours had passed, dinner had been something of a trial. It was not Nigel's place to protest what he had agreed to, once Marian's father had given it his permission; and Marian had taxed her skill at conversation to its utmost and beyond in the last few hours, for she could see the thoughts slipping like fishes behind her father's watery eyes, and knew that if she once let him say what he opened his mouth to say several times, she could yet lose what she had gained.

Reda had followed where Marian led, and had made her own inconsequential observations when Marian had paused for breath or for inspiration. But her eyes were blank, and Marian did not know what she thought of the plan for tomorrow; nor, as her friend, would Marian try the tricks on her that she had used upon her father and her suitor. And so she only asked: "You *will* come tomorrow?"

Reda pressed Marian's hand to her side briefly and said, "I will come," but her voice was flat.

After a minute, and half a flight of stairs, Constance twittering away at Beatrix behind them, Marian said, "You do not care for it."

Reda was silent for so long that Marian thought she would get no answer. She and Reda shared a bedroom, but the other women were supposed to attend to their needs before they retired to their own bedchamber, and when she was in the mood Marian enjoyed making the attentions difficult for Beatrix, who so hated the idea that she should have to attend anyone but herself. On this evening Marian asked the merest token from her women, and Reda nothing at all; Marian dismissed them quickly.

Reda sat, hands folded, on her bed. Marian looked at her and then went to the window, which she had not allowed Hawise to close, and leaned out over the sill. The stars were bright tonight, and the air tasted better in her throat than the wine at dinner had. She closed her eyes and thought that it was not her voice that was hoarse from the strain of the evening past, but her mind; and wished that the breeze could blow behind her eyes. . . . Blow away thoughts of Robin. She opened her eyes. Even if Robin had not existed, she could never have married Nigel. But if Robin had not existed, she might have gone already to a convent, where she might look at the stars every night without her heart's hurting for someone who looked at the same stars and might not be thinking of her as he did so.

She heard footfalls behind her. She turned as, without looking at her friend, Reda sat down on the sill beside her, and looked out over the quiet garden and the wall and trees beyond. The square plot where the herbs grew was a paler green against the shadows, as if it glowed faintly in its own light. When Reda had first come to live with them she had been horrified at Marian's fondness for the night air, which everyone knew was poisonous; perhaps it was Marian's own obvious health that changed her mind, or merely the realization that Marian was as stubborn as earth or stone or fire when she chose. But Reda did not shudder now when Marian shoved at the curtains as though she would like to open the entire wall to the out-of-doors, and had even learnt to like the cool herb-scented draught that wandered through their window. She still sniffed at it cautiously, though, as if she might notice poison in the air in time to duck back and slam the shutters closed against it.

"It does not matter if I approve or not, does it?" said Reda. "You have chosen your line and mean to keep it, as you have done this long time past. If there was a time when I, or your father, might have changed you, I missed it."

Marian was silent.

"Perhaps," said Reda, "were I as you are, I would do the same. I do not know."

"I will be grateful for your presence tomorrow," said Marian humbly.

"Yes, I believe you," Reda said thoughtfully. "Sometimes I envy you knowing so clearly what you want. It is why Beatrix hates you, you know, for she does not know, and can only see that she must wait on you because you are the lord's daughter. It would comfort her to believe that it is being the lord's daughter that gives you that surety, but it is her misfortune not to be stupid, and so her hatred is difficult for her. It twists in her hands, and bites her."

"I suppose I do know what I want," said Marian sadly, "but I do not see much hope that I shall get it. There is not much in that to be envious of."

"I know that too," said Reda gently.

Marian made a face, and rubbed her hand over her aching eyes. "Then what is the use of knowing?" she said. "For you or for me."

Reda looked into her friend's face as if she would read her fortune there. Marian's heart beat suddenly faster, as if she would, and that Reda's next words would tell it to her. But what Reda said was: "I do not know you, for all the years I have spent daily in your company. We are not much alike. I would have married Nigel. Come; we must go to bed. You will need your wits about you tomorrow."

CHAPTER FIFTEEN

f they decide to obey Sir Richard after all, our bright career is reaching a swift and brutal end," said Robin lightly.

Much said, "These folk have no illusions about what kind of master Beautement would be, with the sheriff standing behind him and telling him when to breathe and what clothes to put on. For love they might obey Sir Richard, had they less to lose—or nothing to hope for. Those whose hearts hurt the worst will remember that they do their good master a service by disobeying him now."

"I believe you," said Robin; "but I have a mastery of the art of worrying that is a burden to me if I may not use it." He looked up at the clear blue sky, which hurt his eyes; he wished for green.

A small hunch-backed old man materialized from behind a hedgerow. "Sir," he said, looking around at them. His eye fell on Little John, and his face brightened. "I bring you the news you look for," he said. "The sheriff has come, and his men are placed as Robin Hood said they would be; but we have two men for each of his, and three for the biggest ones." He grinned, showing more gaps than teeth. "None so big as you; we'd need four for you."

"And Sir Richard?" said Robin.

The man's smile vanished. "He's up in his hall, with the sheriff, and Beautement, and a few of Beautement's greasy hangers-on, and the sheriff's men that aren't standing around stiff as pokers and looking like fools outside; and there are some visitors for Sir Richard who came today too."

"Visitors?" said Robin sharply.

The man's shoulders rose and fell. "Aye. That's what I know. A lady and an old man and a young one; and another lady, and maybe a few folk with 'em. Friends of Sir Richard's, who want to bear him away with 'em when all's done. A kind thought: Sir Richard might have leprosy for all his great friends have stood beside him these last weeks. And these visitors have put the sheriff off his stride, for which alone they're welcome to us. He can't gloat as much as he wanted; 'twould be impolite with ladies present." The man grinned again, and spat.

Robin was amused, despite the suspicion that had immediately presented itself to him. "The sheriff standing on the wrong foot is always good news to me," he said.

"You'll be Robin Hood himself, sir?" said the old man.

"I am," said Robin. "And you are?"

"William," he said. "Old William. I was a clerk till I got too old and my hand knotted up; but Sir Richard has kept me this eight years for nothing. I know what would come to me, did Beautement become my lord."

It was curiously quiet as they approached Mapperley. There were cattle and sheep grazing in some of the fields, and corn ripening in others, and turnip tops visible in one near the way they took; perhaps it was only that Robin and his band knew what they approached, but to them the silence pressed in upon them as the clear blue sky had done since they stepped out from under Sherwood's green leaves. Even the short streets of the little village that huddled under the castle walls were deserted; they saw one or two skinny dogs, who slunk away from them.

When they crossed into the outer bailey they at last saw some folk: sheriff's men, who stared as Robin and those with him entered the unguarded gate. They did not try to stop them, but they did not look as comfortable as the minions of a conquering and unconquerable force should look. As the Sherwood outlaws came further into the bailey grounds, one or two of the sheriff's men began to drift around behind them, toward the gate; whereupon three or four of Sir Richard's folk began to drift in a like manner. Robin's careful eye tallied up as Old William had predicted; the sheriff's men were outnumbered here by slightly better than two to one, and while the sheriff's men were better dressed and armed, Sir Richard's men looked the more earnest of purpose.

A few of the local men were unconvincingly posed as shepherds to a few of Sir Richard's beasts grouped for the purpose; several were engaged in horse-breaking, which to any accustomed eye was confusing the well-broken horse being worked. But the watchfulness of the scene was so plain that the thud of the horse's hoofs, and the occasional voice, were startling.

It was worse inside the main court. A porter hailed them half-heartedly at the gate; but when Robin said, "We have business with Sir Richard and Blaise de Beautement," he made no further question, and the outlaws walked on. Here were more sheriff's men standing around looking utterly ill at ease, as if perhaps they were suddenly possessed of a few more arms and legs than they were accustomed to, and did not know how to dispose them. And here were thicker and more watchful clots of Sir Richard's peasantry. The blacksmith was banging away at a simple horse-shoe, so the size of his audience was surprising; but his audience was paying poor attention, and most were looking over their shoulders. Indeed, the blacksmith was not well attending either, for the iron under his hammer was becoming brittle with the long and needless working. All the horses in Sir Richard's stable seemed to need hand-walking today; and all the hawks in his hawk house were individually carried out to take the sun.

When the Sherwood folk came to the inner ward, the same atmosphere prevailed; and not a one of the sheriff's horses was tied, for each was held by a grim-faced peasant—several of whom looked as if they'd never been so close to a horse before.

Not all the horses belonged to the sheriff or to Beautement; there was another little group slightly to one side, their trappings less gaudy, and perhaps even a little well-worn for fashion, but aristocratic nonetheless. "Marian," said Will, under his breath. "What will she be at?"

Rafe said quietly, "Whatever it is, she will do it handsomely."

Will, thinking of the girl who had climbed trees and torn her skirts like his own little sister, said, "I hope so."

No one here asked their business; no one asked what name should be announced; but when they reached the Great Hall they were obviously anticipated, and the tableau opened out a little to let them in.

Sir Richard, drawn and haggard and looking twice his years, stood with his head bowed and his hands cupped with a curious desolate emptiness, as if they would never hold anything again. He wore a green tunic very similar to the ones favoured by the outlaws of Sherwood; but his, while of a better cloth, hung less well upon his stooped shoulders than upon any of Robin's folk. The sheriff was standing behind the great table, where Sir Richard was wont to sit; and Robin's fists closed involuntarily at the sight, for at the table itself, in Sir Richard's very chair, was a thin, pink-eyed man in a long dingy robe trimmed in fur: this would be Beautement.

The sheriff's expression as he looked at the new arrivals was mixed of lust and fear and uncertainty; and Robin remembered that Old William had spoken of other visitors whose unexpected arrival had put the sheriff out already—whose identity he had guessed even before he saw the horses outside and recognised the blaze-faced bay. He tried to keep his eyes fixed on the sheriff but they would not obey him; against his will they slid to the other end of the table.

Marian sat there, with her hands crossed gracefully in her lap, and her curly hair smoothed back under a riband; he could only see the top of her head, and the beautiful slope of her neck. . . . He could not remember when last he had seen her in a dress; this one was the colour of dark amber, with embroidered cuffs, and a yoke of some fancy needlework across the breasts; the skirt fell in long thick folds, hiding her feet. He wondered if she was beautiful, or if only in his eyes she gleamed in the sunlight.

With her was her father, who sat staring like one stricken at the girlhood friends of his daughter; for Much stood at Robin's elbow on the one hand, and Will moved up and stood beside Little John at the other. The man's face was bloodless, and in his slow and fearful mind the truth of his daughter's absences was inexorably emerging from the shadows where he had banished it.

Beside him sat a sad-faced woman a little older than Marian; and over Marian's chair, half-crouched like a dog protecting a bone, stood a young man Robin guessed must be Nigel. He, too, looked at the outlaws as if his worst suspicions were being confirmed, but Robin feared any outburst he might make less than anything Marian's father might say, for he could call too many of them by name.

"A merry meeting," said Robin; and Sir Richard stirred, as if a long-forgotten voice were disturbing a bitter dream. "I am glad we came not too late."

The sheriff opened his mouth, and his men, who had been ranged around the walls of the room, took a long step forward. But the sheriff said nothing after all, and they paused again, leaning on their lances and looking silly; committed to leaving their lounging against the walls but having no command to follow.

"For we have come in time, have we not?" said Robin; and he unhooked the purse at his belt. Little John did the same. "We are here to buy back the mortgages on Sir Richard's lands, which I understand are otherwise forfeit. We would have come to you sooner—sir—" said Robin to the sheriff, who stared over his head, "but we have a quaint dislike for Nottingham town, where the streets are narrow and we cannot catch our breath." And at Robin's words there was some clinking of hauberks against sword-hilts and lance-butts against flagstones.

Sir Richard moved now; his hands clasped, and his head rose and turned toward Robin. Robin's name had already shaped itself on his lips when some spark of his native wit returned to him, and instead he said formally, "Sir, I know not what you mean by this; but these debts are my own, and I ask no aid; my lands are forfeit."

"I think not," said Robin. "You may call them mine, if you wish, rather than yours, but they are no longer Beautement's; and I hire you now and forever as my administrator. I have no wish to oversee this holding, which would be too great a responsibility to a—yeoman—like myself."

"And if I choose not to accept?" said Beautement, querulously. "For the worth of the lands I know, and I mislike the look of your purses."

"And the hands that hold them!" cried the sheriff at last. "Seize them!" But he was too late; for there was an arrow at the throat of every one of his men before he finished saying the words; and there were Much and Will and Little John and Robin left over, smiling faintly, their hands loose at their sides.

"How unkind," said Robin mournfully. "But see! All is not lost; our gold is good." And he and Little John upended their purses on the table; and a lovely bright heap of gold and jewels spilled twinkling out. A bar of sunlight from a high window lay diagonally across the table, and the outlaws' ransom fell across it, as if the table were divided per saltire, and Sir Richard should gain a new coat of arms by the day's business.

"Thief!" gobbled the sheriff, seizing a ring. *"Thief!* This was taken from the hand of Sir Nicholas not a month past!"

"Indeed?" said Robin. "How curious. For it bears upon it—you see," he said, taking it delicately from the sheriff's shaking hand so that their fingers did not touch, "it bears the sigil mark of an old Saxon family, and I know they cherished it very dearly. So dearly, I think," he said, smiling, "that you must be mistaken; for only to another Saxon's hand would they have yielded it up. But they will, I am sure, take comfort in the fact that it has fallen to Norman hands at last to save a fellow Saxon from harm.

"And these must be the mortgages?" Robin continued, bending closer to the table to look at the heavy vellum pages lying before Beautement. "Yes. I shall take these, for they are mine now; and I have a bard who will be happy to scrape them clean, for he has been pining for something to commit his lyrics to; and so yet another person's heart shall be gladdened by our meeting this day."

"Gladdened?" the sheriff said thickly. "I shall be gladdened by the sight of you and your foul crew hanging from my gibbet!"

"I am sorry to disappoint you," said Robin. "Surely there must be some other thing to please you; for life is short enough—for both of us."

"Short enough!" said the sheriff; "within these walls you have the upper hand; but you shall not leave these gates alive."

"For shame," said Marian, rising from her chair with a sweep of amber skirts. "How can you speak so? I know naught of what happens here, though I see you know each other past this day's meeting and in no friendly attitude; but I see also that this man," and she made a tiny bow toward Robin, "has offered good price for Sir Richard's mortgages; and I cannot see that your claim is not satisfied."

She turned gracefully to Sir Richard, who still looked dazed. "I congratulate you, sir, on your good fortune; not merely in the regaining of your property and by it your life and livelihood," she said with the faintest clear stress, "but in the having of so good a friend as this man." Her eyes, perfectly cool and indifferent, met Robin's briefly; and if looks could kill, thought Robin, Nigel would have pounded several holes in my heart by now. Marian looked back to Sir Richard. "At so happy an occasion"—the sheriff twitched—"I wish to cause no distress"—the

153

sheriff twitched again—"but I hope that regaining your own home will not make you a stranger to ours. Our invitation is still sincere even if it is no longer necessary."

There was a tiny pause, in which the loudest noise was the sheriff's breathing. His men were still caught in their awkward poses, half at the fraudulent ease of soldiers in a situation that should not call for their skill, and half on useless guard from the arrow-points held steadily at the hollows of their throats. The outlaws looked relaxed, as if they stood around with their arrows notched and their bows pulled back for hours daily, just, perhaps, in practice—or in anticipation of such occasions as this one. The sheriff hauled violently at his tunic, which had a tendency to ruck up over a belly grown too big for it.

Marian turned so smoothly to Robin that perhaps only the sheriff and the outlaws standing nearest heard Beautement begin to say, "But—"

"I would have your name, sir," said Marian. "I would thank you by name for a good friend we share."

"My name is Robin," said Robin Hood; "Robin, son of Robert, forester, once, in the king's service."

"And so you are a good king's man," said Marian. "I am glad to know this." There was a strangled noise like a sob behind her; the sheriff's men looked miserably to their leader. "But I could have no doubt by this generous deed."

"It is not fit," said Sir Richard slowly, "that you, my lady, should offer my thanks first. I can only beg that my—my oppression of mind these recent weeks has had a—an adverse effect on my manners. I thank you from my deepest heart." His eyes still looked blank, but he fixed them on Robin's face, and straightened his back, and did not look at Beautement or the sheriff. Robin could guess that it took all his self-command not to; for it was not yet clear to Robin, or, doubtless, to Sir Richard, that gold and impudence would carry this day. And while Robin knew that Marian provided a leaden weight upon the sheriff's behaviour, and that by her presence there might yet be no blood shed and no one of Sir Richard's loyal folk taken for siding with outlaws against the law of England, still he wished her far away from this dangerous show.

"May I offer you—refreshment?" said Sir Richard. He looked around, as if a meal might materialize at his elbow as a confirmation of the miracle this doomed day had brought him. One of his people stepped forward, braving the red-hot gaze of the sheriff, and said to Sir Richard, "My lord?"

Robin said, "We thank you, but we have—other duties, which bid us not tarry. But we hope to see you again, and soon, and under less—er—mortal circumstances. On that day we shall be glad to eat and drink—and to laugh—with you."

Sir Richard's eyes seemed at last to focus, and the faintest beginning of a smile touched his mouth. "I shall look forward to it."

"We too should be leaving," said Marian; "you will see us to your gate, will you not? Perhaps the looking at what is again yours without question will please you." Her words flew like butterflies through the vibrant air of the hall; and the company was quiet, as if watching them.

There was definitely a smile on Sir Richard's face now, but it was a small one, and not entirely pleasant. "I shall of course escort you off my property," he said, and his eyes swept round the room, and took in the fact that the sheriff's men were outnumbered better than two to one by his own folk; and that at the moment there were arrows at their throats besides.

"Perhaps all my guests would do me the great service of letting me bide alone just now," said Sir Richard; "I have, you understand, much to attend to, now that my lands are my own once more. I have been sadly careless of late, for the grief that was upon me. I fear I would be a poor host."

Beautement stood up uncertainly; his lower lip trembled like a child's. He seemed not to notice or remember the gold strewn upon the table in front of him; it was the sheriff who stuffed it back into the two purses, and stood gripping them in his two hands.

A moment longer he stood, glaring, Beautement a little to one side; Robin watched as his eyes roved over his own men, then Robin's, and, last, upon Marian. There his gaze lingered for a heartbeat or two, and his nostrils flared—not a pretty sight when the nose is long and red, thought Robin—and his bristly eyebrows drew together so fiercely that his deep-set eyes almost disappeared beneath them. Then he stamped down off the dais and made for the door as if blindly, bumbling close to one arm-bent archer, Eva, who slid silkily aside without ever letting her arrow waver from her prisoner's throat. When the sheriff's bulk was outlined by the sunlight of the doorway, Robin's folk stepped back, to let the sheriff's men follow him; but they did not slacken their bow-strings. Beautement hurried after the sheriff, eyes on the floor, anxious not to be the last to leave, for fear, perhaps, of an arrow stinging his heel to hurry him on his way. Robin's bow seemed to chafe his shoulder at the thought.

Nigel and Aethelreda stood up; and, Marian's father trailing behind them, looking like a man who has narrowly missed the gallows and is not sure yet of his fate, came up to the little group before the dais.

"We will give them a few minutes to get well on their way," said Sir Richard; his folk were slipping out now also, in some apparent speed; and Robin's folk began to ease their arrows. "I believe the word will go round that at the last defeat we have won a victory, and the sheriff will not choose to tarry. Then I will take you to my gate—unless you might now agree to stay? I beg you will. I believe my kitchens have kept themselves in good order without my attention, and I owe you a meal at least."

Robin shook his head. "It may not be true that it is duty that takes us away in haste, but wisdom will do as well. The sheriff will not love me for this day's work, and I wish to be back to my own—er—lands before he decides what to do about it."

"I do not seek graceful protestations," said Sir Richard, "and my gratitude is none the less for the asking of this question. But great heavens, man, what made you do this? You must know there's a price on your head, and no small one at that—and on yours," he added, looking at Little John, "as I would guess you must be John Little."

Marian shivered, and Nigel laid a hand on her arm, and murmured something to her; and Robin had to repress a desire to lay his own hands upon Nigel's shoulders and throw him out the door.

"If you have heard that much of us, then perhaps you have heard more," said Robin. "It seemed worth risking a little to come to the aid of the one true Saxon lord who lives in Sherwood's shadow." He wondered where Nigel's estate might march; and then he thought, the man detests me already; let him make something of it if he will. But Nigel was silent, and Robin kept his eyes on Sir Richard.

"If you call this risking a little, then I want to know no more of how you spend your days," said Sir Richard. "But I thank you again . . ."

Robin interrupted: "Thank us no more if you would please us with it. Were your extremity any less, we would not have come thus to your aid; for the aid of rogues is not without its own price, or so I fear the sheriff will wish to make you believe.

"Tell us this instead: that what by—as I may call it—sleight of hand you have won, you will keep. And hold."

A shadow crossed Sir Richard's face. "You may be sure that I will hold it." He was silent, and when he spoke again it was as though he pulled the thought out one word at a time: "My sorrow has been great, and as it grew upon me, the sheriff has made it grow the greater. The simple gaining of my lands, victory enough as that would be, was not enough for one of his metal. I will not forget. I have tried, perhaps, to forget some things; but this I will never forget."

Robin said gently, "There might have been an easier way to do what we have done this day, but we are rough folk and not ready-witted. I feared the danger I put you in by drawing you out of another. That Saxon ring is not the only jewel the sheriff will recognise. But if we are lucky—and if you, perhaps, will pretend to forget some things—he may concentrate his efforts on me."

"You mean that he is a coward? Aye," said Sir Richard. "This is one of the things I have learnt. I had thought, or chosen to let myself think, he was merely over-fond of luxury. But if I cannot thank you more, let me say this to you: if you ever have need of a true friend, I am he; and this castle, you know, has never been taken. Walter!" he said, and turned away at once. The young man in livery who had answered his lord's call before stepped up again. "Have them bring Windwing out," said Sir Richard. "I have it in mind to ride with my guests a little way.

"And you, my dear," he said to Marian. "I hope there will be no ill effects of this day's visit for you and yours."

Marian smiled her cool aristocratic smile. "How could there be?" she said. "Will the sheriff hold me responsible for seeing his discomfiture?" She spoke lightly while Nigel watched, his hand again on her arm.

"How could there be?" said Sir Richard, nearly matching her tone. "But I think perhaps you would do well not to go visiting our sheriff, if you are again in the mood for visiting, for some little time. I know that the sheriff does not like to be reminded of—discomfiture; and this sample of it, I think, will prick him hardily."

Marian smiled again, almost sleepily, as if Nigel's hand on her arm were a yoke that bore her down. "If the mood for visiting comes upon me again soon, I shall come to you first."

They moved to the door; outside, a great grey horse was being led up. "You do not ride, I think?" Sir Richard said to Robin.

"No," said Robin; "I have it in my mind some day to breed a horse that can climb trees; until then I find it more convenient to go on foot."

"Climb trees?" said Nigel, in a voice that suggested that he was judge and jury and gaol-house keeper, and that he enjoyed his work.

Robin said, "My folk and I lead a somewhat—idle life. We spend some amount of time lying comfortably in the branches that our great English oaks see fit to provide us. Horses, however, love meadows best."

"I should miss riding," Marian put in, as if making conversation.

"No fit husband for you would expect you to give it up," said Nigel, through his teeth.

"My people are unaccustomed to riding," said Robin thoughtfully. "Most of us, I think, do not miss what we do not know."

Sir Richard beckoned to the men holding the horses, and the little procession went on foot, with the horses being led after; quite the parade, thought Robin, and a pity the sheriff is not here to appreciate it.

"Not all of us are ignorant of horse-flesh, however," said Will. "Are we, Rafe? A fine animal, sir," to Sir Richard.

"And you are?" said Nigel to Will, turning his gaol-house eye from Robin.

"I am Will," said Will cheerfully; "Will Scarlet, as I am called now, who was once . . . well, no matter. I remember you, Nigel; you always cried when we were playing tag, and you got knocked down. You used to call us bullies. And I remember once you put sand in our soup," he went on reminiscently, "and we tried to drown you in it, and we might have succeeded if old Anna hadn't come in just then."

Nigel stopped dead where he stood. Robin looked at him, thinking that he had the face of someone who would put sand in the soup.

"So—! Will, you call yourself? I remember Will of Norwell, and his foul young cousins, all of whom thought it great sport to set upon the one of their number who was thin and weak—"

"You were never great sport," said Will. "I assure you."

"I remember you," Nigel went on as if he had not heard. "And I remember that that Will of Norwell forsook family and loyalty and lawful obedience when *they* would not be bullied to suit his whim, and ran off, and skulks now in the wild wood, with others of his stripe."

"Sir Richard, you cannot know who your saviour is, or . . ."

"Next time, Will, I shall leave you at home," said Robin, as Nigel blustered himself into silence in his attempt to phrase his condemnation the most roundly. "I thought Much was the only one of us who needed a gag."

Sir Richard said, "I cannot condone their methods in all cases, sir; but I cannot condone our sheriff either, and in this case I choose, as men will, the sin that pleases me most. I am grateful to Robin, and to Will—whose tongue does need curbing, I think; I see how he might have decided to turn outlaw—and to these people, these outlaws, as they are called. And I feel no shame at my gratitude."

"Your debts were debts of honour, and these men have no honour!" cried Nigel.

"Do they not?" said Sir Richard gently. "Was it honourable to divest me of my lands for wanting to save the life of my son?"

Nigel opened and closed his mouth a few times, but even his piety was unequal to the task of condemning a man's son to his face. He then turned on Marian. She was trying to look female and negligible, which was more difficult for her than speaking out against the sheriff had been. She had her face a little turned away, but she had not managed to droop.

"And you! You defended these renegades! You spoke against the man who embodies justice—"

"Justice?" Marian snapped, turning round and looking Nigel in the eyes with a glitter in her own. "If he is the embodiment of justice then I am Queen Eleanor. I spoke as I saw fit; as I saw fit to offer Sir Richard some token of friendship. . . ."

"Token," sneered Nigel. "Interesting that you should think to offer tokens on the day that these outlaws should appear—"

Robin stepped forward, struck Nigel on the chin with his curled fist, and knocked him down.

"How little things change," murmured Will, unabashed. "A pity Hugh and Edmund are not here."

Sir Richard grabbed Robin's arm as Nigel shook himself and began to climb to his feet. "I believe, sir, that you owe the lady an apology, even if my friend here was a little hasty in the asking."

"Apologise?" squeaked Nigel. He swayed awkwardly upright, but hurled himself at Robin without hesitation. Robin went down with a grunt, and the two thrashed about for a moment or two, while the jaws of the horse-leaders dropped, and their eyes brightened. But it was over quickly; Robin was soon sitting on Nigel's breast and banging his head briskly against the ground.

"Oh, my," said Sir Richard, and went to break them up. None of the outlaws moved, although Marian's father took a step or two, sideways, as if he was not certain where he wished to go. Marian stepped too, but forward, to stand by Will, and say quietly in his ear: "This is not correct of me, but I find in me no sorrow that I am to be relieved of Nigel's admiration. Though in truth he had some cause to hate you, you know. You *were* bullies."

Marian's father stumbled in Sir Richard's wake and was now attempting to brush Nigel down; Sir Richard had turned away to grasp Robin by the shoulders and was saying something, rather fiercely, in an undertone. Robin looked blank.

"Do not clench your fists, my dear," said Will; "it is not seemly, and I believe that work is over for today. And I do not recall that either you or—or Sess minded our bullying."

Marian sighed, and relaxed her fingers. "It might be simpler merely to have a price on one's head. And Sess and I learnt to climb trees very young, which was beneath Nigel's dignity. He's always had trouble with his dignity, that one."

"Which is the real reason he will not trouble you after today," said Will; "and little to do with your espousal of an outlaw perspective. And we might have been less bullying out-of-doors if he had been less bullying indoors. Adding figures came easily to him, as—as—"

"As drowning people in the soup came easily to you," said Marian.

She moved away as Nigel, with her father on his arm, babbling anxiously in his ear, approached them. "We will take our leave now," said Nigel, meeting no one's eye; and he brandished his hand imperiously at the horse-holders, who came up, eyes politely on the ground and lips firmly held in a straight line.

Fortunately Marian could mount without assistance, for Nigel offered none, and her horse-holder did not know how. Aethelreda stood a moment, a little at a loss, and then the tall fair-haired outlaw was at her elbow, smiling down on her. "If you will permit the unclean touch of a rogue's hands to the bottom of your boot, my lady," he said. Aethelreda, amused, put her foot trustingly enough in his cupped hands, and she was lifted to her saddle with an ease she had not felt since her riding-master set her upon her first pony when she was four years old. "Thank you," she said. "Some grace your rogue's life has spared you, Will."

He stood a moment beside her, looking up now as she looked down. "Some grace, I guess," he said. "But for old friendship's sake, Reda, say 'granted,' not 'spared.' "

Reda shook her head, and Will said, almost pleadingly: "My wits are no quicker than they were those many years ago, but would it have been any better for the recognition I saw dawning in Nigel's eyes to come after we parted? For I know the—the strength of Nigel's opinions of old, and here at least they were made—short." Reda still said nothing, and after a pause Will said, "Tell Marian I am sorry."

"I will tell her," said Reda. "But it changes nothing."

Will said, "You would have stopped us drowning him in the soup, too, had you been there, Reda, would you not?"

"I would," said Reda. "He is not a kind man, I grant you, Will Scarlet, but he keeps his promises."

"And I do not?" said Will. "Perhaps you are right. I would have said rather that there are promises I wish I had had the opportunity to make."

"That is what Marian would say, too," said Reda, and nudged her horse with her heels.

"Good-bye, Sir Richard," said Marian.

"Good-bye," said Sir Richard. "Your welcome here is always good."

"I will remember," said Marian, but her face was troubled. She did not look at Robin, nor at Will; she turned her horse's head and rode away, and the others followed, Nigel crouched a little, as if some portions of his anatomy pained him.

"If I were not grateful to you," said Sir Richard; "if, indeed, after this morning's work I would not lay down my life for you should you ask it, I would now have you thrashed and thrown in the dungeon for a few days to cool off. You, Robin—and you too, Will—that was appallingly ill done." He turned abruptly on his villeins, who were standing where Marian's party had left them. "I shan't want you—no, nor Windwing either—now.

"For heaven's sake, man, have you *no* sense?" he said to Robin. "It is not surprising that you must bait the sheriff as part of your rivalry —stupid it is, for he must pursue you till one of you pays with his death —but not surprising. But how could you expose your lady so? Do you not realise that but for her presence here, the sheriff's men might be riding back to Nottingham with your heads on stakes?"

"It is not—" began Will.

"They outnumbered you nearly twenty to one. You are very quick and clever with your bowstrings, and I've no doubt blood would have been spilt generously—my hall would have smelt like a charnelhouse for weeks," he said, and there was no smile about him. "And I see that my folk had been subverted by you, and I daresay they would have sided with you, which gave you the numbers again; but peasants know little of fighting. You scorn the sheriff's men, but you have need of caution—you won today, whether you like it or no, by hiding behind a woman's skirts. That you should then betray the woman for the sake of baiting a foolish little man whose worst fault is a lack of humour . . . I'm ashamed of you."

"Nigel is such a *weasel*," said Will. "We've done her a favour, getting rid of him for her."

Sir Richard ignored this, staring at Robin, who was staring at his feet. "I love her, you see," he said at last, indistinctly.

Sir Richard grimaced. "A fine way you have of showing it."

"A fine thing I should love her at all, do you not think?" Robin said, looking up.

Sir Richard's expression did not change, but the sharpness softened a little. "I cannot help you there, except to say that she obviously loves you too, and perhaps you are as stupid as that poor man you have just been rubbing into the earth and therefore not entirely accountable for your actions.

"Oh—go away. Perhaps we may meet on some happier day in future."

Robin began tentatively, "In Sherwood—"

Sir Richard grunted a laugh. "Some day when I feel like eating treasonous venison I shall wander deep into Sherwood and wait to be rescued —or set upon."

"Good-bye," said Robin, subdued.

Sir Richard hesitated. "Thank you—I do thank you. I do not disavow my gratitude. And you still make the finest arrows I have ever seen." He turned on his heel and walked back toward his gate. The outlaws looked after him. His folk were going back to their homes and their tasks; the village was no longer silent. Some were singing; some were drunk.

"Let us get away from here," said Robin. "I do not think the sheriff will have any stomach for us today, but that will not last long. We have preparations to make."

CHAPTER SIXTEEN

Robin knew why Will had spoken as he had; and Will's words had some excuse, which was more than could be said for Robin's subsequent behaviour. Perhaps it was the sting of a guilty conscience that made Robin pay acute attention to what Sir Richard had had to say on parting. But it was true that in the preparations for the confrontation at Mapperley Robin had chosen not to think too carefully about the aftermath. He knew now that he had been too blithe, and had let too many innocents share the danger. When the dozen who had gone on the adventure returned and whistled the all-clear, and the rest of the company began drifting (and, in some cases, stomping and crashing) back in to Greentree, Robin looked around him and thought bleak thoughts. The idea that anything resembling a community could form out of reach of the sheriff, even in the tangled fastnesses of Sherwood, was absurd; and it put the real outlaws at greater risk. Sir Richard was right; they had openly scorned the sheriff in a way they had avoided previously; even the theft of St Clair's bride was little to this. The sheriff would not forget. With so many of his own men witness to it, he could not afford to forget.

And so Robin spent the last of the outlaws' coin filling the pockets of most of his folk as a preliminary to sending them away. There was always a rather more than less precarious balance between what news their spy system brought of honest work elsewhere, work that could be done openly under the sun, and what folk were available or suitable for it. Robin felt now that to be in Sherwood was the greater risk against the possibility that reputed work would prove illusory; and as they had done rather better in their high-road robbing than Robin had bothered, or perhaps wished, to take note of, he was able to provide everyone with enough ready money that they might bear themselves in relative comfort through some weeks of travelling. All the gold and jewelry had gone to pay Sir Richard's debt; what remained, conveniently, was the smaller coin that ordinary folk might carry without too many awkward questions being asked.

Greentree's population dwindled as parties were sent off—not always willingly—to safer places. There had been barely two score of them to begin with. Then there were thirty; then a single score . . . at sixteen the attrition halted.

"It means less privy duty," said Much one night. "The only thing left is for you to start exiling *us*," he added crossly, "and none of the rest of us is going to go voluntarily, so stop casting that speculative eye around, will you? The rows you had with Edward and Col are nothing compared to the trouble us red-eyed drooling-fanged last-ditch die-hards could give you."

Robin's speculative eye rested most often on Alan and Marjorie. There were few enough women left, and there had never been many. Even Matilda had been sent on, and she was missed. She had a gift for getting things done; no one shirked privy duty when Matilda's eye was upon them. Eva and Sibyl had stayed; they were as stubborn as Robin himself, their arrows flew almost as truly as Marian's, and he still would not, as Much said, exile them when they were determined to stay. "Time enough to take up something like our old lives again—if we can —when the king comes home. I'll not live with Normans till then; I love an oak tree better," said Eva.

Eva had briefly been a maidservant in Nottingham; but she was too young and too beautiful not to catch the sheriff's eye. Except for the long red hair she refused to cut, it was hard to see her now as the frightened, soft-faced woman who had appeared (to Robin's horror and dismay) at Growling Falls and flatly refused to be sent on. Sibyl had taken her part, and Eva had thrown herself into the learning of the outlaw trade with a stoic single-mindedness that had, at last, impressed even Much.

Cecil would not discuss being sent away, although, young as he was (however young that was), Robin would have liked to try. He had gone white-faced when Robin had suggested it to him; but he did not deign to answer his leader's remarks and, short of tying him up, Robin could not make him listen. On this occasion he merely faded into the undergrowth, in his now notorious manner, and for days after would disappear if Robin even looked at him twice. "If he's a runaway aristocrat, as you think," said Will cheerfully, "he's no good for anything anyway, so why bother? He has no training for you to sell. I suppose he could go for a soldier, but—speaking as one who knows something about runaway aristocrats—he wouldn't like it. I, of course, think he's a myth, since I've still not met him."

Alan-a-dale struck a minor chord softly on his lute, and began to sing.

Which brought Robin back to Marjorie again. Marjorie was a sore point. Robin had refused to back any aid to Will's sister, and Will was not merely a member of the band but one he valued among the highest. Sess's fate remained unknown; there was a thread of rumour that she had by herself escaped, or run away, but the family abruptly became so close-mouthed that not even Beatrix had been able to wheedle or claw a reliable tale from the Norwell lady's-maids. All that was certain was that Sir Aubrey remained unwed. No one mentioned sisters in Will's hearing, not even Much, who had little tact and several sisters; and the whispers about a rescue against Robin's wishes had died away to silence. Will's good nature appeared to harbour no resentment against Marjorie, who had been rescued; and Robin—as Marian had long ago predicted—could have no doubt of his loyalty to their company.

But his conscience obsessively repeated to him that while their company owed a great deal to Will Scarlet, it owed very little to Alan-a-dale, whose own continued presence among them was rather a sore point as well. Either or both Alan and Marjorie found wandering through Sherwood would, in the normal way, have been sent on as fast as possible. But both Robin and his conscience had to admit that St Clair's coin had been a major portion of the reckoning paid to Beautement; Alan's music was good for morale and—everyone *liked* Marjorie, even those who still found Alan's artistic temperament a bit much upon occasion. Marjorie looked as if a good breeze would knock her over, and yet none ever did. She never had tantrums, was never sick, and had borne up under Matilda's gimlet eye with better spirit than anyone else ever had.

He should send them away nonetheless. Keeping Greentree cheerful was not a vital occupation. A lord might have hundreds of villeins and servants before he indulged himself with a resident minstrel; and there were fourteen outlaws left—plus the resident minstrel and his wife.

Alan's face had lit up at the sight of the vellum pages—not long to contain mortgages—very similarly to the way he had become radiant at Robin's grudging agreement to steal Marjorie away from St Clair; that kind of simple joy was rare enough anywhere, Robin thought, and was perhaps no more out of place for being contained in Greentree. And while Alan could not pull the longbow as strongly as Little John—nor even as Robin—he stood guard as alertly as any of them.

He should still send them away. This was no place for such as they. Was it? And where could he send them? What lord in his right mind, with safer choices available, would prefer to cast his protection over a minstrel who had stolen the bride of as bad-tempered a Norman as St Clair? The Saxon lords that were left were, more often than not, hanging on by their finger-ends; Alan's talents were not enough to outweigh the probability of making St Clair an enemy.

"—and a tiresome myth at that," Will said. "I only dignify him as a myth because I have sometimes seen Little John's shadow bearing rather more, and smaller, arms and legs than are necessary for himself alone; but there's always a sudden breeze in the nearest cover and the shadow rights itself when I approach."

"I don't think—" began Robin; and then there was a loud rustling in the bushes—much louder than was allowed so near the camp: branches breaking, muffled but raised and furious voices—or one voice. The lot of them at Greentree had leaped to their feet and, feeling for their weapons, begun sliding toward the shadows, when Robin realised that the furious voice was familiar; even more familiar was the sound of a second voice, in brief, irritated expostulation. It had taken him some moments to recognise either because he had never heard either in such a passion. . . . "Little John," said Robin, clearly and distinctly, "if you and Cecil do not leave off making such a noise at once I will shoot you myself."

The outlaws around him all froze, looking at one another in surprise and dismay. Little John's evenness of temper, and Cecil's silence, were so well-known to them that they felt a shiver of fear. The quiet emanating, after Robin's words, from the undergrowth was now one of some final, terrible battle of wills; and then Cecil burst into the firelight as if propelled by a mangonel; and Little John followed at a somewhat more leisurely pace, but with a lowering brow.

"We made a little discovery today," said Little John. "Rather, perhaps, an interesting one."

"I won't leave," said Cecil, on his hands and knees, near the broken ring of the standing outlaws, where he had stumbled and fallen after his abrupt entrance. He took a deep breath, half a sob. "I *won't leave*."

"I don't believe you've been asked to—at least not recently," said Robin, who went over to pick him up. "I suppose this ferocity must bear upon the nature of the discovery?"

Cecil writhed out of Robin's hands as he tried to draw him up and near to one of the logs they used as seats; but not before his face had been clearly lit by the fire, with the other outlaws looking on curiously.

"Cecily," breathed Will, and if Little John had not at that moment grabbed his protégé's shoulders, the young person known as Cecil would have dived once again for the shadows under the trees.

"Sess—you—" Will began, and took a step nearer. He looked hurt and glad and worried and hopeful and furious all at once.

Cecil, or Cecily, threw up a hand as if expecting a blow, and shrank back, as much behind Little John as his hands on her shoulders would allow: Little John was holding her much as one might hold a wolf-cub: straight-armed and wary. "I won't leave," she said. "I don't care what you say. I am worth my salt. You can't send me away—I couldn't stay," she went on, confusedly; "you know what Sir Aubrey is; the very thought of him made me sick, till I could not eat, and they put off the wedding because they said I was sick." Little John's hands relaxed a little. Cecily was speaking half to her brother and half to the others, glancing nervously around as if any one of them might tie her up and carry her back to her old life if she was not careful; and she both leaned into Little John's grasp and seemed to want to hold herself aloof from it. Him she avoided looking at; but perhaps it was only that turning to see his face would be too awkward.

Her voice went higher and higher and she spoke faster and faster. "Father said that if I would not have Sir Aubrey he would not have me; and so to go on saying 'no' would avail me nothing. What could I do? I thought of jumping off the watch-tower, but that made me even sicker than the thought of Sir Aubrey. And then . . . you disappeared." She swallowed. "And I remembered what you had been saying. . . ."

Will took another step toward her. "If you touch me I'll knock you down," she said to him quite calmly.

"She might just do it, you know," said Little John. "I've been teaching him—her—to handle a larger opponent."

"You left me behind," said Cecily, standing stiffly between Little John's hands, to Will. "You could have taken me with you."

There was a silence. "I did not think . . ." Will began again.

"No, you did not think," said Cecily. "It was all very well for you to go around gnashing your teeth and clenching your fists about the Normans, and looking doomed and heroic—it was not you who had to marry one. Oh, it might have come to that," she went on, in a tone of voice so dry it burned; "but you were only the second son, and you would not have been handed over to your Norman *wife* like—like—" Her voice broke and her head dropped, but Will came no nearer. To the ground she said, "It was hard enough to pick up what you had learnt about the outlaws in Sherwood. I did not like listening at key-holes, but I had no choice. If I had known you meant to go so quickly I would have confronted you sooner, and then it was too late."

After a little silence, Will said, hesitantly, "But—there are other women in this camp. Once you were here—"

"Why have I gone on pretending to be a boy?" Cecily said, and her voice flared out again as it had when she first plunged into the firelight ring. "How many of us are left? There have been those who would have stayed, had you let them. Perhaps Matilda and Nell had no better right to stay than Edward and Ben and Col; I don't know. But . . . Eva and Sibyl speak mostly to each other, and they have each other to guard their backs—and they're yeomen's daughters. Marjorie . . . Marjorie scrubbed pots for Matilda till Matilda was sent away and now she scrubs pots alone because no one has taught her to do anything else. She's a *lady*. But she has Alan. . . . And they have all lived in Sherwood longer than I."

Cecily turned on her teacher then, turned with the sharp litheness of an enemy. His hands dropped, and she took two steps backward, away from him. "Would you so freely have taught me to use a staff, and to throw larger opponents, and to leap out of trees upon them, had I been Cecily—Lady Cecily of Norwell—these weeks past?"

Robin turned away. There was a little silence, and Little John said, heavily, "No. I would not."

Cecily gave a little shiver, and faced the fire again, and to it she whispered, "And what has become of the only lady of Greentree who could string her own bow?"

"I'm sorry," said Will. " 'Twas but a fortnight ago I told Reda there were promises I wish I had had the chance to make. If it is revenge you have wanted, you have had it, for not a day has passed since I left our father's house that I have not thought of you; particularly after I heard that you were gone too, and no one knew where."

"Marian half-guessed," said Cecily. "Marjorie has half-guessed too, I think." She was a slight figure, her shoulders slumped, staring into the fire. She raised her head at last, and looked straight at her brother for the first time. "I have thought of you every day too," she said; "I have thought, every time I fled from you, of how much I missed you. . . ." Her voice trailed away, and Will held out his arms, and Cecily went to him. They stood silently, and he stroked her ragged hair, and she sighed and leaned against him as if exhausted.

Much said, "One mystery solved. Might one ask how"—to Little John—"you came to so—er—upsetting a discovery?"

Cecily stirred in her brother's arms and Little John looked thoughtful. "No," he said. "No, I don't think I'll tell you."

Cecily backed away from her brother, looking down at her tunic. "It's true, it only works if you pretty much look like a boy in the first place." She caught her brother's eye. "But I have always been a good archer, haven't I?"

Will put an arm around her again, as if to reassure himself that she was real. "I should know; I'm the one who got whipped for letting you use my old bow. . . . But how could you not tell me? How could you let me go on thinking . . . Did you really believe I would try to have you sent home?"

She lifted her shoulders. "Would you not?"

"*No.* I would not have sent you to Sir Aubrey."

Robin said, "Will is tactfully not mentioning that he thought of trying to rescue you when he heard that you had locked your door and refused to come out and say your wedding vows."

Will looked uncomfortable. "Will is also tactfully not mentioning that he believed that his sister was planning to go through with it, which is his bad reason for abandoning her."

Cecily smiled a dismal little smile. "You could not have rescued me," she said. "And I knew what you thought. You thought I was like the rest of the family after all. . . . I misjudged you, too; I did not think you would act so quickly."

"Still . . ." began Will. "Then—but—"

"But by the telling I would still have lost my teacher," said Cecily, "and without my teacher, I would have lost my place. Is it not so, Robin Hood?"

Robin looked at her thoughtfully. "I cannot answer that honestly," he said. "I—there is some truth to what you say. If that does not satisfy you, then you must go on thinking of us what you will. But whether your means were fair or not, you have bought and served your apprenticeship, and proved your place among us. I was blind to why you reminded me of Will; but do you think, these last weeks, if I had decided that you must leave us, that I could not have forced you to listen to me?"

Little John, watching her standing next to her brother, half-glowering in the old Cecil manner and half-comforted by Robin's words, saw for a moment what it had been like for her as Will's little sister. Some of what she was good at, and some of what she was bad at, as his pupil, came clear to him in that moment; and something else came clear to him too, but he set it aside so quickly that he allowed himself not to recognise it for what it was.

"And," added Robin more lightly, "you pass the basic requirement, which is to be a better archer than your leader." Cecily stopped glowering to look surprised. "Come now, that's the most open secret here, that I am the worst archer of us all."

"And speaking of archers," said Little John, "the sheriff's contest is tomorrow."

"Which we are all staying very far away from," said Robin. "Why do you bring it up?"

"I think," said Little John slowly, "that it is not wise that we do not go." There was a rustle from several of the other outlaws. "There are currents in Nottingham that I do not like, that I think we would do well to watch; and they will be well worth watching at such a grand event."

Robin frowned. "We have no one to spare," he said. "You know how

171

tight-stretched we are now. Those coming off watch are tired; I would not ask anyone to risk it."

"I have not had a hard sennight," said Little John; "it has just happened that way. I could go."

"You know since Lucy married that wine-merchant that Rafe's news of the town has been thin," said Much. "The thinness shows especially now, since we bought Beautement off."

"You are too visible," said Robin to Little John.

Little John shook his head. "Not on fair day. I will go as a wrestler; there will be other men as big as me."

"Do you know *how* to wrestle?" said Much.

"Yes, small man, I do. I once earned a few coins at it. I can probably do so again."

Robin stood in troubled thought.

"Besides," said Little John. He rubbed his well-forested chin. "I thought to shave. No sensible wrestler would wear a beard; and I have worn this one since before there was a price on my head. I will put a little colour on my face, and no one will notice that I had a beard very recently."

"You would be better not to go alone, even so," said Will slowly.

Little John looked at Will, and then at Cecily, who was staring fixedly at her toes, and back to Robin. He said, "Cecily could come with me, as my assistant; she could carry my cloak, and collect the coins. We will look very ordinary that way." He looked back at Cecily, who appeared to be chewing on the insides of both cheeks. "We are accustomed to each other, and that will also show to our advantage. She will understand what to do when it needs doing."

Cecily looked up at last, but now it was Little John who would not look at her. She risked a glance at Robin, who was watching her quizzically. She dropped her eyes again at once.

"Very well," said Robin. "I do not like it, but I see we may have a need of it. Stay as far from trouble as you can; I do not like sending anyone to Nottingham on the day the sheriff hopes to spring the trap for me and mine."

CHAPTER SEVENTEEN

Cecily pulled a blanket from the heap folded up at the front of the little half-cave and went off into the fringe of forest between Greentree and the first guard post to find a suitable tree to sleep in or under. She had spent most of her nights over the last several weeks curled up against Little John's back, but she was too astonished at her luck of being chosen by her hero to accompany him to Nottingham on the morrow—however logical a choice it was—to risk forcing any decisions about potentially sticky topics. She told herself that he had chosen her because she, like he, had had a comparatively easy sennight—he should know, they had spent most of it together—but that got her no farther forward about anything else, and she could argue meaning both ways.

The men who were regularly paired for guard duty often slept together; Eva and Sibyl slept together—even Alan and Marjorie had slept with the others after their wedding night. The little turf hut given over to them that first night was too necessary for its original purposes. Robin had reluctantly compromised his rule about (even relatively) permanent structures to let them build it—if you could call dirt, stone, turf, and a few wood braces building; Jocelin denied it was anything of the sort—after nearly everything they owned was chewed up by non-hibernating mice and other uninvited visitors during their first winter. Even now there were a good many tunics and blankets that were a trifle scalloped around the edges. Cecily was wearing one of the former, and one of the latter was over her arm as she meditated on her choice of trees.

She thought of the delicate flush on Marjorie's cheekbones once after she and Alan had been away from Greentree on no particular errand for a little time: "Just for a walk," she had said, somewhat anxiously, to Matilda, upon their return. "We—we see so little of each other because there is always so much work to do." This had been only ten days or so before. Cecily had been scrounging for more to eat; she and Little John had come in from a double term of watch after their relief had been disabled by a forester's arrow in the hand, and she had felt as if she could eat the bark off a tree. Matilda was cutting bread for her, and Cecily had clearly seen the odd, kindly, wistful little smile that had crossed Matilda's face. "Do you think I am going to scold you? I had a young husband myself once." To Cecily: "No, you may not eat a raw turnip. Here, Marjorie, now you're back, start peeling these, and chop this lad's fingers if he gets in your way."

There is *no reason* I should remember that just now, Cecily thought, and stalked into the shadows.

Little John was never very communicative, but he was as silent as a stone the next morning. Cecily crept back into the camp before dawn and was heating water for one of Sibyl's curious herb infusions over a tiny corner of the banked fire she'd kicked and blown into life. Simon was on duty nearby; she'd seen him when she creaked down from her tree. The best tree in the world was not meant for sleeping in, and she'd made a good bit of noise in the process of trying to wake her muscles out of the knots they'd twisted themselves into overnight. Simon had not been by last evening when she and Little John had crashed into Greentree; perhaps it was her own anxieties that made her think that his face was too blank and the question he did not ask about why she had spent the night in a tree was too loud.

She poured the water, arranged some bread near enough the embers to scorch but not catch fire, and looked up at Little John. She was so accustomed to his step, to his bulk, that it took a moment to notice his face; and when she did . . . It was, she thought, rather like the moment it took to realize one had cut one's finger as one stared dumbly at the first drop of blood on the knife-blade. You know it is going to hurt quite a lot in a minute.

He squatted down beside her without a word. This was not unusual, but his not meeting her eyes was, and her heart rose up in her throat for a moment in fear that he planned to tell her she could not go with him today. His lower face looked unnaturally pink from close at hand. Most of the men had beards kept cut off short near their chins; a few, like Robin and Will, kept themselves shaved by every day or two begging a little hot water from the pot of it Matilda, and now Marjorie, usually kept simmering. "It's not the knife against my skin I dislike," Much had said once; "it's Matilda's ironical eye."

"If I could grow anything that looked like a beard," said Robin, somewhat indistinctly, through shut teeth, "I would probably forego this bit of self-inflicted misery. But one's vanity reveals itself in strange ways."

Little John's face looked rather peeled. They passed the infusion between them as they had many times before, and shared the crunchy bread. Cecily's heart slowed down to its usual pace, and she thought, I could follow him if he tries to leave me behind. Last night he asked Robin to let me go with him; they will not miss me here.

Little John stood up; now he did let his eyes rest briefly on Cecily's anxious, upturned face; but his expression was unreadable. It wasn't just the beard, she thought, and sprang up. He picked up a bundle and set off in the direction that would bring them at last to Nottingham. She hurried to walk beside him, where he could not help but notice her, and he said no word suggesting that she remain behind; he said no word of any kind. She had soon to drop back for the sake of making her way neatly through the tree limbs and vine leaves that clutched at them. Perhaps it was her own oppression of spirits, for he was often silent. But his silence on this day weighed on her heart.

In walking they were a good match, for her legs were long, and she'd always taken strides as long and quick as she could as a kind of protest against being compelled to wear skirts. Walking with her brother had been good practice, for he was nearly as tall as Little John. What Little John had had to teach her was to walk quietly. She was not a bad pupil —in this or in anything else he had chosen to teach her—but her mind tended to wander from the immediate repetitive question of where to put each foot, while Little John, it seemed to her, never stepped absent-mindedly on a twig. Perhaps his feet had their own eyes. She'd complained once to him—weeks ago—that he must be made of air, not flesh, for no one so large could walk so quietly. That had been before he had begun to teach her how to throw an opponent bigger than herself with her hands instead of her staff, and before she'd found out how heavy he could be when the lesson was going against her.

"Flesh enough," he'd said at the time, "flesh and blood and bone. Or did you think that was Much last night whose blanket you were stealing? I learnt to walk quietly because I needed to learn so badly. Have you not noticed how noisy squirrels are, and how quiet the deer?"

"I am not a squirrel," she'd said, a trifle sulkily.

"No," he agreed. "You cannot leap half so far."

But Little John's bare chin was sunk upon his breast this morning, and she could think of nothing to say; the best she could do was to walk as silently as she was able, to remember past lessons as perfectly as she could, as an indication that . . . her thoughts stopped here. It was hard not to keep glancing at his face when the undergrowth permitted; when his profile appeared over his shoulder as he held a whippy branch back for her to grab. His beard was the sort that grew up within a couple of fingers' breadth of his eyes, and it was nearly black, darker even than his dark hair. Now she had discovered that he had cheekbones and a chin; and there were long deep lines on either side of his mouth.

Humphrey almost challenged them when it took him a moment to recognise the tall smooth-faced man walking beside Cecil. "Wrestling, eh?" he said, looking at Little John's shoulders. "Nay, I'd not willingly stand up against you. Drink some ale for me, though, will you? I don't miss much, living in trees; but I miss the good ale."

They had come most of their way to Nottingham without a word between them. Little John paused, and caught one of Cecily's sidelong looks. He put a hand to his face. "I feel a draught," he said ruefully. He let the bundle down off his back. "Time for the rest of our disguise, I think." He knelt, which then put him well below Cecily's eye level as she stood beside him, to untie the bundle; hesitated; and looked up at her. "You haven't said how I look."

She was silent a moment, looking down, and he began to smile, as if involuntarily. The lines around his mouth looked suddenly merry, and his smile was nothing like what it had been behind the beard. "That bad, eh?" he said.

She shook her head; the throb like a cut finger had been hurting all morning, but it was nothing she wished to tell him about. "I don't know. Different."

He stayed as he was a moment longer, head thrown back, eyes holding hers. There was a little gap in the trees where he had chosen to stop, and the early sun was on his face. "You have no call to complain about my appearing suddenly different."

She smiled a little. "No. I didn't say anything about that."

He sank back on his heels, and began to pull at the knots of his bundle. "Was it so awful—what you ran from?"

She sat down beside him; he'd never asked her about her history before. She had, in fact, dreaded that he might, because she had not wanted to do any further lying; the essential lie of her name and her gender was hard enough to bear. She'd thought daily of what would happen when she was finally discovered, for it never occurred to her that she would not be discovered. Even if the laces on her tunic had not chosen to give at the same moment that the thin-worn spot on her shirt had decided to tear, she would not have been able to avoid her brother forever. To make herself sleep at night she had told herself the story of the lady This or That, who'd led her husband's knights into battle while he was away on the Crusades; led them and won, too. She knew several stories like that which had come to her father's castle. They were always her favourites, and she believed them fiercely while her father and her brothers scoffed at them as minstrel's fantasies.

Somehow they rang hollow to her at midnight in Sherwood. She had been grateful and ashamed at once for the natural reticence of the outlaws, their easy willingness to leave someone so visibly troubled by memory kindly alone. She had never understood why they had trusted her when she was so mistrustful herself; how had Robin known that her guilty secret was no threat to them? She had wanted to confess during every sleepless night she had—had occasionally gone so far as to creep out of the cave and look for Robin, who seemed to her never to sleep at all, but to spend the nights investigating the corners of Greentree, or whittling by the fire, or going on long mysterious walks through the trees. But she never had. The thought of Marian always stopped her.

She found herself choosing words carefully, for fear of saying too much, even now. "It seemed so to me. I had enough to eat, and I know that that . . . makes me different from most of us. But I could not eat it. You had your livelihood taken from you; my life was to be given to someone I hated."

"It is perhaps another form of starvation," he said, "although I would have said there was no other form of starvation, those months ago when Robin found me." He looked at her, and she bit her lip against asking him what he thought of her now. "But then I did not think," he continued, "till I knew—Marian, that a lady could shoot straight, or not mind the calluses on her fingers—or learn to stand guard duty, and handle a staff." Cecily thought she perceived a twinkle, but was not sure. "You may be grateful that I had known Marian some time before Cecil appeared, and had known Cecil some time before Cecily— appeared. Else I might have tied her in a sack and left her for the foresters to find."

Cecily sighed. "Well, you do see why it was Cecil."

"I see," said Little John. "I do not exactly pardon you, but I do see." He had unfolded the bundle, and set various things aside, and now handed her a red tunic. "It was simply my fate to be saddled with you. I have long thought Fate has a tricky sense of humour."

Cecily remembered, some weeks ago, when the talk at the fireside had come round to the absent Little John and how he had resisted—and never quite given up resisting—the presence of women in the camp. Cecily was in the tree she used on the occasions when Will or Marian was present; she could neither see nor be seen, but she could hear quite clearly. Her blood had run cold at this. "I'm glad I was here before him," said Marian, "or we might none of us have got through. There's a lot of him to get around."

"It's a tunic," said Little John. Cecily found herself holding it out in front of her as if uncertain of its identity. She shook herself, lowered her arms. "Yes."

"What ill thoughts were you thinking, not of the tunic, then?" said Little John, and she heard herself saying, "Friar Tuck said that you did not care for women because you had had your heart broken." Her tongue stopped just before she added what Marian had said next: "In his slow, methodical, deep-eyed, immovable way—I think he likes having things to be against. I *pity* the woman who tries to break that heart."

"I've not had my heart broken," said Little John, calmly. "I had three silly sisters and, briefly, a silly wife—who left when I first got into trouble. She was relieved to have the excuse, and the demesne court was relieved to grant it her; she had by that time a more suitable husband in her eye. That was several years ago. Now, turn that tunic right-side up, if you have recognised it yet, and put it on. We must look pretty fine to compete with the crowds today. If I've forgotten how to wrestle, then we can be shabby again. There's hose for you too; what you're wearing didn't fit you even before you started tearing them to shreds."

She pulled her tunic off, self-consciously; she'd hastily patched her shirt that morning (too late now) and was wearing a shift beneath it as well. Muffled in pulling the new tunic over her head, she almost didn't hear Little John ask: "What was the man you were to marry like?"

"A toad," she said violently, re-emerging. "He had no neck, and a dome-shaped head with no hair on it, and very large poppy eyes. . . . He was even a kind of pale green, I think, though they tell me he is very fierce in battle."

Little John laughed, and she looked at him reproachfully. "I do not blame you for not wanting to marry a toad," he said gravely, and pulled his own tunic off. She said, so quietly that he might not have heard her, "And he would not talk to me." She thought: I don't think he cared if I knew how to talk.

Little John pulled his shirt off after the tunic and then picked up a small pot of something which she now recognised as tallow. "If you would attend to my back, I will deal with the rest of me," he said. "A wrestler should be a little slippery."

He offered her the pot, one long bare arm stretched out toward her, the pot cupped in his broad palm; she took it from him daintily, her fingertips not touching his hand; and he turned and sat just before her, his head a little bowed. She noticed that he'd trimmed his hair when he cut off his beard. He was so close to her that she was conscious of the warmth of his skin. Blindly she dipped into the pot with her fingers, slapped some of the soft grease on Little John's back, and began to smooth it out. "Careful," said Little John. "That's all there is, and there is a lot of me."

"The dogs will follow you," she said, her voice a little high.

"So long as none decides to try a taste," he said. "Use your hands, for pity's sake. My brother used to do this for me, and he would nearly knock me over."

"You must have been smaller then," she said. She began to use the palms of her hands, rubbing the long round muscles in a circular motion, using the heels of her hands around the shoulder-blades, running the edge of her palm down the spine. She was not so young that she did

179

not know what was happening to her: why her heart was beating too fast, why her breath came hard; why there was a knot in the pit of her stomach which spread into a terrifying warmth over her lower belly and thighs. She knew, and tried to pretend she was Little John's brother, and failed.

"That should do," she said, after a few of the simultaneously longest and shortest minutes of her life; and Little John moved away from her, and turned to pick up the grease pot. She absent-mindedly went to rub her sticky hands down the front of her bright new tunic, when there was an exclamation from her companion and her arms were nearly jerked out of their sockets as Little John grabbed her wrists. "Not on the tunic! Have you no sense?" He rubbed each of her hands down each of his forearms, and she closed her eyes briefly and thought about fraternal relationships, and then Little John said: "Here—are you all right? I am sorry, did I hurt you?"

"Not nearly as much as all the bruises from my quarterstaff lessons, my friend; a mere dislocated shoulder or two is but nothing," she said with a fair imitation of her usual tone.

He dropped her hands. "Fortunately you are a fast healer," he said. "But you look unwell. Are you afraid of our adventure today? Robin may be right that we are wrong to risk ourselves this way." He rubbed at one sticky forearm. "I do not know but that I feel uneasy myself."

She shook her head. "A little. No, not really. Robin is always right about that kind of thing, but I still want to go with you."

"You need not."

Her stomach was beginning to feel like a stomach again; the cramp was fading to a queer unfamiliar ache that she did not care for but could live with; and all of her began to feel on more familiar territory. "Stop trying to protect our youngest and weakest member," she said equably. "You have already invited me, and I wish to go."

He looked at her a moment longer, but when she lifted her eyes to meet his something happened to his face, and he turned away, and picked up the little pot of tallow again. Cecily pulled on her new hose —which fit her much better than her old ones—and then began to tear bits of leaves into littler bits while she waited for Little John to finish his own preparations; and put her mind to what they might see today in Nottingham.

CHAPTER EIGHTEEN

hey could hear the noise of an unusually large crowd before they reached the main road. They were so accustomed not only to the relative silence of the woods, where loud noises were liable to be wild boars or king's foresters, but to the sense of being outlaws, that it took them a conscious effort of will to step out and join the throng of holiday-makers and people with wares to sell on the way to the Nottingham Fair.

Little John was noticed at once; in a sky-blue cloak he could hardly be missed. Cecily's eyes had bulged when he shook it out, last, from the bundle he had carried from Greentree, and swept it on. He grinned at her expression. "We're supposed to draw attention, remember? And the lad I took this from is on his way to Scotland." By the time they arrived at the outskirts of the town, where the commons was already thick with little booths and bright-dressed jongleurs and acrobats tumbling between them, Little John had gathered a following.

The first match was barely a match at all. The other man came up to Little John's collarbone, and Little John, to Cecily's eyes with some embarrassment, took him gingerly up at his long arms' length, tied him in one or two knots, and laid him tenderly on the ground. Cecily passed her hat around for coins in something of a daze; the two of them were immediately offered the first of the ale that Humphrey had told them to drink for him; but Little John refused politely and Cecily did the same.

They moved slowly along the commons; Little John stopped once or twice to flatten another would-be wrestler, while Cecily held the sky-blue cape. Her hat was soon sagging from the coins it carried. "I guess you haven't forgotten how," said Cecily.

"Mmph," said Little John. "I don't know yet whether I have or not; these poor fools are just the strong men from their villages; they are no contest. After they've worn me down a little, one of the real wrestlers will appear from somewhere and challenge me." He looked down at her. "But your hat is already heavy, is it not? We don't want to attract cut-purses; that's not what we're here for."

"Besides, one of them might recognise us," said Cecily.

"There's that," agreed Little John, and stopped at a horse trough to pour some water over his head. The sun was hot, particularly on faces accustomed to the forest shadows.

"You'll get your nice cape wet," suggested Cecily.

"Water will *dry*," said Little John. "You watch yourself and leave me to watch myself."

"Sir," murmured Cecily.

They did not have to ask many questions for the people who flocked around to watch Little John to give them the current gossip; the two of them were obviously not from Nottingham, and the town was buzzing with the tale of Sir Richard of the Lea, and Robin Hood, and the sheriff's fury.

"Robin Hood is more than man," said one goodwife seriously.

Cecily said with real curiosity, "What is he, then?"

The woman lowered her voice. "He's an elemental, of course, child. I see by your face you're of good Saxon stock. Robin Hood is one of the old gods come back to save England from the Normans."

The man lounging outside her stall with acorns under cups for unwary folk to bet on, said, "That's why he has to come to the archery contest, and the sheriff knows it. Why, you don't suppose the sheriff wouldn't have caught him a fortnight ago at Mapperley if he'd been an ordinary man, do you? I've just been up there—the folk are all so pleased to have their own master back they are in a mood to spend coin freely—and they all say that Robin came with a handful of men. It's not canny."

"The sheriff hung three robbers this week," the woman said comfortably; Cecily found herself swallowing rather hard. "You can see 'em hanging over the gate to the sheriff's house."

"There," said the man, as if that settled it.

"And what if this Robin Hood does not come to the fair today?" Cecily asked.

"He will," said the woman.

The man shrugged and moved his acorn from under one cup, consideringly, to another. "If he does not, then the sheriff has won."

"Won *what?*" said Cecily, half irritable and half apprehensive, to Little John, as they moved on.

Little John lifted his shoulders briefly. "I'm not sure; but part of why we've survived this long is because the foresters themselves half-believe this elemental stuff—and half want to, as it excuses them. Even ordinary outlaws, you know, when found, tend to sell their lives rather dearly to their captors."

"But to risk your life for a golden arrow? What could any of us do with a golden arrow? It's silly," said Cecily.

Little John looked at her as he had the first time she'd tried to block with her staff and he'd knocked her down. " 'Twas an arrow made Robin Hood an outlaw. Don't forget. The sheriff hasn't. These people have not."

The archery ground was already filling up; the three-sided tent, with the dais beneath, was set up nearer the mark where the archers would stand than to the targets that would tell who won the prize—as if the sheriff were more eager to see who came than to determine who shot well. There were practise targets set up a little to one side, and a few folk were sighting along their bowstrings and smoothing their arrows. One bored-looking man in the sheriff's livery was standing by the practise field, but when one of the archers shouted to him to move one of the marks farther down, to make the possibility of practice more like the coming contest, the man slouched over to the nearest straw target with infinite reluctance, dragged it a few feet only, and left. The archer who'd shouted and another man hauled the wooden frame back themselves.

Little John and Cecily drifted over to stand near some of the minstrels and acrobats who were wearing clothing similar to their own, so as to be a little less conspicuous. The proximity of the sheriff's tent, even empty as it was at present, made them both uncomfortable. One of the wrestlers Little John had defeated came up to him and asked, as if idly, where he was going from Nottingham. Little John gave a vague answer; they'd earned enough today that they would perhaps lie a night or two at the inn here before they moved on.

"I hope you're as good at wrestling fleas, then," said the man. He had put a plain green shirt over his wrestler's garb and looked almost ordinary, except, perhaps, for the easy, alert way he moved—as if he might leap into a back flip at any moment. He might make a good outlaw, thought Cecily. "I hoped perhaps I could interest you in joining us; I am more an acrobat than a wrestler—as you may have noticed—and I would be glad to give it up in your favour. We might," he added, eyeing Little John with a certain wistfulness, "use you in the acrobatics as well; we had a strong man once, but he left us a year ago to marry a farm girl, and waste himself on ploughing."

"I thank you for your offer," said Little John, "but I think not. We—have not had good luck travelling in company."

"Jealousy?" said the man in green. "I am not surprised. I can tell you we are not like that—we even played our old strong man's wedding for free—but you may not believe me. Perhaps—" the man hesitated— "perhaps we'll call on you at the inn tomorrow, after you've had a chance to think on it?"

"If we meet you at the inn," said Little John gravely, "we would be happy to speak to you further."

Silence began to make its way through the crowd, in a twisty, snake-like manner; Cecily turned to look where the others were looking and saw a man she could guess was the sheriff, from the size of both his girth and the gold chain around his neck, approaching the dais with a grandly dressed party of courtiers. The party included two ladies, whose long brilliant skirts belled out in the breeze. It was a pretty picture, but Cecily remembered what it felt like, and stamped one hose-clad leg in satisfaction.

"The wind will do the archers no good," said the man in green.

Little John grunted. "I know little of archery; but I have thought before that it is a matter of luck as much as skill; as most contests of arms are."

"Arms and legs," said the man, smiling; "it was skill that defeated me, not ill luck. But I think I agree with you here. Arrows are malicious mites, with wills of their own."

"Aye," said Little John, and fell silent, frowning; he was looking toward the archers lining up for the first target. There was a goodly number of them; one or two wore the sheriff's livery, but the most conspicuous group among them were the king's foresters, who made up nearly half the number of the whole.

"God help any outlaw trying to pull the sheriff's nose in that group," said the green man.

"You have heard the rumours that Robin Hood will try?" said Cecily bluntly.

"Aye. Have not we all? And a fool he is, I say, if he falls for so foolish a lure."

"You speak treason, or near to it," said Little John gently; "for are we not to hope that the sheriff will succeed?"

"You're no Norman," said the green man, "or I would not be here talking to you; even their money smells bad. Why should I hope a Saxon who has found a way to elude the Normans' hold will fall back into it? And now if I've passed the test, will you think of joining our company?"

Little John smiled. "I did not mean a test, exactly, but you are right that we are not Norman."

"And have little cause to love them," Cecily put in, and Little John turned to look at her quellingly.

The green man grinned. "I like your assistant, but you feed him too well; he would not talk to strangers so easily if he'd had your experience."

"He has had his own experience," said Little John; "but it is true that I think about tying his tongue in a knot at least daily."

The first archers were taking their turns; the foresters all shot well enough to go to the second round; a number of other folk did as well, including at least one lady.

"The only child of Sir Waleran, and it had to be a daughter," said the green man; "but he is doing what he can with her instead of giving up quietly—or siring a bastard on some woman who can conceive sons."

Cecily had her mouth open when Little John's foot descended on hers, and she hissed instead, and bit her tongue as her jaws snapped together. "Rmph," she said, as the herald bellowed that the second round would begin at once.

About half the original number of archers stood up to shoot; including one ordinary-looking man with an extraordinarily long-handed bow, whose appearance at the mark caused Little John's hand to drop to Cecily's shoulder. She was still nursing her crushed foot, but she looked up. There was nothing about this man to draw attention: of medium height, curling brown hair visible under a rough hat—and an excellent shot: the arrow sank into the heart of the target almost before you saw him lift his bow. Something about the way he walked, though —and the long bow . . . It couldn't be. Little John's fingers tightened.

"If that's Robin," said the green man, "he could have the sense not to draw quite so well till it was necessary."

It wasn't Robin, of course, thought Cecily, because he doesn't shoot that well. But there was still something—the way the man caught the eye for no reason; the same something that Robin had.

"He seems to be alone," observed the green man; "perhaps at least he chooses to risk only himself." He shook his head. "He *is* a fool, and I'm sorry for it; but then . . ."

Cecily said, despite Little John's fingers, "Then—?"

"You like this outlaw, don't you?" said the green man. "And your master does not approve, which is wise of him. Perhaps yon Robin Hood has heard of what the sheriff has in mind if this contest does not catch him, and decided that this is the easier way for the folk he loves and would spare sharing his fate."

"Easier?" said Cecily in alarm.

"Have you heard of Guy of Gisbourne?" said the green man.

Little John's head snapped around. The second round was over; the field of contestants was again cut by half; it still included Sir Waleran's only daughter, several foresters, and the brown-haired man who drew the eye for no reason.

"Ah, you have heard," said the green man with satisfaction; "and have heard the right stories too."

"I have not," said Cecily. "Tell me."

"Guy of Gisbourne is a kind of paid assassin," said the green man, with a certain involuntary relish. " 'Tis said he is the younger son of an old lord up north who hated him, and since he had nothing to lose, as he saw it, has gone in for hiring out to cut up other folk's enemies. He was in Palestine for a while, the stories say, and he was sent home in disgrace for being too bloodthirsty. He'd kill off a Saracen they might have held for ransom, and he threw someone's child off a battlement in Acre because it annoyed him."

"The sheriff has hired him to track Robin Hood?" squeaked Cecily.

186

"Aye. And his band of cutthroats, all of them as charming and civilized as Guy himself, I believe. Even in Sherwood, Guy will find his quarry; the stories say that Guy doesn't sleep, and he finds his men by smelling the heat of their blood. I don't know about that, but there's something uncanny about him nonetheless."

Uncanny. What the bauble-seller had said of Robin.

The third round went more slowly, for all that there were fewer archers; for each one shot only after carefully lining up the mark and sighting long down the length of the arrow before releasing the string. Several of the foresters missed nonetheless and were disqualified. One of them wanted to argue about it, but the sheriff raised one hand and then made a violent and highly suggestive gesture with the other, and the man subsided.

Sir Waleran's daughter, two foresters, and the brown-haired man were left. The watching crowd had a curious kind of hush over it, and there was some movement to press in closer, which sheriff's men immediately appeared from behind the sheriff's tent to prevent. The crowd became restless, and the fourth round was delayed a little till it quieted; despite the sheriff's men, who seemed to have received uncharacteristic orders not to be too rough, the crowd had contrived to shift forward by a few yards. Its edges were now even with the sheriff's tent.

Little John, Cecily, and the green man had not moved. They were all three taller than the average, and even Cecily could see over most of the heads of the crowd; and she felt frozen to her place besides.

"We are not the only ones who think that's Robin Hood," said the green man. "There will be trouble if the sheriff tries to take him."

It's not Robin, thought Cecily. It's Marian.

The brown-haired man shot last. The target was now set so far away that Cecily could see the center mark only as a bright blot of colour; but she saw when the two foresters' arrows went wide, and struck outside the blot. The breeze had picked up, and seemed to be coming from all directions at once; and a particularly fierce gust rushed over the crowd as Sir Waleran's daughter released her string. The arrow should have gone to the heart of the mark, thought Cecily, as the breeze fanned her right cheek; even so it struck within the left edge of the blot. The crowd sighed.

And the breeze died. In a dead calm the brown-haired man stepped up, sighted tranquilly along his string, and released his arrow. The faintest breath of wind whispered overhead as the arrow struck the center of the target, as if it were in response to the arrow's flight; as if the archer might be one of the old gods of England come back.

There was a commotion in the sheriff's tent, and then a tall man leaped over the barrier, and drew his sword, ringing, from the scabbard he held in his other hand. The scabbard he dropped to the ground as he said, "I challenge you, Robin Hood, to single combat. I, Guy of Gisbourne, have come a long way to face you!"

Little John dropped the attention-drawing blue cloak as Cecily was pulling her bright-red tunic over her head. When she reappeared she saw the green man pulling the laces out of his shirt. "Here," he said to Little John. "You'll be a bit less noticeable in this."

The crowd had muttered for a moment as the archer named Robin Hood stood a moment blankly, bow slack in his hand, staring at his challenger; then it rushed forward with a roar.

"Pity he wouldn't consider just putting an arrow in that man's black heart and doing England a favour," said the man who was no longer green. The unlaced shirt barely fit across Little John's shoulders, but it did make him look less like a wrestler and more like any member of the crowd who happened to be very tall. "Thank you," said Little John.

"I won't look for you at the inn," said the man.

It was hard to make their way through the crowd, even with Little John as a battering ram. But then there was a cry, and the crowd heaved backward; Cecily was almost knocked off her feet, but she hooked a hand into Little John's waistband and hung on. Little John surged forward and to one side, and Cecily broke free and found herself suddenly at the edge of a little clearing, ringed by shocked and frightened faces.

The archer named Robin Hood was on his knees, his bow on the ground beside him, one hand pressed to his side, where Cecily could see the red drops welling mercilessly between the fingers. The crowd looked from him to the suffused face of Guy of Gisbourne, standing with his sword outstretched, the point of it glazed red. "Stand back!" he cried. "You have this stroke on your heads; would you try for another?"

At that moment, though, Guy of Gisbourne himself staggered to the side as Little John slammed into him. Cecily snarled, "Your belt, man!" to a gaping minstrel with a trailing sash. She pulled it off him and he made no demur, and she darted forward and caught Marian as she slumped to the ground.

"Not quite what I anticipated," murmured Marian.

"Hold on," said Cecily, half weeping; "we're getting you out of here."

Marian's eyes flickered open. "Sess? What an odd dream I'm having. Why have you cut your hair? What odd clothes you are wearing—as if you were a boy. That shirt looks like something Robin's men might wear. Don't fall in love with an outlaw, Cecily; it makes you lose your common sense."

Cecily bound the sash as tightly as she could about Marian's ribs and belly. "Press here," she said to her. "Can you?"

"My fingers seem so far away," said Marian. "I will try. Poor child, I am more than an armful for you, aren't I?"

Cecily pulled Marian's other arm around her shoulders, hauled her against her own hip and thigh as best she could, and began to draw her upright, as quickly as she dared; Marian's face was very white, but her fingers pressed dutifully against the spreading red stain upon the minstrel's sash.

No one from the onlookers stepped forward to help Cecily, but none tried to stop her either. She was dimly aware that Little John and Guy were grappling near at hand, and something narrow and shining slithered past her feet, but she dared not drop Marian to seize it. "You!" she said, catching the eye of a young man too slow to avoid hers. "Take that sword and *throw* it!"

He stared at her, but Cecily was burning up with fear and sorrow and fury, and after a moment he took three steps forward and picked up the sword. There was a bellow from Guy and a terrible thump as someone hit the ground very close behind Cecily. She let go of Marian's arm and slid her own under Marian's knees, and lifted. She had muscles she didn't know about yet from her quarterstaff work with Little John; and her blood was up, and she lifted her old friend without strain. "Throw it as far as you can!" she cried to the man now uneasily holding the sword. As if compelled by some force other than his own will, he raised his arm stiffly and flung the sword—awkwardly but with some strength —and the crowd beneath its trajectory ducked and swayed away from it like a field of corn under a wind. Cecily started forward with her burden, and the people before her parted to let her through.

CHAPTER NINETEEN

ecily became aware of some commotion on the edge of the crowd. There was still an unbroken circle of onlookers around the space where Marian had fallen, and Cecily, with Guy and Little John at her back, was making in a direction away from the sheriff's dais. But she realised that as the crowd seemed to have hemmed them in, it was also, in its shock-stricken way, keeping the sheriff's men out. It had been only minutes since Guy had cried his challenge; the sheriff's men would start slashing their way through the crowd if it did not give way soon. And as she framed the thought, she began to hear the sound of cudgels cracking across heads and ribs, and to register what the sound was. While the worst of it was still to one side of her, she wondered what she was carrying Marian toward.

And suddenly there was someone at her elbow, and a voice she knew said, "This way." She had begun to follow before she identified the voice: it was the green man. "I've brought our waggon close up. Hurry."

She hurried; he went before her, to ease her way as he could. They broke through the edge of the crowd; there was one sheriff's man immediately visible. He turned toward them, raised his staff, and opened his mouth to give a shout; but his eyes went blank, his jaw fell slack, and he crumpled forward on his face. An acrobat in yellow hose was standing just behind him, a rock in his hand.

The confusion at the edge of the crowd would be a wide-scale brawl soon. Under almost any other circumstances so many sheriff's men and foresters could have brought a crowd even this size quickly under their control, but the circumstances were unusual. Many local folk, and some not so local, had a soft spot for Robin Hood equalling the hard spot of grudge they bore toward the sheriff; and a few of the visitors had seen their own villages burnt by Guy of Gisbourne and were inclined to appreciate the possibility of seeing him brought low.

Another man in livery came rushing up toward his fallen comrade, and a member of the crowd who had till then been watching idly thrust a foot out at the last moment. The man fell sprawling, rolled over, and sat up to shout at the one who had tripped him, or for help; but he disappeared from view as several of the crowd jumped on him. The brawl was beginning.

Where was Little John? thought Cecily, as the green man said again, "Hurry. Shall I take him for you?" Cecily shook her head and made her feet go faster. The sword was gone, but what if Guy had a dagger hidden? Many of Robin's outlaws did; would not an outlaw-hunter do the same? The tumult around her was growing; soon Little John would not be able to get out even if he was hale enough to try. What if—

"Here," said the green man, and touched her elbow. A small, brightly painted if a trifle worn-looking caravan was pulled up just before them, drawn by an elderly and shaggy pony. The canvas curtain at the rear of the waggon was pulled to one side, and several minstrels and acrobats stood near.

"It was my master you wanted to steal," gasped Cecily; Marian was taken out of her arms and lifted gently into the dark interior of the waggon.

"If we have you, he is sure to follow," said the green man, with a flicker of humour. "Now you."

Cecily stepped up to the waggon. Perhaps they were being stolen; but she could not get far without help, not with Marian hurt and . . . "But where is he?"

"I am going to look for him. You stay under cover; you've been noticed." He smiled briefly. "If you could order folk to toss pennies the way you order them to throw swords, you would be even more valuable to us than your master." He said to the others: "You start out of here. There'll be others leaving, to get away from what's going to be a grand mopping-up once the sheriff gets the upper hand. Gerard, you come with me." The green man and the man in yellow hose made off purposefully toward the spreading mêlée. Small knots of fighting men were separating from the crowd and rolling individually on the turf; there was a great deal of noise, and the green man had almost to shout.

"You heard 'im, love," said one of the women of the troupe. "You get in there now." There were chucking noises and the slap of reins to get the pony moving, and the waggon began to lurch forward. But Cecily, rather than ducking through the canvas doorway, stayed on the outside step and put a hand out to cling to the frame, still looking toward the shattering crowd.

"I know," said a young man in a short embroidered surcoat. "He can have my spare suit, and then he can walk abroad with the rest of us. Make way," he added, and jumped lightly onto the frame beside Cecily.

"If he promises to mind his manners," said the woman anxiously, looking back over her shoulder; but there was no one visible in livery, or none unoccupied enough to give another players' waggon any trouble.

The young man in the surcoat was making rustling and gentle thumping noises; Cecily turned around in time to be hit in the face with another embroidered surcoat, though not so fine a one as what the young man was wearing. "Put that on. You've become my twin." He frowned, staring at her chest, and Cecily nervously put her hands up to where her bound breasts were. "You've blood on your shirt," he said. "Here—wipe it first; I don't want it on my coat." She took the rag he offered her, but they both turned to where Marian lay. There was a small dark figure crouched beside her—Cecily had a moment to notice how very *full* the waggon was—who was drawing some kind of coverlet over her.

"Do you know any doctoring?" Cecily asked; but the young man shook his head. "Dislocated joints and cracked ribs, that's about all. Bind 'em up and leave 'em alone. Not sword wounds."

Marian moaned, and the small dark figure put out a small hand and wiped her face with a cloth. "Annie'll do what any of us can do." Cecily noticed that Annie's other hand was pressed against the pad of bloody cloth on Marian's side and stomach, that once had been a minstrel's sash; the coverlet was rumpled to one side to leave the wound clear. "Are you going to put that coat on and help us look for your master or not?"

Cecily put it on, and they left the waggon together. "Try not to look so wild," said the young man. "You look guilty of any crime."

Cecily tried to relax her face. "Why are you doing this for us?"

The young man shrugged. "Our master—that's Henry, who you were with—liked yours." He gave a brief grin. "Takes all kinds. Henry doesn't usually like getting bent backwards and forwards like a stick of dried meat being torn in half, but we have been looking for a strong man to help in our tumbling, and your master didn't hurt him, and he could've. That's what really got Henry's attention. And . . ." He paused. "We've come across Guy of Gisbourne's trail once before; two friends of ours died of it."

He looked around. "Mary's not watching—come on, quick."

They bolted back for the crowd. The young man might have tried to lead her, but she never noticed; she burrowed into the ranks of struggling men like a badger into the side of a bank; and the young man followed her or didn't.

She was smacked and kicked and thrust this way and that; she heard a seam of her coat rip. She lost track of which way she was going, and she half-paused, as much as she could in the human maelstrom that seethed around her. Then she heard a familiar shout, and turned toward it.

The shout was one of warning, and it was not addressed to her. A little knot of foresters had hold of Little John—she saw him now. One of his eyes was swollen nearly shut, and blood ran down his cheek, and the foresters clung to him like hounds at a boar. The man he shouted at was the green man, who ducked aside in time for another man to bowl past him, lose his balance, and plummet into Little John and his attackers. Little John went down.

Cecily found herself on her hands and knees, groping for rocks. Her knee found one, her hands two more; she stuffed them violently into her pockets, which had not been made for such use. Then her groping hand found a greater prize—a knife; and her fingers grasped it just as an accidental foot caught her under the hinge of her jaw and tossed her over backward.

She clung to the knife, though when she staggered to her feet and opened her hand to examine her prize she discovered that the base of the blade had sunk into the base of her forefinger, just above the palm, and her hand was slippery with blood. She wiped it down the side of her borrowed coat, and dove back into the human sea, aiming for the point where she had last seen Little John.

193

She almost tripped over him. Her jaw hurt and her head felt funny; she stood swaying on her feet a moment, waiting for the mass of green forester backs to come into focus as separate human bodies. She fished out one of her rocks, waited for an opening, and flung it with all her strength at the bare throat of one of the men. He collapsed, rolled to one side, and lay still without a sound. She saw one of Little John's legs come into view as the man fell away. The leg drew itself up with a snap and kneed a soft spot in another man, who gasped but did not let go. As he threw his head back, another of Cecily's rocks caught him full square in the cheek. He gave a gargling cry, and let go of Little John to paw at his face.

Little John half-rolled; there were only two clinging to him now—one of them looking wildly around for reinforcements. The other man seemed to be clutching at something she could not see; he had an arm around Little John's neck, and clung to him so tightly she could not get a clear shot with her last stone. Someone else knocked into her from behind, and when she turned back again she'd come some way around the edge of the space where Little John was fighting for his freedom, and now she could see what the man clinging to his back was groping for: a knife.

She saw the glint of the rising blade as she took two steps forward, seized the arm, and buried her own small knife into the spot just above the forester's collarbone.

There was a rush of crimson before her eyes, and her head spun; and she barely realised it when Little John, shaking off his last assailant like a fly, sprang to his feet, seized her round the belly with one arm, and ran.

There was dirt and blood and tallow matted in the hair of his chest; he had shifted her up and against him as he ran through the thinning crowd, dodging around knots of fighting. She came to herself half-crushed, her aching head pounding with every thump of his running footsteps; then she heard the green man's voice, and Little John paused. Cecily half-opened her eyes, conscious of the hot, sick-making smell of fresh blood, too near and too heavy, and the sound of Little John's heart thundering in her left ear. The right side of her face was stiff and sticky, and when she moved her right hand she guessed that the blood-smell was coming mostly from her.

The green man and Gerard in his yellow hose and the young man in the surcoat were all there suddenly; the green man was saying, "—you are a *mess*," and then, "set him down; that blood's mostly yours and the man's he stuck the knife into."

She was set down gingerly, and she clung to the arms that had held her, because the world was still heaving under her feet; and then a voice, not Little John's, said, "Stand still"—and a bucket of water was thrown over them.

She gasped something, and the green man swam into focus before her streaming eyes and said, "I thought that wasn't your blood. Scrub off with this; we can't stand around or they'll catch us again." He gave her and Little John a rough length of flannel each and she rubbed her face and arms. "You've ruined Osbert's second-best coat, my lad," the green man said, and sighed. "But then my green shirt seems to have disappeared entirely. How's the eye?"

Little John's face re-emerged from behind the towel. There was the beginning of a fine purple ring around one eye, but the cut was on the cheekbone, a safe distance away.

"Good. Let's go." He set off trotting toward the road out of town. Cecily's head was still swimming, and as she took her second step she stumbled. Little John stopped immediately.

"No, don't carry me," she said, and put a hand on his arm. The green man and Gerard and Osbert were already several yards away. The arm under her fingers was streaked with black grease where the fighting— and the flannel—hadn't quite rubbed it away. "You *are* a mess," she said.

"You haven't seen yourself, my friend," said Little John. "Can you run? We dare not stand."

"Yes." Cecily blinked, willing the air to stop shimmering.

"While I think of it," said Little John. She looked up. "Thank you."

"Oh." For a moment she remembered the flash of the other man's knife, of Little John's body arching back as the man dragged at his head, Little John's newly shaven throat white through the dirt, and the man's bared teeth, as though he would rather use them than the blade in his hand; the arc of that descending hand broken by Cecily's own hand, and the burst of blood. . . . "Oh. Brothers in arms and that." She swallowed. Again the scene played itself over to her: the other man's knife, Little John's throat, the burst of blood; the knife, the throat, the blood. . . .

"Not quite brothers," said Little John.

Not quite brothers. She banished the scene to her nightmares, where she knew it would find her again. Not quite brothers. "If I can lean on you we can still catch them up."

They set off. "Marian?" said Little John. "In their waggon," replied Cecily. And in answer to the unspoken second question: "She's alive."

If the green man thought it odd that the wrestler he had taken a liking to was running hand in hand with his assistant, he said nothing, and merely bundled them into the back of the waggon with orders to be quiet. "You are not to so much as put a nose out till I tell you to. It's too obvious that you've been in the thickest of it, which does not go well with the picture of peaceful players making the best of their way from other people's troubles—besides, we've wasted enough clothing on you already. Annie, are there any clean shirts left? Or I'll have to hide too."

Annie shuffled toward the rear of the waggon long enough to hand Henry another shirt; but beyond one long look, unreadable in the waggon's shade, she did not acknowledge the two newest passengers. She went back to her place by the pallet where Marian lay, and said no word. Marian was asleep or unconscious.

It was not an agreeable journey. There was very little room even on the floor; Little John sat down as best he could, bending his back as if it hurt him and folding his long legs up like the incongruous limbs of a child's jumping jack. Cecily curled up beside him. She was stiff and sore also, but there was less of her to fold. She leaned against Little John; there wasn't room not to. The motion of the waggon was slow and rough and noisy; the wooden wheels ground mercilessly through every rut, the wooden frame groaned, and many of the obscure bundles stowed in the waggon ticked and jangled and mumbled together with every lurch. Cecily's head throbbed, and with the noise, the cramps in her muscles, and the unsteady movement, she began to feel rather sick.

She tried to find a more acceptable position, and Little John's voice from the almost-darkness next to her whispered, "Are you as uncomfortable as I am?"

"I must be," she whispered back. "It's not being able to see, not knowing what's happening, that's as bad as the bruises."

"Aye," he agreed.

She turned round a little, and had the misfortune to knock her swollen jaw against a shadow that unexpectedly proved solid. She hissed involuntarily. Little John touched her shoulder.

"You're hurt."

"Just clumsy," she said, trying to feel the place; it felt unpleasantly hot and squashy.

"Show me." He raised his hand and almost put her eye out when the waggon rolled into another rut.

She took his fingers and guided them to her jaw. He touched her so lightly she barely felt it; her jaw felt cold and numb in waves at the same time as it was hot and swollen. She tried to press her teeth together against whatever was rising in her throat, without involving her jaw muscles. "Somebody's foot," she said.

"It's not broken, I think," he said.

"One casualty is enough," she said; Marian, lying several feet away, was invisible in the darkness.

Cecily eventually found a different, marginally less desperately uncomfortable way to curl up, and the rocking and creaking of the waggon began to blur together, and it occurred to her that she was mortally tired.

She woke up because the waggon stopped; and as she heard Little John catch his breath she realised that she'd been dimly aware of his steady, slightly raspy breath over her face as he, too, slept. Her head (the sound cheek down) had come to rest on his knee, and slid down to be cradled by the curve between his hip and half-drawn-up leg. As she tried to sit up, his arm fell away from her shoulders.

"Ho there," came a soft voice from outside. "We'll stop here, I think. Anyone want to stretch his legs?"

Cecily half-fell into the green man's waiting arms. Even Little John needed a steadying hand. Mary tied up the canvas curtain, and Annie stood up and hobbled toward the light, twilight now, just enough daylight left to scratch a hasty campfire together without the aid of a lantern.

"How is he?" said the green man.

Annie shook her head, and Cecily blurted, "Not—dead?"

Annie looked at her with what might have been sympathy; it was hard to tell. Her face was a network of wrinkles, and she looked happy and sad and angry and abstracted all at once. "Nay—not dead. Not yet. But not good."

The young man whose second-best coat Cecily ruined had laid aside the coat he had been wearing and was plying his flint. A small blaze of dry grass lit Henry's frown. "I—"

Little John said, "We appreciate all you have done for us. We'll trouble your hospitality little longer if"—he looked around—"you'll give us some idea of where you have brought us."

Henry said, half-dignified and half-annoyed, "I'm not trying to turn you out, man; have some supper with us, and we'll talk." He paused and looked at Little John. "Well, no. We probably won't talk. I'll talk, and your lad will burst out occasionally, and you'll say as little as you can. But we've come this far. I demand as payment for the trouble you've given us—there's a ruined coat and lost shirt between us, as you should remember—that you stay a little longer and eat with us."

"But—" began Cecily.

"I don't think another hour will make much difference to your friend one way or another," said Henry. "If he's not dead yet he's not for dying at once; and before you start dragging him off through the trees, he might be grateful to lie quietly for a little time."

"We are on the track for Sherwood," said Little John, having recognised some landmark Cecily did not know. He sounded almost accusatory.

"You're members of Robin Hood's band, are you not?" said Henry, with badly feigned innocence. "I thought you'd be pleased."

"We can take he—him to Tuck," said Cecily to Little John.

"Friar Tuck," said Henry. "Yes, I can take you very near his dwelling; we have met with him ere now and he has always been most kind. Indeed, he gave us some salves for bruised muscles that are the best I've ever used." He grimaced. "I have lately needed to use them more than I care for."

Little John was silent.

"I can get nowhere with you, can I?" Henry said sadly. "Probably you will not even tell me if you are the one named Little John?"

Little John said slowly, "Is he so famous, this Little John, that he stands out in the tales of Robin Hood's outlaws?"

Henry said wistfully, "He stands out at least by reason of being as tall as a well-grown oak."

Mary, and the young man Gerard of the yellow hose, and the waggon driver, who proved a young woman in a faded blue skirt, were pulling a variety of goods out of the waggon, and unpacking with the absent-minded briskness of long familiarity. Annie crouched by the little fire, feeding it slowly with twigs, while Mary arranged a frame over it so that a pot might hang suspended. Osbert disappeared, carrying a bucket.

"We might bring our—friend—out of his dark bed, and let us see what food and fire may do," said Henry. Little John and Cecily exchanged glances, and then Cecily, being closer, stepped up into the waggon again. She heard Marian murmur and stir, and she made her way by touch back to where she lay. "Marian," she whispered.

"Nay," Marian said clearly, " 'twill do you no good, sirrah, for my heart is already given, to the outlaw of the greenwood."

"Oh dear," said Cecily. Little John had followed her, and was stooping at her shoulder. "What do we tell them?"

"We tell them we want a sling," said Little John. "Stay here with her."

Cecily knelt, helpless and uncomfortable, at Marian's side. She thought to check the sash she'd wrapped around the wound, but as her fingers touched the rough, crusted cloth, Marian shivered and cried out, and Cecily jerked her hand away. She tried to take hope from its stiffness; perhaps the wound had stopped bleeding. She touched one of Marian's hands; it felt hot and strange, and it skittered away from her fingers, though Marian did not cry out again.

She could hear a muted argument going on outside. She closed her eyes a moment. Her nap had not refreshed her, and she felt as if her limbs were made of old and rotten wood: creaky and unreliable. She moved her jaw experimentally; that, she thought hopefully, was maybe a little bit better.

The waggon dipped protestingly under Little John's weight. He was carrying a long folded cloth. "Take her shoulders—gently." Marian bucked once against the hands upon her, and then went limp, and they eased her onto the blanket. They half-carried, half-slid her along the crowded floor of the waggon, trying not to jolt or bend her; eased her out the door and onto the greensward. The blanket ends were bunched and sticky in Cecily's fingers in her effort to keep the heavy cloth pulled taut.

Osbert was stripping the leaves off new-cut ash poles and Gerard was untwisting a piece of rope into twine. Mary came forward with a thick needle, to start holes for the twine, and they began to rope the poles to either side of the blanket without disturbing the occupant. Cecily noticed that all the players kept stealing sidelong looks at the face of the person they thought was Robin Hood, and she wondered what they thought. Robin and Marian were much of a size, and the leather tunic Marian wore disguised her lighter shoulders and her breasts; her hands were as sinewy as any archer's; and her face was grimy, and genderless in the tension of pain.

Henry was standing, arms folded, looking upset, to one side, doing nothing to help or to hinder. Cecily picked up the dipper from the bucket Osbert had filled at the spring she could hear close by, and knelt by Marian again. She sprinkled water on her hot face, and dribbled a little of it at her lips. Marian's glazed eyes opened and seemed to try to focus. Cecily said hesitantly, "Can you sit up?" She slid a slow arm under Marian's shoulders. Marian grimaced but did not protest; and Little John knelt at her other side and supported the small of her back. Her right hand—the one farther from the wound—came up to steady the cup Cecily held before her. She drank, and sighed, and her eyes rested on Cecily. "Don't try to talk," Cecily said hastily; a bit of a smile crossed Marian's face, and her lips shaped silent words that might have been "I won't."

Mary had finished one side, bending under Little John's long arm to prick the last holes; Little John thrust the pole into the loops and tightened the lashings. Cecily got up to let Mary begin the other side. She should take the needle away from Mary and do the work herself, but she was tired—so tired. As if Mary knew what she was thinking, she looked up and smiled; and Cecily smiled gratefully back. She drank a dipper of water herself, rolling it carefully around inside her sore cheek, and, seeing Henry staring at her, scowled right back at him. His face fell a little more, half-puckered, like a disappointed child's. "At least eat something—or take food with you," he said, trying to sound bitter and sounding only unhappy.

Little John looked up. "So long as we stay with you we endanger you. You saved our lives; we know that. The only thanks we are able to offer you is to leave you as quickly as we can. The hair on my nape tells me we are followed even now; and we cannot trust that no one noticed our leaving with you. I have found that what you most want to be over-looked will be seen, even if many other things are happening at the same time. There is something terribly attractive about any action that one wants not to be observed." He got up to reach for the other pole. He found a knot on it that was liable to catch on the blanket; Osbert offered him his short knife. The blade twinkled briefly in Little John's hand, and Cecily remembered again, with a shock like a kick, the twinkle of a blade in her own hand that had not been only a nightmare, and her stomach roiled, and she thought she was going to be sick. She sat down abruptly, till the curtain of red before her eyes faded.

Henry said, "Your lad is weak with weariness and hunger; he will be no good to you if he collapses."

"I am not," said Cecily, but her voice sounded not only weak but petulant; and she would not explain the nightmare. Let them think it was hunger.

Little John said with great gentleness: "This is what it is to be an outlaw."

The pot over the fire had begun to steam. Annie dug in a sack brought off the waggon, and dumped some wooden bowls and chunks of bread on the ground near the fire; the loaves thumped together with a noise like stones. Annie dropped a chunk in each bowl and began to pour the soup over it; she came very deliberately to Cecily's side with the first bowl and offered it to her as if she was expecting refusal. But Cecily took it, hoping Little John would wait long enough that the broth could soften the bread; her jaw wasn't up to much chewing. She looked into Annie's face, trying to smile, and saw there, quite clearly, kindness, and then she was suddenly even more tired, and the tears prickled behind her eyes.

Henry got the second bowl.

Cecily stabbed at the bread with her finger, willing it to crumble;

Little John took his bowl with a grave "Thank you," and began to eat at once. Cecily picked up her bowl and was going to go to Marian, but a gnarled little hand pressed down on her shoulder and dark wrinkled skirts whisked past her, and Annie was squatting by Marian with a bowl and a spoon.

Little John was finished too soon; Cecily gulped the broth and stuffed the sticky bread into a pocket for later, and rose to her feet. She did not know if she was merely infected by Little John's anxiety, but she found that she too was restless, and did not after all wish to stay by this quiet fire and drowse and nurse her bruises. Little John bent to pick up the two poles of Marian's rough litter, and Henry said, "Wait—I almost forgot." He reached an arm around the corner of the waggon's canvas door, and pulled out a little bag. "This is yours," he said, and held out —Cecily's hat. She looked at it in amazement. "You dropped it when you dropped your tunic," he said. He shook it, and it jingled with the coins Little John had earned as a wrestler, a few centuries ago. "Take it."

Cecily shook her head, and Henry took a step toward her. "No," said Little John. "We'll not take it. It is little enough to give you for our lives; but at least it may go some way to buying you a new shirt and jacket."

Henry said uncomfortably, "I do not care about that; the shirt was old, and Osbert ruins his coats as often as anyone could do it for him. You may have need of money."

Cecily shook her head again, but no words came to her. Again it was Little John who answered: "What lies next before us has little to do with money."

Henry dropped his outstretched arm, and Cecily turned away and seized her ends of the poles; she was at Marian's feet, that Marian's head might ride the higher. They lifted Marian smoothly; she was surprised again at her friend's light weight, though she knew the weight would become that of millstones and mountains before the night was out. She tried to fix it in her memory that she had initially thought Marian no great burden, so she might think of it later.

Henry said, "And will you not tell me even at parting—are you Little John?"

Little John said quietly, "Yes, I am he."

"And"—more wistfully—"is that Robin Hood?"

Cecily was staring at Marian's face, remembering how pretty she had always thought her, how gay and strong she had always been; she had been equal to anything the boys might do, equal as if she gave it no thought; she did what she chose. While Cecily, a few years younger, stumbled in her wake and loved and envied her. The matted hair curled around her forehead now, the smears of mud and blood on her face made her nearly unrecognisable; and never before had her cheeks been hollow. "The shooting you saw today was Robin Hood's shooting," said Little John, in a tone suggesting that Henry was foolish to ask.

Henry understood what he was supposed to understand, and he looked a little embarrassed, but he said, "We are not entirely unknown in this area. If you ask the tavern-keeper at the inn on the road to Smithdale he will get word to Henry who leads a troop of travelling players. We usually winter with Sir Michael, at Highwall." Henry almost smiled. "And we could still use a strong man. But remember that there is always a place with us for someone who needs it."

Little John nodded. "We will remember; and I shall tell Robin, and he will be grateful, as we are grateful to you now. Forgive us for leaving you with so little courtesy."

Henry shrugged, and the last anger smoothed out of his face. "Of course. Go with our good wishes."

But Little John was only half-listening to Henry. Cecily heard it too, a far-off confused sound which might have been horses galloping. Without another word Little John turned so that he led them, the litter between and Cecily behind, and they plunged into the trees.

CHAPTER TWENTY

arian moaned and stirred. Cecily tried to make her bent
elbows take as much of the jolting as she could, but it was not easy.
They trotted on for some time, Little John apparently smelling his way,
for it was soon too dark to see clearly; but he rarely stumbled or
swerved. Cecily panted in his wake, expecting at any moment to have
to beg humiliatingly for a pause to breathe; and her feet went on picking
themselves up just high enough to avoid being tangled by roots and
rocks. But perhaps he knew her limits—or his own; for she never came
quite to that point, and they walked and trotted and walked again into
the dark hours.

They stopped once, to drink at a stream. Little John said briefly,
"Stonebrook; we're above the Small Falls here," and Cecily suddenly
understood where they were, and that they were quartering their way
through a small corner of Sherwood—and with some chance of coming
to Friar Tuck before they fell down with exhaustion.

When they went on it was at a gentler pace, but they still covered
much ground. Cecily's shoulders ached and her finger joints were on
fire, and she had blisters starting. They stopped a second time and
Cecily offered Little John half her bread, but he shook his head. "I've
eaten mine."

It was full night now, and as Cecily slumped against a tree and ate
her bread in ragged mouthfuls Little John paced carefully around them,
peering at the sky where the trees would let him. "Do you know where
we are?" Cecily asked, and realised she was too tired to care overmuch
what he replied. She still could not chew, and had to hold the hard bread
in her mouth till it began to disintegrate on its own.

There was a glint of teeth in the shifting starlight. "I hope so. I dare
not wait till dawn, for Marian's sake if not ours. If the breeze has veered
much, I could be leading us past Friar Tuck. I would be happier if the

moon would rise, but wishing will not hurry her. And here I should be finding one of our marked trees, and I am not."

Cecily, on the ground, had a slightly different angle of sight, and her eyes had grown accustomed to the shadows of the trees. "Yes, you are," she said dreamily. "There. Perhaps the last storm displaced it."

Little John followed her pointing finger, and there indeed was the little device of braided twigs that the outlaws sometimes used to mark a path. It had broken off and fallen from its high place into a bush, and there lay almost hidden but for the rustle of evening wind across the shadows.

"Ah." Little John heaved a sigh that told Cecily he was more worried than he was admitting.

They arrived at Friar Tuck's cottage soon after; there was one long questioning bay from one of the dogs, but they knew most of Robin's band. Little John and Cecily were old friends, and the dogs came up to thwack their thighs with their great brutal tails. Tuck knew his dogs' voices and recognised the single query that meant the arrival of a friend, and his door opened before Little John and Cecily had got close enough to knock.

"Why—?" he began, and saw the litter. "Come in," he said. "I will risk a fire."

He had one ready laid for such an extremity, and it caught and flared up at once. Cecily shivered; it was her thoughts that made her cold more than the gentle air—or a reasonable fear of the conditions of Tuck's roof and fire-hole, despite Jocelin's attentions—but cold she was. Tuck knelt by the litter, which they had laid upon the floor as they could, and hissed between his teeth. "Marian," he said. "What happened?" He began to raid a small cupboard as Little John told him.

"Guy of Gisbourne," said Tuck, dismayed; "that is the worst news yet. Folk see things so differently." He had knelt again, and was delicately cutting at the sash around Marian's body.

"All who were there today, save us two, I think, believe they saw Robin Hood," said Little John.

"Ah," said Friar Tuck. "I believe you, and yet that is not what I meant."

Cecily was foggily aware that Tuck was saying something important, but she could not make herself understand. "What do you mean?" she said.

"There is water in that tun by the door. Bring me some," said Tuck; and when she had done so, he said, "Have you asked Robin Hood who he is?"

Cecily said, puzzled, watching Tuck's deft hands, "No. I would not."

"Have you asked yourself who he is?"

Cecily said slowly, "He—he is our leader."

"The leader of a band of outlaws," said Friar Tuck, "who live leanly in Sherwood. And did you hear the folk today talk of this Robin Hood whom they saw shooting his arrows into the target better than anyone else?"

"They spoke of him—as if he were not human," Cecily said, thinking of the woman selling trinkets. "She said he was one of the Old Ones, come to save England."

"Robin Hood would not agree, I think," said Friar Tuck, laying back the clotted cloth; Marian gasped and murmured, and one of the dogs whined outside the door.

"No," said Cecily, shocked.

"I would not agree with either Robin or your fairground tale-teller," said the friar. "And Marian, I guess, agrees with me, or she would not be here." He added softly, "But, my dear, was it worth your life to make the tale come true?"

"But—" said Cecily, and could think of no words to follow.

Friar Tuck said kindly, but with some humour, "Ask me about the meaning of life, or anything else you choose. Tales are as much the necessary fabric of our lives as our bodies are. There are blankets in that chest; pull them out and lie down beside it; there is just room for you, I think, as you are the smaller. Little John, I will trouble you to help me bring my mattress here by the fire, and then if Cecil will let you have any of the blankets, you can sleep too. There should be space enough where the mattress lay, although I may require you to keep your feet tucked up."

"They will look here," said Little John.

"Not tonight," said Friar Tuck. "Only an outlaw could find his way to me on a night with no moon. I will not let you move her further tonight anyway; tomorrow we will decide what to do—early tomorrow, I promise you. Perhaps we should all four—and the dogs—go to ground in the little bolt-hole you and Robin arranged for me after the good baron had cause to hate me. Perhaps I will merely send you. I have not decided. Go to sleep."

Cecily said, struggling to keep her eyelids open a minute longer, "You —say—four—of us. Then Marian will live through this night."

There was a pause long enough to notice, before Tuck said, "I believe so. In all events, you can do nothing about it; you have done your turn, and it is now mine. Go to sleep. I dislike repeating myself."

Smells haunted Cecily's dreams: bright sharp smells of green spring and bitter herbs, and grim smells of blood and death, but nothing woke her for several hours, till her stomach observed that she was now smelling *food*, and then her eyes came stiffly open.

"Good morning," said Friar Tuck as she sat up. "It is a fine morning, and the dogs are disturbed by no far-off rumble of armed men coming this way. There is bread and cheese and ale on the table and stew on the fire."

"How is Marian?" said Cecily; her voice sounded as rusty as a neglected byrnie.

Tuck shook his head, but his face was not gloomy. "I do not know yet. I may know today; perhaps not till tomorrow. I believe she will live if she can, and that is a great thing."

Cecily looked at Marian's sleeping face, and thought that some of the lines that had been there yesterday were there no longer, and she felt a little hopeful. This left her some freedom to think of other things— like the fact that her clothes chafed her as if she had been wearing them a year. "I would *wash*," she said gruffly; Friar Tuck looked mildly surprised. "You may borrow a change of clothes from me if you do not mind the skirts."

Cecily ducked out of the hut with a roll of Friar Tuck's spare gown under her arm. The dogs were inclined to wish to help her at her bath in the little pool beyond the chapel; and then she had some trouble deciding how to tie (or not tie) the billows of Friar Tuck's robe so that her gender would not inadvertently reveal itself, telling herself first that it didn't matter anyway and then that it did, and then again that it didn't. Little John knew already and Friar Tuck wouldn't care. Probably. He was too busy with Marian anyway. She decided that she couldn't decide and that not deciding was best expressed by not tying. Whereupon she wadded up some of the billows in one hand so they would not catch between her legs and trip her that way (the hem ended well above her ankles) and her wet, reasonably clean, or at least less dirty, clothes in the other, and went back to the hut for breakfast. She found she still hated the feeling of skirts flapping around her, and wondered why Tuck bothered wearing them. It was not as though he did not possess several other individualistic approaches to being a priest and friar.

Little John and Tuck were in the middle of an argument; the friar was shaking his head. "I do not know if that is wise," he said. Little John protested at once: "Would you have him not told?"

Friar Tuck stood looking down at Marian, who was lying very still. "I might," Tuck said at last, "for he can do no good by knowing; you could wait a day, in the hope that I might have good tidings to allay a terrible tale."

"And what if someone hears a tale of Robin Hood shooting at the fair and being wounded by Guy of Gisbourne and rescued by a tall man and a boy? And brings the tale to Sherwood? Cecil and I should be bringing our own tale by this morning. We are the only folk from Greentree who were in Nottingham yesterday, but there are those who love Robin well enough to venture into Sherwood for his sake, or the sake of news of him after what they know they saw."

Friar Tuck took a long minute to answer. "I did not expect to be able to stop you; bad news travels fast, but not so quickly that, were it my choice, I would not risk the delay of one day. I would ask you to bear her to our hiding-place, however, ere you leave; for I do not like the risk of any man coming to inquire of me today about any belly wounds I may have seen recently."

Cecily surprised herself by saying, "Only one of us needs to take news to Robin; and Friar Tuck should be seen about his chapel in the ordinary way. Marian should not be left alone—at very least that she might not wake in the dark and have no one to tell her where she is. I will stay if there is no reason against it."

Little John's smile was so slight and so wry that had he still been wearing a beard she would not have seen it. "It is a good plan and a good thought, but I would rather face twenty foresters than wait in the dark for something that may not come."

Cecily said sadly, through a mouthful of cheese (which required no chewing), "So would I. Ten foresters anyway. But you are the better tracker and the faster, and it is only sensible you should be the one to go."

Robin had not liked the idea of Little John and Cecil—Cecily—going into the sheriff's baited trap; but it was true that since Sir Richard regained his land the air the outlaws breathed seemed thick with the sheriff's hatred, and the leaves seemed to have eyes in them, that had been their friends before.

The loss of Rafe's source of news when Lucy married and moved a town away was a severe one, and came at a particularly bad time from the outlaws' point of view; as if fate had arranged it, the pieces fit so neatly. And Rafe himself, one of the sunnier-tempered members of Greentree, had been trailing around like a lost fawn since Lucy had told him.

"I can't blame her," he said miserably; "I couldn't marry her, now could I? Or I could, I suppose, but what man who loved a woman would ask her to live as we do?"

Robin had overheard this much of a conversation between Rafe and Simon and Jocelin; they had fallen silent when they recognised Robin's step. It might merely have been the end of the conversation anyway, but Robin thought not. What man would ask a woman he loved to live as they did? It was a thought he was only too familiar with.

The other rumour he had heard of late, one he could not decide whether to hope for or not, was that the Lionheart was coming home to England. Richard was a Norman and spoke English like a Frenchman, but he was king. Would he uphold the laws of England or would he be careless of the rights of the English so long as his fellow Normans were happy? Whom would he believe, the sheriff of Nottingham or Robin Hood? Was it, Robin thought dismally, a question worth asking?

It was not just that he was the king. Everyone loved Richard Lionheart, even outlaws hiding in the king's forests. He was tall and blond and heroic, and he had been fighting for the Holy Land, a cause that the

Saxons—except perhaps when there was a sheriff leaning on them too heavily—could love too. Almost everyone seemed to forget his Norman blood when they spoke of him. Maybe Robin had once felt that way too, long ago, when he was still a king's forester himself. But he did not forget it now, just as he feared that if the king did decide to hear the sheriff's complaint of them as true and serious, his outlaws would give up in despair that the Lionheart had turned against them, before any one of them was taken.

Robin had an uneasy day while Little John and Cecily were at the fair; he half-imagined he could hear the crowd from the heart of Sherwood. He listened to his imagination and it sounded like an angry crowd, shouting of cruelty and disaster . . . and then he cursed himself for a fool and was more uneasy than ever. It was not surprising that Little John and Cecily did not return that night; the fair would go on till evening, and if Little John was keeping in his role as a wrestler, he would have proven a popular contestant.

But as the next morning drew on toward noon, Robin gave up all pretence of not being anxious.

It was past noon when there was the cry from the nearest guard that someone bearing news approached. Robin's heart tried to rise and sink simultaneously when he saw Little John come toward him, obviously hale and—when he got a little closer Robin saw some of the bruises, and that the shirt he wore was not his own; it looked like it might fit Friar Tuck. The cut on his cheek did not look like the kind of thing a wrestler should have received. "Where is Cecily?"

"With Marian."

"With Marian?"

Little John hesitated, and Robin took him by the arms and shook him. "Speak, man! What has Marian to do with the news from Nottingham?"

Little John sounded as if he were reciting a speech he had memorized; maybe he was. "At the shooting contest at the fair, one archer stood out among them all as the best. As the final arrow struck the target, a man leaped from the sheriff's tent and challenged the winner, naming Robin Hood. As the crowd had done among themselves already."

"And?" said Robin violently, as Little John paused; but he knew already the end of the story.

Little John's voice was flat. "This man called himself Guy of Gisbourne, and he drew a sword on the archer, who had no sword, and the crowd pressed around the two of them in anger, for they had liked it that Robin Hood should win the sheriff's contest, and did not like Guy. But Guy . . . wounded the archer with the point of his sword."

"Marian," said Robin. "She lives?"

"She lives," said Little John. "She is with Friar Tuck, who would have had me stay the news for a day; he hopes that Marian may rally and we be sure of her by tomorrow. Cecily is with them."

"Is Cecily hurt?" Robin asked; but his lips moved stiffly over the name. Marian was lying wounded by the closing of the sheriff's trap. . . .

"No," said Little John, and touched his purple cheek. "Not to signify. Bruises. There's less of her to resist when a nailed boot steps on her. There was quite a mix-up at the end, when we were getting Marian away." Little John paused.

Robin looked at him, his eyes dark with visions of the day before; of the day to come; of the woman who lay under Friar Tuck's roof.

"Will's little sister saved my life," Little John added as if inconsequentially.

Robin's eyes cleared long enough to stare into the face of his friend. Another stroke upon the sheriff's tally, that he nearly caused the death of Little John. "I am glad of that small favour. And you were right to come straight on; by tomorrow I would have been walking down the main street of Nottingham, shouting your names. Where is now Guy?"

Little John lifted his shoulders. "I do not know. But the tale is that the sheriff has bought him and his men to find the outlaws of Sherwood." After a moment he said, "We were followed out of Nottingham, I believe, but with luck we lost them in Sherwood; no one had come to the chapel by this morning. I do not know if those who followed included Guy; it would be bad luck indeed if he should have chosen our direction to start his search."

"The sort of bad luck we need to expect," said Robin. He had picked up his bow and quiver, which the tension of the day had caused him to have nearer at hand than was his custom at Greentree. His fingers paused over his staff, and then he picked it up slowly, turning it in his hands. "A sword, you said?"

"Aye. A long sword, such as a knight might wear."

Robin said, with a recklessness that Little John did not like at all, "Well, I have no sword; my dagger will have to suffice."

Little John said, "You will not go alone."

"Will I not?" said Robin; but his thoughts were far away. "I do not care. You may come with me if you wish."

Much approached the two of them; Little John's hand was on Robin's arm, but even Little John's grip was not going to detain him long. "Where is Cecily?" he said. "What happens here? I like not either of your faces."

"You will find me at Tuck's chapel," said Robin, stepping away and settling his strung bow over his shoulder; and he was gone through the gap in the trees that served Greentree as a front door—gone at a running pace that a hunted stag might set.

"What?" said Much; and Little John told him.

He finished by saying, "Round up all of us you can, will you? And let us meet at the chapel. Robin will see Marian first, which will delay him a little—I like this mood least of any I have seen. I don't want him left alone—even for these moments I spend in talking with you."

"Guy of Gisbourne," said Much, appalled; but he said it to empty air, for Little John was gone after Robin.

It was a hard journey for Little John, who had had too much of hard journeying in the last two days; but he caught up and kept pace, though he went less quietly than was his usual.

Once, when they stopped to drink at Rosebrook, Little John said, "Do you know who it is you are chasing? You cannot mean to take him as you stand."

Robin said savagely, "I mean to take him with an arrow in the back, if I can. It will be no less a choice than he gave Marian. But I also mean to give myself as many choices as I am able; and even if he is a demon in human form, as they like to say of him—yes, I know the tales—I still believe that I know Sherwood better than he does, which may, I hope, give some length over a longsword's reach."

Robin seemed to flee over the leaf-strewn floor of Sherwood without ever quite setting a foot firmly down; their time back to Friar Tuck was less than Little John's to come to Robin to give the news, and Little John had not lingered by the way. Robin said, almost over his shoulder, to his companion: "There is some method behind my passion for speed besides the love for Marian that you fear may betray me to rashness. Guy is an ill enemy—the worst, I think, that we have had, for the sheriff is only as great an enemy as he can hire other folk to be for him. I am glad now that I have been so merciless in cutting our camp down to so few; that fewer folk are now to be at risk.

"The sooner we confront him the better; I think it will not be numbers that decide the ending to this tale, but luck and perhaps some skill. Guy has the devil's own luck; we will see if the luck that has kept us alive thus far may stand against that dark gentleman's."

They were now close to Tuck's cottage, and Robin dropped to a walk. And he said then, with an expression on his face more like the Robin Hood that his people knew, "And as for meeting Guy alone—did you not leave word with Much for all of us that he could muster to meet at Tuck's chapel, before you came after me?"

Beauty gave the single cry of hound welcome, and Tuck emerged from the chapel path into the meadow, turning to face the way Beauty stood, and said to the trees: "They have gone, they who would ask me of you; you may come out from where you watch in hiding."

"So men did come," said Little John.

Tuck said, smiling, but not so comfortably as was his usual way: "They did; I grow slow and dull in the wilderness. I did not realise how the sheriff's hatred for Robin has grown."

"Marian?" said Robin, as Little John said, "You were not there when we bought back Sir Richard's life from out the sheriff's hand."

"Marian is not well, but no more ill than when Little John left to find you," said Tuck grimly, "—I hope. Now that my last lot of visitors is well on their way"—he and Little John turned to look at the dogs, who were untroubled by any wandering whiff of strangers—"we may go look to her again."

The silence within was perfect as Friar Tuck drew the brush aside from the hidden earthwork; Robin was nearly stepping on his heels with impatience, and it was Robin's hand that yanked open the low, carefully moss-grown door.

There was a brief glint in the darkness within, and then Cecily

---

dropped her dagger-point with a sigh. "You might have identified yourselves," she said; "I am weary of being frightened, these last two days."

"How is she?" said Tuck; Robin had pushed in past him, blinking in
the dark. "A little better, I think," said Cecily. "She has come to herself
enough to know me, once or twice." She stooped, pulling the volumi-
nous skirts of Tuck's spare robe clumsily out of the way. There was the
smell of flint, and then a little rush-light wavered into brightness, and
Robin fell on his knees beside Marian's pallet.

The other three drew quietly outside, and Little John touched the
nape of Cecily's neck with two fingers and said, "You have only learnt
to be tired of fear in the last two days? I am a poor teacher, then."

Cecily wondered that with all else happening she should instantly be
most aware of a whisker-light touch of Little John's hand, and she said,
tiredly enough, "Nay, it is I who was the poor student, for I believed
that my teacher need fear nothing, and I have learnt better."

"I am glad you learnt, ere you died of the ignorance," said Little John;
"but—I wonder if, then, the student has no further use for a teacher so
fallen from perfect strength."

"Oh," she said, too bone-weary to pretend: "I would far rather that
I love you as I saw yesterday I do than that I had gone on worshipping
you as I did not long since." And she turned away hastily, and did not
see that Little John would reach out to her; and, half-running, went to
Tuck's cottage, where she could pull on her half-dry clothes, and become a proper outlaw again. At least, she thought, fighting back tears,
like this I am Cecil, with a place among friends, and a task to do. I am
someone. I wonder if perhaps if I am no longer Cecil, I am no one at all.

"Marian," said Robin; or he meant to say it, but his lips parted and
no sound came. He touched her hand and tried again. "Marian?"

The light was so dim, through the brush that still hung over the
opening to the out-of-doors and in the tiny flicker of flame on the earth
floor, that he could not even be sure that she breathed. He seemed to
have been waiting for hours, gathering up her hand between his, when
he saw that her eyes slowly opened. At first it was the merest glint
between the lashes; then they opened full, and cast about for a moment
as if they did not know why they were being forced to look out; and

then Marian turned her face a little, and looked at him. Her smile looked only wistful and drowsy, as if he had awakened her from a sweet happy dream that she was sorry to lose.

"Robin," she said. "I am glad to see you; yet I fear you are very angry with me."

There was time for three heartbeats between each of her words, and when she said "angry" he had almost forgotten that she had earlier said "you." By the time he remembered, she had gone on, and he had to lean close to hear her: "We had not parted good friends, I fear, when we last met; and I knew if you heard of yesterday it would be the worst of all."

Robin said at random, "I am sure you should not talk so much, but save your strength"; and she smiled into his eyes and fell silent, and then he could think of nothing else to say. He remembered the many times he had told her she must not come back to Greentree and how many times she had ignored him; and how he had come to rely on that —disobedience—because he was as sure that he could not live without her as he was sure that she should not risk another journey into Sherwood.

He remembered seeing her, with her curling hair drawn back smoothly as a lady's should be, in her long amber gown that fell so beautifully around her feet, so near the sheriff, so near mortal danger: danger that he knew she faced for his sake. She had known what she faced and why, but she had known from the beginning, from the first day when she and Much had found him hiding near the place where they had played as children. She had known and had dealt with the knowledge; he had known, and had refused to know, and had left her to bear the weight of responsibility alone, accusing her, to spare himself, of an idealism that in truth none of his band had been guilty of, Marian least of all. He had let her come to him because he wanted her to, while he soothed his conscience by listening to his tongue telling her to go away.

He looked at her, pale and hollow-cheeked; her eyes were sunken as from an illness of many months, and her rich hair was lank and dull; and he thought she was the most beautiful thing he had ever seen, and he knew his heart was breaking. "My dear," he said, crouching beside her, "I am so sorry."

Some look he could not read flitted across her face. "A sore belly seems to make me deaf," she said. "You cannot be apologising for my arrogance and stupidity."

Robin laughed a little, but the laugh made his throat hurt. "No; I do not apologise for your arrogance and stupidity, but for my own."

Her eyes drifted shut, and for a moment he thought she was gone from him, and he stared at her breast till his eyes, now accustomed to the shadows, saw the faint rise and fall of her breathing. But after a few minutes her eyes opened again and she said, "Thank you. We do not make it easy for ourselves, you and I, do we?"

"No," he said. "I love you, Marian."

She gave a tiny gasp, as if she would chuckle and had not the strength. "Well, my love, this wound of mine is worth something after all, to have forced those words out of you after so many years I have longed to hear them. But please, my dearest love, let us learn to be a little softer? I do not like the thought that crisis is our only chance of contact. First you must promise to say what you have just said to me again when I am well."

"I promise," said Robin, "if you promise that Robin Hood will not go again to Nottingham Fair."

"It is an easy promise to make," said Marian, "for I have learnt my lesson. I learnt many things, suddenly, when I felt my own blood sliding between my fingers. But there was a time not long ago when I thought that all you would ever let me have of you was your legend—and—and I might at least use that to some effect." She stopped talking and Robin thought she would spare him the rest; but after a little pause she went on: "I have never made you understand, I think, how the folk outside Sherwood see you; you are too preoccupied with keeping your own folk safe. It was—it was the one thing I could give you, that some of those people should see you as they wished to see you." She paused again, and sighed. "And I liked the idea of doing something stupid and violent. I was feeling stupid and violent."

Robin was silent. Marian's fingers curled weakly around his. "I am weary, Robin, but I am determined to stay alive. Tell me that I have something to look forward to, besides the dangerous and lonely business of the burnishing of a legend."

"Marry me," said Robin. "Stay with me, never leave me. Come with me to the ends of the earth—which I fear will soon be all that's left safe from the sheriff of Nottingham. Will that do?"

"Yes," said Marian, and closed her eyes, and they sat thus for some time.

Robin stirred and looked up as Tuck appeared hesitantly at the door, with a bucket in one hand and a cup in the other. "You should not be tiring my patient," he said, but his voice was kind.

"He does not tire me," said Marian; "I feel stronger now than I have ever felt."

"Ah," said the friar. "I am of course pleased to hear this, but I would prefer you to remain lying down for some while yet till you accustom yourself to all your new strength." He knelt beside Marian and offered her the cup, sliding his hand under her head to make her drinking easier. "That was not water," she said.

"Some of it was water," said Tuck. "Some of it was not. You might sleep now." She closed her eyes as if the lids were of stone, and Tuck dipped a cloth in the bucket and began to wash her face. "Let me," said Robin.

"Very well," said Tuck; "but then you have to go away, for I will not have you here when I change the poultice. You can call Cecil, who has a steady hand and eye for the work, as I discovered this morning. A lad of many parts, that one."

Robin felt as clumsy and uncertain as if he had spent months crouched in a small dark cave, when at last Tuck forced him gently outside. Cecily was hovering not far away and came forward when she saw him. "Tuck wants you," he said. She nodded. "He calls you Cecil."

She nodded again, and gave a flickering smile. "Does it matter? At least now."

Robin stood staring as if at nothing, and she made to go by him, when he said quietly: "It mattered to Marian, what name they used."

Cecily wanted to say, but Friar Tuck doesn't want to kill me. Then she thought of Little John's face tipped back, with the early sun on his beardless skin, saying, "You have no call to complain about my appearing suddenly different"—it had been but yesterday morning. And she remembered that only an hour ago she had told him she loved him. "I will tell Tuck my name," she said, and ducked under the low lintel.

Robin found that he was breathing rather too quickly, as if in anticipation of—of what? What he most wanted was to sight down a bow-string at Guy of Gisbourne's heart. But he felt, meanwhile, like a man waiting for the herald to call the beginning of the contest; like someone who has come to the city gates too early and found them closed, and now waits impatiently for the first trace of dawn in the sky.

He walked slowly down to the little pool beyond the chapel, and there found Little John hurling pebbles; he, too, seemed preoccupied with some thoughts of his own, and needed an effort to turn and acknowledge Robin's presence.

"I feel like a hawk with my hood still on," said Robin.

Little John grunted. "If there was a cloud in the sky, I would be happy to think that there was a storm coming to blame for the prickling of my skin."

"You too?" said Robin.

"Aye. And it was my idea that I should come with you to prevent you from doing anything rash . . . and I cannot sit still, nor begin to give good advice."

"I hate the thought of waiting like a child in a cradle for Guy of Gisbourne to come and find me," said Robin. "I must decide which way is likeliest and go to find him—and yet I do not want to leave Marian, though staying will draw Guy near her."

"He may think his job is already done," said Little John, "and have gone on."

Robin shook his head. "I doubt it. The sheriff would not have gone to such lengths as to hire such a one if he were the sort to leave before he brought Robin Hood's own head to the sheriff's table."

Sweetheart gave the single long cry of a friend approaching, and Much and Rafe appeared, looking warm. Much took a quick look at Robin's face and arranged his own to placidity, trying to disguise the hastiness of his breathing. Rafe hung a little back. "Marian?" said Much, speaking to the air somewhere between Little John and Robin.

"She is not worse," said Robin; and at that moment all three dogs bayed and went on baying. Tuck and Cecily burst out of the earthwork and began feverishly pulling the brush down that concealed it. As Robin turned toward them, Simon appeared as if by magic at Tuck's elbow. Tuck turned away, rubbing his hands along the generous folds of his friar's robe with a hard, set expression on his face so unlike him that he might have been some other friar. Simon and Cecily finished their business hurriedly and melted into the undergrowth as Little John, Much, and Rafe had already done. Robin began to make his way round the far side of the pool, to come upon whatever might appear from that direction; the dogs said that was the direction to look.

There were the delicate but purposeful crunches of outlaw feet on dry leaves all around Tuck's clearing.

CHAPTER TWENTY-ONE

he dogs had gone on baying, their attention focussed on a lesser-used trail somewhat north of the small side-path to Tuck's chapel from the main way to Nottingham. Tuck tried to look like a peace-loving man of God as he went toward the dogs; he tried not to scuttle as well. But his heart misgave him before he saw the troop of heavily armed men collecting around one man at the edge of his clearing. They fanned out, ignoring him, having identified him, looking for someone else who would be a greater threat: a war party, looking for war. Their leader ignored them as they ignored Tuck: a well-trained war party, with a leader who had confidence in them as did they in him.

This leader was a tall man, not so tall or broad as Little John or Will, but with heavy, strong bones visible in his face and in the width of his wrists; and there was no ounce of unnecessary flesh upon him anywhere. The tough, sinewy outlaws would look soft next to this man. And no ounce of unnecessary kindness lay in his heart, either, thought Tuck, looking into the narrow, level-eyed face. He was dressed in hardworn but supple leather, and the mail-shirt that showed beneath the cloth surcoat was dark with use and careful oiling; neither leather creaked nor chain clashed as he moved.

"I am Guy of Gisbourne," he said quietly, pitching his voice to carry across the noise of the dogs; "and I seek a man who was wounded at Nottingham Fair yesterday."

By an effort of will Friar Tuck raised his eyebrows. He said with cautious surprise, "I spoke to a troop of the sheriff's men only this morning about such a man. I have not seen him." He told his conscience, I have not seen *him*. The dogs, who knew all the tones of his voice, redoubled their barking; Beauty's ruff stood up till she looked as large as a pony.

"If your dogs do not cease their caterwauling," Guy of Gisbourne said calmly, "my men will shoot them."

Friar Tuck's mouth dropped open, in honest surprise this time; and then he swallowed convulsively and called his dogs. But his voice creaked as Guy of Gisbourne's armour did not, and for the moment he could not make them mind. He saw one of the men nearest Guy turn to look at the dogs with interest, and feel toward the quiver that hung at his belt for an arrow. Desperately Tuck bellowed, "Beauty! Sweetheart! Brown-eyes! Come *here*; that's enough of you."

They came, reluctantly, muttering in their throats, and sat down around him. But Beauty stood up again almost at once, and paced up and down in front of him, growling and showing her great teeth, her ruff still fully erect.

"That will do," said Guy of Gisbourne composedly. "They need not love me, but I require civility, from man or beast. I ask you again to tell me what you know of a wounded man who escaped Nottingham yesterday."

Tuck said, his voice unpleasantly high in his own ears, "I have told you, I do not—"

He barely saw the gesture that Guy made, but the man who had been watching saw, and fitted an arrow in his bow as quickly as Robin's outlaws used their longbows; and Beauty, pacing, dropped suddenly and soundlessly in her tracks, with an arrow buried in her throat. It happened so quickly and neatly that the other two dogs did not understand what had happened, and looked in puzzlement at the slightly twitching body of their sister. But Friar Tuck knew, and it steadied him, and a coldness came over him as icy as the heart of the man he faced.

There was a listening silence in the trees around him; he knew that those who listened paused only for fear of his one small life. He knew too that the men before him outnumbered the outlaws at best two to one, and that only if Much had gotten word quickly to all of them that were left in Sherwood. He was sorry for the first time in many years that he no longer kept a dagger strapped to the calf of his leg, for he was sure his life was shortly to be forfeit, and he would have liked to strike one blow first. He stared at Beauty, knowing that his face reflected the shock and sorrow that he felt, and that the sorrow would be read by Guy and his men as fear.

"Two men came through here late last night," he said, raising his eyes, "bearing a third man in a litter; this man was sore wounded, by a blade taken a little way in the belly. An inch more and he would have been dead already." Tuck was watching for it, and so saw the flicker in Guy of Gisbourne's eyes when he said this. "They would not stay. I did what I could for the wounded man, but I would not be surprised if he did not live the night. I do not know if they came from Nottingham, but as they came that way," and he nodded toward the trail Guy and his men had not taken, "they may well have done so." He looked down at Beauty again, and tears shadowed his eyes, and when one tipped over the edge of his eyelid and fell down his cheek he did not raise a hand to brush it away.

"That is better, but not good enough," said Guy of Gisbourne. "Or not if you wish to escape your dog's fate. Did you tell of these men to the sheriff's soldiers?"

Tuck shook his head and tried to look truculent. "No. I did not know if this was the man they sought, and they—did not linger."

"Did not offer any persuasion, you mean," said Guy of Gisbourne. "I know that you help the outlaws of Sherwood; perhaps"—and his face closed further as he said this—"you even call their leader friend. How were these three men you saw last night dressed?"

Tuck shut his eyes as if to concentrate, or to shut out the sight of Beauty, sprawled at his feet. "One was very large and wore no shirt; one was just a lad, and wore the remains of what had been an elegant coat. They both looked as if they had been in a brawl; they were bruised and filthy. The wounded man was dressed in plain homespun with a leather tunic over."

Guy grunted. The man who had shot Beauty stood alertly, another arrow loosely in one hand. Tuck looked around, to see what Guy's men were about, remembering to look small and alone and fearful, which came easy, trying not to display any interest in what might be going on immediately behind any trees beyond the clearing, which was not so easy. Although his brain still functioned calmly, he found that he had some difficulty breathing; from one moment to the next he expected . . .

He had turned a little as he looked around, and did not at once notice that Sweetheart had left his side; he recalled his dogs when he heard Sweetheart's growl.

He heard it fractionally before anyone else did, and he spun round, yelling, "Sweetheart, *no!*" as the dog, who had been gently nosing

Beauty's body, crouched and sprang for Guy's throat. Then a number of things happened at once.

Tuck dived for his dog, and got just the end of his tail; they both fell hard, and Tuck heard one arrow whistle past his ear and one more at a little distance, that he could guess had been meant for Sweetheart. Brown-eyes, catching on at last, leaped for the man who had shot Beauty and missed Tuck, and who was now redrawing hastily—not hastily enough, and he went down with a scream. Guy, briefly startled by Sweetheart's lunge, had taken one step backward—enough to save his life, for an arrow hummed past his nose so nearly that he blinked against a feeling that the feathers would brush his eyes.

At once he shouted to his men, rallying them against the new attack; not that they needed much rallying; they would not be in his command if they were not accustomed to such sport as this, and Guy had been sure that Robin's men would be near the old friar's hovel. Where else could they have gone with their wounded master? Which meant their master was also near at hand. . . . Guy's teeth gleamed as he drew his sword.

The friar was still rolling inanely upon the forest floor; Guy thought to cut his throat as he walked past, but he stayed his hand against the possibility that some of his band might need the friar's leechcraft when this business was over. A friar would not be tiresome about tending mercenaries, as laymen sometimes were. These outlaws were a bit more challenging than crushing a village; and they had their master's wound to make them angry—and foolhardy. The next hour or so might prove amusing. He had no doubt of the outcome.

Tuck rolled up onto his knees as soon as he had seen Guy's feet pass by; Sweetheart was already gone into the fray, after one briefest glance of reproach at his master: reproach I deserve, thought Tuck; if there was any chance that he might have succeeded in tearing that man's throat out I should be hung from one of these trees. . . . It may come to that yet, or near enough as makes no difference. He began circumspectly to make his way toward his cottage; for his long-unused dagger was there.

It was hard to see what was going on, or what was to be avoided; there were thumps and crunches echoing from all directions, but the trees absorbed some of the sound, and reflected the rest confusingly, and Tuck could as well hear the faint burble of running water. The occasional arrow flew, but he noticed that the ones he saw were the shorter kind, that belonged to Guy's men—the ones that are missing their marks, he thought hopefully.

He began to realise that much of the crashing he was hearing was of Guy's men searching for their attackers: as he watched, one man of Guy's troop paused, panting and at a loss, at the edge of the clearing, looking wildly around; as he turned to make his way farther back into the concealing shadows, a long slender shaft whistled from nowhere and buried itself in his chest; he fell first to his knees, swayed, and slowly toppled to one side. Tuck abruptly realised that the trees were not such good concealment for men dressed as Guy's men were dressed, with the bright wink of sword-blade and occasional band of colour in a surcoat over the mail-shirts, as for the outlaws. The outlaws wore no mail; but chain did not protect Guy's men from the longbow arrows of Robin's invisible archers.

Tuck picked up the hem of his gown and scurried for his hut. He yanked the door open; one of the leather hinges gave, as it had been threatening to do for some time, under this rough treatment, and the door nearly brained him. He squeezed by it, and felt, with trembling hands, for the dagger in its hiding place: a crack cut into the underside of the table.

There was a shout from outside—a desperate shout. Tuck fumbled his way past the door again with it ringing in his ears.

Guy's men had made an appalling discovery. One of their fellows had died with an arrow in his back, clutching at the underbrush as he fell face down, and carrying it with him as he slid to the ground. The underbrush he held happened to be that disguising the entrance to Marian's haven.

There were two men clearing the earthwork when Tuck heard the cry; one of them was falling with an arrow in his throat, and the other was turning to look where the cry—and the arrow—had come from. Tuck saw Cecil—Cecily—leap out from behind a tree just ahead of an arrow from another of Guy's men, who now rushed up through the trees behind her. Tuck had his mouth open to give a shout of his own, when she turned, dagger in hand, ducked—mostly—under his sword-stroke, and slashed him across the thigh. He was the worse hampered by the branches because of the length of his blade; but both were wounded and each staggered back from the other's blow.

The man by the earthwork was fitting an arrow to his string when

Tuck's dagger caught him under the ear; he had not thought to pay attention to the stumbling approach of the fat little friar. Cecily's opponent paused, perhaps astonished at the sight of the terrified friar of a few minutes ago waving a dagger wet with his companion's blood, and Cecily reeled forward for the final blow. Her left arm was red from the shoulder, and hung limp.

The man fell where he stood when she struck him. She stood swaying on her feet, looking down at the man who would have killed her if he had got his second blow in first; and behind her the leaves erupted and another of Guy's men appeared. Tuck lurched forward, weeping; but from just by where Cecily stood helpless, a large man in a shirt that did not fit him appeared as silently as a ghost; his arrow passed clear through the throat of the running man and hung quivering in the bole of a tree some little distance away, almost before the dead man had finished falling.

Little John caught Cecily as her knees buckled, and Tuck came up to them. Little John was staring into her face with a haunted, hungry expression, as if most of Guy's men were not still seeking them, and liable to find anyone who stayed in one place for more than a moment. Tuck tore Cecily's shirt a little clear of her shoulder and said, "It is not mortal."

Little John said, "It is likely to prove so yet if we cannot hide her." But he said it looking at Cecily, not at Tuck, and he moved not a foot.

Tuck looked frantically around; perhaps they could put her in with Marian. The entrance must be covered up again in all events, and Cecily's shoulder must be tied up or she could bleed to death. And Little John stood like a stone.

Cecily stirred a little in his arms, and her eyes flickered open. Tuck saw the colour rush into her face as she saw who held her. "If we—stand here, they will pick us off—with those foolish little excuses—they have for—bows," she said. "Put me down—*ow*," as she tried to straighten up, and she was quiet a fraction of a minute, and a little blood appeared on her lip where she had bitten it as she tried not to think about her shoulder. Gently, Little John set her feet upon the ground, and she leaned against him, panting. She looked toward the earthwork. "Must —cover that," she said.

"We'll put you in first," said Little John, but Cecily shook her head.

"Tie up my arm, Tuck," she said. "If someone will give me a back to step on, I can get up in a tree and at least cry warning."

"And get shot for your trouble," began Little John; and then Will materialized at his elbow. "Cecily—"

"Just—my shoulder," she said, and made an attempt at a smile. "Why are you—standing there?"

Will shook his head. "We've killed ten—fifteen," he said, looking around him. "Maybe one or two more; the rest of them are skittish, and not so easy as they were. Robin's regrouping—I was to find you. We did not expect—" He was looking at the earthwork.

"Sit down," said Cecily, and did so, dropping so suddenly out of Little John's grasp that he missed easing her down and she hit the ground with a thump that made her give a little cry. "I didn't know," she said, her voice wobbly, "that little things like shoulders could hurt so much."

"Not little," said Tuck, kneeling beside her. "This should be stitched." He looked at Will. "May I risk fetching needle and thread?"

Will said, "Robin's been drawing them deeper into the forest—farther from Marian—and you too, Tuck. Perhaps—"

Little John said, "We'll move back a little way, where we'll not be as easily seen. Will—you could move some brush back over that entrance."

Will opened his mouth to protest; he was, after all, her brother. But he noticed the protective way Little John's arm cradled her good side, and closed his mouth again, looking thoughtful. "Give her some of this, then," he said, dropping a small leather flask at their feet. "The last of the sheriff's brandy. It was not his best, I fear, but 'twill do for the need, and 'twas all Greentree's stores had to offer."

He and Tuck left and returned without incident. "This will hurt," said Tuck.

"It can't hurt more," said Cecily.

"Yes, it can," said Little John.

She looked up at him. "Then I hope I faint," she said. "Because if I do not, I will scream."

She fainted. Little John's forehead was wet by the time Tuck was finished, but Tuck's hand was steady and quick, and of this Cecily would take no harm. "How are the rest of us?" Little John asked Will.

"Two more flesh wounds," said Will; "but this is the worst I've seen. You might still bring your trussing gear, Tuck."

"I shall," said the friar, and began to roll the tiny satchel together again. The three of them heard the shout, not too far distant; and Cecily opened her eyes.

"Up that tree," said Little John sharply; Cecily came to her feet as best she could, ignoring his hand. Tuck hung the brandy flask around her neck. "If you feel faint, sip a little—just a little."

Cecily managed a smile. "I shall try not to fall out of my tree from either faintness or drunkenness," she said. And then, as Little John knelt for her foot, she said, "Wait—" They had come some little distance from the second mercenary she had killed, and her dagger had fallen beside him. She went back, picked it up, carefully not looking at him, wiped the blade on the leaves without ever quite looking at it either, and stuffed it back down her boot-top. Then she stepped on Will's and Little John's cupped hands, and was raised over their heads so that she could step directly on a branch and grab with her one good hand. They left her climbing slowly higher and turned toward the noise of renewed fighting.

Will was the last of them to leave the neighbourhood of the little clearing and the earthwork; he would rather have put his sister inside the latter, although he knew the time it would take to rearrange the turf and the brush over the entrance would be dangerously long. He had felt his shoulder-blades prickling with dreadful anticipation while he had only had a little disarranged brush to attend to. But still he hesitated; and then stooped, and picked up the sword belonging to the man whom Cecily had killed—the sword still red with Cecily's blood. It was a little light for him, but the balance of it was good, and the hilt felt strong and familiar in his hand. And he was running out of arrows. They must all be running out of arrows—and he was the only one of them who knew how to handle a sword. He turned to follow Little John and Tuck.

And one of Guy's men almost ran into him. The man's quiver was empty, and his sword was out, and his eyes were wild. He attacked at once; and Will was glad to find that he still remembered what to do with a sword, borrowed as this one was. His attacker was dismayed to find that his opponent not only carried a sword but knew how to wield it;

and during the first exchange of blows Will believed he would win out soon. But a branch caught fiendishly at his elbow, and he had to give way, blocking with the enemy sword that had cut his sister's shoulder open just minutes before, while another enemy sword engaged him, and threw him back another step. Will was tired, and the man facing him had the strength of desperation, for he knew that no ordinary folk could defeat Guy of Gisbourne and so this Robin Hood must be a demon, and his company demons too. Who ever had heard of a common outlaw who knew how to use a sword? This man fought like an aristocrat—and it was Thomas' blade he carried, which told him what had become of Thomas. . . .

Will stepped backward again as the man thrashed forward, for he had not regained his initial balance—and then stepped on an unseen knob of root, thrusting treacherously upward through the soft leaf-mould; and he stumbled. He might have recovered from the stumble, and he hurled his sword clumsily sideways in a gesture his old teacher would have spanked him with the flat of it for, and blocked his attacker—barely—once again. But as he straightened and turned, a green branch, half-broken by the violence of some other contest this day, whipped free of the ivy that had caught it, and slashed Will across the eyes.

He knew then that his time was up, for he could not see where the next sword-stroke might come from; only that it would come and, because he could not defend himself, that it would kill him.

But his sore and weeping eyes instead saw a small explosion from the undergrowth to his left. His opponent saw it too—but too late; and Marjorie's short staff caught the man under the chin. Good stroke! thought Will, amazed. Who's been teaching her? The man crashed into a tree, his eyes rolled up into his head, and he crumpled. Marjorie stood over him, shivering.

"Thank you," said Will.

"I—you are welcome," said Marjorie. "Have I—have I killed him?"

"No," said Will.

"I took the staff from the hoard, you know," said Marjorie. "Eva has shown me—a little—how to use one. I think—I think we must all be here now. Bartlemey and I were the last." She looked around a little wildly. "All here somewhere. There are"—she took a deep breath—"several bodies in the chapel clearing."

"But none of them ours," said Will encouragingly.

Marjorie almost smiled. "No, none of them ours." She glanced down at the man at her feet and then jerked her eyes up again. "Has anyone sent for Sir Richard?"

Will looked surprised. "Sir Richard? No, I should think not."

"Well, someone should," said Marjorie. "You great idiots, by how many do Guy's men outnumber us? I am no good for this work. I thought—as I had already thought no one else would have—that I would go for him." She gave a little grunt that was not quite a chuckle. "I even know the way from here."

Will looked at her with respect. "Godspeed to you, lady."

Marjorie recognised both the surprise and the respect, and said with a sharpness that surprised Will even more, "Try to keep a few of us alive till I get back, will you?"

"I will try," said Will; and he waited several minutes, till she was well away, before he ran his sword through the heart of the man she had prevented from killing him.

Tuck jogged uncomfortably in Little John's long-legged wake. He heard Sweetheart bay, and a lump rose in his throat in the unexpected happiness of knowing that one of his dogs yet lived, and in fear for what might happen at any moment; but he shook his head as he jogged on. There were too many of his two-legged friends to worry about. Why had he come so far anyway? His place was at his chapel. He was no good at fighting—and the noise, ever nearer, told him that it was not yet time for his little satchel and his skills.

One of Guy's men fell at their feet with a dagger in his belly. Simon leaped after to retrieve it; the man screamed. Tuck closed his eyes and tried to remember how to pray. It seemed a very long time since he had said his morning prayers.

"Guy—Robin," panted Simon.

"He is no demon, you fools," snarled Guy's voice, very near at hand. "He merely was not the winner of the archery contest at Nottingham Fair yesterday."

But Guy's remaining men had had their nerve badly shaken by the events of the last half hour, and while they still outnumbered the outlaws—barely—they were inclined to stay huddled behind their leader, with their heads pulled down and their shoulders hunched up. Guy roared at them: "What do you fear? You have swords, have you not? And have the arrows stopped flying? Are their quivers not empty?"

This was true. Despite the skill of Robin's folk, they had wasted or lost many arrows; and, perhaps, considering the terrain and the comparative numbers of the opposing force, it was not shaming that the outlaws had spent their arrows for a tally of only eighteen of Guy's men as result. But the tide of battle, with Guy to lash his men into rallying, was likely yet to swing to his side. Their numbers were almost even, but Guy's men now had the reach; for the outlaws carried only daggers. The mercenaries' swords were not so long as to be hopeless in a wood; nor were the woods here the tangle that the heart of Sherwood, and Greentree, was. For here were the ways that the foresters walked.

But rout was not yet. The outlaws had no swords; but they did carry staves. Robin stood lightly before Guy of Gisbourne, his bow and empty quiver discarded, his staff at half-ready, to flick up against any blow Guy might offer. Robin's longbows had caused the folk who knew of them to think only of the archery of the outlaws; and Little John's pre-eminence with the staff had cast a little in shadow Robin's own expertise—that, and Robin's stubborn insistence on his not being particularly good at any sort of fighting, which, as such insistence will, became its own prophecy. But Robin was smiling. His good staff would turn any sword cut but the most unlucky; and he was already choosing the place on Guy's face where brow and nose met, where he planned to drive the hardened end of his staff.

There was a scrambling at the rear of Guy's uneasy men, and then they spread out in some semblance of their former tight order, and the fighting became general. Dear God, prayed Friar Tuck. Dear God . . . What can I ask for? A bolt of lightning?

Robin gave back as Guy came on. The sword whistled through the air with a whine as deadly as any arrow, but Robin struck it aside. He gave back again, hoping to make Guy unwarily eager for a killing blow. He struck the sword aside a second time; thrice—but at the third meeting Robin caught the blade at slightly the wrong angle and a chip sprang away, its underside the pallor of raw wood. Guy grinned, but Robin caught the next stroke on one of the iron bands round his staff, and the force behind the blow was so great that the sword reeled back with its edge notched.

Robin almost finished it then. He dived forward, presenting the end of his staff as Guy recoiled to regain his grip; but one of Guy's men flung himself sideways, away from Jocelin, whom Robin caught a glimpse of at the edge of his sight; or against his master's enemy; Robin never knew. But the man fell on him, and bore the two of them to the ground. Guy made a sound of pure anger, and almost slashed his own man where he lay—and Jocelin, who had no staff, had time to leap clear. Robin shook himself free and took a descending sweep from Guy's sword with his staff over his head. He took a chance and rapped Guy's knees, but the blow was wrong; Guy staggered but did not fall, and Robin, recovering, had to duck and jump aside, off balance as he was, and if a convenient branch had not spoiled Guy's aim, that would have been the end of it. The other man did not move so quickly, and as Guy re-engaged Robin, Jocelin darted in behind, his dagger in his hand.

Tuck had drawn back behind a tree. There was no safe place as the men milled awkwardly around, striking and ducking away as they could; while the outlaws better knew the terrain, the swords were very fearsome even when their wielders could not get a clear swing. Tuck tried to see if any of Robin's folk were down; and he remembered that Will had said that there were at least two wounds that needed to be attended to. But if the wounded men were secreted anywhere, he did not know where—and he did not know where Will was to ask. He saw Robin fall, and held his breath—and saw him roll upright again; and closed his eyes when Jocelin's dagger descended.

He clung to the tree he stood behind, for his knees shook under him. He could feel the stiff cold length of his own dagger against the skin of his leg, but he would do no good if he drew it now. He could not even remember strapping it on—after he had cut the throat of the man uncovering the earthwork's entrance. He rested his forehead against the bark of his tree and thought of nothing; but something struck his ribs and he staggered aside, biting back a cry. "Look out, man!" said Will, who had struck him with the hilt of his sword. "Do you think you are invisible? Do you trust that Guy's men will not strike you where you stand because you are a friar?" And then he moved quickly around another tree after the silvery twinkle of another sword gleaming in the green shadows, and Tuck lost him but for the noise of his passage.

Again he felt like a bit of flotsam in a storm, for the sound of battle went on all around him and while his heart beat fast in fear, he could see nothing to run from—or toward. He thought, this is just as it was half an hour ago—has it been half an hour, a day, a year?—perhaps this hour never happened, or has happened many times; perhaps we must go on killing Guy's men, and they us, for all eternity. . . . He thought of Marian, and wondered what she might be guessing in her darkness; he wondered about Cecily, clinging to her tree; and he wondered about his dogs.

The noise around him was moving a little away—moving back toward the clearing by the earthwork and the chapel. He hesitantly let go of his tree, for he had paid little attention to Will after all, and had only crept a little way round the tree he was clutching; and moved to follow. There was a thrashing, low down to one side, and he looked fearfully there and saw one of Guy's men, his breath bubbling pink; Tuck turned away, for there was nothing he could do for him. Even had it been one of Robin's folk he could have done nothing; he knew what he saw in the man's face, and in the spittle upon his lips.

He almost tripped over Simon. He lay motionless, and Tuck knelt despairingly beside him, guessing what he would find. Simon's eyes opened slowly, and his breath whistled between his teeth. "My—staff," he said, and moved one red arm. Tuck thought he wanted to hold it, and groped a little way among the leaves to find it, but when he laid it against Simon's fingers, the fingers curled away. "No," he said. "You—take it." He smiled a ghostly smile. "If you hit someone on the back of the head with it, he will fall down, even if he carries a sword." His voice was so faint Tuck had to lean close to hear him; when his eyes closed again, Tuck saw that the whole of his tunic was stained red, and the leaves upon which he lay.

Tuck picked up the staff and went on.

Sibyl was barely a sword's-length away when Eva fell, but she came too late; she killed the man who had killed her friend, and then she wept, heedless of who might find her still living, with Eva in her arms. But Fate is a curious thing, and no one did find her, though she heard the crashing of other fighting near the place where she knelt, and wiped her friend's damp face with her own dirty sleeve. It took Eva some little time to die, and she wandered in her mind. Sibyl said, "Hush; you will be stronger soon, and I have told Robin to send others for our spell of duty, that you might rest and I might take care of you."

"Thank you," murmured Eva; "It is good to have you here." And Sibyl stayed till the end.

Fate also set Alan-a-dale and Much to fighting side by side. Alan knew the rudiments of sword-play, for he had been a lord's son before he was a bard; and when the last of Robin's outlaws had arrived at the chapel and found the bodies of three dead mercenaries and nothing else, Alan had paused long enough to pick up one of the swords, and thrust it through his belt. Harald and Gilbert ran on ahead, notching their arrows, toward the confused sounds of battle, while Alan was making sure that the blade was not going to cut into his own side by accident, and biting his lip. He knew nothing of battle but the many verses of many ballads, all composed after it was over; he had learnt to shoot, because Robin insisted, but he had rarely shot anything for the cooking fire; the bow over his shoulder felt almost as strange as the sword. He had never struck a man in anger in his life; the one time he had come close, Robin had stopped him, and he knew that Robin had been right, and that he would have died. . . . He thought of Marjorie, back at Greentree with Bartlemey, whose wound was still sore, and who could not walk far or quickly; and he hoped that he was going to see her again soon.

He ran too, holding the blade a little to one side; and ran almost into Much, who had just felled a mercenary with his staff. "I'm glad to see you," panted Much, and there was no sarcasm in his voice; but there was no time for conversation, for two more of Guy's men were upon them, and Much took a sword through his thigh. He fell with a gasp, but his dagger was in his hand, and then in the other man's belly, before that other man could make the final stroke. Alan had pulled his stolen sword free just in time to slice into the second man's shoulder. The man dropped his sword and clutched his shoulder, screaming, falling to his knees, and Alan stared, appalled. *"God,"* said Much, hauling himself upright on one leg and against a tree. He snatched the sword out of Alan's nerveless hand and finished the wounded man.

Alan, taking a deep, shuddering breath, turned to Much, who was going white, and started to say, "Your leg—here, we must tie it up for you at once"—when a third mercenary came upon them. He struck first at Alan, who could not reach an arrow in time; Alan ducked and, without thinking, threw up an arm to protect his face—and felt the blade sink into the palm of his hand. Much, faint and wavering on his one good leg, and with no idea what to do with a sword, took a wild swipe at the man, and managed to catch him under the arm, where his chain-shirt did not protect him; and fell down upon his enemy as he drove the point home.

Tuck, holding Simon's staff awkwardly, went on, back toward the chapel, following the sounds of cries and blows. In a little while he heard two muffled cries: one that sounded like victory and one that sounded like loss. He looked around a shoulder of rock and saw one of Guy's men raising his sword for the final stroke as Rafe dropped the two bits of his broken staff. But the man let his delivery linger a little too long, to enjoy his success; and Tuck brought the smooth knob end of Simon's staff down upon the tender place where the neck's tendons cradle the skull; and he saw the bright blood flower around the staff like petals around a stem, in the moment before the man fell. He and Rafe stared at one another a moment, and Rafe croaked, "Thank you."

"Here—you'll have more use for this," said Tuck, and thrust the sticky knob at Rafe.

"You're doing all right," Rafe said, with a bleak smile that reminded Tuck of Simon's, but he took it anyway. He shifted it from hand to hand for a moment for the feel, and said, not looking at Tuck, "Whose was it?"

"Simon's," said Tuck. Rafe paused a moment longer, and then turned and left Tuck standing.

Tuck averted his eyes from the body of the man he had killed, and reluctantly he followed the way Rafe had gone.

He arrived at the edge of the chapel clearing in time to see the few outlaws that were left on their feet straggling out of the trees to a halt, trying to look as if they had any strength left. Guy and Robin were still fighting, but their steps dragged, and their blows had the stiff, mechanical pace of the practise field. Tuck looked around; four outlaws he saw, but neither Will nor Little John; and he saw none of Guy's men.

And at that moment Robin was a little too clumsy in turning away one of Guy's lagging blows, or perhaps the sword found a weak place at last—the place, perhaps, where it had gouged out a chip earlier—for Robin's staff burst apart with a noise like the end of the world.

Robin made to duck and tumble away, but Guy was too quick for him: victory gave him a last burst of strength, and he seemed to tower over the slight young man he had been hired to kill. The sword drew a line of blood along Robin's jaw till it came neatly to its resting place in the hollow of his throat. Robin straightened up slowly.

"If any one of you takes a step closer," said Guy clearly, "your master dies instantly."

Silence fell. The blood drummed in Tuck's ears; but he was sure that no birds sang anywhere in these trees, and he would not have been surprised if he had found that the stream had stopped running. None of Robin's folk breathed.

"Kneel," said Guy. Robin did not move, and Guy pressed the point of his sword a little harder into Robin's throat. Tuck could see him open his mouth a little to try to get his breath. *"Kneel,"* said Guy, but Robin only rocked back on his heels.

And then, like the bolt of lightning Tuck had not been able to pray for, a dagger came flashing through the leaves—flashing *down*, where Guy could not see it, standing as he stood with his back to one particular tree at the edge of the clearing.

It was not a very good throw. Cecily had had a grisly and painful and terrifying time in the last few seconds, trying to get herself into any position that would give her any shot at all; and then her whole body throbbed so miserably that it was hard to put even her good shoulder into the throw. But throw she did.

And it did what it needed to do. The blade struck Guy's upper arm, below the mail, as he stood with that arm stretched out, and his sword-point pressed into Robin's throat. The force of the blow knocked the point aside, gouging Robin's flesh a little, and Guy was more tired than he knew, for he *dropped* his sword, which he should not have done for so little a thing as a minor flesh wound. He looked, amazed, at the dagger, as it fell to his feet, red with his blood—it was the first blood he had shed this day.

He had only a moment for such thoughts, for Robin's hand slapped up his dagger from its sheath; and Guy of Gisbourne fell with Robin's dagger buried in the place Robin had felt Guy's sword. That little wound leaked blood down Robin's chest to mix with the other dirt and cuts, for it was not the first blood he had lost; and he stood a moment, head bowed and legs braced, staring at his fallen enemy; and he realised his hands were trembling.

CHAPTER TWENTY-TWO

I t was mostly over for the outlaws then; and Tuck's work began. Simon was dead by the time they found him, as was Eva; as were Jocelin and Harald and Humphrey. Alan, despite his own wound, had managed to staunch Much's; Much would live, but he would never walk straight on both legs again. Alan might have lost a finger; it was too early to say. It had been only a glancing blow, or he might have lost the whole hand; as it was, there were tendons severed. Alan was perfectly quiet as Tuck dressed it, but when the friar stole a look at the boy's face, he was crying, the tears flowing silently down the pale cheeks. Tuck's own face puckered in sympathy, but Alan smiled a very old smile and patted Tuck's nearer hand with his one good one. "If I am to lose the use of a few fingers," he said in a steady voice, "why, I must teach Marjorie to play my lute."

The outlaws who were still hale enough were set to tearing cloth to make bandages—no one was willing to use any bits of their fallen enemies' clothing, which put a strain on Tuck's meager resources—and to digging up the friar's cache of food, and throwing anything that could be made more of by adding water into a pot and making soup. Little John, who came back only shortly before Robin decided to send someone to look for the last two unaccounted-for members of the bloody and bedraggled band, appeared carrying an unconscious Will Scarlet over his shoulder. Tuck, holding his breath, felt the lump under Will's ear and decided the skull was not broken. He turned then to the ugly slash above Will's left knee.

Little John paused long enough to tie something around the calf of one leg and one forearm—pushing Tuck's hands aside as he tried to look at the wounds first—and limped out again. Robin, who had been to see Marian, found him searching in the lengthening shadows of late afternoon for arrows. They collected half a dozen still usable ones of their own; they rejected Guy's shorter, clumsy shafts, of which there were a great many more. When they returned to the very rough camp that was spreading out in front of Tuck's cottage, they brought with them two squirrels and two rabbits, and were cheered like heroes.

By then Robin was limping too, and claimed to be surprised when Tuck discovered that one foot had been half cut off. Robin shook his head. "I don't remember it," he said.

"You'll know as much about it as you'll want to by tomorrow morning," said Tuck.

Of those who lived, Marian's was still the worst case, and Tuck had cause to be grateful for this gruesome favour. He used up his small store of candles that night, tending to the wounds of the ten outlaws that were left, while the sweat ran down his face and his eyes blurred with exhaustion. He had no sleep that night, but he did not think this was unfair, for he was the only one of them all who had lost no blood during the past day; and by morning all his patients were at least no worse. A few—Marian among them—looked to be healing.

Tuck was nonetheless luckier than many, for no one got much sleep the night after the battle. Cecily could neither lie still nor move; her shoulder pained her incessantly, and the earthwork's small store of whisky and brandy, which most of the outlaws were happy to apply to, did her no service. She had never tasted the contents of the flask her brother had hung round her neck that day; she had told herself that she would in just another moment, when she could not bear it any longer. Then when that moment passed, she said the same to herself again, and so more moments passed; and then she had seen Guy and Robin in the clearing in front of her tree; and then she had made her way down out of that tree, with Rafe's help, and had given her flask to Tuck. She'd finally tried a sip or two—which did burn distractingly and not unpleasantly on the way down—but then it began to make her queasy.

She drifted in and out of consciousness; her dreams were as dreadful as wakefulness, for she dreamed that someone was pulling her head back to cut her throat, only the pain of it somehow always concentrated in her shoulder. Or she dreamed that her staff was broken and a man with a sword was about to—she awoke with a gasp and a jerk, and the jerk set fire to her shoulder all over again. As the night wore on, she grew more and more tired. . . . She wondered how Marian bore it so patiently.

237

"Her time will come later," said a familiar voice; "it is not so bad for her now because she is too ill to notice so much."

Cecily's eyes came open. Little John was sitting beside her, one of his knees drawn up and one arm around it; his other leg looked as long as a young tree, and there was a rusty-brown bandage, rough as bark, tied below the knee. She tried to sit up, and he slid his unbandaged arm under her with a dexterity that suggested he had dealt with other people's injuries before: "Aye," he said, "you do not suppose we outlaws win all our victories easily, do you?"

She smiled a little, and he picked up a cup that had stood hidden beside him. "I did not want to waken you if there was no need," he said. "But this may help your sleep a little, if only a little, and it will ease the heat of the wound." She drank obediently, though it had a bitter taste. "What is it?"

Little John made the low rumble that passed for his chuckle. "An old farmwife's remedy. My father used it on sore oxen. . . . Our village thought him a great man for the remedy, for we had no oxen to spare."

Cecily said, looking down into the cup, "It smells like what Tuck has been giving Marian."

"It is," said Little John. "It is also good for sore oxen. Tuck says he learnt it from a brother of his order who had learnt it from an alchemist in Constantinople, and I say that the alchemist's mother was from Nottinghamshire."

This did not roil in her stomach as the whisky did, and while it was not exactly true that the pain in her shoulder lessened, it was true that the pain around it lessened, and she could feel the tips of her fingers again, and most of that side of her body felt less hot. "Is your leg very bad?" she said drowsily.

"No," said Little John. "But Tuck seems to think it won't stop bleeding unless I sit down for a while, so I'm sitting down. I'm not wholly sorry for the excuse; I was forgetting the way of sitting down, these last days. Is the draught helping?"

"Yes." She sagged a little more against him, almost contented to have her shoulder hurt, if he would stay by her. The pain still got in the way enough that it was hard to think about anything, but there was a comfort in the sound of his breathing as the throbbing in her ears began to ebb. . . .

She fell asleep, leaning on his chest, and he edged her a little off a particularly painful bruise, leaned his head back against the tree he had propped them up against, and closed his own eyes.

Rafe and Sibyl were the nearest to unhurt of any of the outlaws, and Tuck could not afford to let them rest, although he was pretty sure each of them fell asleep standing up as soon as either stopped moving. Robin and Little John helped as they could, hauling water, chopping wood, even changing poultices; but Little John was limping too hard to disguise and Tuck told him to get off his leg and, preferably, to get some sleep. And shortly after that Tuck put his hand by accident on a bloody axe-handle and snatched at Robin, who had turned indifferently away, pulling back his sleeve and exposing a long slash on his upper arm.

"I don't remember this earlier," said Tuck.

"No?" said Robin in a neutral voice, and Tuck was too busy to pursue it, but merely bound it up and told him it was time for him, too, to try to sleep. Robin never had to tell anyone of his meeting, weaponless and with an armful of dead branches to break up for firewood, with one of Guy's men. The next day, when the burying began, no one questioned the body of another mercenary.

Robin went often to watch for a minute or two by Marian's pallet. There were several folk in the little half-cavern now, but every time he appeared in the doorway her pale face turned toward him. Sometimes he went in to her; sometimes he did not.

"I plan to go on living a while yet," she whispered once. "You might as well attend to other matters."

Dawn came. Tuck and Rafe and Sibyl and Robin fell down where they were and slept.

It was not surprising that they heard nothing.

Something flopped heavily onto Tuck's legs some time in the early morning. Tuck did not leap awake as perhaps he should have; he groaned and with deepest reluctance began to sit up, and to grope down toward the obstruction, whatever it was. It was when his fingers touched fur that his eyes snapped open. Brown-eyes lay there, profoundly asleep. The dog, in his turn, groaned in protest as the legs were withdrawn, but when Tuck buried his face in the filthy ruff the tail thumped the ground once or twice, and a very long tongue curled out to loop around an available wrist. The two of them fell asleep again immediately, Tuck snoring gently into Brown-eyes' nearer ear.

Robin had collapsed beside Marian; she shifted toward the edge of her mattress and trailed a hand over his face; he seized it in one of his and tucked it under his chin. The sound of approaching hoofbeats disturbed neither of them.

Little John and Cecily were nearest the sound, and their guardian instincts shoved them awake, but too late.

Sir Richard flung himself off his horse and shouted despairingly into the air of the clearing, empty but for the bodies of several mercenaries and the five outlaws whose bodies their friends had retrieved. "Are any of you alive?"

Robin came to the entrance of the earthwork on his hands and knees before he found the strength to rise to his feet and stagger toward daylight. Brown-eyes gave one disconsolate howl; Tuck sat up and wondered if he could get up any farther. Little John, a brown and green lump in the undergrowth to Sir Richard's eyes, differentiated himself from his surroundings as he hauled himself up a tree; Cecily emerged from the undergrowth by hauling herself up Little John.

Sir Richard and a few of his men stood, stiff with shock, looking around them. Guy's men and Guy himself lay where they had fallen, and the turf was hacked and bloodied in many places. Sir Richard saw Tuck first; the friar was the only one who had not automatically withdrawn a little way into the trees to sleep. Tuck blinked at the man before him, recognising a friend without being able to remember another thing about him. "What of Robin Hood?" said Sir Richard, his voice sharp with fear. "I heard the news only this morning—Alan-a-dale's *wife* brought it to me before dawn, her feet and face bleeding from travelling in haste at night. Why did you not send to me?"

Robin's voice seemed to echo from the ground by Sir Richard's feet, and it was not only the horse that shied. "We were somewhat pressed for time, and for the use of every available pair of arms."

"Good God, man," said Sir Richard, peering down as Robin clambered out and stood before him, swaying—Sir Richard reached out and grabbed him by the shoulders. Robin winced, but Sir Richard did not drop his hands. "Did you even consider sending to me?" he said fiercely.

"No," said Robin, after a pause. "Not, perhaps, for the reason you think, however."

Sir Richard grunted, and turned to his men. "Don't stand there gaping. You brought shovels, did you not? There are graves to be dug."

"You came prepared," said Robin.

"For almost everything," said Sir Richard; his bow and his sword were slung across the front of his saddle. "Guy of Gisbourne! I did not think to see you standing before me again."

Robin said, "It was a near thing enough."

Rafe said, "Too near."

Robin said, "For all of us." He beckoned to Cecily. "Here is my saviour," he said; "or Guy would have had me after all." But Cecily shook her head and remained where she was. Sir Richard stared, and his brows snapped together, and he stalked over to her as he might toward a villein who had displeased him. Cecily could not square her shoulders, but she raised her head and glowered Cecil's old familiar glower.

"Cecily of Norwell!" said Sir Richard. "You did no honourable thing running from your father's house."

"My father did no honourable thing in forcing me to accept a life I found hideous," flared Cecily, though Sir Richard's face swam through her vision like a trout in a sunlit stream.

"They all think you are dead," said Sir Richard, no whit softened.

"I *am* dead," said Cecily; "they killed me. I am now Cecil of Nowhere, one of Robin Hood's outlaws."

"I know your father," said Sir Richard.

Will said mildly, "You know Marian's father too, as you may recall; I don't see there's more than a farthing's worth between 'em. Or do you wish to call me down too? Again?"

Sir Richard dragged his eyes from Cecily's haggard face and fixed them on Will. "This does not go down well after our last meeting, does it?" A reluctant smile began to pull at the corners of his mouth. "And I stand here before the folk I wish to succour, arguing propriety.

"Forgive me," he said to Cecily, and he bowed to her; and she inclined her upper body a fraction of an inch or so in return, as her shoulder would let her. "And *now*," said Sir Richard forcefully, "you will all come back with me to Mapperley, where I can supply you with food and water and clothing—and beds—and even, perhaps, safety, at least for some little time to come." He folded his arms and looked at Robin.

Robin smiled. "I am too tired to argue, my good friend, so I will merely thank you. I cannot think of anything to do with us, and food and water and clothing—and particularly beds—sound . . . miraculous. Later we can argue about the safety."

"You are a sorry lot of ruffians," said Sir Richard then; and they were, tattered and blood-stained, and not a one of them stood unsupported. The humour left his face and he added, "Is this all there is left of you?"

Robin glanced around. "Nearly. Most have been sent away in the last weeks, as I have expected . . . something. Not, I admit, something like Guy of Gisbourne, but I am glad my imagination failed me in this case."

Sir Richard said softly, "For the rescue you made me the sheriff has sworn for your blood, whatever price it may cost him. You had done better to stay in Sherwood and go on rolling fat bishops off their ponies."

Robin shrugged—gently; he possessed no bone or muscle that did not ache. "I am not sorry for the choice of adventure that gave you back what is yours; I do not know that I will even let you claim that battle as decisive. We would have rolled the wrong bishop sooner or later." He looked around at his filthy, hollow-eyed companions, and added as if speaking to himself: "But the battle we have now won did perhaps lose us the war. I think that we cannot go back to Greentree, and be as we were." He shrugged again—and winced; and brought his eyes back to Sir Richard. "And perhaps it is only the bruises which speak this way."

There was a shout from across the little meadow: two of Sir Richard's men were about to lift the body that in life had been Guy of Gisbourne. Sir Richard recognised the sword that one of the men brought him, and he looked again at Robin; the tale of Guy of Gisbourne was well-known most of the length and breadth of England, and the sword made the tale of Robin's exhausted band suddenly real. Sir Richard took the sword and held it; he seemed also to be holding his breath.

"It was not so noble a fight as one might wish for the minstrel's version," said Robin.

"That depends on your point of view," said Will. "I do suspect that 'Cecily' will prove an awkward rhyme."

Robin did not answer; it was his own passion to face the man that had hurt Marian which he did not like to remember; but his private thoughts need not appear in the minstrel's version either.

Three more men rode into the meadow; the outlaws looked wearily toward them, but they were only more of Sir Richard's men. "Thank fate," murmured Robin to no one in particular; "we could not get out of our own way just now."

One said something to his master in a low voice. "We must get you out of here," said Sir Richard. "Someone has already brought the tale of your day's work to the sheriff; I had hoped this news might travel less fast. Although I expected it to travel less fast because I did not expect so conclusive an ending so quickly. The sheriff may not yet know that his champion is slain, but he knows that his followers have but put to something that looks much like rout—and this chapel, I fear, will be one of the first places he will look. Friar Tuck, I will ask you to come with us; I would not trust the sheriff's temper now even to a priest and friar."

"I would not either," said Tuck sadly. "I thank you for the offer, and I am sorry to say that I accept."

"Someone got away," said Much. "I am sorry for that; it would have been better for us and for England—and for our minstrel—if we had made an end of them all."

I wonder who it was? thought Cecily. And I wonder how he explained having got away?

"How many of you can ride?" said Sir Richard. Several grimaced, but none spoke; many eyes, however, went to the dark half-door that led beneath the knoll behind the chapel.

"Marian," said Robin.

"Marian?" said Sir Richard quickly. "Is she here?"

Robin turned toward the dark opening. "Have you not heard that Guy of Gisbourne thought he had killed Robin Hood at the Nottingham Fair, two days past?"

"Killed?" said Sir Richard.

"She lives," said Robin. "But—"

Tuck, leaning on his dog, said, "I do not like moving her."

"Tell me," said Sir Richard to Robin.

Robin answered, "It is Little John and Cecily's story."

After a pause Little John began reluctantly: "We went to the fair to listen to what the people met there would be saying about the outlaws of Sherwood. And so we were at hand when the winner of the archery contest was struck by Guy of Gisbourne's sword; Guy called out the name of Robin Hood, and the folk around heard. We knew it would not be he, but . . ."

"We brought away whoever it was," said Cecily. "It was Marian."

Sir Richard said, "If the Lionheart had an army made of folk like the outlaws of Sherwood, Saladin would not stand a chance." He spoke in a low voice to the man who had brought him the latest news; the man remounted and left at a canter, ducking over the neck of his horse as it entered the trees. "We will have a litter and horses for the rest of you as soon as we may," Sir Richard said aloud; "and, meanwhile, there are other tasks to attend to."

Simon and Eva and Harald and Humphrey and Jocelin were buried in individual graves; Beauty and Sweetheart were buried together. The bodies of Guy and his men were heaved into one great common hole —dug by the fresh muscles of Sir Richard's folk—and dirt smoothed over them as quickly as the earth could be shifted. Most of the outlaws made to help them, but they moved slowly and stopped often.

As the day wore on Sir Richard grew more anxious; his men caught his impatience and began to trip over each other and curse. Robin said mildly, "You might consider leaving us to our fate; if it overcomes us quickly enough we shall be too tired to notice or care."

Sir Richard snorted. "I might almost be tempted, but I do not think our sheriff is in the mood to let you off with any swift fate. And there is Marian."

When the litter finally arrived, it was a good one, hung on long poles between two horses, and piled with cushions and a feather mattress to ease the jolting as much as possible. It was a slow journey nonetheless. Most of the outlaws were unable to ride faster than a walking pace— most of them would have been unable to ride faster than a walking pace even were they unhurt—nor would Robin have let any of his folk ride on when Marian might need protection from whatever pursued them. And all ears strained toward the possibility of that pursuit.

Several of the outlaws doubled up; the friar, who had the use of all his limbs (not, as he thought to himself, that he knew how to bestow them usefully on horseback), had Much pillion behind him. Both Will and Little John rode with their injured legs across the saddle before them to ease the pressure; Cecily sat sideways behind Little John and gritted her teeth. She could feel every joint of the horse's hind legs and quarters bending and unbending under her; at least it was a broad enough back that she was in little danger of sliding off inadvertently. Little John kept one hand on the reins and the other one over Cecily's hand at his belt.

There was a mournful half-howl, half-whimper from behind them after they had gone a little on their way. Robin, who had no one up with him, looked around. Friar Tuck's face had taken on a look of curious fixity.

"He is hurt in two legs," said Tuck. "I did fear he might not be able to keep pace."

"Mm," said Robin, and turned his horse back. It did not wish to turn back while all its fellows were headed home, and Robin, an inexperienced horseman, had little patience for argument. He dismounted and handed the reins to Tuck. "You mustn't risk—" began the friar, but Robin shook his head.

"Hold this unlovable animal," he said, and plunged back along the trail. Tuck stopped and looked after him. "We could follow him," said Much. Tuck's horse was more cooperative, or perhaps it was because there were two of them now to keep each other company. They met Robin with a dismal and sheepish-looking dog in his arms: indeed there was so much dog it was hard to see much of Robin, who was, as Tuck noticed unhappily, limping badly. "Your foot—" he began.

"I'm glad to see you," Robin panted; "yes, I had rather forgotten about my foot." He thrust his other foot firmly into a stirrup for a brace and heaved the dog across his saddle. Brown-eyes, confused, began to struggle, but Tuck reached out and took hold of the dog's ruff and pulled, and Brown-eyes decided that if his master was a part of this peculiar situation it must be all right, and permitted himself to be pulled. But the horses decided they did not like whatever was going on and began to sidle apart; Much reached out to grab Robin's horse's bridle, almost lost his seat, wrenched his wounded leg, and made a noise not unlike the one that had sent Robin in search of the dog in the first place. But Brown-eyes was stowed at last. Robin gingerly climbed up behind him, and he only looked up with the damp soulful gaze that had given him his name and thumped his tail once across the horse's shoulder. The horse tried to shy but concluded that it wasn't worth it; the path was too narrow and the trees too close. "I wasn't at all certain he was going to let me pick him up," said Robin, as they awkwardly turned again and set off in pursuit of the others; "which, after all that, would have been embarrassing."

"Thank you," said Tuck.

There were men and women herding sheep and cattle and chickens and geese (and children) through the gate into the outer bailey when they arrived; the riders had already noticed that—once again, thought Robin—the village where Sir Richard's villeins lived was curiously empty. The horses were trying to be brisk as they saw home and hay looming nearer, and several of the outlaws gave up all pretence of using the reins, clung to the manes, and wished it to be over quickly.

The porter at the first gate said: "The sheriff's been seen riding with a good many men toward Sherwood; and he looks angrier than a storm-cloud."

"Already?" said Sir Richard. "He travels almost as fast as fear."

"Or as outlaws," said Will.

"Or as friends," said Friar Tuck.

"Our luck," said Robin, "is both much better and much worse than we could have hoped."

"Let us concentrate on the better," said Sir Richard.

"You *are* the better," said Robin, "and we thank you again."

"I recall, not long since, that you disliked being thanked overmuch," said Sir Richard. "I begin to understand the feeling. And I think you might save a little of your gratitude for the young woman who brought the news to your good luck that he was needed."

There was relief on all the faces in Sir Richard's party—and on the faces of those that saw them enter—as the gate was lowered slowly closed behind the last horse, a few laggard chickens squawking out of the way of the hoofs. "Do you think it will come to a siege, then?" said Sir Richard to his seneschal, who appeared at the stable doors as he dismounted. There was nothing but a wistful curiosity in Sir Richard's voice; as if he had asked if it might rain tomorrow when he had thought of going hawking.

The seneschal said, "None of us has much kindness for the sheriff, my lord; nor, I think, he for us. It is well to be prepared."

Sir Richard said dryly, "It *is* well to be prepared. How prepared are we?"

"All our people are accounted for—and we can feed my lord's guests for a goodly span of days," said the seneschal.

"Goodly span enough to send to the king and receive his reply, I wonder?" murmured Sir Richard. "If we knew for sure where to send."

Robin, who had helped his saddle-mate to earth again and then gratefully given the horse over to a stable-boy, heard this. "The *king*?" he said. "Do you buy the tale that the Lionheart loves an adventure so much that he would overlook the number of the king's deer who have found their way into our cooking pots? I do not."

"I wonder," said Sir Richard again. "The Lionheart has some sympathy for boldness—did he not leave England because she was too tame for him, and seek adventure elsewhere?—and little sympathy, I think, for greed. It occurs to me that he might be more sympathetic still to tales of oppression after two years in a German dungeon. It might be worth a try."

"I have a better idea," said Robin. "If our good luck can spare us a sennight to lick our wounds, we will leave him again and look for another forest to get lost in. You once suggested that it would do me good to be thrown in your dungeon to cool off. Perhaps this is the time for it; me and those with me too recognisable. And then you can raise your gate politely and turn a smooth face to the sheriff, while we hide under the straw."

"I would like to ask for clean straw," said Will. "And I would prefer a bolt-hole reasonably free of rats, although that, in a dungeon, is perhaps too much to ask."

"The gate stays closed," said Sir Richard, "and there is no corner of Mapperley's dungeons not extremely well provided with vermin, so I think you will all be happier staying above ground."

"But—" began Robin.

"We can discuss to whom and where to send messages further," interrupted Sir Richard. "But over food, perhaps? I am ready to eat these cobblestones."

CHAPTER TWENTY-THREE

Over the next few days the outlaws ate and rested and began to grow strong again, and to take some interest in their changed surroundings. Marian was out of danger—and as Little John had predicted to Cecily, her convalescence quickly began to chafe at her spirit. Marian and Cecily and Sibyl had been given an apartment together. Sibyl had little to say; she ate when food was placed before her, and spoke when she was addressed directly—when she noticed.

"You have a talent for playing the crabby invalid," said Cecily to Marian, after a day or two. "Why don't you demand that you teach her chess, as a way of passing your time?"

"Thank you," said Marian; "I appreciate that you have our best interests at heart."

Marjorie had come to them on the first day, after greeting her husband, demanding instructions for his care from Friar Tuck, and withstanding being thanked by Robin and Sir Richard, which she did not enjoy. Marian was settled on a low couch in the outer room while several house servants set up extra beds with feather mattresses enough for royalty in the inner chamber, which would serve as the sleeping room. Cecily sat by Marian, while Sibyl stared out the window. Marjorie's eyes rested thoughtfully on Cecily, and she looked up.

"Oh," she said. "I'm Cecily. I'm Will's little sister."

"Yes?" said Marjorie. "That has come out at last, has it?"

"I rather thought you knew," said Cecily.

"I did not *know*," said Marjorie. "But I did wonder—and your eyes did beg me, when they saw me wondering, to give nothing away, so that I had to assume there was something to give."

"Thank you," said Cecily.

Marjorie looked surprised. "Of course," she said, and turned to Marian. "I have had my first lesson in poultices from Friar Tuck," she said. "I already know a good deal about bandages and about pillows, and about broth with wine in it to make you strong again. Can I do anything for you?"

Marian smiled weakly; the journey from Sherwood had felt like centuries to her. "How are you at being snapped at, and having the pillows you've just readjusted thrown at your head?"

"I can learn that too," said Marjorie.

But as those that remained began to recover, their missing comrades loomed larger in their thoughts. Without Jocelin's skills the Sherwood outlaws might never have slept dry; they might all have perished during their first winter, for all that the weather had been comparatively mild. Gilbert had known Simon all his life; their fathers had been friends; the strips they tilled in their lord's fields lay adjacent; they had once courted the same woman, who had married a third man. Humphrey had been teaching Bartlemey to make arrows; Greentree invalids often learnt fletching to keep them quiet—and make them useful—while their injuries healed.

There was a grisly little circle in Robin's mind where his thoughts walked. He should have sent Harald away with the others. He had known—hadn't he?—that Harald had not the woodscraft he needed. Robin had permitted himself to be sentimental because Harald had wished to stay, because Harald had been among the first to come to Sherwood. And it was pleasant and convenient to have someone who could tan skins and work leather at Greentree. He should have sent Harald on; he had not, and it had cost Harald his life.

And Alan's hand. Alan was a musician, and by Robin's carelessness he had lost his music; better that Robin had sent them on with no more than the coins that his other folk were given, with no prospects at all. And yet how could he balance Alan's hand with Much's life—and Marjorie's message to Sir Richard?

"I wish there was a way to tell Red where Simon—where we all went," said Cecily.

Sibyl looked up from the chessboard. "Red will be all right. Foxes are scavengers anyway, and some handsome vixen will find him and teach him about robbing nests and farm-yards."

Marjorie spoke little of Alan. "It is healing perfectly," she said once; "the wound is almost closed. But he cannot move his fingers." Alan said nothing at all, and his lute lay hidden in the deserted Greentree.

Everyone's temper, from sorrow and worry and the itch of healing, grew a little sharp as the days passed. Robin was pacing (jerkily, because of his foot) by the second day; his whole body felt as sore as his slashed foot and arm. "Kindly captivity is still captivity," he said to Little John on the sixth day.

Little John had his leg propped up in the crenellation he leaned on as Robin paced the wall walk, staring toward Nottingham, invisible beyond the spur of Sherwood at the edge of Sir Richard's grazing lands. Little John grunted in agreement; but his own restlessness had more to do with not yet being able to pace—and to the strange shyness that had come over his sometime protégé. Almost he could believe she had never said those words outside the earthwork. . . . He pulled his thoughts away from that unsatisfactory subject for the dozenth time that afternoon, concentrating on the trees and fields before him, idly rubbing at his leg, which was still hot and sore.

"He may not even come here," snarled Robin.

"He'll come," said Little John.

"Then why has he not come before?" said Robin, unreasonably. "The longer Sir Richard's gate stays closed—and I cannot believe this has gone unnoticed—the more obvious it is that he is hiding something. Or someone. We should not be placing him in this danger. . . ."

"That depends on what you want from the confrontation with our friend the sheriff," said Much, who appeared through the doorway, red-faced from climbing stairs on crutches. "If you had in mind that any of us should survive it longer than the gaoling while they built the gallows to hold us all, then Sir Richard's intervention in this matter may well be called timely."

Robin was silent.

"Even Sherwood isn't big enough any more," said Much.

"I fear me that England is no longer big enough," Robin burst out again; "and we have not even had any news."

"That also depends on what you mean by news," said Much. "There has not been time for an answer to any of our messages; they cannot be delivered in a straightforward manner, you know. And we have heard that the sheriff appears to be cutting down half of Sherwood with his sword; his temper has not cooled."

"It's really only me that puts us all in danger," said Robin.

"There's a price on my head too," said Little John mildly. "And I am content to accept the kindly captivity, to keep price and head separate for a little longer."

"You are right, of course," said Robin; "and it is a curious sort of bragging I indulge in. But the sheriff—while he would no doubt like to hang all of you, it is me whom he lies awake nights strangling in his hopes. He would be satisfied with me: with the man whose name is cried in the streets of Nottingham as leader of the Sherwood outlaws."

"See? Your name *should* have been Sheriff's-bane," said Much.

"The rest of you could go away—can go away as soon as we hear something from our other friends. Me he will track . . ."

"Are you on that old tune again?" said Will. "Quite an invalids' gathering, aren't we? Why is it those of us with wounded legs keep looking for stairs to climb?"

"It's the challenge," said Much. "Like that of knocking sense into the thick head of our leader."

"One of the things you insist on leaving out of your calculations is that our absurd and uncomfortable life under Sherwood's wide branches suits some of us," said Will. "Say, Little John, if someone gave you a herd of cattle, would you go back to farming?"

"No," said Little John immediately. "They'd get the pox, and I'd not have rent on quarter day, and soon I'd be an outlaw."

"Nothing would drive me back to my father's hall," said Will; "not even a full pardon. Indeed, particularly not a full pardon, because then I'd be treated as the lord's son again, and if you knew how boring it is, dressing up in frills and a clean shirt every day and praying that a guest will arrive some time soon with a few new jokes. . . . You can even get bored with hunting and hawking occasionally, without the savour of need. I know why the Lionheart went off to Palestine; he couldn't stand it either. All those state dinners. I'd've followed him if I hadn't heard about Sherwood. I wanted to stay in England."

"But you can go home again from Palestine," said Robin. "What *you* are leaving out of your calculations is that we are not going to be able to wait out the sheriff's wrath and go quietly back to our old ways in Sherwood. We have come to our end."

There was a little silence, and then Will said, "You can go home from Palestine if the Saracens don't get you first, or the climate. And then it starts all over again—hunting and hawking and minstrels and feast days —and boredom. Particularly boredom."

"We need a third choice," said Robin. "And my eyes are blind to it."

Much said thoughtfully, "I had never gone hungry till I lived as an outlaw; but I never had a clean shirt every day either. That part sounds very nice. I do not think I would grow bored with it very soon."

"Have Sir Richard's servants been neglecting you?" said Will. "Tell him at once, and their tanned hides will be your new suit."

"No; this is a new suit. You never saw this colour in Sherwood, did you?" said Much, holding out one blue arm. "It is the cleanness itself that itches, I think. It is not the same as fleas at all." He scratched himself gently around the neck.

"You'll be wanting a lace-trimmed shirt soon," said Will.

Little John said, "Hunger is the most boring of all, for it leaves no possibility of anything else."

There was another little pause. "Why doesn't the sheriff come?" said Will. "It has been nearly a sennight, and the closed gate screams for attention."

Robin said dryly, "Sir Richard has had a rumour begun that we are threatening him—that he owes us a favour for our little job a few weeks back, but as a law-abiding citizen he does not wish to give succour to his country's enemies."

"I like it," said Will. "But it won't last."

"I do not understand why we have been left untroubled this long," said Robin. "It is not to the sheriff's credit that he has even pretended to believe it."

Again Will broke the silence: "We should perhaps shift this gloomy meeting to Marian's chamber. She might have some better chance of convincing our blockhead leader of the wisdom of keeping his head from the block."

Robin said dourly, "I fear that the most Marian has learnt this sennight is that the name of Robin Hood has nothing but fear and pain attached to it."

"She has not," said a new voice. Little John turned around as Cecily emerged into the sunlight.

Robin smiled for the first time.

"I dare you to repeat those words to her," said Cecily.

"I dare not," said Robin. "She might grow warm, and her fever is not long gone."

"Look," Will said quietly. There was that in his voice that made them all turn quickly around.

A little train of riders was cantering out of the forest on the road to Sir Richard's castle.

"Shall we go down and see what may be happening?" said Much after a few minutes, while everyone's eyes burned with the strain of trying to identify the riders. There was always the possibility that they had nothing to do with Nottingham or the sheriff, though no one believed this. From such a distance the riders were still mere spots, bouncing to the horses' rhythm; but there was a purposefulness about the horses' gait, and the party clung too close together to be friends coming for an idle visit.

Robin shook his head. "Not just yet. Or at least I do not wish to: I would rather see what I am looking for first. The gate has been closed this long; we need not fear surprise."

So they all stood and stared. Slowly they became aware of heightened activity below them, and voices shouting. But Sir Richard's voice was quite calm when he joined them on the wall walk. "You are observing our approaching guests?"

"Did you know they were so close?" said Robin.

Sir Richard shook his head. "I have been hearing since the afternoon we waited for the litter and the horses to carry you here that the sheriff of Nottingham was hiding behind the next tree, and I fear I had become somewhat jaded. Certainly I heard the message that he was setting out for Mapperley this morning, but I credited this report as I credited it yesterday and the day before. I have wondered daily—hourly—why it is that no one from the sheriff has come to inquire why our gate is closed. . . . I will, however, remember to give Philip a nice young colt for his efforts—and an apology. I fear I was not polite to him this dawn."

It was hard for Cecily to remember that less than a fortnight ago she was serving guard duty as a young outlaw named Cecil. She could remember quite clearly, as she braced against the trunk at her back and sighted an arrow along a forester's cap, and held her breath as she waited for him to pass under her without looking up, that she had thought then it was hard to remember her previous life as a person named Cecily in long skirts. It was probably the constant ache in her shoulder that made her philosophical, and the loss of sleep it compelled, as she could do nothing but be philosophical—or join Marian for some one-armed pillow-hurling—till it healed. But she wondered if whoever it was that she was would stay herself long enough for her to get accustomed again to living in her skin? When she lived in her father's house she had wanted nothing more than to shed that skin permanently; she'd come even to hate it when it became something to be sold to a cold-faced Norman lord. She looked away from the riders and down at her hands, opened the fist of her good hand and stared at the callused palm.

"Why do they never look up?" she had whispered, in her last life, as Cecil, to her teacher, Little John, after the seventh or twentieth king's forester had crept by beneath them, looking searchingly into every bush and shadow.

Little John shrugged. "It is enough for us that they do not."

"For so long as they go on not doing it," said Cecily, peering the way the man had gone. "Surely even foresters must learn eventually that Robin Hood's outlaws like climbing trees?"

Little John said dryly, "The trouble they do not see may not see them. The chances of being gored by a boar one has not seen are still a good bit higher than the chances of being shot by a Robin Hood one has not seen. I have not a high respect for the men we watch for, but I believe they know that to live and let live works better on outlaws than on wild pigs."

"So long as you are not a Norman with a fat purse," said Cecily.

"Just so," said Little John.

The riders grew steadily closer to Mapperley's walls. The sheriff was learning to look up at last.

Little John shifted beside her, leaning on the stonework as he eased his leg. She had without meaning to chosen the gap in the wall nearest his to look through. She remembered her words to him outside the earthwork where Marian lay, and wondered that he would still speak to her after she had betrayed herself so; but events had crowded upon them. She had tried to give him as little opportunity as she could, since they came to Mapperley, to snub her. And it was easy enough, for she slept with Marian and he with the other men. She thought longingly of guard duty, which had been boring and cramped often enough at the time. As she watched the approaching riders she could hear Little John's breathing, sense the bulk of him against the stone—she felt she could discern the human shadow that touched her from the cold hard edge of the shadow the stone threw. . . . What nonsense, she said to herself.

The riders pulled up to a walk to blow their horses.

"That's the sheriff in front, right enough," said Sir Richard. "He always did ride like a sack of meal; no horse can put up with it for long."

She could see the wink of pale faces as they looked up to the high walls of the castle, and she wondered if they could see their watchers, unmoving against pale stone. Robin Hood's outlaws had not lived in Sherwood long enough to train their hunters to look up into the trees; and now they never would.

Little John sighed extravagantly: the frustration of a strong man who watches his enemy approaching and can do nothing.

"Do any of you wish to be present for the exchange of verbal pleasantries that is sure to occur when I decline to raise my gate to my impetuous guest?" said Sir Richard. "To—er—allow for a certain hesitation in the walking speed of certain of our number, we might have need to begin our descent soon."

"That's us," said Much. "Will and Little John and me, we go first, so you can't get ahead of us."

There were a great many folk trying to look casual in the general vicinity of the gate when Sir Richard arrived, the other outlaws among them—including Marian, who had got out of her bed to sit in a chair by the window for the first time the day before. She had persuaded a couple of the junior squires to carry her out in a sedan-chair. All the younger squires and page-boys loved her, and loved the story of the Nottingham Fair, which she had refused to tell them, which made them only worship her the more. She looked thinner and frailer than she had ten days before, but there was some colour back in her face, and her chin set with its old familiar arrogance when she caught Robin's eye. "Should you—" he began.

"Don't even bother to say it," she said.

He looked at her a moment, and then moved near her to take her hand. The junior squires glowered in the background.

The porter had descended from his little chamber, and bowed to Sir Richard. With a straight face he said, "My lord, the sheriff is come to visit his good friend Sir Richard of the Lea, and is saddened by the shut gate, and wishes to inquire of Sir Richard what possible hurt he antici-pates from the peaceful land and folk of England that his good friends meet with so chill a reception?" The man paused and added with a grin, "He also wishes to request your porter's head on a silver plate for not opening the gate at once upon his herald's declaration of his visit. This tale of threatening brigands is all very well, but can't I see he's the sheriff?"

Sir Richard strolled in the most leisurely manner toward the gate, perhaps to give everyone an opportunity to find a good view of the subsequent proceedings. Robin, without a word, caught Marian up in his arms and went gently up the narrow stone steps to the second floor of the gate house, where they could watch through the barred windows there; the others followed. Tuck looked anxious, Rafe eager, and Sibyl looked animated for the first time since Eva's death.

They could hear Sir Richard's voice clearly, though it sounded a little hollow; and clearly they could hear the sheriff's reply—or rather, they could hear what he instructed his herald to say. The ditch before the gate was a narrow one; they heard most of what the sheriff bellowed at his herald before the herald opened his mouth, and they could see the expression—and the colour—of the sheriff's face: the former chol-eric and the latter maroon. He dispensed with his herald's services after the first exchange; he all but danced in his rage at the edge of the ditch.

"Wouldn't it be lovely if he fell in?" said Marian.

"I have heard of your traitorous behaviour!" he howled. "I heard it, but I did not yet believe it—"

"Of course not, his history of kindly and honourable dealings with Sir Richard being borne so strongly in his mind," said Robin.

"I could not believe that a lord of this land—"

"Even a Saxon," said Much.

"—would give succour to a band of common rabble—"

"Definitely Saxon," said Much.

"—indeed, I wonder that I do not find you with your throat cut by this rabble, and all your goods stolen—"

"As we have often stolen yours," Will said cheerfully.

"I cannot understand how you would come to so low a choice as this, to turn your back on the law of this good land, the king's law, to give comfort to the king's enemies—"

There had been some confusion in the bailey yard, but few paid attention, most eyes being riveted upon the spectacle the sheriff of Nottingham made, shaking his plump fists at a cool and unreachable Sir Richard. But Sir Richard paused in the middle of explaining his attitude toward rabble and the king's law, and toward a sheriff who would hire a notorious ruffian like Guy of Gisbourne for any purpose whatsoever and then speak to another man of his decision to harbour cutthroats. "He is not mincing words, our lord, is he?" murmured Will. But there was a certain electricity apparent in the pause, and people began to look behind them. The few watchers left on the south wall were obviously looking intently at something, and there were cries and pointing fingers.

Those in the gate house could not guess what was going forward; they could not see to the south. But now some of the men with the sheriff were looking south; and the news, whatever it was, went quickly from mouth to mouth. The sheriff's fists dropped, and he, too, looked south, facing away from those in the gate house, so they could not see if he watched in hope or in fear.

It seemed a long time but it was not when a gaily caparisoned rider cantered up to Sir Richard's gate. The sheriff's men parted before him like cheese from a knife. Two men rode with him; one carried a banner, the second, some kind of long horn. The second raised his instrument to his lips and blew a brief, merry *ta-ta-ta*; and at that moment the wind caught the banner and snapped it out flat, that its device might clearly be seen by all.

And the herald shouted: "King Richard the Lionheart is come to visit his liege lord Sir Richard of the Lea."

CHAPTER TWENTY-FOUR

he outlaws stumbled down the steps to the gate, to stand near as the portcullis was raised and the drawbridge lowered. The hearts of Robin's folk beat quickly, but the hearts of Sir Richard's folk did too; there were many flushed faces and half-eager, half-fearful looks. No one thought of running away or of hiding; this was the *king*. That was enough, for good or ill.

The king was both very grand and not grand at all. He was tall; perhaps as tall as Will or not quite so tall as Little John. He rode a tall horse with a girth great enough to fill his long legs; and mounted he looked like a giant. But he rode as a man rides when he sits in the saddle every day; and if there was no visible effort on his part to look commanding it was because he did not need to make the effort. Every easy turn of his golden-haired head was regal; the set of his foot in the shining silver stirrup was regal. Even someone who did not know to look for a tall blond man would have picked this man as the leader.

The Lionheart's eyes raked the folk around the gate. His face was long and stern; stern even when he smiled. Cecily, feeling her heart still beating too quickly, could not decide if his smile made her glad or terrified. It was not, she thought, a facile or a comforting smile. Her father had been to Henry's court; Will had once been to the Regent's. "And a colourful and wicked place it was, too," was Will's comment. "I don't know which the more, but I was grateful to be the humblest liege and not expected to linger." But no one she could call friend and ask questions of had been presented to the Lionheart; he was always away from court, before and after he became king, fighting some battle in which he might distinguish himself further as deserving his nickname. She found she half-expected him to have yellow eyes with thin vertical pupils, like a cat's. It was with almost a shock that she noticed, looking at his smile, that his eyes were blue.

The sheriff and his party crept in after the king's men had all passed beneath the gate; but they were a subdued group, and Sir Richard's people barely noticed them. There were not many more of the king's party than of the sheriff's, nor were they conspicuously better attired. The sheriff was known for his material generosity with his favourites, and the Lionheart, for all his love of colour, always looked a little too soldierly for perfect glamour. But the difference in bearing between the two groups was unmistakable; so unmistakable that no one within Sir Richard's protection bothered to put into words the thought that while the king was present they had nothing to fear from the sheriff of Nottingham.

Besides, thought Cecily, the sheriff standing on a box would barely come up to the Lionheart's collarbone. It's hard to look too grand when you're led by someone who looks like a pudding with legs.

Robin was thinking dazedly, What comes to us now? Will the king listen to both sides of our story? He meets kindly with Sir Richard—surely that is a good sign for us. Yet does our host not blanch as he sees the king cross his threshold? The sheriff has many friends, if only because he is the sheriff. If it is not accident—it cannot be accident?—then it is the sheriff's message that has brought the king, and not Sir Richard's; there cannot have been time for Sir Richard's . . . and so he flinches.

A little wryly the thought continued: I was wrong when I said that I should leave here and let my friends stay in comparative safety in my absence; it is they who should have left and I stayed. . . . Well. Come what may. We make our stand here, whatever stand we can, where we are found.

The bustle and clatter of the two great parties passed from the outer bailey to the inner; most of Sir Richard's people followed, some to work and some to gape. The outlaws trailed slowly after, half-fascinated and half-longing for the old simple days of sleeping uncomfortably in trees and fearing discovery. The king and the sheriff and all the grander members of the three households disappeared behind doors soon enough; and the other folk began reluctantly to take themselves off to their proper occupations.

The outlaws were left, feeling rather forlorn, standing in a corner of the inner bailey. Their Sherwood instincts meant they clung automatically to available corners. Marian's sedan-chair was trailing them at a prudent distance; Marian herself was riding on the crossed forearms of Rafe and Robin. She slid down to stand, weakly, and put her arm around Robin's waist. The sedan-chair crept a little closer. The bearers were as in awe of Marian's tongue as they were of anything to do with Robin Hood; and while they felt that Marian could do no wrong, sometimes the right that she did to them hurt.

She looked around at her companions, and an ironic smile appeared on her face. "A sorry lot of gawps we look, to be sure," she said.

Robin closed his still-hanging jaw with a snap, and straightened his back. "We'd best make ourselves tidy," he said; "we'll be called up to account for ourselves some time—dear Fate," he said with some violence. "I only hope it is tonight; I cannot bear the waiting."

Marian said thoughtfully, looking after the vanished company, "I would guess it will be. The Lionheart is not known to be a patient man himself."

"It would be excellent tonic for our self-importance if it should happen that we have nothing to do with his visit," said Will.

Robin grinned. "I should be very glad—but I doubt we could have such luck. Our luck was spent in Sherwood, some days past."

"Nor, I suspect, will we have the luck to find any water-bearers not totally occupied with the king's party," said Much wistfully. "I've grown quite attached to hot water to wash in."

"I'm hungry," said Cecily.

"So am I," said Marian, sounding surprised. "How if I do my failing-invalid performance and have food sent up to my chamber for all of us? There should be some quite good crumbs that fall from the platters tonight, if I can find someone to brave the tumult that must be bursting out in the kitchens just now." She smiled at her chair-bearers, who smiled adoringly back.

"I think you may discover willing sacrifices," said Robin; "and I'll see what I can find out about hot water."

"I do love to be waited on hand and foot," said Much. "This business of being a cripple has its advantages, Marian; you should learn to appreciate them more."

"And then I'll drown you in it," said Robin.

* * *

It was not a merry meal, though Marian was right about the crumbs, and Robin about the staunchness of her chair-bearers. Everyone started whenever there was a noise outside the big outer chamber of the women's apartment, where they had gathered; and there were a good many such noises, mostly scampering, often accompanied by anguished whispers. "I'm expecting someone to reclaim about half the amazing number of feather mattresses they gave us when we arrived," said Marian; but no one did.

Occasionally the din from the dining hall rose to a level they could hear, if dimly, from halfway round the other side of the keep. But mainly the disturbances were from the constant to-ings and fro-ings of the extra squires and body-servants either attached to the guests, or hastily assigned to them. The anguish level was audibly higher in the latter.

Cecily found she was not so hungry as she thought; or that her stomach had shrunk in the meanwhile from increasing dread. She—like Robin, though she did not know it—did not believe the king would be sympathetic to her and her friends. She knew Much's still uncrippled idealism—and her brother's; and she knew that Robin hoped, at least aloud, that the king might listen to the truth, instead of to the sheriff. She did not know what Marian thought; Marian could use her lady's training in ways that Cecily had never been able to learn, and one of her more significant skills was of turning any conversation away from a subject she did not wish to discuss. Cecily wondered what Little John thought.

Perhaps it was because she had known too many lords that Cecily could not believe in a king; it was not as though he were Saxon himself, blond hair or no. She'd heard—from the baron who was to have been her husband—that he barely spoke English; French was his native language and the language of his court. She heard the baron's own hissing accents as she remembered. He had met the king and eaten at his table (so he said). How could she have any confidence in such a king?

She got up abruptly. A dinner in consequence of a king's visit would go on for hours, however unprepared poor Sir Richard was to entertain such a guest. The Lionheart would have brought enough of his own minstrels and his own sweetmeats to turn any meal into a feast; so much generosity—to a nobleman—might be expected of him. She did not think the outlaws would hear their fate till tomorrow at earliest; she also knew how feasts could go on for days, particularly when there were politics being passed with the plates. She wondered how Sir Richard had dealt with the problem of seating the sheriff of Nottingham and his party; and for all her own troubled future, she did not envy the master of Mapperley.

She went to the door that led into the hall. Darkness had fallen, but torches had not yet been lit here, with all the attention centered upon the king. The first royal page-boy who stubbed a toe would set up a howl that would get them lit, but she was not a royal page-boy and had to grope her way—rubbing along the corridor with her right side, in fear of bumping her left—to the stairs that led to the battlements Robin had been pacing a few hours earlier.

She was staring so fiercely at nothing that she did not hear him coming up behind her till he spoke; and with the drag of his wounded leg he was not so quiet as he used to be.

"I hope you see no one else coming to join the party."

For a moment she thought the voice was only in her own head, the product of the concentration of her thoughts; then she turned and saw Little John's outline against the evening sky. He limped forward and leaned on the wall with a sigh. "A glorious company we shall look," he said, "shambling on half-healed legs, or cradling some other wound. How is your shoulder?"

Cecily tipped her head in a half-shake, which was what she had developed over the last week to take the place of a shrug. "It is, as you say, half-healed, which is an improvement." One keeps searching for ease, she did not say, and not finding it, till the memories of no-pain seem only like daydreams. "Think you then that the king will call for us?"

"I do not think of it one way or another. Robin and Marian—and Much and Tuck and your brother—think so."

"Then you do not think so."

"You are too sharp for me."

She could not see his face. "It comes of having sat at my father's table too long and listened and not been allowed to speak," she said.

262

"Whereupon you learnt to guess what was not said by the shadow it cast," Little John said softly. "You are right. But Much and Will talk enough for several men, and I have been most often allowed silence when I wished it."

Cecily said, remembering, "I knew that Will was thinking of going away when he stopped protesting. My father thought that he had given up, and was pleased. He is a stupid man."

Little John said, "You do not think Robin is a stupid man."

She almost laughed. "No. He may be the most terrifying person I have met—because you believe what he tells you even when you know better. And yet I think he would quench that fire in him if he could—perhaps because it throws such dark shadows around the things he does not say. Much isn't stupid either—or even my brother. But I think they are a little—flame-blinded. And I think the Lionheart will not care for a fire that does not burn to the king's laws."

"Aye," said Little John.

There was a silence, till Cecily said curiously: "Why do you follow him? Robin, I mean. I . . ." She stopped.

"You," said Little John. "Why do you follow?"

I asked first, she thought, and sighed, and shifted her shoulder. "I follow because I had so few choices. I thought of them all while I was locked up in my room, before I ran away. I should have been thrown out of a convent, if I didn't go over the wall first; I was too wild—wild with the life I'd led, or not led. I don't sing or anything, and I'm not pretty, or—or tractable. And . . . after I'd followed Will . . .

"But I don't think I ever believed this life would last. I was hoping to wear myself out somehow, to resign myself finally to the convent—to have something to tell over to myself during long hours on my knees. My father would pay, even now, I think, what would be necessary for some sisterhood to take such a fallen creature as I am—hoping that singing Lauds in the middle of every night would keep me docile enough during the days not to get into any more trouble that would embarrass the family." She paused. "And I've woken up every morning since I ran away hoping that I might have one more day of it—even these last days. I think I shall not go to bed tonight at all."

She stopped, dismayed that she had let herself go on in such a way.

While she was trying to compose an apology that would sound un-premeditated, Little John said, "You forget that I am the only other member of our band who has a price on his head. I killed one of the men who came to turn me off my land because I could not pay the Norman tax that was killing me." A little breeze moved down the wall walk, whispering of ghosts and old promises. "I will not say that I did not know my own strength, for I knew it very well; it is the one thing I have always known. You cannot be as large as I am without knowing that everyone else is smaller. I could have hit him less hard, and I did not, and he died. So I, too, had a secret; one known in Sherwood, but one that I could have carried outside perhaps even less well than Cecil might have carried his."

He moved his leg again as Cecily rearranged her elbow. "I too have awakened every morning praying that this life might go on a little longer. I believe in Robin, but I do not believe in what he believes in. I do not believe in the justice of kings. He does not truly believe in it either; but it is a shield against what you called a fire. And he does believe in justice."

"Do you know him so well?" said Cecily.

"I was one of the first," said Little John. "As there are but twelve of us at the end. I remember how he did not believe that what we were doing would last one more day. I would not want to be believed in the way the folk who came to him believed in him. Perhaps that is why I do not. Perhaps that is why he believes in justice."

There was silence again; twilight was passing, and night crept close around them; and Cecily found herself thinking that perhaps—perhaps it would never be dawn again. She said, almost idly, "Why did you follow me up here?"

Little John said nothing for so long that she thought she had not asked the question aloud. But at last he said: "I would like to say that I decided when I saw you leave that I, too, wanted to breathe free air. Perhaps it is that I have never lived within the shadow of such walls before, but I find the weight of them almost stops my breath, and I long for the sound of trees, or at least the touch of wind on my face. I could say that, for it is true." He stopped, musingly. She looked at him sidelong; despite the darkness, she could still see the line of his profile, and she already knew his face by heart, though till less than a fortnight before she had known him only bearded.

"It seems to me that one of two things may happen by the king's coming," he said. "One of them is that I shall be hung by the neck till dead. I do not think the king will find that he needs to see us to pass that judgement."

Cecily shut her thoughts off ferociously.

"If I am lucky I will be sent off to the Holy Land to kill Saracens till they kill me; which will not be long, for I am not much of a fighter. I am only large." He paused again. "As it seems, then, that my future is like to be short, perhaps some things do not matter as they might, like the fact that you are daughter to a lord. I followed you up here tonight to tell you that I love you, for I would not be shamed by the courage of your words to me as you left Marian's bedside a few days ago at Tuck's chapel."

Cecily, who had often felt that her love was rather a devilish thing, looking to unseat or upset her, burst out: "My courage! Dear God, you cannot love me if you say so! It is courage that keeps me silent, that I would not be a burden to you! Is it not pity you feel?"

"Never pity," said Little John with such simplicity that she could not help but believe him. "But allow me some little time to understand why my best student drew me so; I have never been a boy-lover. I was not the one of us wearing a mask."

"Were you not?" said Cecily with some irony.

"You are still a lord's child," said Little John, "and my family has been free for less than a generation; and my first act was to lose our holding."

"But—" Cecily began; but Little John put out his hand, and at the touch of his fingers she fell silent, and she shivered as she had shivered on the morning they went to the fair. Little John said, puzzled, "Are you cold?"

"No," she said. "I want to put my arms around you and hold you so hard you scream for mercy, and I have only one arm to do it with."

"Ah," said Little John, and came to her, and stooped, and kissed her; and her one good hand reached up to pull down on the nape of his neck.

265

CHAPTER TWENTY-FIVE

I t was Robin himself who came to find them a little while later with the message that the king's command had come—already. The two of them stiffened and fell apart as the future presented itself to them again after only a few minutes' happiness. It's not fair, said a little voice in the back of Cecily's mind; they might have let us have one night. But another little voice said: You have had many nights. You are luckier than you deserve. The first little voice said unkindly: What would you have done with your night anyway? He cannot touch your left side and you cannot touch his right. The second voice said, Come to that, where there's a will there's a way.

Cecily pulled her clean tunic as straight as she could over her bandaged shoulder, and Little John gave his leg one last hard scratch.

"You look like you are expecting nothing less than the gibbet," said Robin dryly; Little John looked down at him. Robin was carrying a lit torch; its approaching glow had given them some warning that their warm darkness was about to be invaded.

"So do you," said Little John. Robin smiled; and went first to lead the way.

Robin and Rafe carried Marian again; Tuck brought up the rear. There were only the twelve of them together, plus Tuck himself and Brown-eyes. Brown-eyes had so disdained any contact with the castle dogs that he had been permitted to stay with his master. Tuck curled his fingers in the dog's ruff, not from any sense that he could prevent Brown-eyes from doing anything he might choose to do by physical strength, but just for the comfort of his being there. Brown-eyes, like most of the rest of them, still limped; but also like the rest of them—Tuck thought—he looked a formidable enemy. Brown-eyes had only to bare his teeth to prove his potential dangerousness; something else clung around the human outlaws, something that Tuck, who had become a hermit to get away from such things, could almost smell hanging in the air.

No one wore anything that might be considered a weapon; even the short daggers they cut their meat with had been left behind. Alan and Marjorie held hands; Little John and Cecily walked side by side. When the torchlight fell briefly on Cecily's face, Tuck was saddened by the look he saw there. For all our words we aren't expecting much, are we? he thought.

There was a roar of noise and a dazzle of light when they crossed the courtyard and the squire who had brought them—one of Sir Richard's, who looked as anxious for them as they felt for themselves—pushed the heavy doors open. Men in Sir Richard's and the sheriff's and the king's liveries stood inside; and beyond that was the Great Hall where their fate awaited them. Perhaps it was the unfamiliarity of the noise, and the knowledge that they would have to stand alone in that great bright room and be stared at by many strangers' eyes, but that fate in prospect felt as merciless as the falling edge of Guy of Gisbourne's sword. Cecily wanted her knife in her boot-top just for companionship. As they paused on the doorstep she took a deep breath and tried to settle herself as for combat, or for being knocked down by another tricky blow from Little John that he hadn't taught her yet.

Marian stood, a little shakily, on her own feet; Robin offered her his arm. She was dressed as an outlaw; they all wore the dark leather and rough wool they were accustomed to, though all of them (particularly Much) were cleaner than customary. They had not discussed what they should wear to face the king—with the considerable stores of Sir Richard's wardrobes at their disposal, they might have chosen almost anything. But what they were all wearing when they trailed in to Marian's chamber to stare at their supper and find it hard to eat was their old garb, patched extensively from Sir Richard's goods, but their own old clothes nonetheless.

Tuck's gaze lingered on each in turn. It was hard to remember his first sight of some of them: of Will Scarlet, who had become Will Brown and Green; of Little John, almost as tall as one of the friar's gateway oaks; of Cecily, who had been Cecil then; of Robin, wary and half-hostile even as he came to ask the friar a favour. Robin caught Tuck's eye and said, "Now is your opportunity to ask for a new roof for your chapel."

Robin and Marian went first, Robin adapting his pace to hers; the others followed equally slowly. When Robin and Marian reached the dais where the Lionheart sat with Sir Richard at his right hand, they paused, and the others could see Marian gathering her slight strength for an obeisance to the king. But the Lionheart stood up and came forward, startling them; the other outlaws fanned out behind Robin and Marian, and all halted.

"You need not make me any bows," said the king. "I know of your wounds, and I do not wish to compel any of my subjects to unnecessary pain." No one said anything. Cecily thought: His English is better than Aubrey's.

The Lionheart stepped down from his dais, as lightly as a boy on holiday stepping outdoors with a sunny summer day beckoning him on. Robin and Marian held their ground, but whether deliberately or because Marian was not sure she could step backward without losing her balance, it was hard to tell. "But I will ask of you something I value most in my subjects."

The hall fell silent as soon as the king rose. The tumult had subsided when the outlaws passed the threshold, but new excited whispers had run round the room. When the Lionheart's foot touched the floor, the hush became so profound that the scuffling of the dogs among the floor-rushes for scraps sounded loud; and when a hawk, disturbed by the sudden silence, stirred on its post behind its master's chair, the tiny chime of its bells was shocking.

The Lionheart was half a head taller than Robin or Marian, but he did not come so close to them that they must tip their heads back to look at him. He was smiling a little, the smile sitting both easily and uneasily on his long hard face: the face of a man who is a staunch friend but a stauncher enemy. "I ask," he said, and he did not need to raise his voice for the whole hall to hear him, "for your fealty."

A good many breaths hissed through teeth; the restless hawk spread its wings and cried out. The king did not appear to notice. He looked into Robin's face; and Robin realised that this man meant what he said. "You, called Robin Hood, outlaw of Sherwood Forest and leader of outlaws, breaker of the king's laws and the king's peace, do you now pledge me, your king, your fealty?" He held out his hands, and Robin placed his between them and spoke in a voice as clear as the king's: "I swear."

"Marian of Trafford, and sometime outlaw of Sherwood, loyal friend of the outlaw Robin Hood and breaker of your proper obedience to your lord your father, do you now pledge me, your king, your fealty?"

Marian's voice rang out: "I swear."

"John Little, called Little John, outlaw of Sherwood, do you pledge now your fealty to me your king?"

But Little John looked down upon the king in silence, and did not at once place his hands in the outstretched ones of the Lionheart. "My lord and majesty does not speak all my crimes aloud," Little John said in his low rumble, so that those sitting at the far end of the hall could not be sure of his words. "Does he still wish my fealty?"

"He does," said the Lionheart, his outstretched hands steady; whereupon Little John laid his in them, and said, "I swear."

Cecily was as surprised by the touch of the king's hands as she had been by the colour of his eyes; she would have expected royal flesh to be cold and stiff, more like metal than human skin; instead his hands were warm, and cradled hers almost tenderly. He had stepped close to her, and held his hands lower than he had for the others, that she might not trouble her shoulder. His blue eyes held hers as if he knew her and would remember her; as if he knew exactly from whom he was asking fealty, and that she, Cecily of Norwell, was the specific person who had given it.

When he came at last to Tuck his smile grew a little. Brown-eyes examined him with interest, as if he might be a new sort of thief or blackguard it would prove his duty to chase. "I do not name you outlaw, Friar Tuck, for the friars have long been called to befriend those who are in need of friends when other folk shun them. I think not a few of those standing with you this evening owe their lives to you; and as you choose to stand with these your friends who are outlaws, will you also swear fealty to me?" And Tuck drew his cold fingers out of Brown-eyes' fur to lay them between the king's and say, "I swear."

The Lionheart turned away, moving quickly now, as if the ritual of fealty had given him new energy. He remounted the dais, where he stood looking out across the hall. His expression was the one he had worn when he first rode across the bridge and under Sir Richard's portcullis; he smiled, but he looked as if he did not greatly like what he saw. And for the first time since the king's banner had snapped out

269

flat in the wind that afternoon, Cecily felt a real hope rise up in her heart; for he had looked more kindly upon the outlaws of Sherwood when he asked for their fealty.

The king said to Sir Richard, "I want a small chamber where my newly reinstated vassals and I may speak of their duties."

Sir Richard rose that he might himself lead them. Several of the king's men seated at the high table stood to follow, and the king nodded to them. The sheriff of Nottingham sat at the bottom of that table and stared before him, blankly, like a blind man; as the outlaws followed Sir Richard and the king, Cecily looked into the sheriff's face. It was grey, as grey as Marian's had been when Cecily had caught her in her arms on the day of the fair.

Sir Richard led them to his own private chamber: the room where Robin, not yet of the Hood, had sold him his last arrow as a free man, before the fatal meeting with Tom Moody on the way to another Nottingham Fair, a year and a half ago. Sir Richard stood aside at the door, to let the king and his guests go in alone, but the king gestured that he should join them. The lord of Mapperley looked surprised, and hesitated near his own door, like a servant expecting to be sent on some unnecessary errand, just to make him go away.

Some of the king's servants appeared with chairs from the dining hall; Marian subsided into one immediately, but while the king indicated they might all sit down, none of the rest of Robin's folk chose to do so. Even Much dug his crutches hard under his arms and stayed upright. The king's men all sat—carefully at a little distance from the outlaws, where they had been at pains to instruct the servants to place chairs— but the king himself did not, choosing to prowl up and down the room, between his courtiers and the outlaws; and both sides wondered what was to happen.

The last servant left, closing the door behind him, and the gracious room was suddenly a prison. The hope Cecily had felt a few minutes before was too stubborn to die at once, but it felt itself beset.

The king said without preamble: "You are now mine, to do with as I choose; and what I tell you, you must obey." No one said anything; one or two of the king's men looked relieved. "I might have you ordered hung out on Sir Richard's gibbet at dawn and it should be done; if for no other reason than that you are only twelve and I am king, and those around you would do my bidding." He looked at the outlaws, catching everyone's eyes in turn. "I might at least hang those two of you with the blood of king's men on your hands: Robin Hood and John Little."

The silence stretched out, like a midwinter night, cold and hard. The Lionheart stopped his pacing, and stood with his hand on Sir Richard's desk. "I will not have outlawry running over this country while I am doing Christian business in the south. It is not enough that you have now sworn to me; you must be disposed of somehow—disposed of in such a manner that you will not be tempted to take up your old ways in the green and roofless halls of Sherwood. Your deaths are one such way of certain disposal." Silence fell again; the king picked up a leather pen-holder and examined it as if it were a doubtful peace-offering from a treacherous knight.

"But I have other plans." He set the pen-holder down. They all stared stoically at him. "The sheriff of Nottingham is a fool and a lout; and a cruel and greedy fool and lout. Him I am tempted to hang as I am not tempted to hang this company. I think I will not. I am not yet sure, but I think I will not. I have already given my Regent my opinion of his Regency, that he has not found time from his other pleasures to attend to the matter of the sheriff of Nottingham long since. Perhaps I spare your sheriff because I do not trust the strength of Sir Richard's gibbet, which is old and long unused. Perhaps I spare you because I do not know of a gibbet long enough for twelve at once and would not humble your loyalty to each other by hanging you separately.

"You are doughty fighters and I have need of such. I would have your services as soldiers when I go south again, which shall be as soon as I can raise the money. . . . I go from here to my tax assessors." His smile turned wry. "You will be guests of my court, with the rest of my army, till we set sail. It will be some little while; you will have the time to heal and grow fit.

"And for the breaking of the king's laws," he said softly, "this shall be punishment enough, for I see you love England very much: that it will be years before you see her again." He did not say, *if ever,* yet the outlaws heard the words nonetheless. "I will not let any of you go who can still march and fight till the Holy Land is freed.

"Alan-a-dale." Alan straightened his back as his name was called, but his eyes held no spark of interest. "You are a minstrel."

"It is likely I am one no more," said Alan, raising his bandaged hand. "Not unless I can learn a way to hold down four strings with two fingers."

"A soldier who no longer bears arms is still a soldier," said the king. "Your wound was honourably received and you need have no shame of it; and I do not permit you despair. You can write, can you not?"

"I can," said Alan, surprised.

There was a pause, but the king now had Alan's attention. "You I will permit to stay here in England; I will make you scribe to the new sheriff. For this much I promise all of you: that there will be a new sheriff of Nottingham before I leave Mapperley. Alan-a-dale shall write to his new master's orders, and eat and sleep easily, and rest that hand, and stretch the stiff tendons till they become supple, and play the lute again. If your master is not too demanding, you may, in your free time, write poetry."

Alan did not quite smile.

"And the lady Marjorie will doubtless be useful in such a household as the new sheriff will have."

Marjorie's face was blank as she glanced at Alan.

"And so the king's justice has come to this: that a man shall be rewarded for the taking of another man's bride by an honourable post suitable to his skills. Your friends will think of you from Palestine, and envy you. Perhaps, if your master is very kind, and you have time and more to write poetry, you will also write a letter to your friends. War does upset the mails; but perhaps the letter will arrive, and your friends will read of spring in England, or of the satisfactoriness of the year's harvest—or of comfortable daily household details they will not be able to understand." The king paused again.

"I will do as the king wills," said Alan slowly.

"But?" said the king softly. "An outlaw so newly escaped from the gibbet, and ungrateful already?"

Alan flushed. "Forgive me, sire, I did not mean ungratitude."

"But," repeated the king. "I will hear your but."

Alan looked around a little wildly. "You offer me a reward beyond my deserts. But—for you ask—you would separate us from our friends, to take that reward. Robin Hood and his company gave us each other,

272

and for this we owe these people our lives." He looked at his hand. "My wound may have been honourably received, but it was not—intelligently received. Had I been trained as a—a soldier, I would not now be unable to play my lute." He looked at Marjorie; she was smiling at him, and when he reached his good hand to her, she took it in both hers. "I would never have been a splendid addition to your army as a soldier, majesty, but—but I can write, here or anywhere. In Palestine. Cannot the king's army use another scribe?"

The king said, "I could make you a scribe for the king. But everyone concerned with the king, you know, must expect to pick up a sword or a bow now and then; even my cooks know what to do with a knife besides chop vegetables."

Alan hesitated, looking at Marjorie; and Marjorie said, "And what of me, majesty? I can chop vegetables at least, though I know little enough of the other uses of a knife."

"I would not part a husband from his wife," purred the king, "unless they themselves should wish it."

Marjorie laughed, a surprising sound in that room. "Nay, majesty, if my Alan is to go to Palestine, I come too. There are no estates to manage between the two of us; no convenient reasons for us to separate. I have learnt things, these past months, that I had not expected ever to learn —about what it is like when you have not enough to eat and your neck is stiff from sleeping in the damp. I had not thought that these things might give you choices as well as take them away.

"I write a fair hand too, majesty, unless you would rather have me chopping vegetables. And the heat will be a change from Sherwood."

The king smiled his discomfiting smile. "I did not anticipate finding the king's mercy so . . . instructive.

"Tuck." Tuck started. "You may go or stay as you choose. I do not demand your presence in my army; you were once a wandering friar, I believe, as friars are; but perhaps you feel your wandering days are over, and that all your desires center upon a new roof for the chapel you tend."

Tuck said, stuttering a little: "I had thought so, sire, but I was perhaps mistaken. I nursed the sick once long ago in the land of the Saracen, for the heat and the plague-ridden air did not seem able to grip me, and I spent years there unscathed. I came home at last, for I missed the green grass here too heartily; yet now I think I would miss my friends more."

"Good," said the king. "I would have wished you to answer so; my army has need of your skills. But till a few minutes ago I would not have expected such an answer. . . .

"Much."

Much jerked his eyes away from the empty chair with the cushion on the seat that his leg was begging his dignity to reconsider. "Sire."

"You, too, have been sore wounded—more sorely than my new scribe. Your father, I think, would be glad to see you back at Whitestone."

Much blinked. This was more surprising than the king's knowledge of the roof of Tuck's chapel. "I—that is—are you asking me? My father would take me in, sire, but he has little need of me with three sons-in-law—any one of whom has several inches on me in height and length of reach. And that was before—this." He glanced at his leg. "I will not be carrying many bags and bales in the near future."

"Nor swords and bows either," said the king. "Of the two, I think you would make a better miller than a soldier."

Much said nothing.

"The prospect does not please you? What a stubborn and perverse folk outlaws are. To stay in England and see the turn of her seasons, to eat bread that never has weevils in it, while your old comrades fight for their lives in the heat and dust of the Holy Land? That leg will trouble you your life long, I think; you would be better in England, where when winter bites you would have a warm hearth to sit beside. Old wounds ache strangely in the south, they ache and gape and do not heal.

"Still you say nothing? Perhaps you think, like those who have already spoken, that you would miss your comrades more. Perhaps you wish a choice?"

This time the king let the silence stretch out; and at last Much said, grimly, "I would, majesty. I would have a choice."

"You can write figures neatly in columns that other scribes may read?" the king said. "I have heard that the old miller at Whitestone by Nottingham is so odd as to keep his accounts written down in figures, and I know you are that man's son. Can you do accurate sums?"

"I can," said Much, a little dazedly.

"Then you shall be marshal, and keep accounts for the king's army, and for the sparing of your life and your comrades' you shall tell me when my other marshals would cheat me. Do you like this choice better?"

"I do," said Much. "If I must look forward to spending most of my time hence sitting down, then I am grateful for a function that does not necessarily include Saracens or angry farmers chasing me."

"Gilbert, Rafe, Bartlemey; I offer you no tricky choices. Do I spare you, I wonder, or merely work the king's whim upon you? And Sibyl . . . I plan to take you south, too, to satisfy the king's whim. Blind eyes to certain things have long precedent, in other armies than mine; and I am not, perhaps, very particular about certain things that do not seem to me to be critical.

"Will of Norwell . . . Will Scarlet. If I wished to punish you, in the sense of a judge sending an outlaw to gaol, I should send you home to your father and elder brother. Their tutelage, I believe, you find so little to your liking that even the rough tutelage the Saracens will offer you is preferable. I wonder, therefore, if exile from England is enough for you?" The king paused, looking measuringly at Will. Will met his king's gaze forthrightly; the aristocratic air that had never quite left him, despite so many months as an outlaw, was very much in evidence. "But I think," the king said slowly, consideringly, "that some punishment— some anxiety beyond the prickling of the nape that every soldier must have—shall come to you nonetheless.

"John Little . . ." But the king turned his eyes to Cecily, who stood at Little John's side. "I guess you would go with him, my lady, would you not?"

"I am 'lady' no more," said Cecily; "it is a title I gave up when I left my father's house, and called myself Cecil, and cut my hair. Yes, majesty, I would go with you to the Holy Land to stay near Little John; without him I would still go—if you let me—to be near my comrades."

Will made some gesture, quickly suppressed, but not so quickly that the king—and Will's sister—did not notice. The king let a little pause establish that he *had* noticed.

"I shall not call you lady, as you ask," said the king; "but I do not think I can call you Cecil either. But you and Sibyl will not be the only beardless young men in my army.

"Little John, does this satisfy you also? Is this reward, or the king's whim?"

"I do not ask reward," said Little John. "It is more than I hoped for."

"But you—like so many of your comrades—do not sound glad of your unhoped-for reward."

"Majesty, you are playing with me," said Little John heavily. "I would not be parted from this woman, as you know or guess; and yet is it not the worst nightmare of all to be in mortal danger that your lover shares? For so it shall be in your army."

"A philosopher," said the king. "I am not sure I approve of a soldier philosopher. I might suspect such a man to be led by his thoughts to wonder if it matters which army wins the war."

"You do not know him," Cecily said sharply; "or you would not suggest that he might behave dishonourably."

"He has king's money on his head for some act someone found dishonourable," said the king in his purring voice; "but perhaps you know him better than this someone."

"I know him as well as anyone may know another. Well enough to say what I have said—whatever circumstance may seem to be set to the contrary—and to know the truth of it."

"Hmm," said the Lionheart. "A philosopher and a fire-eater. I had not thought of this either, when I planned what to do with my outlaws."

"Marian of Trafford."

Marian raised her head; her face was pale and her skin damp. "I am no fighter," she said, "no soldier. I have killed the king's deer many times, for arrows go where I choose to send them, and my friends were hungry. But I have loved that archery best when I drew against a straw target that did not fall and bleed when my arrows struck it." She stopped, panting a little; but the king remained silent. "And I have found," she went on, "that I like even less the other side of soldiery; for I have never disliked anything so much as I have disliked this hole in my side."

"It is a discovery that comes to many soldiers," said the Lionheart. " 'Tis where much of the best of my taxes comes from, for when my good soldiers come home to England they become my good farmers and burgesses." He paced the width of the room and back. "But to you, too, Marian of Trafford, I give a choice; and yet what I ask of you might be a thing more hard than soldiering." He stopped, turned, and faced her. "I would make you the new sheriff of Nottingham."

The king's men stirred; they calmed themselves at once, but the looks on their faces faded more slowly.

"It would be easiest," the Lionheart said dreamily, "if I ordered you married to the present sheriff, had him quietly assassinated, and ignored the resulting situation while his relict took capably over."

There was an appalled silence.

"I think I should not do that to you, however. I think, somehow, that such a beginning would give you a distaste for the job. But my advisors"—he turned an ironical eye on his men, who hastily adjusted their expressions to attentive blandness—"keep attempting to impress me with the unwisdom of taking all the best men from England to fight my foreign war, however important they diplomatically concede that foreign war to be."

His advisors all went limp in their chairs.

"Many of my best soldiers, you know, do not survive their wounds, to become my good farmers and burgesses—and sheriffs.

"It would not be easy to make Lady Marian a sheriff; but I am the king, and I would think of a way." Marian opened her mouth, licked her lips, and closed it again. "Speak your mind," said the king. "I am, as I have said, finding this meeting very instructive."

"Such an offer—suggestion—choice—leaves me very little mind to speak with," said Marian, at a loss. "Why do—why does the king think to—to award me such a role?"

The king smiled a carnivorous smile. "I cannot think of better training for important administrative matters than the double life you have led in the last nineteen months. That you did lead it is proof that you could be successful in the situation I now suggest." He added, "Sir Richard made an elegant tale of the buying back of his estates, my lady, in which you were significantly the heroine."

"It was not a role I enjoyed," said Marian.

The Lionheart's eyebrows rose. "I have not and will not speak of enjoyment to any of you. I spoke of punishment—punishment to fit your crimes against the king's peace; punishment to fit my needs, and your abilities."

"You have also spoken of choice," said Marian.

"So I have. May my new sheriff be so sharp with those who wish to curb the king's taxes.

"Robin Hood."

Robin met his king's eyes. Survival, as a soldier of the king in the Holy Land, is what he would hope for, survival as his reward, if he could seize it—to see England again. To see Marian again.

The king said to him, as one comrade to another, "You know your fortune already; you come with me to the south."

"And have I choice, or reward?"

"I begin to think clemency more dangerous than I realised, for you will snap so at the bait I but half-heartedly set out. Perhaps outlaws cannot be broken to service any more than a rogue horse to saddle." He watched Robin's face, and smiled. "I do not frighten you."

To Marian he said: "This is your choice, my lady, and almost, if I were not your king, I would beg your pardon for it." His eyes swung between her and Robin, whose hand lay on her shoulder; the Lionheart's eyes went between them almost irresolutely, if the Lionheart could be irresolute. "My lady, you may stay here, in England, and risk few swords but those of men's tongues, and be a powerful figure in your own land, a king's sheriff, with lackeys to do your bidding. Or . . ." Robin's fingers tightened, and Marian's hand reached up to press down over his. "Or you may risk as your lover risks; you may come to the southlands too, and bear the heat and the stench and the many kinds of death the war and the Saracens bring us—and risk another sword in your side, which you likely would not survive the second time. I have experience of near-mortal wounds, lady. You may lose your country—and I my new sheriff, which does not please me—and perhaps your life; or you may lose your lover. How will you choose?"

"You already know how I will choose," said Marian faintly, "for we outlaws have proved, as you say, instructive. I will go where Robin goes, as you will let me."

"And will Robin let you?" said the Lionheart, as if the question interested him.

Robin said slowly, "If this is my choice, then my choice is that I will no longer try to say her nay. It has taken me almost losing her to make me understand that I cannot. I hope not to lose her; I may at least not lose her to my own stubbornness."

"Prettily said," said the Lionheart. "I am almost moved to forgive you the loss of my new sheriff. And if the two of you together survive the king's stubbornness—unlike my advisors, I believe the Holy Land can be won—you will see he is not ungenerous.

"Sir Richard."

Sir Richard looked up from his post by the door; he had still the slightly bewildered bearing of a servant who awaits a delayed summons. "I do not take you to my war; you earned your peace here now at my father's back, years ago; and you have already learnt my choice between the sheriff of Nottingham and the outlaws of Sherwood, and so I will force from you no price upon that score. I would keep you here besides, to be a strong friend to my new sheriff.

"I give the rest of you news that your host heard only a few hours ago; that I would leave to him in other circumstances, but now cannot. I brought him news that his son was killed under the walls of Palestine shortly before I was released from prison in Germany. It was a good death; a soldier's death."

Sir Richard said nothing; among the outlaws there was the tiniest stir of air, a suppressed sigh, and the thought of all who had known him was the same: A good death to end a bad life.

"This means that Sir Richard's lands are without an heir; and I as king may award them as I see fit. I believe I will choose to declare Robin Hood as heir. I might wait—under other circumstances—to announce such a future to a soldier who might otherwise feel the need to fight the harder to gain the king's notice; but I think in this case I shall rely on this outlaw's honour to stand beside me even with such a prize already in his eye.

"The heir of a lord like Sir Richard might consider himself a suitor for the hand of the lady Marian. I believe there should be time to celebrate such a marriage before we set sail; as I have said, there will be some delay while we gather our new forces, and the money to furnish them for war." He looked again at Robin and Marian, with that same glint of interest in his eye. "May I think that, with kingly insight, I have satisfied both your desires for reward?"

Robin said dryly, "Majesty, you may."

Marian said, "But why?" All eyes turned to her; she stared at the king. "Why? Why do you do this? We are only twelve; and we are not—not an important twelve, in the legions of your subjects. None of us are proven soldiers—or anything else—except our thirteenth, who at least knows how to nurse the soldiers who fall. We are not anything. Anything a king with a war to win should find so—interesting."

"Why," said the Lionheart softly. "Why. Have I not mentioned the king's whim?

"I have been hearing tales of this fellow Robin Hood since before I set foot in England again; someone on the ship crossing the Channel had a story about him. There are many urgent matters that greet a king long absent upon his return to home and court—and duty. Most of them are not interesting. The tales of Robin Hood were very interesting. I am, I admit, a little disappointed that he does not wear seven-league boots and knock down walls by the sound of his voice—that latter talent would be very useful in Palestine—but I will, as kings and other mortals must, deal with what I can get. And any lone man who can, with little more than stubbornness and a few ragged friends, set so much of my aristocracy in a rage, is a man I wish to put to *my* purposes.

"Does this satisfy you as to my reasons? If it does not—I plan to keep all of you close to me. You seem to stick together, like stew in the bottom of a pot. You will have or, I am sure, make opportunity to ask me again. I do not wish to waste Robin Hood's obstinacy, you see. There are those who will feel that keeping such a notorious group together at my back is unwise of me—but I have won things in my life that I treasure ere now by unwisdom.

"And now we shall drink together one toast," said the Lionheart. "To Sir Richard, and to his heir, and to his heir's bride; and to the new soldiers—and scribes, and vegetable-choppers—of the king."

Sir Richard moved away from the wall he leaned on, and threw open the doors of a cabinet near at hand; within were a large carafe of wine and some goblets. "The wine is not worthy of a great occasion," said Sir Richard; "but it is the best I can offer you."

"Then it will do," said the king. Sir Richard himself poured and served: the king first and then, with a faint smile, Robin and Marian; and then the king's men, who, upon outlaws, even pardoned ones, being served before them, had once again failed to look bland and attentive; and then the others. They were one goblet short, and Cecily handed hers back to Sir Richard, and curled her fingers around the base of Little John's cup.

"Health and victory," said the Lionheart; and they all drank.

"And to the king's mercy," said Robin.

"And to comrades," said Cecily.

AFTERWORD

I grew up with Howard Pyle's *Robin Hood* (and with Alfred Noyes' *A Song of Sherwood*). But I was slow to recognise the significance of *authors*, and that therefore Pyle's was a particular version of the tale rather than the tale itself in some absolute sense. Later I read other Robin Hoods; in the last several years, as I worked on mine, I have read over two dozen.

From my first paragraph I have found myself falling into the gaping crevasses in my knowledge of English history. Growing up with Pyle there were several things that simply were the *truth* about Robin Hood. One of them was that he shot a longbow. Another was that he lived in the time of Richard Lionheart. A third was that the sheriff of Nottingham was his chief enemy. Imagine my horror when I discovered that the sheriff of Nottingham did not administer Sherwood Forest; that the English did not commonly use the longbow till about 150 years *after* Richard Lionheart.

I am no historian, and never flattered myself that I would write a story that was historically accurate. I did, however, wish to write something that was, let us say, historically unembarrassing. A cousin of mine, who is an historian, told me that our sense of history in the 20th century is not what it was 700 years ago; we have what we call *the media* now, with the result that history tends to be even-handed and instantaneous. This was some comfort; for example, the English were quietly using the longbow as a hunting weapon long before Edward III faced the French at Crécy, which is when the English longbow enters 20th-century textbooks.

I've read bits of my Robin Hood aloud several times in the last few years; invariably there were questions, not necessarily about the historical veracity of what I was doing, but about why I had chosen this version of the tale over that version—or where this or that portion of the tale had come from. Many people have strong ideas about who Robin was and what he was like; and a lot of our ideas are as incompatible with each other as they are with history. There is a variant in which Robin is a disinherited earl, for example. My Robin has always been a yeoman (yeoman, by the way, is a term that was not generally used till well after the Lionheart's day—because the position that would come to be known as yeoman was not yet widespread). There are even tales of a Robin Hood who did not live in Sherwood Forest.

When I could, I have tried to be historically unembarrassing. When I couldn't. . . . The book that rescued me from the slough of despond is called, simply, *Robin Hood*, written by James C. Holt, a professor of Medieval History at the University of Cambridge. It is a lively and fascinating book, and one of Holt's theses is that the tales of Robin Hood have always reflected what the teller and the audience needed him to be *at the time of the telling*.

Scholars disagree about when the stories were first told; the earliest hints of an historical Robin Hood date around 1260. The first literary reference to him is from *Piers Ploughman* in 1377. But the retellings through the centuries have echoed concurrent preoccupations—not those of a possible historical precedent that existed, and may or may not have been a person named Robin Hood. And the slow accretion of the details that most of us would consider inseparable from any man called Robin Hood is sometimes surprising. Maid Marian did not appear till 1500; nor till about the same time was Robin presented as an honoura-ble outlaw who stole from the rich to give to the poor. And it was not until Sir Walter Scott's *Ivanhoe* in 1819 that Robin was inaugurated as the Saxon champion against the Norman conquerers.

The Outlaws of Sherwood is not the last Robin Hood story any more than it is the first story about an outlaw band living in Sherwood Forest a long time ago. I needed my Robin to carry a longbow—even during the time of Richard Lionheart. I needed him to be a particular kind of hero with a particular set of preoccupations, surrounded by a company of people with preoccupations of their own. My Robin Hood is meant to be neither absolute nor definitive—nor historically satisfying. But I hope my readers may find him and his company persuasive and congen-ial.